Cara Lockwood is a [...] of more than twenty-[...] *I Don't*), which was n[...] movie. She's written [...] for young adults, and [...] into several languages [...] raised in Dallas, Cara now lives near Chicago with her husband and their blended family. Find out more about her at caralockwood.com, friend her on Facebook, Facebook.com/authorcaralockwood, or follow her on Twitter, @caralockwood, or Instagram, Instagram.com/cara_lockwood.

Ever since **Lisa Childs** read her first romance novel—a Mills & Boon story, of course—at the age of eleven, all she's wanted is to be a romance writer. With over forty novels published with Mills & Boon, Lisa is living her dream. She is an award-winning, bestselling romance author! Lisa loves to hear from readers, who can contact her on Facebook, through her website—lisachilds.com—or at her snail mail address: PO Box 139, Marne, MI 49435, USA.

If you liked
Masquerade and *Dating the Rebel*
why not try

The Fiancé by Stefanie London
Her Playboy Crush by Nicola Marsh

Also by Cara Lockwood

Cuffs
The Sex Cure
Double Dare You
Hot Mistake
First Class Sin
Look at Me
No Strings

Also by Lisa Childs

Liaisons International

Dating the Billionaire

Legal Lovers

Legal Seduction
Legal Attraction
Legal Passion
Legal Desire

Discover more at millsandboon.co.uk

MASQUERADE

CARA LOCKWOOD

DATING THE REBEL

LISA CHILDS

MILLS & BOON

First Published in Great Britain 2021
by Mills & Boon, an imprint of HarperCollins*Publishers*
1 London Bridge Street, London, SE1 9GF

Masquerade © 2020 Cara Lockwood

Dating the Rebel © 2020 Lisa Childs

ISBN: 978-0-263-29788-1

MIX
Paper from
responsible sources
FSC® C007454

This book is produced from independently certified FSC™ paper
to ensure responsible forest management.
For more information visit www.harpercollins.co.uk/green.

Printed and bound in Spain
by CPI, Barcelona

MASQUERADE

CARA LOCKWOOD

MILLS & BOON

To PJ, my amazing husband, partner and best friend.

Thank you for making every day better than the last.

CHAPTER ONE

THE THINGS ONE did for love…and revenge, Asha Patel thought as she squeezed between two men in custom-made tuxedos wearing silver masks in the glittering gold ballroom of the Grand Hotel in Stockholm. Everyone, in fact, wore them, except Asha, who was—not so subtly, she realized now—crashing this shindig. Also, a small point, but it *seemed* this might be a black-and-white ball. Everyone wore some combination of one or the other, and her Chanel red strapless gown stood out like a police siren. So much for subtlety.

She moved past a golden column, past the gilded mirror windows lining the walls on either side of the opulent space, feeling like she'd fallen into a costume drama. She checked her reflection in the mirrored windowpanes. She might be standing out like a sore thumb, but she still looked like a damn fine one with the strapless floor-length gown clinging to her curves like a glove. The slinky dress with the thigh-high slit and matching red stilettos suited her perfectly, because she paid her in-demand stylist top dollar to ensure it did.

She wore her long, wavy, nearly black hair down, and it hit midback. She'd kept her makeup heavy and dramatic, her lips the same Chanel red as her dress. She scanned the well-heeled crowd, noticing a few pointed stares in her direction. Not that she cared. She was here to catch her cheating boyfriend, Connor, whom she knew was here was that empty-headed lingerie model, Kayli. She grabbed a glass of champagne from a roving waiter, who also gave her the side-eye and a slight raised eyebrow. Okay, so how was she supposed to know she should be wearing a mask? That *hadn't* been mentioned in Connor's texts to his model mistress, but then, most of his texts included dick pics, so she supposed he was busy doing more important things like trying to get the best lighting for himself.

Asha had been monitoring Connor's phone for weeks. He was the one dumb enough to use her father's app to proposition models. Enlisting the help of one of her father's engineers had been easy. And what she wanted now was to find her boyfriend and tell him to jump off a high balcony. Of course, *boyfriend* was a strong term. Although not as strong as *fiancé,* the word he'd been hinting about with phrases like "ring shopping" and "popping the question."

They'd only been dating three weeks. Hell, they'd not even slept together. Not for lack of Connor's trying. He came in hot and heavy, declaring his love, telling her she was his soul mate, smiling his legendary smile. Except, it became increasingly clear, Connor didn't like brunettes, even though he was one. Clearly, he preferred empty-headed blondes. Asha, whose father immigrated to Seattle from India, and built one of the most successful tech companies in recent years, knew from experience growing up in Seattle that she wasn't everyone's type. How often had she smiled politely when someone called her an "exotic beauty"—making her sound like she came from Mars? But the worst, by far, was discovering that the men declaring love to her were really declaring love to her billion-dollar fortune.

She was here to make Connor pay. And pay he would. Except, glancing around her, with all the guests hiding behind silver eye masks, she realized *finding* Connor and Kayli would be more challenging than she thought. And what *was* this mystery party anyway? Lord help her if she'd stumbled upon some weird kinky sex party. Was Connor into that? Well, he *was* an actor desperate for any publicity he could get. Who knew what he really felt about anything? She glanced around her and saw many of the guests whispering to each other and staring at her. She got the impression they were all talking about her. Her eyes scanned the crowd, but all she saw were masked faces. Impossible to pick out Connor's or anyone else's, unless she knew what the jerk had planned to wear.

"Ms. Patel?" Asha whirled and came face-to-face with a pristine tuxedo shirt and tie, and the dark satin lapel of an expensive black jacket. She looked upwards and saw a strong jaw and full, sensual lips, curved up in a smile. Sharp, cool blue eyes stared at her from beneath the ornate silver-and-gold eye mask he wore. Dark hair rolled back from the mask and curled beneath his ears, thick and soft enough to want to touch.

"How do you know my name?" she asked, suspicious, heart thumping in her chest, because she couldn't shake the feeling she'd been caught red-handed. Not, of course, that that meant anything. She could usually bribe or cajole her way out of any problem. Trespassing had to be among her most minor offenses of late.

"Everyone knows the heiress of The Skycloud—founded by your father?" He spoke with a faint French accent, soft and sexy. "Also, I believe you have more followers than he does on social media." Damn her social media feed, a blessing and a curse. Mostly a blessing, since her influencer powers also made her a decent amount of money. Money that she'd need if she ever wanted to get out from under her father's thumb. "Your reputation proceeds you."

It always did. She'd made her social media reputation as a party girl with loose morals, someone who courted and discarded actors and pop stars on a whim. Some people loved her, some hated her, but they were all *interested.* That's how she kept selling all those mascaras and lips glosses, and how her followers kept growing every day.

"What do you know of my reputation?"

"You're a woman used to getting what she wants." He paused. *Here it comes*, she thought, the moment when he made a remark about how *controversial* she was, how she hopped from bed to bed. She didn't care.

"How so?"

"You point at a man and he usually falls in love with you. Is this not so?" He grinned, slowly, and Asha knew he meant one of the pop songs written about her. It was a lie, of course. When she pointed at men, they did fall in love. Just with her money. Not her.

"That's a slight exaggeration."

"Is it? I am not so sure," the mystery man replied, the French accent a bit thicker now. Asha realized that a hole in the crowd seemed to form around them. People were giving them space. Oddly. And a few were staring in their direction. She wondered why. She turned her attention back to the Frenchman in the tuxedo and gilded mask.

"You seem to have me at a disadvantage, Mr...." she trailed off, trying to figure out if the slant of his mouth, the shade of his eyes, held any clue to his identity. No, she decided, she didn't know him.

"Mathis Durand," he said, and gently took her right hand. He bent over it and laid a gentle kiss above her knuckles, a warm, feather-like touch that made all the nerve endings in her arm come alive. "I am the host of this party."

"The host?" Oh, great. Now she was in trouble. "Well, you see, I'm so very sorry. I've forgotten my mask." Forgotten, or never knew she needed one— what was the difference? "The friend I came with forgot to tell me it was a costume party."

She laughed uneasily. She'd never felt more exposed. Durand didn't join her. He cocked his head to one side.

"The friend? Who is this?"

"Connor Henry."

A slow smile crept across Durand's face. "I do not believe that is true, Ms. Patel. You did not come with Mr. Henry. You are…how do they say in America? Crashing?"

All the guests ceased their own conversations and were simply staring now. Why? Who cared about a single party crasher? Every party had dozens. Didn't they?

"I…" She was about to double down on her lie, because if she knew anything it was that if she acted passionately enough about a bald-faced lie, most people believed it. "I'm a guest."

"You're the guest of no one." The direct contraction startled her. Now she realized too late that bluffing was a mistake. He was the host, after all. Perhaps he *did* personally know…all the hundred or so people who crowded the ballroom. "Shall we talk about this in private?" Durand asked. He took hold of her elbow, a gentle but firm grip, his fingers a shade paler against her golden skin.

"Sure?" she said and he steered her through the crowd, which parted like the Red Sea, the whispers following her as she went. Now, nervous butterflies flapped their wings against her rib cage. Why all the seriousness? He led her to the end of the ballroom, past the enormous crystal chandelier and to the balcony doors beyond. They passed at least three women in low-cut dresses that only seemed to have eyes for Durand. Asha got the impression she was keeping him from flirting with the gorgeous, lithe Nordic model types who were frowning at her as he took her through the balcony doors, and out into the cool summer night in Stockholm. In the distance, Asha could see Strömmen, the innermost part of Saltsjön, a bay of the Baltic Sea. Warm lights dotted the shore of the bay, making it look magical.

Durand closed the heavy, ornate double doors behind them, and then they were alone on the stone balcony, but as darkness never truly fell in Stockholm on summer nights, the ever-present never-quite-set sun meant they needed no man-made lights to see each other. Beneath the gray, slightly pink sky, she noticed the balcony had another, smaller side door, and she wondered where it led.

"Okay, you're right. I crashed your party and I'm sorry," Asha said, hoping that a little groveling might help her case. She needed to find Connor. That is, *if* he hadn't seen her already and booked it out of there. "Surely you have room for one more guest? I'd be happy to pay my way. Of course."

Durand chuckled, the smallest of sounds at the back of his throat. "I do not need your money, Ms. Patel."

"Really?" She'd discovered that the one truth in life was that money *always* talked. And opened doors. And some of the oldest money families sometimes were the poorest. After all, a few of the most famous royal families in the world were happy to use her private jets. She shifted slightly, and she watched as his eyes trailed down her bare shoulder.

"Really." He cocked his head to one side, curious. "What brings you to my party?" She caught the note of possessiveness in his tone. *My party.* There was no mistaking it. "And, please, if we could dispense with the lies and…ah…the theatrics?"

Says the man hiding his face behind a gilded mask.

She glanced up at him, his full face still shrouded by that damn mask, and was tempted to lie. *For fun.*

For a laugh. But she had a feeling this man would see through any petty lies. For once in her life, she decided she'd be honest.

"I'm trying to find Connor Henry. I do know him. He's my…" She hesitated to say *boyfriend,* since they hadn't been dating that long. Plus, after she caught him with his lingerie model, he'd be an *ex-boyfriend.* "Well, we had an understanding. He's deceived me, and he's come here with a woman he also lied to me about, and I want to catch him in that lie."

And make him grovel, and then tell him he's lost me before he ever really had me. Dramatic? Maybe, but he deserves it.

Durand lifted the mask from his face, and Asha's breath caught a little at the back of her throat. The man made gorgeous look ugly. Strong jawline, slim, straight nose, clear blue eyes that looked even darker in the grayish light of never-quite-dusk, even though she knew it was close to midnight.

"That *is* unfortunate. But I am afraid I cannot let you stay." He shook his head slowly, eyes solemn. It took a moment to realize this walking sex god was actually denying her.

"Why not?"

"This is a *members only* event. You must be a member of the Sphinx Society in order to mingle here."

Asha laughed, bright and brittle, but seeing the

serious look on Durand's face, she realized her mistake. He was *serious.*

"What is the Sphinx Society? Some kind of sex club?"

Now it was Durand's turn to laugh. "Hardly. It's one of the oldest societies in the world. We helped *build* this hotel. You know, in that ballroom the very first Nobel Prize ceremony and award banquet was held in 1901?"

"Really?" Asha faked interest. She cared little about history, unless it concerned her personally. What could dusty old facts do to help her, anyway? What she wanted to do was get into that ballroom and find Connor. And if kissing up to this exceptionally sexy Frenchman was the way to do it, then she would. She actually didn't mind, truth be told. She loved pretty things. Durand was the one who ought to be the movie star. She moved closer to the man, eyes never leaving his. If he wasn't interested in money, then maybe he was interested in her attention. Most men were. And she wasn't afraid to take advantage, either. "Tell me more."

Durand's dark eyebrows raised a millimeter. She bit her lip, and he studied her mouth. Good.

"The King of Sweden uses this hotel for his official business, as do all the Swedish royals," Durand said.

"Tell me more about the Sphinx Society." She ran one perfect red nail down his immaculately tailored lapel. He watched the bloodred tip against the black fabric. She didn't exactly care about the society, or its history, but if this man wanted to crow about it, and indulging him got her what she wanted, then she was happy to do it. Not all of her reputation was exaggerated. Men might not fall in love with her at first sight, but they often fell into lust.

"You either know about the Sphinx Society or you don't. There's no *telling* someone about it." Durand was interested, she could tell, just as she knew that now his gaze lingered a bit too long on the neckline of her strapless dress.

"How about…you help me join?" She was so close to him now that if she rocked up on her stilettos, she could kiss his lips. She took his hand and put it open-palmed on her slim waist. He let her. His eyes met hers, the dark pupils in them crowding out his gray-blue irises. *Yes, that's it. Want me. You know you do.*

"Membership is by invitation only."

She studied his eyes. "I can think of one way to get an invitation."

She reached up and slid her hand behind the back of his neck, and then pulled him down to her lips. Asha knew how to play this game—to a point. Most men turned into jelly with a kiss and little more. She'd never really had to go farther than she'd liked. And, to be honest, she'd only ever had a handful of lovers her whole life. Unlike what the tabloids said.

According to them, she was one of the world's biggest whores. Using her body and her money to get famous men to do what she wanted. She'd been accused of all kinds of nonsense, all the allegations no rich man would have to confront. After all, rich men were supposed to have revolving doors on their bedrooms. Rich women? Not so much.

Not that any of what was said about her was true, anyway.

But she used it all to her advantage. Played up the role. Men loved it. And she typically got what she wanted in the process. Now she pressed her lips to his. She was the aggressor, and yet the man took possession of her mouth as if it always belonged to him. Damn, he knew how to use his lips, gently, over hers, coaxing her mouth open, his tongue meeting hers. He tasted like fine champagne, and something more…expensive. He deepened the kiss with a gentle lash of his tongue, teasing her, drawing out her hunger, and for a second, she lost herself. Forgot *she* was the one trying to seduce *him*. He seemed to hold all the power, and she seemed to be losing her edge. All she wanted was more of his mouth. More of his body. More of everything. His mouth on hers, driving her, tasting her, made her head spin, made her body buzz with want. He opened the floodgates in her, and her desire roared out, white rapids of pure energy.

And she wasn't the only one affected by the kiss,

either. She could feel Durand's own body stiffen, feel his own lust rising as she pressed her belly against him. Yes, he wanted her, too. Wanted her badly. She pulled away at last, panting, her heart pounding in her chest, her mind buzzing with all kinds of feelings, none of them having to do with Connor or the party or anything other than Durand's talented, talented mouth. She met his gaze, and he, too, seemed a little stunned. Her chest heaved as she struggled to get her breathing under control. Hell, after a kiss like that, he'd have to let her in. She couldn't see how he could deny her entrance to this party after a white-hot encounter like that, and the promise of more to come. A small smile quirked the corner of his sensual, knowing mouth.

"Thank you for that, Ms. Patel." He wiped the corner of his mouth with one finger, the light of desire flickering in his eyes. "That was...exquisite."

The way he looked at her now made the air catch in her throat. Was he going to pull her into his arms for another kiss? God, she hoped so. Her whole body vibrated with desire for his mouth against hers once more.

"I'm afraid, however, that you can't stay at my party," he said, voice low. "I'm going to have to ask you to leave."

CHAPTER TWO

A WEEK LATER, Durand found himself staring out of his office window in his well-heeled Sphinx Society office, with a perfect view of the Eiffel Tower rising up from the Paris skyline. The breathtaking view, especially with a cloudless summer sky behind it, and his window open to the warm French sunshine, normally calmed him, but today all he could think about was the taste of Asha Patel's lips. He couldn't understand why a simple kiss would linger with him so long. But the invitation in the woman's dark eyes, the way she'd looked at him, lingered in his mind. For a split second, he'd seen right through her expert attempt at seduction, seen her true desire there on her face and felt it in her lips. The memory made his groin tighten.

"Mr. Durand?" The voice of his assistant, Madelyn, broke his reverie. The stunning blonde with her hair neatly up, carried a tray with his morning espresso. He nodded swiftly, and she moved in, leaving the tray on the small table between the two Queen Anne chairs sitting near the window. "Do you need anything else at the moment?"

She waited, red lips pursed, her hands clasped in front of her. She'd changed quite a bit since he'd first hired her, a college dropout who'd been disinherited by her father, a prominent Parisian whose wife disapproved of him supporting his illegitimate daughter. In some ways, Durand had saved her, though Madelyn was resourceful and would've done just fine on her own. Madelyn, he knew, was grateful for the chance to work with him and had, over the last five years, grown to have feelings for him. Though she'd never acknowledged them, and he'd never take advantage, he felt them there all the same.

A sticky situation, to be sure, but Durand never mixed business with pleasure. He always looked elsewhere for distraction and felt it was unseemly to take advantage of an unfair power dynamic. Many of his colleagues had been taken by surprise with #MeToo. But Durand always thought it had been wrong to abuse one's power. He always believed a woman was not truly free to consent if her paycheck was being signed by the man who invited her into his bed.

Durand picked up the small espresso cup, keeping his eyes on the tower. He thought about Asha's cheating boyfriend, that actor, Connor. "Yes. I'll need to revoke the membership of Connor Henry."

Madelyn raised a single blond eyebrow, the only evidence of surprise. "What should I tell him is the reason?"

He thought about the fact that Connor cheated on Asha. Normally this wasn't something that rose to Durand's interest. Men cheated all the time. It wasn't his job to police their behaviors. But…when a member's behavior *brought* chaos to his society, or to one of the parties, then it became his business. Connor should've known Asha would take it personally. He should've guessed Asha would follow him or should've simply taken better care to keep his whereabouts secret.

And Connor hadn't even bothered to try to clean it up with Durand himself. No, he'd taken one look at Asha and fled. The coward. Durand had heard from security that the action star had bolted out the kitchen door, his model date in tow, the second he'd seen Asha in the ballroom.

He could cancel Connor's membership for simply causing this little headache. He'd revoked memberships for less. He told himself getting rid of Connor was simply a smart move, and the one way to avoid inviting Asha and another outburst to a future party. But in reality, he simply didn't like the man. Didn't like that he took Asha for granted, and that he'd be stupid enough to cheat on her in plain sight.

"Ungentlemanly conduct," Durand said at last, turning from the window. It was a broad enough category that could include revealing society secrets, such as the location of one of the society's events.

"He might challenge your decision," Madelyn suggested.

"Let him." Durand waved a hand, dismissive, as he sipped at his rich espresso. He wasn't afraid of a man who lacked the balls to face his girlfriend and own up to his bad behavior. Besides, ultimately, this was, and always would be, *his* club, and he made the rules. There was no board, no oversight committee, no appeals court. He was judge and jury, and that's the way he liked it. He'd spent his entire life trailing after his successful but distant father, hoping for approval, which he'd never get. It had taken most of his life to realize that sad truth.

So instead, he spent his time working on proving his father wrong. He wasn't the disappointment his dour father believed, even though he'd tried hard to forget all about him after he had a string of new children with various mistresses and second and third and fourth wives across the globe. One of those other sons was named heir to his billion-dollar shipping and logistics business. Durand and his mother were left nearly penniless after his parents divorced when Durand was just fourteen. Durand made back all of his father's fortune—and more—using his connections and his wit to take over the Sphinx Society. Members paid handsomely, not only for the privilege to socialize, but also for the powerful business and political connections Durand offered. More than one billionaire-dollar deal had been struck in a Sphinx Society cigar room. He'd started as a board member—as one of the only things his father gave his mother in the divorce settlement—and had consolidated his power, updated the once aging group into a coveted invitation once more. He wouldn't let some lowly action star like Connor Henry be a distraction.

"And we have more important things to worry about. I'll be sending you potential venues for the Masquerade Ball. That'll be all."

"Yes, sir." Madelyn bowed her head and ducked out of his office.

The Masquerade Ball. This most opulent, most extravagant gathering of the society all year. It also happened to be one of the worst kept secrets among the upper echelon. Old money and new money vied for invitations to the ball, and not *every* society member received a black-and-gold envelope. Only *certain* members would know of the super-secret location of this year's most coveted event. Planning the event took months and poring over the society's ample membership list for the best and most deserving candidates. At the Masquerade, nearly anything was possible. Once, a live elephant mingled with the guests in Bali. In Milan, each guest received an engraved platinum bracelet designed by one of the brightest figures in fashion. In Egypt, guests sipped champagne in the shadow of the Pyramid of Giza.

Each year became more extravagant, more dazzling than the last, the guests working hard to top their extravagant costumes each year. But it wasn't just the stunts of the party that occupied Durand's mind. It was also the delicate balance of guests, the way he worked hard to deliberately pair together the right people. Sure, there was the spectacle, but the Masquerade was also where billion-dollar business deals got struck, love stories were made, and feuding families reconciled. That was the part that Durand loved the most.

Durand turned away from the window, glancing at the original Monet hanging above his polished, ornate gold-and-black antique desk, once used by King Louis XV in the Palace of Versailles. The golden clawed feet and ornate golden figures of women on either side, holding up pitchers and grapes, was ostentatious to be sure, but Durand liked exactly that about it. He also very much liked the fact that it stood as a reminder to him not to grow too egotistical, or too lazy. King Louis XV's extravagances and his weak rule, after all, helped sow the seeds of discord in France and led to the French Revolution.

As he took a seat behind the massive desk, loud voices from behind his office door captured his attention. There were at least two of them, and they were angry. Madelyn, he heard, was doing her best to shoo them out, but Durand felt the need to intervene. He wouldn't let his assistant be abused like this.

He swung open his door only to see Asha Patel, dressed in a fetching white linen strapless A-line sundress and matching strappy wedges, a large-brimmed straw hat shielding half of her face. She looked more like a starlet ready for her movie debut than an heiress. Most of them lacked Asha's striking natural beauty. They often used money to hide their flaws, but from Durand's watchful eye, he didn't see any. Her beauty, in fact, took his breath away—a cliché to be sure, one that he'd never believed possible, but the breath caught in his throat as his eyes roved her generous curves, her golden-almond-colored skin, her flawlessly lined dark, soulful eyes—a lighter brown than he remembered, a rich golden brown.

Two men in expensive suits flanked her, both carrying briefcases and the egotistical air of attorneys looking to sue. They were middle-aged and graying, with pudgy middles and faces fleshy from too much expensive wine, which meant they relished fights just like these. He'd met their kind before.

"What's the meaning of this?" Durand demanded, but kept his eyes on Asha. Asha met his gaze and lifted her chin in good old-fashioned defiance. Resentment flashed in her eyes. So, it seemed, she still had sore feelings about him for escorting her out of his party.

"I'm sorry, sir," Madelyn cried, eyes wide, a phone receiver in her hand, as she no doubt prepared to dial security. A blond hair fell loose from her normally pristinely pinned chignon. "They are insisting on seeing you. I told them you have many appointments today."

Durand eyed Asha, who glared at him, eyes flashing. He loved the way her bottom lip trembled just slightly—nerves? Anger? He wondered.

"I have come with my attorneys," she said. "And I'd like to discuss the issue of membership in the Sphinx Society."

So little Miss Disruption was back, and demanding entry into *his* club? He ought to throw her and her attorneys out on the street. Yet something about the defiant rise of her chin made him hesitate. Perhaps he could toy with her a little first. If she wanted to play a little game, maybe he'd indulge her. Cat and mouse was one of his favorite pastimes.

Durand chuckled low in his throat.

"You really think you can bully your way into my club, Ms. Patel?" He smiled slowly, almost relishing the challenge. It had been years since someone was bold enough to defy him openly. Perhaps she didn't know who she was dealing with. Yet.

"You owe me a meeting, Mr. Durand." Asha's dark eyes flashed. Look at that sense of entitlement. It was almost sexy, if it wasn't so obviously the temper tantrum of a spoiled heiress used to bullying people to get what she wanted.

"Oh, I assure you that I don't *owe* you anything." Durand made sure that people who demanded things from him regretted that decision. Even gorgeous heiresses. Or maybe, especially gorgeous heiresses.

Madelyn hovered in the background, still holding the receiver of the phone. "Shall I notify security, sir?" Her blue eyes were filled with concern as she clutched the phone.

Durand glanced at his assistant, and then back at Asha.

"I'll see Ms. Patel, but *without* her entourage." He met the gaze of each of the lawyers, who blinked back at him coldly with their nearly lifeless eyes.

"Ms. Patel," protested one of the pudgy, middle-aged men in their overpriced suits. "I strongly advise—"

She held up a perfectly manicured hand and the attorney instantly fell silent. "No, Robert. I'll allow it."

Allow it, as if she was royalty and not a new money tech heiress. Oh, my. Durand would enjoy this. New money so often lived under the mistaken impression that money, once made, lasted forever. Only heirs of vanishing old money knew the truth: you were always one or two bad investments away from losing it all. Or a single divorce, in Durand's case. A divorce that diverted his father's attention and resources to other children.

Madelyn slowly returned the receiver to the cradle, expressionless, although Durand suspected she would've preferred to kick out the beautiful heiress. Did she suspect Durand's interest?

And, so what if she did? Madelyn knew to keep her feelings under control. He'd never encouraged her, though technically, he hadn't disabused her of the notion either. He thought they understood that their working relationship had no room for tender feelings.

Durand stepped back from his ornately carved door and swept out his arm as Asha moved past, her Louis Vuitton purse clasped beneath one elbow, a trail of expensive perfume stretching out behind her. Madelyn sent him a worried glance before focusing on the attorneys in the waiting room.

"If those two so much as sneeze, feel free to call security," Durand instructed. The lawyers glowered at him quietly, but eventually sat on the gold antique love seats near the front door of his office. Madelyn gave him a reassuring nod and went back to her computer. Durand stepped into his office and closed the door behind him. Asha stood at the over-sized window, staring at the Eiffel Tower.

"That's quite a view," she said, turning around slowly, soaking it in.

"The view, mademoiselle, pales to your beauty," he said, easily. It was the truth. She glanced at him, suddenly, color rising in her cheeks. She wasn't expecting a compliment, though it was easy enough to give. She was far more beautiful than a metal tower in the distance, no matter how famous that tower might be.

"Do you think flattery will get you somewhere?" she challenged, recovering her composure. Durand liked to watch the struggle, liked to watch her try to keep her balance. This was going to be fun.

"I am simply being honest, mademoiselle," he said. "French men appreciate natural beauty."

"Do they? Is that all they appreciate?" She raised an eyebrow in challenge as she took off her sun-hat, freeing her long dark locks. He watched as they cascaded down her bare shoulders, soft enough and silky enough to beg for his touch. The sunlight danced in her hair, revealing merlot highlights. He could feel the power in her beauty calling to him, a siren's song, no doubt, an invitation to crash himself against the rocks. He'd need to keep his head. He'd need to be careful.

"Please, won't you have a seat?" he asked.

She picked one of his red velvet Queen Anne

chairs, her white dress stark against its bloodred fabric and painted gold accents.

"Quite the office you have here."

"I'm partial to antiques—to furniture with history," Durand said, indifferent, as he perched on the edge of his ornate desk, made over 250 years ago. "History is everything. Those who ignore history do so at their own peril."

"I do not care for history," Asha told him boldly. "I care about the future. Making my own path."

"And you think you can make your own path in a vacuum? Without knowing where you came from?"

She smiled at him but did not answer. Instead, she studied the golden accented desk. "Did that desk...belong to... King Louis XV?"

Durand couldn't help but be impressed. "You know antiques?"

She smiled, switching tacks, away from annoyed, entitled heiress and to...coy, flirty one. "Perhaps I just know *you,* Mr. Durand. I did a little research on you."

"About my proclivities in furnishing my office?"

"Among *other* things." She raised a solitary dark and perfectly manicured eyebrow. "You like to leave a trail of hearts in your wake."

He laughed a little. "That is not my fault if one is offered to me. I do not steal them, if that's what you're implying."

"So you just use your charms until you get what

you want and throw women away like disposable towels?" Asha shook her head slowly. "That is so… old-fashioned. Maybe you are a little *too* obsessed with history. You act like a relict, a playboy of the 1950s."

Durand laughed, unable to stop himself. Since when had a woman openly insulted him so? Not that he could recall. "You think I'm a relic?" An amused smile danced on his face. "And you believe that insulting me will get you what you want?"

Asha shrugged one shoulder. "I do not believe in flattery, as you do. Flattery is kissing someone's ass. I believe in a more direct approach."

"Is that so? Is that why you lied to me in Sweden? About being Connor's date."

Asha swept her black hair off one shoulder. "I didn't say I *never* lied. I said I don't believe in kissing asses."

He almost laughed but caught himself. "So you are trying to insult me?"

"Wouldn't you have to have *shame* to be insulted, monsieur?" She grinned.

She was using her wiles again, just like that night at the party on the balcony. The way she sat now, her head tilted just so, leaning forward just a tad so he could see the hint of cleavage in her square neckline. Leaning forward to give him the best possible view, that she no doubt practiced before one of her mirrors in her hotel room. He tried not to linger too

long there. He couldn't afford to get distracted. He
needed to stay on his toes. She wasn't going to get
the best of him. He'd make sure of that.

"You have a reputation, too." He met her dark-
eyed gaze. "A man-eater. A woman who leaves broken hearts in her wake. How many pop stars have
written heartbreak songs about you? Too many to
count, and on at least three continents."

She picked a piece of lint off her skirt, looking
nonplussed. "And?"

"And… I'm not sure how much of the gossip
should be believed, but I've read you are a woman
who has appetites even…greater than most men."

A small flush colored her cheekbones, a bit of
color that most might have missed, but Durand
prided himself on reading people, on being able to
detect even the slightest hint of emotion. She was…
embarrassed. Not quite the reaction he'd expected
from the world's most famous and unapologetic
party girl. But she was quickly trying to hide the
shame with bravado. She squared her shoulders and
looked him in the eye.

"What is wrong with a woman wanting what a
man wants?" she challenged.

"Absolutely nothing," Durand said.

Asha leaned forward even more, revealing more
of the top curve of her golden-tan breasts, her skin
the color of a perfect creamy latte. He tried to avoid
her neckline, but found himself drawn to it again

and again. By design. She knew what men liked. That much was obvious. He studied it all: the ridge of her collarbone made him want to lay feather kisses on it, the flawless golden-tinted skin, the cleavage—plunging. Still, of the traps he'd seen laid for him, this was a truly, beautiful trap. He could see why so many men fell for it. The woman's body begged to be touched. Begged to be explored.

"Well, then. We know each other at least," he added, and with great strength of will stopped staring at her flesh. He hated that it had such an effect on him. Yet he wondered if her appetites could match his. He was a man who liked to explore every crevice of a woman, who felt sex wasn't sex unless it was a complete mind and body experience. Would she be able to meet him? Keep up? He wondered.

"As much as I'd love to talk about me, I believe we have business to discuss," Asha said, shifting gears. "I'd like to be a member of the Sphinx Society."

"Yes, well, there's one problem with that," Durand said as he moved from his desk and sat in the Queen Anne chair opposite her own. Now, face-to-face, it was her beautiful, watchful brown eyes that distracted him and not her delicate tan shoulders and beautiful skin. She was so very small, so very delicate, even her hands, which she kept neatly folded on her knees. "You need an *invitation* to join, and I'm afraid you do *not* have one of those." He cleared his throat, his gaze never leaving hers.

"You seem to have a problem with always showing up uninvited."

Annoyance tugged at the corner of her mouth. "Do I? Well, I'm not the kind of woman who waits around hoping to be rescued," she said. "I'm a woman who goes after what she wants."

"Indeed." One of her sexiest qualities, he thought. Like so many brash Americans, she seemed to believe that sheer force of will could make anything happen. Except there was wishful thinking, and then there was brutal reality. The French knew all about brutal reality. "But in this case, I'm afraid, you can't just muscle your way in. No matter how American, nor how *rich* you may be."

"My lawyers say…"

"Your lawyers have no sway here. This is a private club. I am its owner, and I decide who joins. Period. *C'est comme ça.*" Durand leaned back in his chair.

She reached out and put her hand on his knee, the meaning and invitation impossible to miss. He felt a jolt from the top of his knee to the pads of his feet, as if her very touch was electrified. His whole body hummed with nervous energy, every nerve ending acutely aware of the woman's hands, of where else he'd like them to be on his body. A hunger came to life in his belly, a hunger for *this woman*. "Are you sure there's nothing I can do to persuade you?"

For a second, he couldn't respond. His brain had

shut off, and in its place was just primitive, base need. A need for this woman's hands on his body. A need to put his hands on hers, a primal hunger pervading his being to taste her, to taste all of her. He wanted badly to kiss her again, to have her breathless in his arms, to make her moan.

No. To make her beg.

If she'd had so many men before him, then he'd make damn sure he was the one she'd never forget. It almost felt like a challenge he couldn't ignore. A ripe, perfect grape in need of plucking.

He studied her hand on his knee, hoping she couldn't know the effect it was having on him right now, the unsettling need she'd awakened, the yawning need.

"We could…how do you say…fuck? Right here?" He spread out his hands to show the expensive Persian rug beneath their feet. He had no intention whatsoever of taking her here, on his office floor, in full range of Madelyn and her army of attorneys, but *she* did not know that. She assumed he was an uncouth playboy relic, so he'd act like one.

The offer took Asha by surprise. He saw the flicker of—was it panic?—cross her face. She withdrew her hand from his knee. Interesting, then. The woman who supposedly had no shame, with a reputation for being the world's most vicious man-eater, might actually be…shy? When he called her on her advances…she withdrew? Perhaps that meant she wasn't as confident as she appeared. Maybe she was bluffing. Maybe all that bluster about being a woman unashamed about her appetite might not be completely true? It would explain her unease when he'd mentioned her reputation.

"Here?" Asha scoffed. "But my lawyers are right outside…"

"Let them hear us. Who cares what they think?" Durand pressed. "Surely not a woman as bold as you."

Pink crept up into her cheeks. She was *blushing*. Oh, this was perfect. Truly perfect. He'd put her back on her heels. The way she shifted in her seat made her seem like more of a prude than a party girl. Maybe it had all been an act, the worldly seductress nothing more than a blushing innocent.

And now that he had her retreating, he'd press his advantage.

"Yes, well…" Asha's attention darted to the door, which did not have a lock. So she'd clocked that. And it made her uncomfortable. She definitely wasn't the wild seductress of her reputation. Yet somehow, that fact made her…even more seductive.

"Did you not want to make this transaction? I thought that is what you came here for." He reached out and stroked her cheek, her chin, his finger trailing down the side of her neck. His motive unmistakable.

"Well, of course I do, but…" She bit her lip. She was trying to come up with an excuse. He would let her try.

"But…?" he prompted.

"Well, how can we have *decent* sex here?" She swept her hand across the sunlit room of his office. "And with people hearing."

"That makes you embarrassed?"

"No." She lied. He could tell by the way her gaze darted away from his.

"The blush on your cheeks and the way you won't meet my eye tells me otherwise, I'm afraid."

Asha coughed and stood, turning her back to him so she could glare at the Eiffel Tower. "I am not embarrassed."

"Do you always lie about such things?" This was extraordinary. A seductress with *shame*. A man-eater with performance anxiety. Oh, my, my. What would he discover about her next?

"No," she snapped. "If you want sex for the membership then, fine." She whirled, eyes furi-ous, as she angrily tugged at the side zipper of her sundress, as if she planned to peel off her clothes and get this over with. As if it were a bothersome exercise. That was a bit insulting, to be honest. Du-rand didn't want to be a chore. He'd make sure he wasn't. Not to her or anyone else.

"No, no, no, ma chère." He stood and stopped

her from undressing herself in a rage. "I tease you. I do not mean to make you give yourself to me."

"You don't?" Now she was utterly confused.

"I told you that I do not accept *gifts* of this nature in exchange for membership."

"Then…" She blinked fast, her brain catching up to the reality. "You are just teasing me? Playing with me?"

He was. "I am just having a bit of fun."

"At my expense." She tugged up her zipper and angrily crossed her arms on her chest. "So I am wasting my time, then? You won't give me a membership?"

"I did not say that." He grinned. "But there might be one thing you could do." He leaned even closer to her, so now they were less than a foot apart. Her eyes grew wide, excited even, at the prospect of her trap working.

"Anything," she murmured, voice low but cautious. Her perfume filled his nose and drove him a little bit wild. How he'd love to get beneath that designer scent to her skin. Her real self.

He smiled slowly. "You are willing to do…whatever I ask?"

"Yes," she nodded frantically. "Whatever you want."

"You could say '*please.*'"

She laughed, a sexy, throaty laugh. But he didn't join her. It was time to teach this impatient, brash, *full-of-herself* American some manners. When she realized he was serious, the laugh died in her throat.

"You mean it?" she managed.

Durand cocked his head to one side but said nothing. "Those are my terms." He shrugged one shoulder. "How do you Americans say? Take them…or leave them?"

"You mock me." Now Asha's lips flattened in disapproval. Anger danced once more in her eyes.

"On the contrary, Ms. Patel. I'm only trying to see if you have any humility."

Asha stood, sweeping her white skirt across his knee. "I'll not be insulted like this," she said. "Next you'll ask me to beg."

"Perhaps." Durand couldn't help himself. He chuckled, low in his throat. Making her beg *would* be so very satisfying.

"I don't beg." Asha set her lips in a thin, determined line.

"Perhaps you have not met the man strong enough to make you *want* to beg," Durand offered. He sat back in his chair and interlaced his fingers across his knee. "Surely, saying *please* is an easy exchange for a membership you want so much?" Durand almost enjoyed watching her squirm. He could see her fight with herself: her pride on the one side, her desire to get her way on the other. He loved it. Loved watching her inner battle. She *was* intriguing, and he honestly wasn't sure at that moment which side of her would win. Durand, who could read people better than anyone he knew, couldn't predict this little heiress. Maybe that's why he found her so intriguing.

"If I say please, what guarantee do I have that you're serious? That you'll give me what I want?"

Durand raised both eyebrows. "Why, none at all. You simply will have to trust me."

Asha weighed his offer for just a split second.

"You're impossible." She snatched her bag from the chair and stomped to his door. Durand stood as well, still grinning.

"No. I believe I am just the one…how do you say…holding all the cards?"

Asha let out a disgusted grunt and, glaring at him, opened his office door with such force, it banged against the line of first edition books on his shelf. Asha swept out without a backward glance, and her attorneys, surprised, scrambled to their feet to follow her out of the office.

"How rude," Madelyn exclaimed in French as she stood, surprised. "I hope she has learned the lesson that she can't just demand everything she wants."

"Somehow, I don't think she's learned that at all," Durand said. "I have a sneaking suspicion I'll be seeing her again. Sooner rather than later."

CHAPTER THREE

ASHA SIPPED CHAMPAGNE from a crystal flute, staring out the window of one of her father's private jets as they headed upwards to cruising altitude. She stewed in the anger that still bubbled in her belly. How dare Durand toy with her? She wasn't some dumb socialite, or another kind of woman that likely had no other ambition than to worm her way into his bed. Asha studied the puffy white clouds above Paris and fumed. She'd never been so soundly rejected in all of her life. Never been so *dismissed* as inconsequential by anyone, and she'd met the Queen of England. If anyone had the right to give her the cold shoulder, it was the Queen. Not Mathis Durand. So what that his family made their fortune in the shipping business: more than a century ago, his father hadn't earned his money, but inherited it. Her father defied much greater odds to build a tech empire today.

She understood all too well the tension between

old money and new money. She *had* gone to one of the East Coast's most revered girls' boarding schools. Asha knew firsthand that money didn't solve all problems. Not among the old money elite who felt it was their job to keep newcomers out, especially ones who weren't the "right" race. She remembered the taunts some of the meaner girls had leveled at her, taunts about the color of her skin, the fact that her family came from India, the horrible nicknames that stuck with her through a whole year. She knew what they were trying to tell her: her skin was brown, she was new money, and she would never be welcomed into their social circles, circles with a legacy that stretched back generations to the families who were now household names, who'd built America. In their eyes, there wasn't any room for newcomers, especially those who looked different than them. But she'd proved them wrong. She'd survived it all. She'd outmaneuvered the bullies. She'd left that damn school as one of the most popular girls. Hell, she'd been *class president*. And she wasn't about to be laid low by the owner of a private club, no matter how entitled he believed he was. She'd come too far for that.

Asha watched Paris fade as the plane rose higher in the clouds, and the Eiffel Tower grew ever smaller until she could see it no more. The worst part of all was how easily he seemed not to care about her advances, how he seemed immune to her charms. It was insulting on many levels, but most of all because *she* was most definitely *not* immune to his. Even now, she remembered the determined and experienced way his lips had moved on hers, the way a simple kiss on the balcony in Sweden had electrified her entire body. But rather than being keen on repeating the experience, Durand seemed not to care. Was that how he kissed every woman he met? Did she really offer him nothing new? She thought of the women who eyed him at that party, as if he were a juicy steak they intended to devour. Maybe not. Maybe she hadn't made an impression on him.

Damn him, then.

Still, it was the sting of his rejection that burned. He'd hinted he wanted to take her, there in his office, but when she'd finally agreed...he'd told her no. Men didn't reject her. She rejected *them*. Did she use sex *appeal* to get what she wanted? Sure. Had she done that unfortunate fast food commercial naked, wearing only suds and playing up her sex kitten image? Sure she had, but it had just been for fun, a lark. When it came to men actually getting into her bed, she was...picky. Beyond picky. Downright particular.

Truth be known, she often rejected them long before even the first kiss. Ironic, then, she had such a reputation for sleeping around. It was all her ex-suitors bemoaning her on their social media accounts, implying more happened than did. Just like Connor. Hell, they'd only ever heavy petted across their clothes before he found the need to two-time her with a model. But it worked for his public profile: player plays the player. She didn't care what people said about her. Besides, being a bad girl had its perks. Typically, she could get away with more.

Not to mention that it was one way to rebel a little against her tight-fisted father. She didn't mind that at all.

She set the almost empty champagne glass down in the round, gold-lined holder in the polished wooden arm of her chair. Asha glanced at her phone. On her father's plane, the pilot allowed her to keep it on for the duration of the flight. One of the many perks of private travel.

I expect to see you tomorrow at the board meeting.

She sighed. She wouldn't be going to his board meeting in San Jose. She was headed to London. To one of Durand's next parties. She'd seen the party on his assistant's computer screen because she'd been too slow to hide it. She had her own priorities, and they didn't include sitting in on earnings meetings or charming members of the board on her father's behalf. Besides, her father had long since made it clear that she was to be *seen* and not *heard* at the board meetings. He called all the shots. Her father: the control freak.

I'm not coming. You know why.

Her phone rang then.

"Why can't you come?" Her father's clipped British accent came through the line crystal clear with his disapproval.

"Have you considered my proposal about cutting emissions for the entire company?" she asked him.

He sighed, irritated. "No, you know that our bottom line…"

"Or…letting our warehouse workers organize?"

Her father let out a groan. "You know that would kill our bottom line. We've talked about it and we decided."

"No, *you* decided." This was the problem with trying to work with her father. He made all the rules, and all the decisions, and wasn't much even in the frame of mind to debate issues, either. He wanted her to be a part of the business, but only as a child at the Thanksgiving table generations ago—to be seen, not heard.

"Asha. Please. Should I cut off your funds? I don't want to do it, but if you won't meet the family obligations…"

She glanced out her small window as the private plane glided over the fluffy clouds below.

"Go ahead." This was met with shocked silence. Good. She wasn't just a trophy her father got to sit at the board table. She was a smart woman with her own ideas. Her own goals.

"You can't be serious. You won't have the money to do your absurd socializing. All those ridiculous videos you make…all those parties. When are you going to settle down and get serious?"

"Those videos make a lot of money, Father." So did her new cosmetics line, and her legion of followers who wanted to know about every new outfit she donned, every new party she went to. They'd make sure she didn't go hungry. "This image you hate so much funds all those parties."

"You couldn't survive without me and you know it. You do not want me to cut you off." Her father still couldn't believe it. But then again, he'd always tried to control her with money.

"You're wrong, Dad. I don't *need* your money. I've not been living on your money for some time." That felt good to say. After years of trying to work her way out from under his thumb, of dreaming of real independence, she was finally really doing it.

"The very plane you're on is *my* plane."

She glanced around the gilded interior. Sure, she'd miss the private jets. But she could still afford to fly first class, commercial. And she would. It wasn't all *that* much of a sacrifice. She could forgo his private cars, too. There were such things as rideshares, after all.

"H-how did you…" Her father sputtered on the line, truly amazed. Well, let him be amazed. He'd been so wrapped up in trying to get her to take a more prominent role in his company that he'd not noticed she'd already struck out on her own. She didn't want to carry on his legacy. She wanted to forge her own path. She just wasn't sure what that might be—yet. If she took over her father's company, she'd just be a legacy kid for her whole life. She wanted to have something that was uniquely her own.

"Because I worked hard, Dad. I learned that from you." She glanced upwards at the roof of the private jet.

"You are making money from the social media… things you do?" Her father still sounded shocked.

"Yes. Those things make money. So do the cosmetics I sell."

Her father made a frustrated sound. "But the woman on your accounts…that is not you, Asha."

Asha sighed. "It's a persona. Nothing more. And it's very, very profitable."

"I don't understand why you have to be *someone else* to make money. I am always myself. I do not pretend to be someone else."

"You're you, Dad."

"Yes. That's the whole point." Her father sucked in a frustrated breath. "I want you to take a bigger role in The Skycloud, Asha. You know this. Please. Do it for me, if not for the money."

Her father's voice had softened, and she did realize how much this meant to him. On some level, she understood this. Knew that he only wanted to make sure the business he'd created lived on in the family. Yet this wasn't *her* dream, and she had to somehow make him understand that.

"Dad, I really can't…"

"No. Don't tell me a final no. Think about it."

"Dad." Asha sighed in frustration.

"Just *think* about it. Do that for me."

"Fine," she said, relenting, even though she knew this only delayed the inevitable. Asha had thought about it. Her answer was no, but she was still working out a way to tell her father this. He'd built the company from the ground up, and she was his only natural heir. But tech stocks and new ways to track user data online just didn't appeal to her. She wanted to do something else with her life. She just wasn't sure what yet.

"What's to think about? I want you by my side."

"Yes, but…" She wanted to walk her own path. Yet she was having trouble breaking the news to her father. She would. One of these days. Just not now. "We'll just talk about it later. By the way, have you ever heard of the Sphinx Society?"

"No. What is it? A restaurant?"

Asha laughed. "It's a club. For the elite."

Her father clucked his tongue, sounding disapproving. "Sounds like a reason for rich people to pat themselves on the back." Her father didn't believe in status or the *look* of things. He was too busy taking over the world, one single-day delivery at a time.

"So you're not a member?" she prodded.

"No. Why waste my time with vanity projects? I have real work to do."

Somehow, the fact that her father *wasn't* a member made her want membership even more. It would be one more step to staking out her little claim on the world. Besides, she wanted nothing better than to somehow get the best of Durand. She wasn't going to take no for an answer. Boarding school had taught her that you either fight for your rightful place in the world or you just let the world walk all over you.

Not to mention, reporting from one of his invite-only parties was exactly what her followers would go crazy over. She'd be even more popular. She'd sell even more mascaras. Win-win.

Then she hung up and began thinking about just how she was going to get past security at the *next* Sphinx Society party that next evening at the

British Museum in London. She knew this because she'd managed to plant a bug on Madelyn's computer during her little meeting with Durand. Turns out, it wasn't all a bust.

To London, she planned to go. And she couldn't wait to see the look of shock on Durand's face when she showed up uninvited. Again.

The Egyptian sculpture gallery at the British Museum the next evening was awash in low purple light and filled with guests—in masks—wearing the trademark white and black, as they sipped champagne and chatted among themselves. Asha wondered why everyone was required to be black and white, and told herself she'd file away the question for Durand later. Was he allergic to color? Still, this time, she came prepared, wearing a tight-fitting, shimmering black dress with a plunging neckline and a matching black glittering mask across her eyes, but all she could do was gape at the surroundings: massive Egyptian sculptures dotted the exhibit, making her feel small. Ramesses II, among others, and then…the main attraction at the center of the room, the Rosetta Stone standing in a large glass display case, the very stone that made translation of the hieroglyphics possible. History here was impossible to ignore. It screamed from every glassed-in exhibit, from the statues of the

Parthenon to upstairs, where Cleopatra's mummy lay entombed in a display case. Treasures lay here from all over the world, history shouting from every corner. No wonder Durand picked this place, Asha thought. He and his obsession with history.

Asha had never been to the British Museum before, and certainly not after hours where all the rich and glittering guests wore formal designer clothes. She scanned the crowd for Durand, but failed to find him amid the many dozens of men with dark hair swept back, masks across their faces that hid most of the true identities as they moved past the giant six-feet-tall golden vases, palm fronds splayed at the top, like the world's most expensive palm trees. She stared at the enormous bust of Ramesses II, and the old black-and-white photos of the original archeologists about two hundred years ago, taking the statue from a temple. Asha wondered who gave them the right to take the statues. Why was Ramesses here at all, and not in a museum in Cairo?

"Impressive, isn't he?" a familiar voice whispered in her ear, the French accent faint but unmistakable.

She turned to see Durand, hiding behind a silver mask, his white tuxedo impeccable. Even though half his face was covered, she'd know that crooked smile anywhere. They were the perfect mix, it seemed: he in white and she in black. She felt her heart tock up a notch and hated that the very presence of him sent blood flowing straight to her thighs. She was only glad he couldn't read her mind.

"I was just wondering what gave them the right to take all these treasures. Don't they really belong at home, in Egypt?"

Durand's sensual mouth tugged up to a smile. "Ah, you Americans. Still so troubled by colonialism."

"Well, we *were* colonies. The wound's still a little fresh."

"These treasures are well taken care of," Durand said. "If they were left, they might have been destroyed."

"Or maybe it's because *history* is written by the victors, so they believe artifacts belong to them, too."

"Is that why you don't like history, Ms. Patel?"

"Maybe," Asha said, not even sure herself why seeing these world treasures bothered her so much. After all, they were spectacular, and on display free to the public. Except, of course, during glitzy parties, where the super-rich gathered with their expensive champagne and used the backdrop to socialize. "I just don't think the British Empire should decide where these treasures reside."

"The British aren't all too blame. Take the Rosetta Stone." Durand nodded behind them to the tablet in the case, the one with hieroglyphics and Greek. "It was found by French soldiers."

"And yet it's here. In London."

Durand shrugged slightly as he took a step closer. "Well, the stone belongs here. But you, Miss Patel, I'm afraid, you're once again without an invitation."

Durand put his hand on the small of her back, just a tiny bit of pressure. His hand felt big and warm and strong, and she had to fight an urge to lean into his touch. A shiver ran down her spine.

"Perhaps we should discuss your trespassing in private."

"I'd rather discuss how you'll be approving my *membership* in private." Durand smiled, amused.

"You are an optimist, aren't you?" Durand moved her away from the Egyptian statues and Asha let him steer her.

"More like I'm always determined to get my way," she said, as Durand led her out into the Great Court, the giant open circular heart of the museum, and as a nearby sign proclaimed, the largest enclosed "public square" in Europe. High above them, latticed steel over glass sheltered them from the night air. The stars in the sky were covered by clouds. Soon, he took her directly into the massive cylindrical building at the center, and inside, she found herself in an enormous reading room. Up above, a domed ceiling with a single circular glass window showed the dark night sky. The lights, already dimmed, gave the room a solemn feel, and large drapes across furniture and a scaffolding for construction sat against some of the shelves.

"This part of the museum has been closed for some time, and they're renovating it now," he said. "We won't be disturbed here."

He closed the brass double doors behind them, and a little bolt of excitement traveled from her head to her toes. She was alone with him here in the dim light of the circular room, most of the furniture hidden beneath tarps, and she wondered just what that meant. Could she explore the electric connection with him? Could she—finally—convince him by any means necessary that she deserved a society membership? She felt a tremor of nerves through her arms and down her fingertips. She really wasn't like her online persona, the one who jumped men on a whim. It was simply a mask she wore, like the one across her eyes right at this moment. Yet neither one was making her feel very brave at the moment. Still, she wanted this. More than she'd wanted most anything she could remember. She wanted the membership, but beyond that, she wanted Durand. His hands on her. She'd happily sacrifice her body to him if that meant getting what she wanted. And part of her knew it would be no sacrifice at all.

She turned to him and took off her mask, slowly.

"If you want to get me alone, Mr. Durand, all you needed to do was ask." She laughed at her own joke as she took a step closer to him. He didn't move and kept his blue eyes on her. She reached up and took the edges of his mask, and he let her. Might as well play to her reputation. Men loved it. She could do brash and brazen all day.

His eyes swept her slowly from head to toe, taking in her entire body, lingering at her plunging neckline. She grinned. Men. So predictable. Maybe this wouldn't be the challenge she thought. She arched her back, ever so slightly, giving him a better angle, glad she'd opted not to wear a bra beneath the thin-strapped dress. Eventually, he pulled his gaze away from her body and studied her eyes.

"I want a membership," she said, feeling confident now. "I want an invitation." Above their heads, in the circular skylight, the moon broke free of the clouds, sending a silver light into the room, brightening the dimness.

Durand slid his hands into his pockets, rocked back a little on his heels. "You cannot demand either, I'm afraid."

"I'm not *demanding*. I'm *asking*. Nicely." She took a step back from him. Now was the time to offer what most men wanted. She didn't have to give herself, not really, just a little peek, a little tease. Men were usually so easily swayed. Easily distracted. And she could play the role they wanted. She'd just pretend. Like she usually did. "I know you said you do not usually accept *gifts,* yet would you make an exception?"

Except, of course, she did expect something in return.

She'd hadn't forgotten the debacle of his office, where he'd called her bluff about sex. This time, she was ready. She wouldn't be blindsided, because this time she'd be the one to make the first move, the one to keep him off guard. Asha moved one strap of her dress down her right shoulder, slipping her arm out of it. Then, she eased the left strap down. She let the top half of the dress fall to her hips, the cool air of the room brushing across her chest, making her brown nipples stand at attention. Asha stood, topless, watching him as his eyes roved her bare skin, as his mouth tightened with want. She saw his arms stiffen, as if he were trying to fight the urge to touch her. Let him fight. It was a fight he would lose. She knew men enjoyed her body. Knew what her gravity-defying breasts did to their libidos. She knew her best angles and strongest assets and exactly how to use them. She also knew that a mere touch, a mere glimpse, and most men were putty in her hands. Men, in her experience, were simple and predicable.

Now, she stepped closer, reaching out her hand and grasping his wrist. She pulled his hand upwards to her right breast, putting his hand beneath it. He didn't fight her. Couldn't seem to fight her, as he touched her, firmly, but gently, cupping her.

He flicked his thumb across her nipple, causing it to harden even more.

"Please?" she whispered then, as he stared at her pointed nipple. "Isn't that what you wanted? Me to beg?"

Her voice was so low, almost a hoarse whisper, that she wasn't sure at first if he'd heard her. But then, he looked up at her face. She could read him like an open book, a book that spelled out want. Desire. Need. She could feel it thrumming in him, a live wire, snapping with electric power. Want was a dangerous thing, she knew. Want made people do things against their interests, made them make foolish decisions. Hadn't her father told her a thousand times that the key to being successful in business was not to let emotions rule? Durand was fighting his own desire. She could see it in his face as he struggled to keep it completely expressionless. He held her as if weighing his options, knowing the route he'd take might just be inevitable.

Then, he shook his head slowly. He lowered his hand and backed away from her.

She couldn't help but raise her eyebrows in surprise. This wasn't what she expected. Not at all. She was supposed to be the one in control, not him. Never him.

"You can't use your body to get what you want, Ms. Patel," Durand said after a beat, but his voice came out a little bit hoarse, a little strained, as if the effort of holding himself back took every bit of willpower he had. "I will not make an exception."

She moved to him, trailing a fingernail down the front of his shirt, and brushed the fly of his white tuxedo pants.

"Oh, it's not my body I plan to use to get what I want." A tempting smile curved the edges of her red lips. "It's yours."

She flattened her palm against the front of his fly, feeling him very much alive, very much ready for more. Some men needed *more* persuasion, and perhaps he was that kind of man. A hand job, then, she thought. Easy enough. As she rubbed him, she fanned the flames of his desire. She could see it in his eyes, the struggle. Could see how much effort it took for him not to move. Yet the only way for him to stop this, she knew, was to leave her in this room. Leave her, bare chested, her hand on the fabric against his cock, and she didn't know any man with that kind of willpower. She rubbed him harder, feeling him come alive, strain against the fabric. She knew exactly what would drive him wild. What drove every man wild. She undid the latch of his pants, sliding his zipper down. Her heart thudded in her chest, but she could do this. Just because she was used to playacting, flirting from afar, didn't mean she was a virgin with no skills. She reached in and found him bare, found him ready, found him so very, very thick.

She wrapped her hand around him and his lips parted, his pupils growing big and dark. She knew what she needed to do. Knew that despite his apparent sophistication, Durand, in the end, was like any other man, led by his cock. This was going to be easier than she thought. She'd have the membership in no time, and she'd be able to file Durand under one of many challenges met and answered. She worked him with her hand, delighting in how much her touch affected him. Soon he'd been begging *her* to join the society. She had no doubt about that. Good, she thought. All according to plan. A few more minutes, and the society membership would be hers.

But then, he took her by the wrist, freezing her motion. She glanced up at him, surprised, but before she could protest, he'd lowered his mouth to hers, hungry. She matched his appetite, her mouth open to his, her tongue lashing his. He tasted like champagne, and something more dangerous, a power she hadn't anticipated. But somewhere in the kiss, her game became serious. She was no longer the one in control. He deepened the kiss, pulling her to him with a strong hand to the small of her back. Her nipples pressed against his stiff tuxedo jacket, and his hardness against her lower abdomen pressed against the shimmering, thin fabric of her dress. Now he was taking off his jacket, shrugging out of it, lips still on hers. And she found herself forgetting, for a minute, what she was doing here, why she was here, and all she wanted was his hands on her.

Maybe she'd need more than a hand job. Hell, maybe she'd even enjoy it. A dirty little quickie right here in the dark. It went against her usual strategy, but this was an unusual situation. Maybe she could let herself go enough to enjoy it. Her few real lovers hadn't always been able to make her come, and too often, she'd been left unsatisfied. That's why she preferred to reject them first, before she found that her body wouldn't cooperate with her own mind, that she couldn't reach the finish line, even as her partners sprinted right past it. The irony of the fact that Ms. Party Girl couldn't really climax wasn't lost on her. She realized how ridiculous the situation was, but it was the truth. She'd worked hard to craft her persona, the face she showed to the world. But it wasn't her true self.

Durand's kiss told her that he wouldn't be fooled. He demanded her whole mouth, hell, her whole body in that kiss. He wouldn't let her hide. Wouldn't let her pretend. Maybe Durand would be different than other men. Maybe she'd even let him try.

She worked his shirt buttons, hungrily taking his mouth, and he inched down her bare lower back, finding the zipper of her expensive dress. In seconds, the dress dropped to the floor, in a pool by her red-soled stiletto Christian Louboutins.

Now she stood naked before him, wearing only a lacy thong. He still wore his shirt, though she'd gotten half the buttons undone, the muscled shape of his chest visible in the low light. She itched to touch his bare skin and wanted to put her hands in his shirt.

But then, his hands rested on her hips as he moved her backward, as she carefully stepped out of her dress. His lips demanded more of her, and they moved back into the room, until the ridge of a table hit the back of her upper thighs. In one quick motion, he'd lifted her up on the table. His mouth trailed down her neck then, down the front of her chest, and his tongue found her nipples. She gasped as he took one in his mouth, gently, the pressure of his teeth on the edge creating a pool of want between her legs. Now it was her turn to feel desire burning in her belly, to feel the rage of need churning in her.

She forgot completely about the Sphinx Society, about her little game with Durand. About how she needed to be in control. Now, all she wanted was his hands and his mouth and everything he could give her. And she wanted it now. Asha opened her thighs and pulled him closer to her. All that separated him and her was the thin little stretch of lacy fabric of her thong. In that moment, she didn't even think about consequences: about protection or about whether or not she'd actually even get the membership she so wanted. All she knew was that she burned for this man in a way she hadn't burned for anyone. Perhaps ever.

She wanted him. And she rarely wanted anyone.

She could feel him pressing against her pelvic bone, could feel the thick weight of him against her as he shifted his attention to the most delicate spot on her throat.

"Yes," she whispered as she glanced up at the full moon overhead in the circle of paned glass in the domed ceiling. "I want you inside me."

He pressed harder against the thin fabric, and his hands went to the edges of her thong. She suddenly wanted him to rip it away, the passion between them burning so hot he couldn't help himself. Yet Durand hesitated.

Why? Her brain burned with impatience. Her whole body simmered with need. Now this wasn't a game, wasn't about any membership, it was about something deeper and more primal. It was about her want.

And then, he backed away from her. Cold air hit her bare body. She blinked fast in the near darkness. What was he doing?

She struggled to understand why as she watched him tuck himself inside his fly and zip his pants.

"I'm afraid I cannot accept this…" He glanced at her bare chest, her nearly naked body, prostrate on the table. "Bribe. Beautiful…and tempting…

though it may be. Especially since I know this isn't
you, Asha."

She froze then. Feeling more than naked. Feeling vulnerable. "What do you mean?"

"You are playacting. You are wearing a mask of
your own choosing."

"No, I'm not." At least, she wasn't now. Maybe
it had started as a game, but the pounding of her
heart in her chest was real, the thumping of want
in her belly as true as it got.

He took another step backward and grabbed the
tuxedo jacket across a nearby chair. He dusted it off.
His composure was returning, bit by bit.

"I'll allow you time to compose yourself, Ms.
Patel. Then I'll have someone escort you out."

With that, he turned on his heel and left her,
nearly naked, completely unsatisfied, and hot with
embarrassment—and want. She panted, wondering
what the hell had just happened. Somehow, he'd
seen through her tactics, seen to the slightly scared,
intimidated woman beneath. But how? She couldn't
be that obvious. She was too good at acting for him
to know the truth. Wasn't she?

But, God, the worst of it was, she wasn't even
pretending. Her thighs were slick with want, and
her pulse beat hard in her temples. Her body had
responded to him honestly. His tongue had ignited
a white-hot fire in her belly.

And then, he'd walked away. Could it be that

he found her…lacking? That he didn't want her as much as she wanted him? Could he sense that her body was somehow wrong, that unlike other women, she couldn't climax so easily? Her own insecurities ate at her.

Or…was it just as he said, that he was a man determined not to be bribed?

Asha didn't know what to believe, but the rejection burned. He didn't find her sexy? The look in his eyes told her otherwise, and yet…here she was. Alone and abandoned.

This would *not* be tolerated, she thought, as she hopped off the table and snatched her dress angrily off the floor. Her hurt and insecurities dissolved beneath a tidal wave of fury. She'd never been treated this way. She wouldn't *allow* it. Not now. Not ever.

CHAPTER FOUR

DURAND COULDN'T CONCENTRATE on anything his assistant, Madelyn, was saying in the makeshift office of the penthouse suite in the Savoy Hotel in London. His large windows overlooked the Thames, and in the distance, the London Eye circled slowly, taking tourists upwards to view the city. He barely noticed them or the inside of his posh suite with the plush white couches and golden pillows facing a green marble fireplace as Madelyn went over the last of the bills from the night before. They were supposed to be tying up loose ends from the party, but his mind was elsewhere. Durand was consumed, too busy remembering the feel of Asha's bare breasts in his hands. Heavy. Soft. Perfect.

And the bright light of triumph in her eyes when she worked him, made him hard for her.

"Mr. Durand?" Madelyn's soft voice found him. She had her hands poised on her keyboard. "Should

I reach out to our usual vendor about catering for the big ball?"

"Yes," Durand managed. "Sure, Madelyn. That would be great."

"Is everything all right, sir?" Madelyn, wearing a pristine gray wool fitted blazer and a slim-fit skirt, sat with her legs pressed together on the small love seat, her laptop perched on her knees. Her blond hair was up in a tight French twist.

"Yes, Madelyn. Sorry. I'm just a bit…distracted." That was the understatement of the year. All he could think about were Asha's big dark eyes, wide with want for him, and the taste of her delicious mouth. How he'd only barely restrained himself from taking exactly what she offered him. He'd been so very close to falling into her trap. He refused to be another one of the woman's famous conquests, one more love-struck boy in her wake. He was no boy. He was a man—a man used to being in control. A man who'd worked his entire life to consolidate power, to outmaneuver his enemies, and to show the world he had no weaknesses, especially ones that revolved around feelings and wants. He'd long since learned to control those.

And then Asha Patel strolled into his life and wreaked havoc, dive-bombed his self-control, made him second-guess everything. Because he'd never had a woman he wanted so badly before. He always prided himself on being a man who could take or leave promises of the flesh. After all, one woman was very much like another.

Until Asha.

Asha, who he guessed that the very second he gave in to her, fell into her bed and promised her a membership, would dance out of his life, laughing as she went. And he could not risk that. She was a formidable foe, and one that couldn't be underestimated.

Yet something about the way she kissed, the way she'd pressed her body against his, told him that maybe she wasn't quite as experienced as she claimed. He couldn't say how he knew, exactly, just that the reality of the woman was different than the reputation. There were layers to her that he hadn't expected. Delightful little surprises.

Maybe that was why she stirred such passion in him. Because, God, how he'd wanted her. Like he'd wanted no one in his entire life.

"So, the tallies, sir? Are they suitable?" Madelyn held the bills in her hand from the British Museum and the Savoy. Work this morning seemed pointless.

"Yes," he said, waving his hand, not bothering to double-check the totals. These details didn't interest him this morning. All he wanted was Asha. And he felt as if rejecting her last night was a mistake.

Asha was a proud woman, and he'd rejected her: twice. What were the odds she tried for a third time? But if he were truly honest with himself, he worried that he wouldn't be able to fend off a third advance. He wanted her. Wanted her the way he'd never wanted a woman before. It felt primal, chemical, like their fate was somehow entwined in their DNA. He'd never felt want this powerful before. Never felt like it was out of his control.

Durand prided himself on his self-control. He wasn't like other men who let their petty vices rule their lives. No. Durand's father had taught him to be mentally strong in the usual way rich fathers did: by ignoring him. He knew that was part of the reason he'd taken a small, meaningless society and turned it into a force to be reckoned with. To get noticed. To keep people's notice. To have a place where *he* made the rules. And he so loved the rules.

Asha, on the other hand, hated rules. She clearly looked to circumvent them at every turn. In some ways, he knew that this was all a game to her. All she wanted was a membership, and after she got it, well, he suspected she would disappear from his life forever. And he worried that he didn't want her to leave. Not at all.

"Sir?"

Durand blinked again, realizing that Madelyn had been speaking and he hadn't been listening.

"Yes?"

"Will that be all, sir? Or did you want me to fetch

you some tea?" Madelyn was standing now, laptop folded against her chest.

"No, thank you. And, yes, that will be all." Madelyn nodded once and headed towards the door, no doubt to head back to her own hotel room to finish making the calls and setting up appointments. He needed to concentrate, needed to clear his mind of thoughts of Asha, but the harder he tried, the more he failed. Madelyn hesitated at the door.

"Uh, one more thing, Mr. Durand."

He glanced up. "Yes?"

"Ms. Patel has been calling Sphinx Society board members this morning."

"Excuse me?" The Sphinx Society had a board, just like any other private firm, but it was largely ceremonial. Durand himself owned the lion's share of the company. The board really just worked to give more prominent members a larger role. Durand ultimately still made the big decisions.

"Yes, sir." Madelyn hesitated, seemingly surprised by his sudden pointed interest. "She's trying to bribe them so that she can get a membership."

"You knew about this and you didn't tell me?" Durand felt anger rising in him, uncharacteristically. Normally, he never lost his cool, but he didn't like that Asha was making moves without him knowing about it. He wanted to know everything she planned. Hell, if he were honest, he just wanted to know everything about her.

"I'm sorry, Mr. Durand." Madelyn couldn't meet his gaze. ."I—I didn't think it rose to a level—" She looked up at him and swallowed the rest of her sentence. "I mean, she can't bribe the board. They work for you. And even if she did, she won't get an invitation to the club without your direct consent."

"Yes. But I'd still like to be informed." Everything Madelyn said was true, but he still wanted to know what Asha was doing, especially if she was talking to his board. What was she saying? What was she accusing him of? And more importantly…had she given up on trying to win him over entirely? He didn't like that idea. Not one bit. And yet…he admired her resolve, her determination to circumvent him. He'd seen through her playacting, and called her on it, and yet…she still wasn't giving up.

Most people would run home, embarrassed, but not Asha. She had determination. She was stubborn. Stupidly stubborn, and part of him admired her for it. The more he told her no, the more she was determined to get her way. Intriguing.

"You have taken an interest in Ms. Patel?" Madelyn asked, as she struggled to keep both face and voice neutral.

"A passing interest," he said, wondering if that were even true. Asha seemed never far from his thoughts. He was already more interested than he should be. That might be dangerous.

"Yes. Of course." Madelyn looked at the floor, once again working hard to keep her face blank. "I'll keep you informed."

He glanced at his downtrodden assistant, feeling guilty. "It's not your fault. Asha is…" he struggled to find the right words "…a unique case."

"Yes, sir." Madelyn still wasn't looking at him as she turned the knob of the door.

"Wait, Madelyn." Madelyn paused at the door, glancing back at him, hopeful.

"Yes, sir?"

"Can you get me the contact information for Asha Patel, please."

A look of confusion passed across Madelyn's face. "Are you sure, sir? If you just ignore her, she'll go away."

That's only a little bit of what Durand was afraid of. He didn't want her to go away. He wanted her in his bed.

"Just her contact information, please."

"Yes, sir. Right away." Madelyn nodded and then headed out the door, her body language stiffer, her demeanor curt. Durand knew why, but he didn't want to think about his assistant being jealous. Didn't want to deal with her crush at the moment. After Madelyn quietly closed the door behind her, he walked over to the love seat and sank into it. He grabbed his tablet on the coffee table and began doing research on Asha. Objectively, she would be a fine fit for the Sphinx Society. She was no doubt prestigious enough, and she'd created her own cosmetics company, successful in its own right, though no company right now could be remotely as successful as her father's Cloud. It owned most of the market share and seemed intent on gobbling up what was left.

The problem was that so many young, rich heirs like herself were so intent on their social media presence that Durand knew it rattled some of his more privacy-seeking members. The Sphinx Society prided itself on secrecy, after all. The masks were just one of the ways its members could mingle anonymously. The Society took its duty of keeping parties secret and its members' identities secret a top priority. Social media sensations were all but barred from the gatherings. No one trusted them to keep the Society's secrets.

Not that there were many to keep.

He didn't run underground S&M dungeons, or secret meetings for powerful people to rule the world. This was simply a fun distraction, a way for members to feel safe and secure, to let go and have a good time. He pulled up images of Asha, and immediately felt a surge of lust run through him. She was gorgeous, yes, but why this pull? Why did he want her so very badly? He pulled up an image from one of her social media accounts. She was on the beach, wearing a barely-there bikini, her beau-

tiful, perfect bronzed skin darker beneath the sun.
The curves of her body made his own respond, as
he remembered how soft she'd felt in his arms. How
pliant. Willing. Eager.

Eager to play you, an inner voice told him. He
couldn't know whether she was really attracted to
him or whether this was all a game to her.

He knew that, and yet, he still wanted her.
Wanted her badly. He could feel his body stiffen,
felt the urge to skim the fly of his own pants. Was
he really considering *pleasuring* himself to this
photo of her? Right here in his hotel room?

Maybe.

A message appeared on the screen of his tablet
from his assistant, with Madelyn's phone number
and email.

Durand didn't hesitate. He picked up his phone
and dialed her number. He was shocked to discover
that she answered on the second ring. Who answered their cell phones from unknown numbers,
he wondered?

"Hello?" she said, and her voice, so smooth, like
honey, reverberated through his lower abdomen.
Even the woman's voice was all sex.

"Ms. Patel," he began. "This is Mathis Durand."

A pause met him on the other end of the line.
He wondered, briefly, if she planned to hang up on
him. It was risky calling her like this. He knew it.
He had, after all, rebuffed her advances the day be-

fore. Would she yell at him? Unleash her temper? Or would she be too curious?

"What can I do for you, *Mr.* Durand?" Her tone sounded guarded. So, curiosity won out, he thought. But she was holding yelling or hanging up in reserve. He could guess that much.

"I understand you've been calling my board," he said. He stood and walked to the window of his suite. He watched a boat full of tourists sail down the Thames beneath the big white Ferris wheel.

"Does that trouble you?" The teasing note in her voice both irritated and aroused him at the same time. He fought within himself for control.

"No, Ms. Patel. You don't trouble me. Not at all." That was a lie. She troubled him quite a bit. In all the right ways. That was the problem. "I'm calling because I was wondering if you'd care to join me for dinner tonight."

"Dinner?" she couldn't keep the surprise from her voice. Good. Keep her off balance. That was the only way to win. "And why would I do that?"

"I was hoping to discuss the possibility of your membership. Into the Sphinx Society."

Asha went silent on the other end of the phone.

"What time?" she asked.

"Say 7 o'clock?"

"I think I could squeeze you in," she said, barely able to keep the excitement from her voice. She did want a membership, and badly. He wondered why it meant so much to her and told himself he'd use this evening to find out. "Where shall we dine?"

"Society business can't be discussed in public," he said.

"Is that a rule?" The amusement was back in her voice.

"So, I'd suggest my hotel suite."

"Would you now?" Durand realized too late that it sounded as if he planned a tryst in exchange for her membership. Which he wasn't. This was no quid pro quo. He would never barter for sex. It was beneath him. He never asked for sexual favors. Hell, he never needed to.

"We will only discuss business, I assure you." He felt his own face grow hot and wondered why Asha always made him feel off balance.

"Yes. Yes. Of course." She laughed, the hard edge of a challenge in it. "I'll be there, Mr. Durand."

CHAPTER FIVE

ASHA ARRIVED TWO minutes early at Durand's hotel suite door, butterflies rioting in her stomach, a swarm of them fluttering their tense, anxious wings. She pressed her hands against the thin fabric of her fitted gold cocktail dress that hit above the knee. The shiny fabric clung to her curves and the tiny straps over her almond-colored shoulders were largely decorative. She picked the dress knowing that it flattered, knowing that men would tend to stare at her when she wore it. She knew the effect it had and hoped that Durand fell under the same spell.

She wore slinky, strappy stilettos on her feet, knew that they made her calves flex in a way that men liked. She'd wrapped her dark, nearly black hair up in a French twist, and wore sparkling, dangling earrings she thought drew just the right amount of attention to the curve of her neck. Asha took a deep breath to steady her nerves. She told herself that this was exactly what she wanted: a membership, whatever the cost, and she ought to be relieved that Durand was motivated by the same things as every other man: sex and money.

Though she knew he couldn't be distracted with small things, a simple hand job or a little flash of flesh wouldn't do it. She'd have to go farther. Give her whole self. But she didn't even care about sleeping with him to get what she wanted. No. It wasn't that she didn't care. It might be that she cared too much. She *wanted* this. She worried she'd even jump into bed with him without the membership. She wanted to feel the man's hands on her body. Wanted to grind against him until their bodies became slick with sweat. She was actually *looking forward to it.* And that was a far more dangerous game. How often had men disappointed her? More times than she'd like to count. Then, when she'd fail to be pleased, it was *her* fault somehow.

Frigid.

That was the word one of them used, after, when he'd failed to make her climax. She worked hard to keep men at bay since then. She played to their fantasies of her, she remained in control, and then no one could ever find *her* lacking.

Now she needed to focus. Keep her eyes on the prize: the membership into the Sphinx Society. Durand probably wouldn't be anything special, and it was no good to get her hopes up. She lifted her fist and rapped hard on the double door of Durand's suite. Judging by the lack of doors down the hallway, she assumed the suite must take up the bulk of the corner of this floor of the Savoy Hotel.

Durand opened the door and Asha glanced up at his face, her mouth going suddenly dry. He was more handsome than she remembered, and this time, wore no mask. His dark wavy hair perfectly combed, his sharp blue eyes assessing. He wore a stiff oxford button-down, with three of the top buttons undone. She could see the hint of tanned chest there, and itched to run her hands inside his shirt, feel his smooth, muscled pecs beneath her fingers. He cleared his throat and she realized she was staring at his open shirt collar. Not exactly the best way to play her cards close to the vest.

"Would you care to come in?" He stepped backward, arm sweeping wide, to let her into his enormous luxury suite. She stepped inside, glancing about, but keenly aware of Durand's eyes as they swept her from head to toe. His gaze felt like heat she could feel.

"Wow. This is some place." Asha was used to opulence. After all, she had billions at her disposal, but this had the feel of old-world money. Mirrored walls gave the impression that the suite—largely decorated in white and gold—was much larger. She could see at least three large rooms, and none of them contained a bed. A living area, complete

with green marbled fireplace adorned with golden
antique statues, and two large white couches met
her as she stepped into the room, framed by antique golden floor lamps. A small hallway led to
a study with a glass desk and workspace with a
wall of shelves containing leather-bound books, and
beyond that, a dining table with four plush white
chairs. The dining table was already set with a silver candelabra and fine china. Near the table sat
a rolling cart with what she assumed must be dinner, hidden behind plates covered by ornate silver
domes.

"I'm impressed," she managed as she stepped
further inside, hesitating near the foyer table filled
with a large yellow-and-white bouquet of roses.
She trailed her fingers across the cool white marble tabletop. As she turned the corner, she saw a
black-and-gold bar near the dining room, on it, sat
a chilled bottle of open champagne.

"Would you like a glass of Dom Pérignon?"
Durand asked, his French accent even more pro-
nounced as he mentioned the famous champagne.

Asha raised an eyebrow. The butterflies in her
stomach hadn't calmed, and if anything, were still
flapping around like maniacs. Maybe a drink would
help calm her nerves. "Yes, thank you. I'd like that."

Durand passed close on her left, and he brushed
her arm ever so slightly. She felt a little chill run up
her arm as she watched him stride purposefully to

the bar, his legs long and lean in black pants that hugged him in all the right places. He was a man who kept himself in excellent shape. She appreciated that. So many wealthy men felt they deserved to let themselves go. Not Durand. She watched as he lifted the bottle out of the golden bucket and poured them each a foaming serving in a crystal flute. He handed it to her and her fingers brushed his as she took it. He raised his glass.

"To new friends," he said, and touched his rim to hers with a high-pitched plink.

"I hope to be more than friends," she said, feeling a little brazen as she met his gaze. If she could hide behind her persona, then maybe she had a chance of pulling this off. She knew what she was here for. She needed to keep reminding herself of that.

He stared at her a beat without answering, a playful smile tugging the corners of his lips. No matter how hard he tried to keep aloof, Asha could sense his growing desire for her, see it in the sparkle in his eye.

"Why do you do that?" he asked her and took a sip of his champagne.

"Do what?"

"Play the vixen."

"Who says I'm playing?" Her heart thudded now, the butterflies in a full-out panic in her stomach.

"I'm a good reader of people. I can tell." The

way he was studying her made her believe him. She could not read him and wondered for the briefest of seconds if he'd brought her here just to reject her once more. Her body vibrated with the knowledge that this night would end with their clothes on the floor, but now, her mind intervened. What if she'd read all the signals wrong? What if she'd come here only to be humiliated?

"We all act. After all, isn't that why you have these parties? Where all your guests can wear masks?"

A slow smile spread on Durand's face. "Touché," he conceded.

He was staring at her, and she'd forgotten to breathe. She inhaled, pushing the troubling thoughts from her mind. Surely not. Surely the man could feel the energy between them. It felt immovable, like gravity.

She took a sip of her own glass. The expensive bubbles hit her tongue with an explosion of flavor.

"This is delicious," she murmured, leaning against the bar.

"It should be. Dom Pérignon invented champagne." He held up his glass to the light, studying the bubbles flowing to the service. "Did you know he was a French Benedictine monk? His vineyard at the abbey produced phenomenal white wine in the 1600s at a time when almost all wine in France was red."

"Really? A monk?" She glanced at her own glass. "I guess he had a lot of time on his hands, what with taking all those vows of silence."

Durand laughed a little. "Probably true. Many think he also added the bubbles to the wine, but that came later."

"I like the bubbles," Asha said, taking a long sip. She'd drunk just half the glass and already she could feel a happy buzz beginning at the back of her brain. "This must be expensive."

He glanced over the rim of his glass at her. "Does everything need a price tag to be valued?"

"No," she said after a moment. "But doesn't money make the world go round? People care about how much things cost. That's why they want to drive expensive cars, and own expensive bags."

"Money isn't everything."

"Says the billionaire," she joked.

Durand laughed, showing even white teeth, as the low roar of his amusement rumbled in her belly. She liked making him laugh. She wanted to do it again.

"I think history is more important than money. It's better to know where we come from than to know how much it cost to get here," he added. "So tell me about your own history, Ms. Patel. Who made you the woman you are today?"

"Why is history so important?" The past, to her, was filled with disappointment, like the bullies who tormented her in boarding school. Much better to bury those memories than relive them.

"History is everything. Tell me one thing about you. Something pivotal."

"You first."

Durand shrugged one shoulder. "Very well. I believe history is so important because that's the only legacy my father left to me. He had many mistresses. My mother...she...well, she is French. She understood when she married him—into his very wealthy family—that he'd not be faithful. It was expected he'd stray. What she didn't expect was for him to fall in love with one of them." Durand frowned and stared at his champagne glass. "She told him he could have as many mistresses as he wanted, as long as he came back to her."

"But he didn't come back."

"That's right. One day, he stayed with one of them. Wanted to begin a new family. He divorced my mother, left her hardly anything. The only thing he ever gave me was his board seat to the Sphinx Society. So he gave me history, but...no money." Durand's mouth set in a thin line. "And just a few years after that divorce, Mother died. Heart attack, the doctors said, but I think it was a broken heart."

"That's horrible." Asha felt her heart break for Durand, a man who was all but alone in the world, his mother gone and his father absent. And he hadn't just been alone, he'd been penniless. She'd always assumed he'd inherited his money, but now it was clear he'd had to build it all up. Himself. "How did you afford this?" She glanced around the hotel suite, and at the expensive bottle of champagne chilling.

"I turned Sphinx Society membership into something everyone coveted, and I grew an empire, because of history."

Asha took a step closer to him and he glanced down at her, his blue eyes determined. She suddenly had a new appreciation for the man. He hadn't been born with a silver spoon in his mouth. Or, at least, he'd had it knocked out and had to get his own.

"That's impressive," she said.

He smiled slightly. "That's just necessity," he said. "I did what I had to do."

"What does your father think about it?"

He grinned, even bigger. "My father is not a member. So, he doesn't get a say about it." He seemed to relish the power and that made Asha laugh. She could understand wanting to buck a little against the edicts of an all-powerful father.

She was beginning to understand Durand a bit more. He was a man with something to prove. Just like she was a woman out to do the same.

"Is that so? I guess the tables have turned then. I envy you that."

"Does your father make demands on you?" Durand asked.

"Often." She sighed. "He wants me to be his one and only heir. I don't want the responsibility."

"Don't want it, or worried you can't handle it?" Durand studied her and she felt as if he could see straight through her. Why could he seem to get right to the center of her, but she managed to be able to fool so many others? His insightfulness was unnerving.

"Maybe both," she said. "But it is my father's company, not mine. I want to make something of my own."

"And you worry if you take it over, it'll be somehow diminished."

"No. Well...possibly." Was that it? Was she telling herself she wanted to forge her own path but in reality she was just worried about being measured against her father and coming up lacking? "Enough about The Skycloud. The Skycloud bores me."

"Does it? What doesn't bore you?" He grinned.

"You," she said, the honesty surprising even herself.

"Really?" The sparkle in his blue eyes grew brighter. "Then, by all means, let's sit down and talk about me."

Asha laughed.

"Would that be to your liking, Ms. Patel?" He

motioned towards the table with his nearly empty champagne glass.

"If we're going to be friends, you should call me Asha." She glanced at him and grinned, noticing his lips twitch.

"All right." He paused, the look in his eyes unreadable. "Asha." She loved how her name rolled off his tongue, how his French accent seemed to caress the vowels. "Would you care to sit?"

He gestured to the table and she nodded, walking towards it. He moved easily and pulled out a plush white chair. She sat and he walked around to the other side of the small round table. He grabbed the bottle of champagne and refilled each of their glasses. Then he opened the first silver cover and revealed a plate of chicken and vegetables.

"Coq au vin," he announced.

The warm smell of chicken in wine hit Asha's nose, making her stomach grumble. He put the plate before her, and then a plate on his side of the table. As he slid into his seat, Asha couldn't help but admire the way he moved, as his strong hands took the white linen napkin and gently laid it on his lap.

"Bon appétit," he declared.

"Bon appétit," she echoed back.

"So tell me, Ms.—" He caught himself. "Tell me, Asha." Her name in his mouth raised the hairs on the back of her neck. "Tell me why you don't care for history."

"History is in the past." She put her own linen napkin in hers. "I'm about looking towards the future."

"What's in your past that you hate so much?" he studied her. Asha felt suddenly on display.

"It hasn't been easy to live in my father's shadow." She said it softly, so softly she wondered if Durand even heard. He studied her.

"I can imagine. Money does not solve the problems most people think it does."

"And sometimes it creates new ones."

Durand laughed. "Yes, indeed. What problems did it create for you?"

"Boarding school bullies." She surprised herself with her own candor. She hadn't admitted to anyone about being bullied at boarding school. Not her father. Not her best friends at home. No one.

Durand clicked his tongue. "They were jealous of you."

"They thought very, very powerful and rich people should be blond. And blue-eyed." She remembered the endless taunts, the smirks, behind her back, the nicknames. "They called me *Slumdog Millionaire.*"

"Ah." Durand nodded, as if understanding. "People are scared of what they don't understand, and they're even more scared when it has more money than they do. Your father could no doubt buy them over many times."

Asha laughed. "Yes, he could."

"What did you do about these bullies?"

She glanced at her almost empty champagne glass. "I never backed down. Whatever group they didn't want me to be in, I made sure I was in."

Durand laughed, a low chuckle in his throat. "You thrived on conflict, then."

"I wasn't going to let them win. I had as much right to be in their clubs as they did."

Durand nodded. "True. So, then, is that why you want to become a member of the Sphinx Society so badly?"

Asha studied Durand. "Maybe." Could this be the reason she was so determined to keep going— to get access to a place denied to her? It was about a matter of principle. She didn't take "no" well.

"Initially, as you know, I wanted to catch my boy—" she stopped and corrected herself "—now, ex-boyfriend in the act of cheating."

"Yes, about Connor." Durand swiped his lips with his linen napkin. "I was curious about why you were so jealous…about a man you'd not slept with?"

Asha felt like she'd been slapped. As if Durand could see past her defenses. How did he know that? How did he know Connor was one of those men she'd toyed with, but never let into her bedroom?

"Who told you that?"

Durand's mouth quirked up in a smile. "Connor himself. It was his defense. He didn't think he ought to be kicked out of the society for ungentlemanly conduct when you were…as he said…'a tease.'"

"That's a distasteful term. That's a pillar of rape culture," she managed, her heart thudding as she felt exposed. Vulnerable.

Durand arched an eyebrow. "Yes, well, he is no gentleman."

Asha's mind whirled. Connor was telling her secrets to Durand, and she didn't like it. Also, Durand had stuck up for her? "So you expelled Connor from the club. Why?" she asked.

"Our members should have better sense than to insult someone as beautiful and intriguing as you." He met her gaze, and for a second Asha couldn't say anything. The man was definitely flirting with her, but she wondered if it was a game, or if he really believed what he said.

"Is that why you don't want me in your club? Because I'm so beautiful and intriguing?" she teased.

"Oh, I want you in my society, Asha." He paused, letting this sink in. "I want you very much."

She froze, glass halfway to her lips. Her stomach knotted as she met his stark blue gaze, the want in it suddenly real. He was telling the truth. She felt a tingling at the back of her neck. She realized it was her own excitement. Not just at the possibility of being invited into an elite group, but because she wanted to be invited into *his* life, see behind the curtain he so carefully used to block outsiders.

"Then why…deny me? You've told me no three times." The rejection, actually, still stung.

"You needed to hear a no," he said. "I doubt you've heard it very often."

She felt a flash of anger, heat at the back of her neck. This was far too close to the truth for her liking. "So you're the king then? Ordering us all around? What gives you the right to tell me what to do?"

Durand leaned forward and his knee touched hers at the side of the table. "Because I'm the one who made the Sphinx Society what it is. I say who joins and who doesn't."

"Maybe I'll form my own group then. Keep you out of it," she threatened, her fingers tightening on the stem of her champagne glass.

A slow smile spread across his face. "It won't be very interesting without me in it."

That's what Asha was afraid of, if she was honest.

"So, why am I here? If you're just going to reject me again?"

Durand reached out and touched her knee. His hand felt like hot flame on her bare skin.

"Who said I'm going to reject you?"

"Isn't that what you like to do? It's not *me* that's the tease. You're a tease."

He raised an eyebrow, amused as he withdrew his hand from her knee. "Am I?" He took a bite of his chicken and chewed thoughtfully, as she waited for what he'd say next. That she was out of the society forever? That there was no way he'd even consider allowing her entry? "I don't think you're telling me the whole truth about why you want to be in this club. I don't think it's just because you don't like being told no."

"I don't like being told no."

"Yes, but there's more to this." He glanced at her, and she felt almost naked, as if he could see straight through her clothes, straight through her defenses. He took his heavy linen napkin from his lap and patted the corners of his mouth. "I have a proposition for you."

She felt hope swell in her chest. Hope and nerves. Was this where they got down to business? Finally. Sex for membership. A simple transaction that she was more than willing to make. More than willing. She was looking forward to it.

"Yes?" She left her fork at the edge of her plate, her appetite suddenly disappearing.

"I will give you a membership... If..."

She leaned forward in her chair.

"If you admit to me that the reason you want to join this club is because you want *me*."

Asha laughed, but inside, she felt uncertain. Felt as if he could somehow read her mind.

"I want to make Connor feel bad."

"You've long since forgotten about Connor," Durand said, calling her bluff. This was true. She'd barely given Connor another thought since that day in Sweden when she'd met Durand. "Maybe I'm just here to make a transaction," she said, bluffing. "Maybe this is just all about me trading sex— or whatever you might want—for membership."

Durand's smile grew bigger as he reached out and took her hand. She felt the jolt of contact in her toes. "We both know that's not true. We both know that if I invited you into my bed tonight—no guarantee of membership—you'd come. Willingly. Dare I say…even…happily?"

Asha's heart ticked up a notch.

"You're full of yourself," she managed, but panic began to well in her stomach. Panic that he was right. And that she wasn't in control of this game. Maybe never had been.

"Maybe." He squeezed her hand. "Or maybe, I just know people. Why didn't you take Connor into your bed? He is handsome, no? Famous? Sought after?"

She didn't like being put on the spot like this. "Yes. He is."

"And you were attracted to him."

She glanced down at her plate. "Yes."

"So, why did you not have sex with him?"

So many reasons. She knew if she had sex with him, he'd stop paying attention. But, even more than that, she feared he'd disappoint her. Like every other man. Because inside, she worried that she was *frigid,* a block of ice that would never melt for any man.

"Men are more interesting before they get into my bed than after."

Durand seemed to take this as a direct challenge. "Is that so? Be honest with me. We wear no masks here."

Asha took a shaky sip of her champagne. She felt oddly unencumbered, being brutally honest for once. "I've not met a man who pleased me. Not really."

There. She said it. Her dirty little secret. Of her handful of lovers, none had ever made her come through intercourse. One had managed with his hand, after many clumsy tries. None had managed with their mouths, but, in fairness, only one had ever tried. She'd been amazed at the number of men who found it distasteful. They all expected *her* to please them. But when it came to the other way around? It always seemed a begrudging duty.

A smug smile tugged at the corners of Durand's mouth. "You mean to say, you have not climaxed?"

"Oh, I've climaxed." Asha thought about all the times she'd done it herself. "But typically only at my own hand."

Durand laughed then, a dark rumble of a laugh. "Is that why you run through men so quickly? Because all you have had are inept ones?"

"I find men are always inept in the end."

Durand's blue eyes sparkled. "You have not had the right man, Asha."

"And you are, then? The right man?" she challenged him. Men always said that. They always lied. Then, they always blamed her in the end.

"Oh, I believe I am." He said it with such confidence, even Asha partly believed him. She wanted to believe him.

"How can you be so sure?" she asked, because deep down, she always felt there was something wrong with her. That she really didn't feel pleasure with men because…she was lacking somehow.

"Do you feel the connection between us?"

Oh, she felt it all right. Asha blinked fast, clutching the stem of her champagne glass as she sat across the table from what could be the sexiest man she'd ever met. Sure, he was an egotistical maniac, but that was part of his appeal. The way he was looking at her right now, the way he was studying her, daring her to contradict him, made her want to try.

"I just want a membership," she said, lifting her hand from his. She reached over and touched his knee, the pressure she put there unmistakable. "And I'm willing to…sacrifice for it."

Durand clucked his tongue. "Oh, Asha. We both know it won't be any sacrifice. Trust me on that. You have had some pitiful lovers. But all that changes. Tonight."

CHAPTER SIX

ASHA'S HEART WAS truly beating a mile a minute in her chest as she stared at Durand. The rest of the food on her plate would go uneaten while she sat across from him in the small dining room in his hotel suite. Could he deliver on his promise? Could he show her pleasure that no other man had? She realized she wanted him to try. Had wanted it damn near since the first time he'd kicked her out of his party. Yet part of her, also a small part, rooted for him to fail. There was something about Durand, and not just his impressive physique, or his stark blue eyes, or that sexy French accent, that made her want to bring him down a peg.

"You are going to be the man who finally convinces me that they're worth something?" she challenged. "What if *I'm* the one who blows your mind? Not the other way around?"

His gaze slid slowly down from her face to her cleavage, on display for him in her plunging neckline. "I know you will, Asha."

"So?" She let him stare, enjoyed the attention. "Do we have a deal?" She let the words hang there. All he had to do was say yes. All he had to do was nod his head, and then she'd pounce. Then, they'd get on with what she'd come here for.

Durand ran his finger up her arm, raising goose bumps. "No," he said, meeting her gaze. "We don't have a deal."

"What?" Asha was stunned. Wasn't this what she was here for? Sex for membership? Cold disappointment rushed down her throat, forming a hard ball. She let his knee go and stood, pushing her seat away from the table, the legs of the chair almost catching in the carpet. She walked to the black-and-gold bar, hands shaking. Durand followed her. She could feel the heat of his body as he stood behind her, so close that his breath tickled the back of her bare neck.

"I mean, that I want *you*, Asha, but separate from any membership. Separate from the Sphinx Society. I want *all* of you. One night. It has nothing to do with the society or the membership. But you have to give your body to me. One night. You have to give over everything. That's the only way you're going to have the pleasure you deserve."

"And if I don't?" she asked, still facing away from him, still not willing to turn around.

"Then you won't know what it is to truly climax. To truly let yourself go."

Asha had to admit to herself that she was curious. Durand was so confident. More confident than any other man she'd ever met. But all of her lovers had failed. Granted, there hadn't been that many of them, but even so. He laid a kiss on the base of her neck. A bolt of desire ran straight down her back.

Asha tried to laugh, but it came out as a little gasp. "So, you want to have sex, even though you'll probably just reject my membership anyway? What kind of deal is that?"

"The only one you'll get," he said and nuzzled her neck, making all the hairs stand up there. "I won't pay you with a membership. I'll pay you with a night of pleasure you'll never forget. You have a passion in you, Asha. You and I are the same. Nothing is ever enough."

That might be true. Maybe he was the one who could make her feel something real. Make her body work in ways that it was supposed to work. How often had she felt shame after sex with the few she'd taken to her bed? How often had she felt it was *her* fault that none of their tricks would work? So often.

"You say men have not satisfied you, but I guarantee I will." He kissed her earlobe, flicking the edge of it with his tongue. She gasped a bit, the gentle touch sending shockwaves through her body. She felt a want for him deep in her belly, a want that burned hot. His words were so seductive. Did she have a flame within her? Did she burn with desire? Maybe she wasn't *frigid*. Maybe she just needed the right man.

"How can you be so sure?" she asked. He sucked her neck ever so slowly. She gasped. He reached up and loosened the twist of her hair. It tumbled down her shoulders. He swiped it to one side and kissed her earlobe.

"I know you," he said. "I know what you need. Give yourself to me. One night. No acting. No masks. Just you." He put his hands on her waist and pulled her to him, flattening her back against his hard stomach. She leaned into him, naturally, her body sinking into his. He reached around her, laying his hand on her bare knee. He moved upwards, ever upwards, taking the hem of her dress upwards, too. He stroked her inner thigh, his hot hand an invitation and a promise. She spread her legs, offering a path for his hand, and he found the mound beneath her expensive silk underwear. He ran a finger down the seam, and she shivered, her breath coming faster now.

"I can feel how much you want me, Asha," he murmured in her ear, as he slipped deftly beneath the fabric, the soft pad of his index finger stroking her gently. "You're ready for me. Admit it, yes? You want me, as I want you."

"I..." She didn't want to admit it. She didn't want to give in. She knew her body wanted him, could feel her want, wet between her legs, and now, his hand stoking that white-hot flame. But admitting this felt like defeat. Felt like she was handing him everything he wanted. It made her feel too vulnerable. Because what if a fire didn't burn in her? What if inside, she was, as she feared, a block of ice? Just like the other lovers had said?

"I can feel the fire in you," he whispered, seductive words. "The other men you've known have been afraid of it. That's why you tire of them so easily. I know just how you feel."

Did he? Did he know?

"Other men won't know what to do with you. With that desire. I do. I know. Let me feed those flames." He pushed against her back, showing her just how much he did want her. She could feel his hefty bulge against her lower back and it made her knees weak. He worked her with his fingers, softly, gently, with a determination that told her he'd make her his. And that's what she wanted right at this moment. Wanted him. Needed him. Something was building inside her, some deep desire, some unlocked want, with the gentle flick of his finger against her.

"I... I..." Her breath came fast. The building of pressure between her thighs. God, was she going to come right here? The man's hand beneath her skirt was going to be enough to push her over the edge? Never had a man touched her like this. Gentle, insistent, knowing. For the first time she worried he might just be the man to break through her barriers, to make her enjoy sex like she'd never done before. She moved with him, arching into his hand, her body making it obvious how much it wanted his touch, how much it needed him.

"Give yourself to me," he demanded. His voice in her ear, in her mind, taking control.

She was going to come. She was going to come right here, against the bar, Durand's hands on her. And then, he stopped, suddenly, whisking his hand away. Her body whined its discontent. She needed that release, needed what his hands would give her. She'd never felt desire like this for a man. Not with any of her other lovers.

"Let the fire grow," he growled, harsher now. She turned and now she was staring into his blue eyes, and saw the determination there, the grit. He put one of his fingers in his mouth. "I can taste you," he said. "I can taste your need."

Her lips parted then. Her thighs burned, and her clit throbbed. She knew he spoke the truth. Knew that he could read the want in her eyes, in her body. She'd never before seen a man so determined to get behind her defenses. Yes. She needed him.

"Yes," she admitted finally, her voice hoarse. "You can have me. One night." She felt like a raw nerve, exposed, and yet, her body would let her answer no other way. She was giving herself to him in a way she'd never given herself to any man. But, she told herself, it was for one night.

"Good," he said, and whisked her into his arms, kissing her open mouth, his tongue lashing hers, both in punishment and in pleasure. Her own mouth opened for him, and took his tongue again, and again, her own meeting his in the most primal of ways. He tasted like something she always wanted, something she always needed. His fingers found the side zipper of her dress and she wanted them there. Wanted all the fabric gone. He slowly moved the zipper down, almost too slowly. He moved a strap of the dress off her shoulder and kissed her bare skin there. She'd gone braless.

He stood back and studied her nearly naked form.

"You're beautiful," he said, his eyes drinking her in. She could see the want in them, the desire, and it fueled her own hunger. He took a step forward and lifted her up on the bar as if she weighed nothing. She went, shocked, as he spread her knees, the hem of her dress hiked up to her waist. His hands were on her underwear, tugging them downward. She felt her own heartbeat in her clit, thudding to an ancient beat.

"I want to taste you again," he said, meeting her eyes, and then he dipped down between her knees, his tongue finding her need. His expert tongue caressed her pulsing want and her mind went wild with desire, like nothing she'd ever felt before. The flames felt like they'd consume her from the inside out. She let out a shriek, and clutched his thick hair, holding on for dear life. Her chocolate brown nipples formed hard peaks as Durand devoured her— there was no other way to describe it. It was if he wanted all of her, stoking her fire with his tongue, building it, a wildfire that threatened to rage out of control. Her back arched, and a cry ripped from her throat. He knew what he was doing. More than knew what he was doing. She felt completely out of control. He knew what her body wanted, knew how to control it, knew how to take her home.

He whipped her with his tongue, bullying her body into submission. But she wanted this. She handed over control to him, handed him her body, and then she came. An explosion of pleasure burst in her mind, her body shuddering with the spasms of pleasure as she cried out, a hoarse cry of surrender.

Her heart beat frantically, and she couldn't catch her breath as Durand lifted his head from between her thighs.

"Now, your body belongs to me," he promised, and she believed him. Whatever she had, she'd give him. Her body was his to control. For this night, anyway. He lifted her then, and she wrapped her jellied legs around him, the muscles in them still quivering, as she held tight to his neck. He walked her through the impressive suite, into the massive bedroom, and laid her on his king-sized bed, pushing aside the white furry throw on the high-thread-count comforter. She sank into the soft bed, nude and vulnerable, feeling the soft sheets on her bare back.

"Tell me," he told her.

"Tell you what?" she asked, raising herself on her elbows.

"That your body is mine. For this night. That you will give yourself to me completely. Because I know this is what you want, no?"

He undressed himself, his nimble fingers undoing the buttons of his expensive shirt. Her breath caught in her throat when she saw his expansive, muscular chest. Lean and cut from hours in the gym. The man took pride in his body. And she admired that. Yes, she did want him. And she wanted to give herself to him—in every way possible.

She nodded. "Yes," she managed, a croak. "My body is yours."

"That's right." He stepped out of his pants, coming away with a condom he'd stashed in his pocket. So the man was planning for this. He'd come ready. More than ready, she realized, as she saw all of him, saw his want, both in his eyes and his hard cock. She leaned forward then, wrapping her arms around him. He groaned, his eyes never leaving hers.

"It's my turn," she said, and then she took him

in her mouth. She wanted to do this. Wanted to show him that she, too, could stoke his flame. She worked his shaft with her hands as she wet the tip of him with her tongue. He groaned, leaning into her, his eyes focused on every move she made. She took him deep and he groaned again, once more, growing even harder in her mouth. Then, he withdrew, gasping.

"You're going to make me come," he murmured, voice low, pupils wide, the want on his face evident. She could see his mounting desire, feel the restraint in his stiff fingertips. She wanted him to let go, wanted him to go wild. She'd make him, too. She reached out with her hand and clasped him.

"That's the idea," she growled, arching an eyebrow. "You need to come."

He pushed her down on the bed as he ripped open the condom package, and rolled the thin latex down the length of him. "No, no, ma chère. You, first."

"I—" But he was already on top of her, his mouth on hers, and then with one strong thrust was inside her, filling her, stretching her, taking her breath away. She arched her back into his movement, his delicious weight on her chest. She clawed at his back, groans of pleasure escaping her mouth, as his tongue once more found hers. He was in control, ever in control, the pace, the depth, all him, even as she rocked her hips to meet his, as she tried to take him ever deeper. She wanted to swallow him, own him, make him cry out with need.

And then, he'd rolled to the side, and she was on top of him. He clutched her heavy breasts, stroking a thumb possessively over one nipple. She arched her back once more as he clutched her, holding on tightly. She loved the feel of his hands on her, loved the strength of them. Their eyes met, and for a second, she fell into that stark blue ocean. An ocean of want. Of need. For her.

He spoke French in her ear, and it felt like a caress. So sexy. So fluid.

"Come for me, Asha," he told her in English, a soft command. "I want to see your face when you come. Burn. Burn bright."

She'd never done such a thing before. Hell, never had the chance, as she'd never had a man's cock make her come before. Could she even do it? He pressed deeper into her, raising his own hips, and she rocked harder, faster. She felt desire build in her, as it had built in the past, though she'd never made it to the end, never found a way to push through. Would she tonight?

"Your body belongs to me tonight," he reminded her, sending electric pleasure through her veins. She liked that idea. Being his. Just for one night. His fingers found her clit then, as she rocked on top of him, his expert fingers teasing her, flicking her, making her lose her mind. He played the perfect rhythm as she found herself rushing to the edge of the waterfall, in a raft she could no longer control. She hit the lip and descended downward in a white rush of heat. Her head jerked back, and her mouth fell open as she cried out, riding him ever harder and deeper until the rush faded. She collapsed on top of him, her hair splayed across his bare chest, gasping for air.

"You're going to kill me."

"If you can die of pleasure, then, yes, I will," he murmured into her hair. "You belong to me, remember?"

"Just for tonight," she told him. That's all she could give.

He pulled away, searching for her eyes. "Yes," he managed, eventually. "Just for tonight." He pushed her off him. "And tonight, I will explore every part of your body." He ran his finger down her side, and across her bare hip. His fingers roamed between her bare legs. "I will have you every way I can," he promised. And then he'd set her up on her hands and knees, and he was behind her, his flesh heavy against the back of her legs, the promise of much more to come. He entered her with a hard thrust and she gasped, as he squeezed her hips. It felt primal, animalistic, the way he drove into her, but she loved it. Loved how he took control, how he seemed to grow ever bigger inside her. Her breasts bounced with each rocking movement, heavy. Just when she thought she might come again, he switched positions once more, tossing her on her back, and pulling her to the edge of the bed. He took her legs and lifted them, putting them up against his shoulders.

She was helpless on her back, her feet in the air, his hands clutching her ankles. She'd never done anything like this before, never done much out of the way of missionary and occasional cowgirl. For all her tough talk, she'd not had much experience in the bedroom, not with a man like this, a man who seemed to know every position of the Kama Sutra, and wanted to show her every one.

"You are mine," he told her, as he worked inside her, ever harder, ever deeper.

And she forgot in that moment to add, *for tonight*. Because in that moment, she was his. Her body was his to control. And she knew she'd come again. Because he'd will it.

"Yes," she gasped, because she couldn't help it. He'd made her his. Completely.

CHAPTER SEVEN

ASHA WOKE THE next morning to a ray of sunlight streaming in through the gap in the curtains of Durand's hotel suite. She reached out her hand across the enormous bed but found it cold and empty. She sat up, blinking, realizing she was naked in Durand's bed, alone.

"Durand?" she called, but no one answered. Where was he? They'd spent almost the entire night exploring each other's bodies, and he'd made her come—again and again. He'd shown her positions she hadn't even thought about, much less tried, and she'd realized with certainty that she was not frigid on the inside at all. She was a ball of flame ready to ignite the second he touched her. All her adult life, she thought *she'd* been the problem. Now, she realized, she'd just never met a man with enough experience to please her, enough care to learn how her own body worked to satisfy her.

But now, that man was gone. She pulled herself from bed, noticing her dress from the night before hanging in the adjoining closet. Her stilettos on the floor beneath. There were no other clothes there, though. She was too groggy to wonder why, as she dragged the white cover sheet from the bed and wrapped it beneath her armpits, in case she wasn't alone. On bare feet, she padded to the bedroom door, which she found closed, and opened it, accosted by even brighter sunlight from open windows. She blinked, wondering what time it was. A clock on the wall in the sitting room said nearly noon. She'd slept six hours or so. Six hours since the weak light of dawn had filtered into their bedroom, when Durand had curled up behind her, spooning her and nuzzling her neck. Had it all been a dream? Surely not.

No. The delicious soreness between her legs told her none of it had been a dream.

"Hello? Anyone here?" she called to the other rooms of the suite. She could see the open dining room and part of the bar. No one answered, and she heard no sounds, and realized she was alone. A pit formed at the bottom of her stomach. Durand had told her he'd own her for one night. And, it seemed, he meant it. There was no sign of him. She ran to the closet near the bathroom and opened it wide. Even his clothes were gone. Not a single piece of luggage, either. She was surprised she felt so… empty. So disappointed. How had Durand managed to do all this and leave without her hearing?

Then again, she knew how: she'd been exhausted, her body pushed to its limits by Mathis Durand.

Had he even planned to say goodbye? She'd been the one to agree to one night. No more than a night. She'd never in a million years imagined he'd be so good at making her body respond to his touch, never imagined a man existed who could make her come so easily, so fully…and so many damn times in a row. Until she'd been with Durand, she hadn't even *realized* she could be multiorgasmic. She'd thought women who did that were simply faking. Now, she realized, they weren't.

But the man who'd done that, who'd lit her fire, was gone. She already felt like mourning him, and that wasn't like her. Since when did she ever let a man truly get under her skin? Sure, she'd flown halfway across the globe to humiliate Connor, but that wasn't because she truly cared about him. That was just a matter of principle, about protecting her brand. She wanted to see Durand because her body craved his touch. Because she wanted to hear his sexy voice in her ear, smell his spicy scent.

Asha walked onward, cotton sheet dragging behind her, to the dining room. She expected to see the remnants of their dinner last night, but instead, the table sported a brand-new tray with a simple breakfast of a croissant, a soft-boiled egg in a stand, and a pot of coffee next to a white cup and saucer. A single white rose sat in a vase on the tray, and

next to it, a white square box large enough to fit
a pair of shoes, tied with a red ribbon. A card sat
near it, signed by Durand. It read:

> Merci beaucoup for an amazing night, chérie.
> I look forward to seeing you in Berlin.

Berlin? What did he mean? She ripped off the
bloodred ribbon of the box and eagerly opened it,
feeling like she used to as a child on Christmas
morning. Inside, she saw a golden mask, and beneath that, an official invitation to the Sphinx Society's next party in Berlin in two weeks' time. Her
mind whirled and she felt her thighs warm. He'd
invited her to the next party. She'd see him again.
Maybe it wasn't just one night after all.

She studied the thick, embossed invitation, and
saw that she was, indeed, a guest. This wasn't an
offer of full membership, but an offer to the party.
She guessed she'd take what she could get, especially if it gave her an excuse to see Durand again.
Asha sat at the table and poured herself coffee, plotting about what she might wear in Berlin, mentally rearranging her schedule to accommodate a
trip to Germany. She felt a brightness in her chest.
Could she wait the two weeks to see him again? Or
would she need to see him sooner? The wheels of
her mind turned as she crossed her legs, reminded
of the delicious soreness there, remembering how

Durand had possessed her, had made sure he'd explored every millimeter of her body.

Already, she could feel the passion grow in her lower belly, the passion for him. Her want. She took a bite of the croissant, plotting about what she might be able to do to see him in the meantime. Yes, she would figure it out. Because she wasn't a patient woman. When she wanted something, she went after it.

She heard the automatic key open the lock of the main door of the suite with a telltale beep and sat up, back ramrod straight as she dropped the croissant on the plate. Asha grinned to herself, thinking that maybe Durand couldn't wait, either. Maybe he couldn't keep his vow of one night. The idea that he'd come running back to her this same day, just as eager as she, warmed her. She stood, dragging the sheet with her, but then deciding perhaps what Durand should see was her half-naked, Asha dropped the sheet to her waist as the door swung open.

And a beautiful blond French woman wearing a tight-fitting pin-striped gray suit walked in.

Shocked, Asha tugged up her sheet, but not quite in time. She'd given the woman an eyeful.

The woman seemed unfazed. "You must be Ms. Patel?" she asked, her French accent faint, just like Durand's. She seemed unperturbed, her beautiful poreless face mostly unreadable.

"Uh...yes, and who are you?" Asha tightened

her grip on the sheet beneath her armpits, her face burning with embarrassment.

The mystery woman smiled, but the smile didn't quite reach her eyes. "I am Madelyn. Mr. Durand's assistant. I am here to tell you that you are welcome to stay. Until 4 p.m., but after that…" She let her voice trail off. "I'm afraid you will no longer have access to this suite."

"Oh." Asha tried to regain some of her dignity. It was embarrassing enough getting caught half-naked by Durand's employee, a situation made more embarrassing by the fact that she seemed to be here to kick her out. Her manner was ice-cold. Did Durand intend this less than warm welcome? Asha glanced towards the bedroom, where she knew her clothes were neatly hanging in the hotel closet. "That's fine." She clutched the sheet to her chest, expecting Madelyn to leave. But she didn't. She walked further into the room. Bold wiry thing. Asha noticed her waif-like body, as opposite of her curves as one could get. The kind that fashion magazines and casting producers loved. She wondered if Durand also liked her delicate frame, sans body fat, and sans curves.

Asha watched, stunned, as Madelyn brushed past her, not caring that she was wearing nothing but a sheet, as she bustled into the room, sat down on the couch, and pulled her laptop from her case. She set the laptop on the coffee table and booted it up, even as she laid out a few pages on the glass table.

"What are you doing?" Asha asked her.

"I'm working," Madelyn said, curtly, very much a woman staking out her territory. "This is the office while we're away, and I need to send a few messages." She glanced up at Asha, stark blue eyes cold.

"You can't work in your own room?" Asha asked, her blood pressure starting to rise.

Madelyn didn't answer at first, choosing to focus on her laptop. Then, after a beat, she glanced up. "I realize this might be awkward for you, but not for me. I've worked for Mr. Durand for years, and I know his…" she gave Asha a slow sweep with her judgmental gaze "…proclivities. This isn't the first time I've worked in a hotel room with a naked woman in it."

Madelyn's words hit home in a way Asha didn't expect. They felt like a sudden blow that stole all the air from her lungs. Sure, she knew a man like Durand no doubt had lovers. A man didn't get that talented without experience. But hearing the cavalier way Madelyn talked about former conquests made her feel small. And Asha hated feeling small.

"I'm not just any woman." She wasn't, either. What they had, she knew, wasn't just like any other hookup. It had been special. She knew it in her heart. Plus, no one had the gall to talk to her like this: dismissive. Not since boarding school.

"Really?" Madelyn glanced up from her laptop. "You zink you are special?" Her accent got a little thicker now. "You zink he has not had…an exotique like you before? Believe me, he has. Many times."

"Exotique?"

"Yes, or as you say in English. Exotic, yes?"

Asha's belly burned with anger. *Exotic* was a word she hated—dismissive of her skin, of her as a person. Exotic was a backhanded compliment, the kind she'd get at those dances in boarding school, when the girls' schools and boys' schools would get together in gym. It was a word a boy would use to describe her, when he had no intention of ever letting her meet his parents. Exotic implied there was only one standard of beauty, and everything else fell into the category of foreign and strange.

"Exotic is what you call a bird. Not a person," Asha said.

Madelyn laughed, bitter, sounding almost like a woman who'd been hurt by Durand herself. Had they…slept together?

"Zhat iz not how Durand zees it." She shrugged. Asha hoped Madelyn was lying. Durand didn't seem like the kind of man who kept a tally of the sorts of bodies he'd had in his bed, treating his mattress like a color wheel that needed to be filled in. Asha knew some men like that. Men who whis-

pered, "I've never had an Indian woman before."
As if she should be flattered.

Durand wasn't like that. Was he? He'd explored
her body as if it mattered, as if it were important, as
if it was something precious. Asha felt in her bones
Madelyn was wrong. And yet…her words planted
a smidgen of doubt in the back of her mind. What
if she was wrong about Durand? What if he only
did see her as "exotique"?

"No matter," Asha said. "You're going to leave
now, so I can get dressed." She might be nearly
naked. She might be just one of another of Durand's
many one-night stands, but she'd be damned if she'd
let herself be ordered around and embarrassed by
this rude and probably jealous assistant. Nobody
treated her like that. Not those stuck-up girls at
boarding school, or anyone else. She didn't care
about the judgment. She was a woman of power
in her own right.

Madelyn glanced up but didn't move. "You are
asking me?"

"I am telling you." Asha padded to the door in
her bare feet, put her hand on the handle. "Or would
you like me to call Durand? Tell him you are bothering one of his 'exotiques'? He wouldn't be happy
about that."

The color drained from Madelyn's face. Asha
had hit a soft spot. Good.

Madelyn packed away her laptop, stiffly, and

jammed the papers in a file that she tucked under one arm. She stood on her expensive stilettos and walked towards the door. Asha swung it open for her, thinking that she hoped it hit her on the way out. As she swept by, sinking her heels angrily into the carpet as she went, Asha called, "See you in Berlin."

Madelyn froze in the hallway, her knuckles going white on the handle of her briefcase. Looked like she didn't know about the invite to Berlin. Good, Asha thought. *Point for me.* She slammed the door with a flourish, and this time, she locked the safety latch across the door frame. No model-thin assistants were going to interrupt her again. Smiling to herself, she decided to draw herself a bath in the enormous bathroom offering the clawfoot soaking tub. She had until four, and she planned to make the most of it. Maybe room service, even. She wondered if they had caviar. Or, even better, more of that very delicious and very expensive champagne. She smiled wickedly as she plotted to run up Durand's bill. Her smile grew bigger. Maybe *she* would decide when she would leave.

Maybe she would send a message to Durand. If he wanted her out, then he'd have to come and tell her himself.

Nobody bullied Asha Patel.

Nobody.

CHAPTER EIGHT

THE NEXT DAY, Durand sat in his personal gym, a sleek glass-and-chrome room above his office in Paris, and tried to focus on the bicep curls with his free weights. But all he could think about as he sat on the bench before the wall of mirrors was the night he spent with Asha Patel. The woman's body was…exquisite. There was no other word for it. Perfectly curved, perfectly molded to seem to fit his own body, and the way she'd opened up for him, like a flower in the spring. She'd held nothing back, just as he asked, and watching her find herself was…truly amazing. Even now, he felt his groin grow tight at the memory, felt the want in him blossoming. He dropped the free weight on the ground with a loud clunk, exasperated. He did everything he could to keep his mind off Asha, but no matter what, his thoughts always found her. Her and her delicious body.

Durand still couldn't believe her lack of true

sexual gratification. What man was so inept they couldn't pleasure her? She was so willing. So damn willing. All it took was a little patience, exploring the ways she herself liked to be touched, letting her show him what felt good. Women knew their bodies best and it was always wise to trust them. To listen. It was about listening to her body, understanding what she liked, and she'd come. Easily. She'd come, again and again. Her body came alive beneath his touch, and the sheer astonishment on her face had been priceless.

He'd known the second she'd climaxed the first time that her admission had been no ruse. She'd been telling the truth. Before him, she'd never truly experienced sex the way it should be: pure, bold, satisfying. Her previous lovers had been selfish and unworthy of her. He'd felt like her teacher, but more, that she'd taught him what it was like to be vulnerable, to truly need someone. He felt like he'd deflowered a virgin and because he had, part of her belonged to him.

The possessiveness took him by surprise. Never had he felt as if he should own a woman. Obviously, people could not own people, but he'd never felt a connection to someone like this. Asha was the first woman in a long while, perhaps ever, that he wanted back in is bed. He'd only just begun to teach her what pleasures they could explore together. There was so much more he wanted to show her. So much he wanted to see her experience. The idea of stopping that felt like asking him to stop breathing. He couldn't do it. Wouldn't do it. Because…why? They fit together so amazingly well. Why stop? But he knew this was a worrisome feeling. This need that was building in him, need for Asha. He prided himself on never needing anyone. Never feeling so connected to another person that that want controlled him.

He'd promised to own her for a night, but now he worried that she owned *him*.

And not just for a night.

He met his own gaze in the mirror and wondered what the hell he was doing. Falling in love? He scoffed at his own reflection. Love was for romantics. Amateurs. Men who couldn't keep their feelings in check. Durand was not one of those men. Not someone who'd fall prey to the weaknesses of the heart. He typically never ventured beyond a *cinq a sept*, simply translated, a 5 to 7 p.m., a casual relationship, like one might have to one's work. Yet, somewhere deeper, he knew Asha wasn't a *cinq a sept*. She was a flower that had opened—*for him*. He'd done that. No other man.

In fact, the idea of another man coming after him made his stomach tighten, made him feel possessive.

And that was the problem. Because he'd spent a lifetime carefully cultivating his Frenchman-who'd-sworn-off-love image, the elusive playboy who never gave his heart to any one woman. What kind of mystery society owner would he be if he married? Had a family? Part of the appeal of the Sphinx Society was being free of constraints, of living life outside the typical rules. If he married, settled down, he'd be like every other man. Besides, if he were honest with himself, love scared him. He knew exactly how love could ruin a man. Look at his father. If he'd only just kept his feelings in check, only just kept his various relationships with his mistresses strictly *cinq a sept,* he wouldn't have divorced his mother and ruined their lives. She'd died brokenhearted. Doctors said it was a coronary, but Durand knew his mother, and knew the damage love had done to her. He'd sworn never to let the emotion get to him, never to let love blind him to more important things, like wealth and reputation. Durand spent his whole life honoring history, and that included his mother's.

He shook his head at his own shirtless reflection, and the foolishness he saw there. He was not going to risk his entire empire for love. Wasn't going to risk his sanity, either, for a woman who could still be after a membership to the Sphinx Society. So why couldn't he stop thinking about her?

He stood, grabbed a folded hand towel from a nearby table, and swiped it across his face and the back of his neck. What he needed was a cold shower and something to take his mind off of Asha Patel.

A soft knock came at the door frame of his personal gym. He glanced up to see Madelyn standing there, tentative. Madelyn was hardly ever tentative. She must be delivering bad news.

"Sir? I'm sorry to bother you," she said in French, as her face grew pink. He realized it was because he was shirtless as she snuck a look at his bare chest. He stood and grabbed his T-shirt that was draped across a nearby chair. No need to give her false hope. He never would sleep with her, no matter how big her crush on him grew. He pulled the T-shirt over his head.

"Yes, Madelyn?" he asked, impatient. His gym hours should be free of interruption, but sometimes business could not wait.

The pink receded from her cheeks as she glanced down at her tablet that she held tightly. "I've got word from the Savoy."

"Yes?"

Now, Madelyn looked extremely uncomfortable. "I'm afraid..." She swallowed. "Ms. Patel is refusing to leave your suite."

At the very mention of Asha's name, Durand felt white-hot electricity shoot down his spine. Asha Patel, the woman who wouldn't leave his thoughts. Or, it seemed, his hotel room.

"What do you mean, 'refusing'?"

"She told the hotel manager that she'll only leave if she speaks to you first. She's also…" Madelyn glanced at the email on her tablet, the color deepening in her cheeks. "Sir, she's running up an impressive bill. Champagne, caviar. Spa treatments."

"How much?"

"More than $5,000, sir, mostly from ordering the Savoy's most expensive champagne bottles."

Durand frowned. What on earth was that little minx doing? Had he not satisfied her? Had he not offered an invitation to his next party? Why on earth was she acting like a jilted lover? Unless…

"Did you deliver the box with the invitation?" Durand asked, voice clipped. He observed his assistant carefully. Madelyn shifted uncomfortably on her expensive crocodile leather heels. She did not meet his gaze. She was hiding something.

"Yes," she said, voice soft. "And I relayed your message. About checkout time." She wasn't telling him the whole truth. He could feel her guilt from where he stood. He'd known her so long he could read her every expression.

"And you delivered the message…*nicely*." Durand took a step closer to his assistant. He didn't care if he was covered in sweat. She glanced up once at him, tentatively.

"Yes," she said. "But of course." She stuck her chin out, daring him to contradict her.

In that moment, he realized that Madelyn could have told Asha most anything.

"What did you tell her?" Durand demanded. His heart ticked up a notch. Madelyn's damn schoolgirl crush was getting to be a problem, Durand realized. It was becoming truly bothersome.

"What I *always* tell your women." Madelyn raised a defiant eyebrow. "We have business to conduct, no? We have the next party to plan."

Durand let out an exasperated sigh. "Asha isn't just any woman." The words were out of his mouth before he could stop them. Surprise bloomed on Madelyn's face. Surprise—and dismay. But these words were true. Asha wasn't just any woman. It was about time that he made peace with that.

"You can't be serious," Madelyn began. "She's a spoiled heir. A…"

"No more." Durand waved his hand impatiently. He was tired of Madelyn's jealousy.

"Shall I allow the Savoy to call the London Police? They will make sure she leaves." Madelyn had composed herself and now was back to being all business.

"No," Durand said, surprising himself with the ferocity in his voice. He blew out a frustrated breath and turned away from his headstrong assistant. The last thing on earth he wanted was for the police to come and take Asha. She'd never forgive him that humiliation. And, he wondered, would she even forgive him sending Madelyn to tell her to leave?

Madelyn seemed surprised. "Shall I call Ms. Patel directly, then, and relay a message?"

"No." Durand stared at his assistant. "*You* will not be relaying any more messages to Ms. Patel."

Now Madelyn seemed truly taken aback. He'd never challenged her before because, he realized, he'd never cared how Madelyn handled things. As long as they were handled. He'd given her too wide a berth these last few years. Let her get territorial, and why not? He never cared to see most women he slept with a second or third time. He'd relied on Madelyn to clean up the morning after, however she saw fit. He'd been fine with that, until now. Asha was different. Asha wasn't a woman to dismiss out of hand.

"No. You're going to book me on the next flight to London," Durand demanded. Then, he eyed his assistant. "But first, you're going to tell me, *verbatim*, everything you told Asha."

CHAPTER NINE

ASHA LAY IN a thick white cotton robe, her bare feet dangling from the white love seat in Durand's suite at the Savoy the next morning, as she dipped an oversized strawberry into her flute of bubbling champagne and took a bite. This was the kind of breakfast she could get used to: fresh fruit and off-the-charts expensive champagne. Her head fell back on the pillow, nearly dislodging the hasty bun she'd made with her tangled hair that morning. Asha knew she should think about leaving. She'd overstayed her welcome and she'd had to unplug the phone so the front desk wouldn't call. And the maids had been by five times already this morning. Soon enough, security would come knocking on her door, no doubt. And she was pretty sure this fruit from yesterday and the champagne chilling in the mini-bar was the last room service she'd get for some time. Actually, the front desk had made that clear the last time she'd called down. If she didn't

offer her own method of payment, no more hos-
pitality would be offered to her by the Savoy. She
could pay, but she didn't want to. What she wanted
was to teach Durand a lesson.

She told herself, of course, it wasn't that she was
just licking her own wounds, nursing her pride,
hurt from being told by his cold-hearted assistant
she was just one more conquest among dozens, one
more *exotique.* He needed to be brought down a peg
or two. So did his mean-spirited, jealous assistant…
what was her name? Megan? Marie? Some *M*-name.

She heard the automatic key at the suite's door,
and then someone try to open it, but the safety lock
was latched in place. Then, came a stern knock.
It was probably Savoy management again, maybe
with security this time. They'd ask her to leave,
no doubt. Well, she'd damn well leave when she
wanted. And not a minute before.

"Asha?" came a deep rumble of a voice she instantly recognized. Faint French accent. Durand.

She sat up, and her hand flew to her hair. She
caught her reflection in the mirrored wall adja-
cent to the living room. She rushed to it, fluffing
her hair and pinching her cheeks. She'd forgone
makeup. And clothes, for that matter. She wore only
the robe and had been quite comfortable for the
last two days.

She swept to the suite's main door. "Durand?"
she asked, tentative, as she pressed her eye to the

peephole. It looked as if he were alone. No security. No hotel management. Just Durand in a sleek, expensive gray suit, no tie, crisp white shirt open at the throat, one hand behind his back, looking sexy as hell. He almost seemed to meet her gaze through the peephole, flashing a wry grin.

"Asha, my chérie. Let me in."

Her fingers found their way to the dead bolt, but then she hesitated. Durand sent his assistant to humiliate her. Now, he swept in after two days and all was forgiven? She opened the safety bolt just wide enough to open the door two inches. She craned her neck to meet Durand's gaze, just as he revealed the hand he hid behind his back. He held a single perfect red rose. She'd expected him to be angry, not contrite. The approach threw her for a minute, and she took the rose, smelling its sweet fragrance.

"May I come in?" Durand asked, but the tone of his voice made her doubt she could actually refuse him. She felt the bass of his voice in her toes. She closed the door to free the safety bolt and let the door swing free. Durand strode in, perfect dark hair combed back from his forehead, and eyed the golden room-service tray on the glass coffee table, complete with a half-empty bottle of champagne and picked-over strawberries. There was another empty tray on the dining room table with a half-eaten filet mignon, a tray filled with crackers and an empty jar of caviar.

A slow smile spread across his face. "Making yourself comfortable, Ms. Patel?" His ice-blue eyes met hers, and she felt a shiver down her spine.

"Are we back to formalities?" She almost felt disappointed. Why was he so cold and distant? She wasn't sure what she expected. Durand to rush in and kiss her passionately? Toss off her robe and show her all the many, many delights he'd shown her earlier in the week? No. But maybe she'd been hoping he would.

"I'm not sure I'd call you—how do you say it in English? squatting?—in my hotel room, a formality." He spread his hands, his big, strong hands, and Asha remembered what they felt like on her body. Strong and sexy.

"No, but it's the *least* I could do since I was so rudely left. Without a proper goodbye." She knew she sounded like a pouting toddler, but she didn't care.

Durand raised a dark eyebrow. "I left you a lovely invitation. And a mask."

"And sent in your secretary to do your dirty work." She remembered his assistant's cold manner, the way she'd delivered the news she needed to leave. "She was *not* lovely. Not at all." Asha jabbed a fist into her hip for emphasis. Durand studied the neckline of her robe, which she realized was open low enough to reveal the top curves of her breasts.

Good. Let him look. Let him remember what he left behind.

"Yes, I spoke with her." Durand frowned. "My apologies for the manner in which she delivered my message. I'm afraid I wasn't so specific about *how* she ought to deliver the news. That was my error."

Asha nodded. It was, indeed, but the things his assistant had told her still burned. "She called me… *exotique*? Do you collect women, Mr. Durand, like some men do tigers?" A small strand of hair fell across her cheek and she tucked it behind one ear. Her bun felt in danger of falling, her hair feeling heavy at the base of her neck.

Durand laughed as he walked to the white sofa and sat, crossing his long, muscular legs, his pant legs fitting them tightly. She remembered his strong limbs entangled in hers beneath the sheets of the bed. "No. Not at all. I enjoy women. Of all races and nationalities."

Asha paced in front of him as he watched her long, tanned bare legs part her fluffy white robe. "Even French blondes?" Asha stopped in front of him, the coffee table the only piece of furniture between them.

He raised an eyebrow and she felt she'd somehow given him ammunition, but she couldn't help herself. She'd seen the territorial look on his assistant's face, could almost feel the woman's jealousy.

"No." Durand didn't blink. Didn't even look away. "Not the French blonde you mean."

"She's in love with you," Asha said. She'd come to that conclusion after replaying the conversation they'd had in her mind. The secretary who seemed a little bit too territorial, a little too involved for her interest to be purely professional.

Durand didn't look surprised, either. So he knew about her feelings. Interesting.

Durand worked to keep his face neutral. "Does that bother you?"

"No," she said too quickly. Too forcefully. It even sounded to her ears like a lie. Durand stood and walked around the table, and soon was beside her. He stepped closer, so close that she smelled him, the hint of his distinctive soap, his clean skin. She found herself leaning into him, despite her better intentions.

"I think it does bother you," he said after a beat. "I think you are jealous."

"No, I'm not." She wouldn't look him in the eye. Couldn't.

Durand put his hands around her arms, squeezing her ever so gently through her sleeves. She was suddenly very much aware that she wore nothing beneath the robe, and from the way he glanced down the V of the robe's neckline, Durand was, too.

"You should be honest with me, Asha." He pulled her against him. She felt the hardness of his chest.

"Why?"

He dipped down and nuzzled her neck. She felt a shiver of desire run down the backs of her bare legs. He knew just how to touch her, just how to awaken the want deep inside her.

"Because I know you're jealous." She arched her back, pressing against him, overwhelmed with his gentle touch, with his delicious scent, with the promise of the pleasure she knew he could deliver. Suddenly, the idea of clothes, even a robe, seemed stupidly impractical. What she wanted was his hands on her bare skin.

"How?" she murmured, as he laid gentle kisses beneath her ear. Her breath caught in her throat. She yearned to taste him, to devour his mouth. He was teasing her, and it was driving her wild.

He met her gaze. "Because you are throwing a fit. Because you want my attention."

"I'm not throwing a fit." She pushed him away and crossed the room, her face feeling hot, her neck burning. But she could not escape the truth of his words.

"You are, ma chère. You are throwing a fit, no? You want my attention. And now you have it." He crossed to her, embracing her from behind. She wanted to resist, but instead, found herself leaning into him, as he gave a hard tug on the belt of her robe. Soon it fell open, revealing miles of bare skin. He cupped both breasts from behind, kneading them reverently, so that her nipples grew hard against his palms.

"Yes," she murmured, the admission slipping from her lips without her realizing it.

"You are only pretending to be angry. You are only pretending that you can resist me," he whispered in her ear. His hand slipped from her breast, skimmed down her stomach and cupped her from the front, possessive. He teased her with the soft pad of his finger, caressing her, making her swell with want. Her body responded instantly, as if she'd been made for him. She arched herself, leaning into his touch.

A squeal of pleasure escaped her.

"I offered you one night, but you want more. Isn't that so?"

"No. I—I don't," she lied. "I don't care about you."

"Another lie. I thought we agreed not to lie to one another. Not to wear masks." Durand laughed, a growl in his belly. "You very obviously care." He tightened his grip around her waist. "You want me, ma chère. You want this." His caress drove her wild with need. When she could stand it no more, she turned in his arms and kissed him, openmouthed and fierce, her anger, her desire, her jealousy, all a powerful mixture that fueled her passion, driving her to devour him. His hands slipped into her open robe, against her bare back, and he pulled her close against him, so that she could feel his growing need. His hands drifted down, cupping her bare bottom as she wound her hands around the back of his neck. He tasted like everything she'd ever wanted, everything she'd ever needed, this man who could light a spark in her, a spark that threatened to burn her to ash. "You need me."

"I don't need anyone," she managed.

"Another lie."

Durand maneuvered her to the couch and whirled her around once more. He took the belt of her robe and freed it, and then covered her eyes, tying it tightly behind her head.

"What are…"

"Trust me," he murmured in her ear, a promise. A threat? She shivered with anticipation as she realized she could see nothing, that she was completely in Durand's power. Exactly where she wanted to be. He positioned her so that her hands were splayed across the back of the couch, her legs shoulder-width apart. Her breathing grew shallow as she waited, listened, felt helpless and vulnerable. Durand was as a quiet as a panther, though she could sense him in the room, prowling, his eyes on her bare body, her exposed skin. He pinched her left nipple, softly, making her shriek in surprise.

"What are you doing, Durand?" she cried, shocked.

"You like throwing fits? Playing games? Then

we will play a game," he told her, this time caressing her right cheek. She whirled but could see nothing, hear nothing. She moved one hand, and his
came down on hers, steading her against the couch.
"Stay where you are, Asha." His voice was a command, a delicious command. Normally she hated
to be bossed around, but somehow…letting Durand
do it was sexy. Beyond sexy. White-hot. Her lips
parted as she anticipated where he might touch her
next. Her legs shook in anticipation. Being deprived
of sight, she had no idea what he planned to do, and
it made her slick with want.

She heard his zipper then, and thought she heard
his belt hit the ground, probably with his pants, as
well. Was he going to take her like this? She
couldn't see. Couldn't do anything. Her palms flat
as she faced the back of the couch, waiting.

His palm hit her bare bottom, a playful slap, and
she squealed in shock. He'd…spanked her. Actually…spanked her. No one had ever dared. No one
but Durand. He'd positioned her to do just this:
hands splayed on the back of the couch, backside
vulnerable. She twisted a little.

"Durand!" she cried in protest.

"Stay where you are," he demanded, righting
her once more. And he gave the other cheek a slap.
Playful. Not hard. Enough to let her know he was
in control, enough to send white-hot desire through
her veins, to set off every nerve ending in her body.

"You have been a bad girl, Asha. Playing these games. Lying to me."

"I—I did not lie," she protested, in the direction of his voice, behind her.

"You said you were not jealous of Madelyn, no? That is a lie." His breath was on her neck, and she shivered, feeling him so close behind her that his bare knee touched the back of her leg. "Admit it."

"I…" Was she going to tell this man that she was jealous? That she was jealous of Madelyn's affections, that she was jealous that she was his trusted assistant? It was all so stupid. "I'm not jealous."

He flicked her hip with his fingernail, a small sting. "You lie." He spanked her once more, harder this time, and she gave a little yelp. Then he rubbed her bare bottom with his hand, soothing the contact, as he kissed her neck. It was a possessive kiss. He grabbed the back of her blindfold, the lose tails of her robe's belt, moving her face upwards. Her heart raced.

"Tell me the truth. Are you jealous?"

"Yes," she gasped.

"Because you want me." He clutched at the tie of her blindfold.

"Yes," she managed, heart thumping hard in her chest. She couldn't see his face, the robe's thick belt stopping all but the faintest of light around the edges, and she wondered how he'd taken her admission.

"And you need me," he said, his voice deep and demanding. She could feel his thick, hard cock against her lower back. A promise of what was to come.

"Yes." Her voice sounded like a mere croak, a whispered admission of the truth. She did need him.

"Good," he murmured, moving against her back. "Because I need you, too. So very much." And then, he entered her from behind, filling her up, shocking her with the hard movement that sent her legs apart, made her whole body open for him. He sent her against the back of the couch, each of his thrusts pushing her deep into the rich upholstery, as he took her again and again, harder and deeper. She cried out, unable to stop herself, as he reached around to her front and found her swollen clit, and she nearly burst into a thousand glimmering pieces. She climaxed and so did he, two animals unable to help themselves, as they let loose two distinct cries of ecstasy.

She couldn't help but think they were made for each other, that no two people had ever been so suited for one another, so perfectly.

Instantly, Durand collapsed against her, and he removed her blindfold. He laid a dozen tender kisses on her neck, the disciplinarian gone, and in its place, a man who craved a gentle touch. He slipped off the condom he'd worn and tossed it into a nearby gilded trash can. Then he wrapped her in his arms, gently, and she went, feeling as if a mutual apology spanned between them, that the fight, such as it was, was over.

"Did I hurt you?" he asked, holding her tightly as the two walked around the edge of the couch and sank into it.

"No," she said, remembering the slap of his hand against her backside. "Though no one ever dared to spank me before," she murmured into his bare chest.

"Perhaps that is why you are so spoiled," he teased.

"I'm not spoiled," Asha cried.

"Only the very spoiled would say that," he whispered into her hair, as he pulled her tighter to him. She laughed, and buried her face into his chest, into his warmth. "I did not hurt you, did I?"

"No," she said.

"I only want to show you...the many ways sex can be," he said. "You have had such inept lovers. Such fools. There's so much you have missed."

"And you will be my teacher?"

Durand kissed her head. "If you let me, ma chère. You hold all the power."

"I do?"

"Women always do." He ran a hand gently through her hair. "You will be my undoing." His voice sounded almost pained.

"Why?"

"Because you are like no other woman on earth," he said. "Because you have crawled under my skin, made a home there."

Asha flattened her palm against his chest, feeling scared....and vindicated all at once. So she wasn't the only one who felt the connection between them, the white-hot chemistry. He felt it, too.

"So, I am not just an *exotique*?"

"No." His arm tightened. "You are much more than that. *L'appétit vient en mangeant.*"

"What does that mean?"

"*Appetite comes with eating.* It's a French saying about obsession. The more you have, the more you want."

"You're obsessed with me?" Asha laughed a little, delighted. "Does that mean you won't let me out of your sight?" Asha teased, pressing her cheek against his chest. She felt a warmth in her belly grow outward, and realized it was her own feelings for him growing.

"Maybe," Durand admitted. "I am obsessed with you, and you are obsessed with membership, is this not so?"

For Asha, their relationship was anything but transactional, and she knew that now, knew it the moment he'd taken her into his bed.

"The membership isn't what I'm after," she murmured.

Durand shifted, sitting up a bit, and Asha lifted

her head from his chest. "No?" Durand raised one eyebrow in surprise. She met his blue gaze.

"No. I want something…more."

Durand searched her eyes for a moment, and she expected him to respond in kind. But instead, he pulled her down for a kiss. His lips met hers, possessive and hungry. Yet part of her, a small part, felt like she'd revealed too much. That she'd tipped her hand. She pulled back from the kiss.

"And what about you?" she asked him, feeling the oily coating of insecurity line her stomach. Did he want her, too? Or was this a game to him? "What do you want?"

He searched her eyes for a minute. "Before you came into my life, I thought I knew. But now…" He trailed off, frowned. "I promised myself I would never fall in love."

"Why not?" Asha felt pressure in her chest, as if someone had hold of her heart and was giving it a squeeze.

"It is my image, no? The Frenchman who swore off love. But love isn't very practical. Love can be dangerous. Look at what happened to my mother… to my father… I cannot ignore that."

"But you're not your father."

"Don't we all become our parents? At some point or another?"

Asha rested her chin on his chest. "You fear you can't be faithful to a woman? Is that it?"

"I have never tried to be faithful to a woman," Durand admitted, voice seeming a bit distant. "So I do not know."

Asha felt a small sliver of hurt at his words. Would he not even want to *try* for her sake? It was the one thing she demanded from a man, any man: loyalty.

"I cannot be with a man if he won't be faithful to me." After all, she'd flown halfway across the globe to confront Connor, and they'd not even slept together yet. "It's my one absolutely unbreakable rule."

"Ah? So you *do* follow at least one rule. I thought you just liked to break them."

He was being evasive, but what did she expect? Asha felt her chest tighten even more, but she told herself she was being foolish. Silly. A schoolgirl. What did she care if Durand loved her? Loved anyone? After such a short time with this man, she was thinking they could have a future? And what future would that be, she wondered? A man who prided himself on never committing to anyone, whose assistant even told her how often he had trysts with many women. Many *exotiques*. Asha knew exactly the kind of man Durand was, one that never gave his heart to anyone. Hadn't she known that long before she'd let him into her bed? She'd been playing with fire the whole time, so why now, when he admitted he never planned to love another, should she be disappointed?

She was no fool.

Except in that moment, Asha realized, she was already falling for him. Half in love with him already. And that made her a fool.

"I believe love only ends in loss," he said, even as he stroked her hair.

"Maybe it doesn't have to," she managed.

"Why are you such an advocate for love?"

"Why are you so against it?" Asha countered. "It seems to me that maybe you're fighting a little too hard. The playboy bachelor protests a little too much."

"You think I am bluffing?"

"You certainly seem intent on letting everyone know just how much you hate love. Perhaps you're trying to challenge someone to convince you otherwise."

Durand clucked his tongue. "And you are that woman?"

"Maybe. Maybe not. I only know that I'm not the only one pretending to be something I'm not."

Now Durand laughed out loud, a big belly laugh.

"It sounds to me like you're falling in love with me. Are you falling in love with me?" he asked. In that moment, Asha could show her hand. She could be honest with him. Yet something in her held back the truth. She wouldn't give him the power of knowing he had control over her. She was used to dealing with powerful men. Her father for one, and she knew that giving them the upper hand never ended well. She'd have to keep him guessing if she ever wanted to hope to maintain power in the relationship. Because, in every relationship, there was always a dominant and a submissive. One who held the power, and one who obeyed. That had always been her experience.

"Of course not," Asha lied and then covered it with a brash laugh. Because deep in her heart she knew, she was falling for this man. Falling hard. Or was this just what happened to every woman who was truly pleasured in bed by a man? Maybe all she really wanted was his touch, the touch that felt so reverential, as if he worshipped her body from head to toe. Maybe it was that that she was falling in love with and not the man. After all, what did she really know about him? Besides, in the end, didn't all men eventually disappoint her? Didn't they all lose their ability to please?

Durand went quiet then.

"Falling in love with you would be foolish," she added. He was the man who'd sworn off love, after all, even if part of her thought it was a little bit bluster. Who could cut out love from their life? No one Asha knew.

"You think so?" he demanded, pulling away

from her, and studying her eyes. "But what if I am already falling in love with you?"

Asha told herself Durand's question was just a ploy, just a way to manipulate her or keep her off balance. And yet, as she stared at his blue eyes, so earnest, so honest, she found it hard to believe he wasn't telling the truth. And if that was the truth of his feelings, the mere idea made her giddy. She wanted this. She wanted him to be in love with her, the way she'd wanted no man to love her before. And she realized it was all because she had feelings for him. Perhaps she was already in love with him.

This would not do. How could she love a man who'd sworn never to love? If anything, her history had taught her that men couldn't be changed. Not by a woman. By themselves, maybe, but not by a woman.

"What would you say to that?" he asked her. "What would you say if I told you I loved you? That I would try to be the faithful man you need?"

"I would say that the *what if* at the beginning of the sentence means you aren't serious."

"Oh, I am serious," he teased. "Let me show you how serious," he added and pulled her close to him, pressing his lips gently against hers.

CHAPTER TEN

DURAND AND ASHA extended their stay at the Savoy far longer than was prudent for either of them, locked together in bed, forgetting all passage of time. Eventually, the two parted, as the call of planning the next party in Berlin demanded Durand's attention. Asha returned to her apartment in London, and Durand went on to Berlin, to scout out the venue, and answer Madelyn's ever more insistent demands that he come for final approval of the facilities. She wasn't wrong. The ball needed his attention.

Durand hated being apart from Asha and realized that her influence had grown to touch every aspect of his life. He wanted her more than he'd ever wanted another. Their nights apart gnawed at him, made him toss and turn through many sleepless hours. He was growing obsessed, and he had only just started to realize this might be what his father had felt when he'd left his mother. Could it be? Could he have been taken by emotions this overwhelming? Had he been too hard on his father all these years?

And yet, he'd never committed to a woman, never had a child, never left them to follow his lust or his love, or whatever emotion overwhelmed his sense. He was free to indulge in love, since he had no obligations. All he had was his own vow that he wouldn't let love rule his life.

And yet, here love was. Keeping him up at night. Making him forget his responsibilities to the Sphinx Society, soaking up every last thought in his brain. Durand had thought that he'd been the one to teach Asha about the intricacies of sexual pleasure, but she, he realized, was the one teaching *him* about love.

The days the two were apart seemed endless, but eventually, Asha flew to Berlin.

Durand waited in the Berlin Airport mid-morning for Asha to pass through customs. He'd driven there himself to pick her up, shocking Madelyn, who'd never seen him take on such a lowly duty himself, but the fact was, he needed to see Asha again and did not want to wait for the taxi to bring her to him. It had been a little more than a week, and he itched to hold her in his arms. He wanted to spend all of his time with the woman who seemed to have bewitched him. There was no other word for it. He was under her spell.

Falling in love with you would be foolish.

Her words had hurt him more than he'd like to admit. He shouldn't care that she'd said it, flippantly. After all, since when did he want a woman mooning over him? Falling in love? Wasn't that what he'd tried to avoid his whole life?

Yet Asha was different. He needed her in a way he'd never needed a woman. That unnerved him, but what worried him even more was a nagging feeling that she wasn't as serious about him as he was about her, that at the heart of things, this was just a game to her. He needed to convince her otherwise. He just wasn't sure how.

He watched as tourists poured through the customs doors, dragging their luggage behind them, glancing at the unfamiliar signs, looking for their rideshares and taxis. He grew impatient as different people walked by him, none of them the one he wanted to see. He scanned the crowd, looking for Asha's beautiful black hair, her gorgeous tan complexion, her amazing curves. They invaded his thoughts during the day and his fantasies at night. He'd only half joked about her being an obsession. Now he feared that's exactly what she'd become. He'd thought that the week they'd spent together in London would scratch the itch he'd had, and that he could move on, but instead, his want for her…hell, his need for her, just seemed to grow. He knew he was getting in too deep. Knew he was playing with fire, but he couldn't help it.

She was like no woman he'd ever met. So gorgeous, so stubborn. So deliciously responsive in bed, and he loved the idea of opening up her world, showing her what she might have missed all those years with all those selfish lovers. There was, indeed, so much the two could explore together, so many pleasures awaiting her—and him. The idea made him feel delirious. And possessive. But it was more than her body that intrigued him. It was also her mind. Her fight, her determination, they wiggled their way into his brain, told him she was more like him than he knew. When someone told him he couldn't do something, couldn't have something, that just made him want it more. That's why he'd taken the one thing his father had left him and turned it into everything. Because he wanted to show his father that he wouldn't just survive. He'd thrive. That's why he'd vowed to himself he'd never make his father's mistakes: putting love above all else.

But then came Asha. Blowing his plans apart.

He scanned the crowds walking through the doors, into the lobby of the airport. Asha had taken a commercial flight from London to Berlin. First class, of course, but as it turned out, since her father was squeezing her luxuries, he'd taken away the private jet when she'd refused to attend a company meeting. Durand wanted to know more about that. He of all people knew how tricky relationships with fathers could be.

Asha swept through the glass doors of customs looking even more stunning than he remembered. She wore a white skintight skirt and a colorful sleeveless blouse, big oversized sunglasses on top of her head. The instant he saw her, feet clad in strappy sandals as she pulled her rolling carry-on behind her, he moved quickly, his body taking over, as he swept her into his arms and kissed her. She tasted like everything he needed. Everything that had ever been missing in his life. She tasted like a purpose. His cock came to life instantly.

"I missed you," he murmured as he released her, but kept his arms around the small of her back. It felt like admitting weakness, but he did it anyway. She grinned up at him.

"Did you now?" Her lips parted and he wanted suddenly to whisk her away from this public place, hide her away in his Hotel Adlon Kempinski suite, and hibernate there until fall.

"Shall we go to my hotel?" His fingers itched to peel off her clothes, to taste her skin, to inhale her scent. He felt like an addict right then, an addict needing his fix.

She smiled. "I've never been to Berlin before, and you want to hide me away in your hotel?" Now she was playing coy. Why? He knew that she needed his touch as much as she needed his. Why pretend otherwise?

He squeezed her waist tighter, pressing her against him, so that she could feel just how much he wanted her. His groin ached with need. *Zut alors*, his whole body ached. Surely she could feel that.

"Yes," he growled. "I want to keep you in my hotel all week. Naked. Doing my bidding."

Asha laughed. "Show me Berlin first. Or I might never see it." Now he realized she had a plan of some kind. A plan he didn't like.

"You want to play tourist?" Durand felt the bitter taste of disappointment at the back of his tongue. Who cared about touring the city when he'd much rather be exploring the twists and turns of her perfect body?

"I'd at least like to eat. I skipped breakfast today."

"We could order room service." Images of him feeding her strawberries, naked, in his bed, flashed through his mind.

"Take me out first," Asha demanded, but a playful smile twitched at the corner of her pink lips. "Then, to your hotel. Something tells me we'll have plenty of time to try out room service."

Durand couldn't agree more. Once he got her into his bed, he'd not let her out again.

Asha took no pleasure in the disappointment that flickered in Durand's eyes as he took the handle of her rolling bag and led her out of the high-ceilinged sleek, modern terminal of the Berlin airport, beneath the red decorative red metal ribbon lattice hanging from the ceiling. She'd decided that she needed to try to resist heading back to his hotel room, because there, for certain, he held all the power. She knew this, knew that she'd be unable to resist his touch, since it had brought to life a need she never knew she'd ever had in her body. And then, she'd just fall deeper in love with him. Or lust. Honestly, she wasn't sure she could tell the difference anymore. She was obsessed, she knew that much. She spent every moment thinking of him, or stalking him online, or reading gossip columns about him. The man who never had a serious relationship in his life, the Frenchman who swore off love.

And that made him even more of a challenge. She hated that she wanted to convert him, like some romance novel heroine, but there she was. She liked the idea of being the one woman he couldn't resist. There still remained this stupid little flame of hope in her breast. She was the one who might be able to change him. She had no idea why she thought she could. Maybe it was the way he was looking at her now as they walked through the airport, the way he held her elbow firmly, possessively. Maybe he did this with every woman he met. Every *exotique*. Maybe they were all playthings for him. Maybe he

made them all feel worshipped and adored, right
up until the day he refused to return their calls. He
tended to leave a trail of broken hearts in his wake.
Asha wasn't about to add to that pile. She would
be no one's fool.

What she needed to do was put the brakes on.
Keep out of his bed for a microsecond so she could
hang on to her wits. Get to know the man behind
the amazing hands and mouth and cock, to decide
if this was real, or just…want. It was easy to love
him in bed, where his body controlled hers, where
her want ran riot, but what about out of it? Maybe
if she got to know the man better, he'd lose some
of his power, lose some of his draw. After all, Asha
knew, men, in the end, were almost always a disappointment.

No sooner had they walked out of the airport
than a driver pulled up in a black Mercedes, and a
well-dressed twenty-something German in a suit
got out, hastily grabbed Asha's bag, and stowed it
in the large trunk of the car.

"*Danke schön*," Durand told his driver, and then
proceeded to give him further instructions in German. Asha had no idea what they were saying, but
the man opened the back door of the Mercedes, and
Durand ushered her in.

They drove through the streets of Berlin on the
sunny summer morning, the blue sky partly cov-

ered in clouds. Durand reached out and took her hand, bringing it to his lips and kissing it.

"There's still time to tell him to turn around and take us to the hotel," he murmured, his voice as sexy as she remembered, tinged with that faint hint of French. She wanted to. Badly. But she needed to rein in her desires, or they'd run her life. And she couldn't afford to let that happen. She'd never willingly given over such control to anyone, and she wasn't going to do that now, with a playboy who'd vowed never to love one woman his whole life.

She was giving him too much power. She'd never intended to stay in that hotel room in London with him for a whole week, but she'd done it, without even realizing how much time had passed. Whenever he touched her, she felt powerless. That scared her. She wanted him, yes, but she wanted him on her terms.

"I am hungry, and *you* can wait. It's like you want to eat dessert first." She tugged her hand away and gave him a playful swat.

"What is wrong with that? Especially when *you* are the dessert." Durand let her hand go, moving his fingers down to her bare knee, caressing it ever so gently. She felt an electric current run right up her thighs, felt the power of his touch. He stroked the inside of her bare knee, working his finger up her thigh. She shivered. Her breath came a little quicker, a little faster, and she wondered if she'd be able to tamp down her own desire.

"You mustn't spoil your appetite," she warned him.

He gently squeezed her upper thigh. "When it comes to you, I don't know that I can ever have my fill. *Plus on a, plus on veut avoir.*"

"What does that mean?" she asked, uncertain.

"The more you have, the more you want," he whispered, leaning over and nuzzling her neck. She moaned, just a little, unable to help herself.

She pulled away, managing to fight against the rising need in her belly. She glanced at him, sharply, seeing honesty in his blue gaze. And a little bit of surprise. Maybe this wasn't just some come-on line, something he said to all the women to make them fall at his feet. Yet part of her wondered.

She leaned forward and gently straightened his tie. "Then, I'm worth waiting for," she whispered, aware that he watched her lips as she spoke, aware of how much he wanted to kiss them. He'd have to wait.

"Oui, ma chère. Worth the wait." He sat back then and folded his hands on his lap, but she saw the twitch of frustration at the corner of his lip. Good. Maybe she'd get under his skin this time. Maybe she'd be the one with the power.

She wanted to show him that they were more than just passion. They were something deeper than that.

The car slid through the crowded streets of Berlin, the sun beaming down on the gray sidewalks. Eventually, the black car pulled over and let them out. Durand took her by the hand, as they strolled along the sidewalk beneath the bright summer Berlin sun. He nodded to the left.

"That's Checkpoint Charlie," he said, nodding to the white booth situated on an island in the middle of a bustling Berlin street. Sandbags lined one edge of the booth, and a crowd of tourists stood near it, taking pictures, standing beneath an original black-and-white sign that read, "You are now leaving the American Sector."

"Wow," Asha said, recalling a little bit about the Cold War she'd learned in history in college: the Berlin wall that once separated communist East Berlin from democratic West. He held her hand as they walked. Then, he stopped her, nodding downward. "See? This is where the wall used to be." Oversized stones in the sidewalk marked the wall, labeled *Berliner Mauer 1961-1989*. Asha put her feet on either side of the cobble stones. "Wait, let me take your picture," he said, and pulled out his phone.

She smiled, feet apart, and he snapped the picture.

"Belle," he said, and pulled her to him. He kissed her on the lips, a quick peck, but a tingle ran down her spine. "You are too beautiful not to kiss," he told her as he wrapped his arm around her shoulders, pulling her to him as they walked to the restaurant, a sleek modern affair serving tapas. The host seated them in a small corner booth near the window so they could watch the tourists posing together in front of Checkpoint Charlie.

"Is this all right?" Durand asked her as she frowned at the menu, which was largely in Spanish. "It's a new restaurant in Berlin. Two Michelin stars."

"I... I don't have tapas that often," Asha admitted.

"Do you mind if I order for us?"

"No. Please." Asha folded the menu, and then proceeded to watch Durand address the waitress in Spanish. She'd never quite felt so worldly before: she about to eat tapas, in Berlin, with a Frenchman. That had to be a first. Plus, he seemed to be fluent in at least four languages.

After the waitress had taken their order and left, Asha leaned forward. "How many languages do you know?" she asked him.

"Four fluently. Seven passably." Durand shrugged. "It was part of my education. Plus, it helps to be able to speak to my society members in their native tongues." She thought of Durand's talented tongue, and realized it had more uses than just languages. Delicious uses. She pushed the thought away, though he seemed to read her mind, anyway. He glanced at her, raising an eyebrow. "Though I feel our bodies do not need words, no?"

"Now you sound like a stereotypical Frenchman." She laughed.

"What is wrong with that?" Durand said, and they both laughed.

"So…you learned languages…at school? Where?" She needed to get this conversation back on track.

Durand took her hand on the table, holding it possessively. "Why do you wish to know?"

"I want to know more about you." She wanted him to open up to her. To show her more than just delights in the bedroom. She wanted to know what made this mysterious man tick. He seemed to be a riot of contradictions: one minute, he was cool and aloof and in control, and the next, he was a lover who couldn't seem to get enough of her. She'd begun to understand his body very, very well, but what she wanted to explore was his mind. Maybe then, if she knew him better, she could balance her feelings, which even she knew were growing wildly out of control.

A playful smile pulled at the corners of Durand's sensual mouth. "What do you want to know?"

"For starters, if you've ever been in love."

The waitress came then with two glasses of sangria. Asha took hers gratefully. Durand sipped at his, pensive.

"I told you before," he said, somber now, an edge to his voice, "love only ends in pain. I've spent my life avoiding it."

"Love exists, Durand, no matter how much you try to deny it."

"It killed my mother and made my father…a terrible man." Durand shrugged. "I know it exists. I just don't believe it works the way most people think it does."

"How does it work?" Asha took a sip of her ruby-red sangria, the tart, fruit-infused wine tickling her tongue.

"Most people only *think* they are in love. But, really, they are just in lust. Or in obsession. Or suffer from loneliness. Or it's just about ego. It's not love. We give love too much power these days. People believe they have no immunity. That they must suffer whatever love dictates for them. But that's not how love should be. Love is in our control."

"I disagree." Asha put down her glass and then dabbed at the edges of her mouth with her napkin. "Sometimes feelings grow bigger than you want them to grow. And that's what makes them so beautiful in the end. The fact we can't really control them. Not completely." She couldn't meet his gaze for fear he'd read the truth in her eyes. That she was in love with him. More than she'd like.

"You think you know love? Because you followed your ex-boyfriend to my party? Is that love?"

Asha laughed bitterly. "No, that is not love. I never loved Connor."

"Then what do you mean? Who do you love?" There was a challenge in the bend of his eyebrow, the slant of his mouth. It was as if he already knew exactly what she was thinking. But that was impossible. He could read her body, yes, but not her mind, she told herself. That was still hers to control.

"Do you want me to tell you that I love *you*, Durand? Is that what all your women tell you right before you lose interest in them?" Asha wasn't going to admit her feelings for this man. Not when he was so stubborn about love, about refusing to believe in the power of it, refusing to give in. She also realized that her own plan of getting to know him, trying to find his flaws so that she, herself, might lose interest, was backfiring. Durand's magnetic presence held her full attention, and all she wanted to do was crawl into the man's bed after this meal and never get out. But she could not let him know that. She could not let him know the kind of power he had over her.

If she did, she'd lose everything. She knew the kind of man Durand was. She also knew exactly the way to keep his interest. By keeping him at arm's length. A man like him knew nothing but the pursuit. A man like him would always lose interest once he caught his prey.

Durand chuckled and took a sip of his sangria.

"You worry I'll lose interest in you?"

Asha laughed. "No." She gave him a slow, deliberate smile. "I'm worried I'll lose interest in you, first. And then you'll be such a bore."

"Bore?" Durand's eyebrow rose as his blue eyes grew sharp at the insult. "You think I'll bore you?"

"Eventually, yes, *all* men bore me." She could see him stiffen. Then a slow smile spread across his face, the relish of a challenge in his eyes. She loved pushing his buttons, loved prodding him. "Eventually, even *you,* Mathis Durand, will run out of tricks."

"Not me, Asha. Not ever." His determined expression made her rethink her challenge, almost made her wonder if she'd gone too far. "You'll never be bored with me."

"Prove it," she challenged him.

CHAPTER ELEVEN

DURAND HELD ASHA'S hand tightly as they swept into the lobby of the five-star Hotel Adlon Kempinski, on the east side of Berlin, an upscale hotel built in 1905. They walked across the white marble floor and in between the plush gray seats, Asha's heart beating loudly in her ears, anticipating what would come next once they made their way upstairs into his bed. She wanted this more than she dared to admit even to herself. She glanced at the signature fountain in the center of the lobby, noting the black elephant heads midway up the fountain's tower.

"The elephant fountain was a famous gift," Durand said as they swept by it on their way to the elevators. "India's Maharaja of Patiala gave the fountain to the owner of the hotel, Lorenz Adlon, in 1930."

"Ah, you and your historical facts," Asha said.

"We all must learn history or be forced to repeat it," he said.

She squeezed his hand tightly. "What if I *like* to repeat certain histories? Like…ours?"

"That, of course, must be the exception to the rule." Durand flashed her a knowing smile as Asha admired the lines of the sculpted elephants that fanned out around the center tower of the fountain. Even in the hotels she was used to, these kinds of artifacts were rare. Durand must be rubbing off on her because she was starting to appreciate antiques.

"And do you always stay at hotels blessed by royalty? First, the King of Sweden, and now the Maharaja of Patiala?"

"Royalty is fascinating to everyone—even Americans," Durand said.

"Is it? I think we fought a revolution because we *weren't* so enamored with the institution," Asha pointed out.

Durand pressed the button of the gilded elevators, and one instantly arrived. He swept Asha in, steering her with a firm hand on her lower back. She was more than aware of the possessiveness in his touch. Her stomach rippled with nerves. She knew when she stepped into the elevator with him that once she was in his suite, she'd be unable to think, to control herself. She'd do whatever he wanted, and she'd like it. The idea of giving away her control frightened—and excited—her. No one made her feel like Durand did. No one lit up her desire, made her nerves come alive, like he did.

"Maybe you Americans regret losing the monarchy...just a little bit. Maybe that's why you are fascinated. Perhaps, even, obsessed."

"You think you know about obsession?" Asha challenged him as the elevator doors slowly closed. Durand hit the button for the penthouse, swiping his key against the sensor on the lighted pad, because not just anyone could take the elevator there.

"Yes, I do." Then, Asha leaned past him and pulled out the elevator stop button. The elevator lurched to a complete stop and the alarm sounded, which she quickly disabled with a flick of the alarm switch.

"What are you doing?" Durand cocked one eyebrow in surprise. "Do you wish to...begin foreplay here?" He spread his arms wide, and grinned.

"Maybe." She moved closer to him and ran her finger down the closed buttons of his shirt. "But first, I want you to tell me..." she glanced up at him "...what you mean to do with me?"

She pressed against him, pushing them both to the wall of the elevator, their lips were millimeters apart. She could almost taste the faint hint of sangria on his tongue. She searched his blue eyes and saw playfulness there.

"I mean to do all kinds of things to you, ma chère. Things I believe you will like." His eyes sparkled. "Things I know you will like."

She stood up on tiptoe and nibbled the bottom of

his lip. "And then?" she asked him. "Do you plan to give me that membership?"

Durand chuckled. "This is no longer about the membership, and we both know it."

He was right. She knew he was right. But she couldn't let him see how much he'd grown to mean to her. How much she was already under his spell. She needed to take back some of her power.

"If you do not plan to give me the membership, then what do you plan to do with me?" The elevator dinged and they tumbled out of it, Durand pulling her into the hallway of the hotel.

"I mean to show you many, many tricks. For many, many hours." They reached his door, and he pulled the keycard from his wallet, swiping it past the sensor. The door unlocked and they were inside, their lips meeting, locked together in a desperate dance. She ran her hand down the front of his pants, feeling him come to life beneath her fingers. Then, she pulled back as he sucked in a breath.

"What if I am the one to show *you* tricks this time? You think you are the only one with skills?"

She slipped down on her knees in the elevator. He stood stock-still, watching her with amused eyes, as she freed him from the confines of his pants. Normally, when she did this, it was simply to get something she wanted. She wanted to make Durand lose his own control, wanted to make him feel what she'd felt during that week in his hotel room.

He seemed to still believe they were casual, when she in her heart knew they were much more. Their connection was something that didn't come along very often. And she was going to prove it to him.

She stroked him, and he grew hard instantly in her hand. The carpet cut into her knees, but she didn't care. She wanted to make him moan, make him lose control, and this was the way to do it. She flicked the head of his cock with her tongue, and he tilted his head back and groaned. This time, she'd be the one in control. This time, she wouldn't be the one to succumb. She wanted to do this. Wanted to drive him wild. If she had to be on her knees, so be it. She flicked her tongue again, rolling around the tip, and then she took him—most of him—in her mouth. He cried out, unable to help himself, as she worked him, using both hands on this shaft, and her mouth and tongue around the head. She read his body silently, read his reactions, knew exactly what to do.

"*Mon dieu*," he breathed, grasping her shoulders. "You will make me come," he warned.

She freed her mouth. "That's the idea," she growled, and then she resumed her work, delighting in how she could control his body, how he was now a slave to the growing climax, how he'd have no choice but to come. She could feel it in his quivering body, how the desire was overtaking his control. But then, he pulled away.

"No, no. I cannot let you," he growled, and swept her up in his arms. He once more zipped up his fly as he hit the buttons of the elevator. The elevator began moving once more, and soon the doors opened to the penthouse. He grabbed her hand and pulled her into the hallway. A few seconds later, they were inside his rooms, an extravagant black-paneled hotel suite, complete with bedroom and dining room. The curtains were open, revealing Berlin's iconic Brandenburg Gate, the stone column structure topped with a statue of the goddess of victory pulled by four horses, the afternoon sun blazing down on it. She didn't care about the view or the lavishness of the suite. All she cared about was Durand.

He led her to the bedroom, his mouth hungry on hers. Suddenly, her plan to control his body evaporated in her mind as his tongue lashed hers, as the want in her grew to a burning need. She felt the soft bed beneath her back. Then he was on top of her, his weight delicious against her. He rolled her on top of him, and then found the zipper at the back of her skirt. Soon, it and her blouse were puddles on the floor, and she wore only lacy, sheer underwear. His fingers couldn't move fast enough, and neither could hers. Their clothes only seemed frustrating barriers to what they both wanted now.

His skin felt hot against hers as his hands roamed her bare body. Her skin came alive beneath her touch, and she moaned, even as he shed the rest of his clothes. He seemed to be ready for her as he reached into the bedside table of the hotel and withdrew a condom. She wondered how many of them he'd stashed there, and then remembered they'd gone through more than she could count in London. Would Berlin be the same? Would it be a blur of amazing sex and a growing sense of dependence on this man she knew so very little about?

But then his lips were on her neck and she forgot why she was so worried. Forgot to fear her growing feelings. All she could do was surrender to his white-hot touch, surrender to the need growing between her legs. She needed him, she realized. Needed this. He worked her body as if it was an instrument he was born to play, and as his hands kneaded her, she moaned, nearly losing herself.

He moved so that she could straddle him, and she sat up on him.

"Do you want to show me more tricks?" he asked.

She grinned wickedly. "Of course I do." She lowered herself down the length of him, taking him in, inch by inch, slowly, deliciously slowly. His blue eyes never left hers, and she could see the want in them, feel his desire grow.

Yes, want me, she thought. *Need* me.

She began moving slowly at first, rocking back

and forth, and he kept his hands on her hips, steadying her and himself.

"Do you want me?" she asked him, her voice a low purr. She kept her hands flat on his muscular chest and could feel his heart pounding as she moved her hips.

"*Oui*," he murmured, his lips parting.

"How much do you want me?"

He closed his eyes as she pulled him deeper, ever deeper, inside her. His blue eyes flicked open.

"Very much," he admitted.

"More than any other?" Now she realized it was her insecurity rising to the surface. Her jealousy. She wanted to be the only one that mattered. She was falling in love with him.

He flipped her over then, so that he had the upper hand.

"Do you want to be wanted more than any other?" he challenged. He withdrew from her, even as her knees fell open. She felt cool air against her thighs, and a disappointing emptiness. He rubbed his tip against her wetness, and she arched her back. He teased her mercilessly, when all she wanted was him inside her. *Now.* "Do you want me to want you, Asha?" he pressed. His thumb found her swollen clit, and she groaned.

"Yes," she managed, meeting his gaze. He pushed in an inch and she gasped. "More," she demanded.

"Admit that you have feelings for me," he said, moving his thumb faster.

"I don't," she lied. And he withdrew completely. This was maddening. He was driving her mad with desire, with lust, with need. She clutched at his arms. "Wait."

He pushed forward again, tip inside her, his thumb working the nerve endings in her swollen center, making her see stars. "Yes?"

"I want you...to want me," she breathed, and he pushed all the way in, touching the deepest part of her.

"I do want you, ma chère. More than I've ever wanted anyone." The admission pushed her towards the edge, and she felt her body awash in relief, and desire, and...love. "Come for me, so I can see your beautiful face."

He worked her harder, and she had no choice. A climax ripped from her, and she shouted, unable to contain the explosion of pure pleasure, as he worked his magic, and she succumbed to his spell. When she opened her eyes, he was looking at her with such reverence, as if she were a priceless work of art. Never had a man gazed upon her like that, and she feared, never would a man gaze upon her like that again.

He stroked her face gently. "Never come like that for anyone but me," he said.

"I'm worried I won't," she admitted, and he

laughed. He moved, flipping her so that he was flat against her back, and he entered her from behind.

"I want to be the best you've ever had, or will have, Asha," he promised her.

"Keep on like this and you will be," she murmured, worried that it might be true. That he would be the best sex she'd ever have, a man who vowed never to love another completely.

He worked faster, clutching her to him, squeezing her breasts in his hands as if holding on to them for support. Unbelievably, her own desire began to rise again. Would she come once more? This was insanity. She never knew her body was capable of this. But only with him. Only with this man. He nibbled her ear from behind and her logical brain completely shut off. Now was not the time to worry about the future. She felt a surge of pressure in her belly, the climax growing there. She was going to come. And so was he. They came together in perfect unison, and then Durand pulled her to him, clutching her like a raft keeping him afloat.

"I need you, Asha, like I've never needed anyone," he growled in her ear. "You are...you are making me want to love you."

"What's stopping you?" she challenged him, feeling a rush of emotion flood her.

"Do you want the membership or my love?" he asked her, nuzzling her neck.

"Maybe I want both," she told him.

"Maybe you can't have either," he murmured.

"Now you're the one who lies," she said, whipping around to face him. "You're the one not being honest with me."

"No?" Durand rolled away, and Asha sat up, fully naked. He stroked her hip and the side of her leg with one tender hand. His eyes roamed her bare body, possessive, appreciative.

"You are already in love with me," she told him. A look of surprise flickered across his face. Surprise and…fear. Had she hit on something true? She'd been teasing, but the look on his face told her maybe there was more to this than she thought. "I can read you, Mathis Durand."

"Yes, you can," he admitted to her, and he pulled her close for a kiss. She broke the contact, blinking. "But I cannot give you all that you want."

Asha pulled away from him. "You can give me what I want. And you will."

Durand laughed. "Do you always get what you want?"

"Always," she said with more confidence than she felt.

"And if I give you my heart, what will you do with it? Will you be careless like you are careless with…the other men in your life?" Durand pulled her to him, and she lay with her cheek against his chest.

"No, I would not be careless," she promised.

"Why would you give me one but not the other?"

"So this is about winning for you, is it?" Durand pressed.

"Is that what you're afraid of?" Asha asked.

"And if I asked you to be mine? Would you be mine? Are you ready to commit to me?" he asked her, rolling on top of her so they were nose to nose.

She blinked fast, her heart ticking up a notch. "What does that mean?" she asked, tentative.

"It means I want you, Asha. Only you. And I want you to be with me. And only me."

"Does this mean you love me?"

His lips parted, and for the briefest of seconds, she thought he'd admit that he did love her. Instead, he swallowed his words. "It means I cannot stand to see you with another man. Any other man," he said.

If he wasn't going to admit he loved her, then she was not going to commit to him, she decided. A wicked smile pulled at the corners of her mouth. "Well, then," she said and drew him near. "You'd better keep an eye on me. Make sure I don't wander."

Durand moved closer. "I intend on it." He glanced at her seriously.

"What makes you think you have the right to that?"

"Because it's true. You've gotten through my defenses." He sucked in a breath. "Asha, I'm powerless against you. I... I..." He paused. "I love you."

CHAPTER TWELVE

DURAND SAW THE look of surprise bloom on Asha's face and wondered if he'd gone too far. What was he even saying? He was falling *in love*? Sure, the two of them lay naked in the hotel bed, their bodies tired yet satisfied, but was this *love*? He'd sworn never to fall in love, but like so many things in life, reality had simply blindsided him. No, Asha had blindsided him. He'd never met a woman like her before, both savvy and calculating, and yet, at the same time, so innocent about so many things. He had told the truth: he was helpless to resist her. He loved her strong will, the way she fought to be included. He admired her fight, her determination not to take "no" for an answer. She was like no woman he'd ever met, and that's why he'd come to care for her. Beyond that. Come to love her. He wasn't just falling in love. He'd already hit bottom.

And she wasn't saying anything. She was staring at him, completely frozen.

"Asha?" he prodded. And then he realized that he'd gone further than she was ready to go. She wasn't ready to say it back to him. He'd overstepped and there was no walking this back. Not now. Not ever.

"I—I don't know what to say," she said, looking uncomfortable. And then he saw the hard truth: he might love her, but she wasn't sure of her own feelings. Not yet. At least, she wasn't willing to share them. He knew her body loved him. Maybe that would have to be enough for now.

"You don't have to say anything," he said quickly, to save his pride. The woman he'd declared his love for, the only woman who'd ever stolen his heart, wasn't prepared to take it.

"Besides, I thought Mathis Durand doesn't believe in love."

"That was before I met you." Durand wasn't going to lie. Not now. Her cold feet right at that instant only made him want her more. It only made him even more determined to convince her that they belonged together. They needed to be together. Now and always. "We are meant to be together, don't you see?"

"Why?"

"We are so alike, you and I. Both fighting for what's ours, it's us against the world." This was the truth of it. They were more alike than they were different.

"You sure it's *us*, not me against you?" she challenged him.

"Don't even joke about that," he growled, suddenly feeling possessive. The woman brought out a side of him that he didn't realize he had. Asha grinned, playfully, teasing him. The woman knew exactly how to push his buttons, how to make him want…more. "If you aren't going to tell me you love me, then you have to promise me you'll not be with another."

Asha blinked fast, and in that second, as he watched the emotions play out on her face, he realized she did care for him. More than she was willing to admit for now.

"You want to be exclusive?" she asked.

He thought about her reputation, of dating whomever she pleased, whenever she pleased, and understood that so much of her public persona wasn't true. "I don't want you to run off to any of your other pop stars or actors."

"You think I do that?" she asked him, eyebrow raised.

"I think that you like to make people think you do." He stroked her bare arm. "I want you, and only you, and I want you to be loyal to me."

"Or…? What will you do?"

He growled and rolled her on her back, climbing atop her so they were nose to nose. "I'll punish you." He nudged her nose with his. "And don't lie," he said, a slow smile spreading across his face. He pressed a bit harder against her. "And you *know* what happens when you lie."

"I'll be punished," she breathed.

"That's right." He pressed harder against her, as his own cock came to life again. He slid between her legs, poised and ready to enter. "So? Tell me you're going to be mine, and only mine." He nudged her and she sucked in a breath, but her eyes never left his.

"For how many nights?" A teasing smile played at the corner of her mouth.

"For as many nights as I say," he managed. And he searched her eyes, waiting for her answer.

"All right," she said at last, after she'd made him wait a ridiculously long few seconds. "But only if you promise...to punish me anyway."

"Of course, ma chère," he said, and then he entered her, hard, and she gasped, wrapping her legs around his lower back. He plunged into her depths, again and again, suddenly sure in the feeling that he'd at last found home.

Durand stood on the interior white balcony overlooking the massive ballroom in the Adlon Hotel, the crystal chandeliers hanging from the thirty-foot ceilings, as his Sphinx Society guests began to arrive and accept glasses of champagne from the elegantly dressed wait staff. This ball bore no dress

code, so attendees wore all manner of colors, and
the growing crowd below was ablaze in greens, reds
and blues. Even some of the men traded in black
tuxedo jackets for colored ones. Durand, however,
wore his favorite black tuxedo jacket and white tie.
He should be watching the flow of guests, making sure the gourmet hors d'oeuvres were ready
to serve, but instead, he was searching the crowd
for Asha. She'd left him that morning, insisting
she needed salon time to ready herself for the ball.
He'd hadn't seen her since early that morning, and
he didn't like to be parted from her.

He wanted her by his side.

Durand played over the conversation he'd had
in bed with Asha days before, worried he'd gone
too far. It was damn near the closest he'd come to
truly committing to one woman. He didn't believe
in monogamy, and yet, he'd gone against that very
core belief by asking Asha to be his. Only his. The
most infuriating thing was: she hadn't given him
a straight answer. *Keep an eye on her?* He wanted
to scoff. She was known for discarding boyfriends
and suitors faster than she could collect them. Plus,
Durand wasn't entirely convinced she wasn't just
playing to win, that she'd walk away from him the
second she got what she wanted: this damn membership.

"Monsieur Durand?" a familiar voice behind
him made him turn. He saw Madelyn, wearing a

very low-cut, very form-fitting stark red dress that matched her lipstick. She had her platinum blond hair up in a French twist, and wore long, dangling diamond earrings. For most men, she'd be an absolute knockout, but he barely noticed her model-thin frame.

"Yes, Madelyn?" he asked, somewhat annoyed. He didn't want problems at the moment, didn't want to think he had a job to do. Instead, he wanted to see Asha. He wanted a real answer about whether or not she'd be faithful to him. Whether or not she'd take his ask seriously. She'd been glib about it, or diverted his attention, but he realized, tonight he needed to know.

"It looks as if we have a few members who failed to RSVP, but they are at the doors, and…"

Durand waved his hand, annoyed. "Let them in." He didn't have time for small problems like this. He needed to focus.

"Some of them have guests, and…they are former members, but not current…"

He sighed, annoyance rippling through him. "I do not care about these petty issues now." He turned and saw the stricken look on her face. He instantly felt guilty. Madelyn was a good assistant and did not deserve his bad mood.

"I am sorry, Madelyn." He reached out and took her hand. She glanced up at him, unsure. "I did not mean to snap at you."

"Are you feeling all right, sir?" she asked him, the uncertainty still in her eyes. "We usually have work meetings the week leading up to a ball, and you've been..."

"I've been engaged elsewhere," he finished. This was none of Madelyn's business, and yet, the look on her face told him she intended to make it her business. She blinked fast. He could see her struggling with the truth, with the jealousy. He'd let this crush of hers go on too long. He'd let it grow right under his nose. Maybe it had been flattering once, but now he realized that it wasn't fair to her or him to let it continue.

"I worry, monsieur, that you are becoming distracted from your work." And from her, the meaning was clear. Not that they ever had a real connection. It had all been in her head, and he was fine with letting her imagine what she would, as long as she worked hard for him. Durand realized how unfair he'd been. And now her feelings were interfering with her job, just as he feared they would.

"That is not your concern," he said.

"Isn't it?" She frowned. "I know you. I know what you're passionate about. You've spent your entire life building this society and you're going to let one woman distract you from it? Take away your focus?"

"My focus is where it needs to be."

"Is that why you invited her to the Berlin Ball? Is that why you look for *that woman* even now? When your focus should be on the other guests?"

Durand glared at Madelyn, feeling his face grow hot. "You forget yourself."

Madelyn lowered her lashes, not meeting his gaze. "My apologies for speaking out of turn, sir."

Durand wondered if the apology was sincere, and then decided he didn't care. Madelyn was a good assistant when she wasn't blinded by her feelings.

"Please don't let it happen again. You and I have a professional relationship—nothing more."

Madelyn nodded once, but still wouldn't look him in the eye.

"Do you understand that?" He took a step to her and lifted her chin with one finger. Her hurt blue eyes met his.

"Yes, I understand, sir."

"Bien. Then get back to work."

"Yes, sir. And there is a matter that needs your attention immediately. The Princess of Sweden wants an audience."

"Her suspension is still in effect," Durand said, sighing and regretting that one night in Prague two years ago. He might have gotten carried away that evening after one too many glasses of champagne. Of course, that was long before Asha.

"Yes, but she's waiting in a sitting room nearby.

She says she won't leave until she speaks directly with you. And she's threatening to call her father."

"Of course she is."

Durand let out a woeful sigh. Work, apparently, did call. He would have to find Asha later. "Fine," he said as he followed Madelyn away from the balcony and towards the sitting room.

Asha arrived in the ballroom wearing a snug, form-fitting golden backless gown, her dark hair wound up in an elaborate twist, diamond earrings hanging from her ears. After a day of spas and pampering, she felt buffed and polished from head to toe, her makeup pristine and not a hair out of place. Not that many could tell about her makeup, as half her face was covered with the golden cat-eye mask Durand had gifted her. It suited her face perfectly, however, the fit comfortable, and she wondered how he'd managed to find a mask that fit her so well. She wore gold from head to toe, and almost worried she might look too much like a walking awards statuette. Though she could tell from the sidelong glances of the men in the room that the form-fitting dress made the impression she wanted. The golden fabric of her dress draped across her lower back, held by two small straps around her shoulders. She opted for no bra and felt like she was pure liquid as she moved. One man eyed her with appreciation as she walked, a man who looked like he might even be a former president. But she didn't care.

The only person she wanted to impress was Mathis Durand. When she stepped into the elegant eggshell-colored ballroom with the crystal chandeliers and soaring ceilings, she searched the crowd for Durand, but found no sign of him.

Where was he?

She took an offered glass of champagne and worked her way through the actors, heirs and dignitaries, their identities all hidden behind gilded masks. Asha should feel glad just to be here with the official invite, smug in the knowledge that she wouldn't be kicked out. She could finally see what all the fuss was about, all the whispers and gossip. Yet all she wanted to do was find Durand.

She was getting soft. There was no other way around it. She took a sip of the expensive champagne and wondered whether she'd ever get her edge back. Durand had gotten under her skin, had become her new obsession. She could think of little else, and worried that she might never think of anything else again. Her organic makeup business almost needed to run itself this month, and she'd let at least half a dozen voice mails from her father go unanswered. All she wanted to do was focus on Durand.

Was this what love was? she thought.

Asha clutched her champagne stem as she moved

through the ball. There was something delicious about being anonymous, about moving through a roomful of powerful people without really knowing who they were, or them knowing her. The din of voices grew louder as more people packed into the room.

Where was Durand?

She flagged down a passing waiter. "*Bitte*, excuse me. *Sprechen zie English*?"

This was the extent of her German, picked up from her travels.

"Yes," the waiter replied, bowing his head.

"Do you know where Monsieur Durand might be?"

"I am sorry, Fraulein." He shook his head. "I do not know."

Asha bit her lip. "Thank you," she murmured, already turning her attention elsewhere. Where was Durand? Then, she caught a glimpse of him walking down the side steps, Madelyn leading the way. *She* wasn't wearing a mask, she noticed. She clutched a tablet to her chest as she led him away. Where was she taking him? Durand's face looked somber as he went. Society business? she wondered.

She decided to follow them. She wondered what it could be. A trespasser? A catering catastrophe? She held back a bit as she followed through the crowd, leading her to a narrow hallway near the kitchen, and a small double-doored office. She hung back as the door opened, peeking around the corner of the small hallway. She saw a striking blonde, wearing nothing but lacy underwear, reach out from the office and drag Durand in. She saw a flash of pale skin and pink nipples through the sheer lace, and then Durand was gone—inside the office. Madelyn stayed outside the door, her back to it, guarding whatever was going on inside.

Asha felt cold and then hot again as a dozen different emotions rushed through her. Anger, jealousy, hurt. Hadn't he just demanded her loyalty, her fidelity in bed? And now he was rushing into a Nordic goddess's arms? Is this what happened at all his parties? Maybe the society was nothing more than his own personal sex club. The thought made bile rise up in her throat. She'd go confront him. She'd tell him that he'd made the last mistake he'd ever make with her. She stalked up to the door, and Madelyn's eyes widened in surprise.

"Let me in," she told the assistant, who narrowed her eyes as she glanced up and down Asha's clinging gold dress.

"I'm afraid I cannot do that," Madelyn said, a triumphant look on her face. She was enjoying this. "Monsieur Durand is occupied at the moment."

"I saw," Asha said, voice clipped. "Let me in. Now."

"I warned you not to get too attached, Ms. Patel," Madelyn said, voice low and blue eyes narrowed.

"You are not the only woman using your body to try to get a membership."

Asha felt like she'd been slapped. The contempt in Madelyn's eyes cut right through her.

"That's not what I'm doing here," she countered.

"Isn't it?" Madelyn raised a knowing eyebrow, and Asha clutched one fist at her side. She wasn't prone to violence, but she had a sudden urge to shove this smug assistant.

"No, it isn't. Now, move aside."

Madelyn caught the attention of a security guard in a black jacket as he walked past the hallway. The black jacket pivoted and headed towards them. "Don't make me have Becker see you out," Madelyn said, nodding at the guard as he approached.

Asha weighed the options of making a scene and hoping Durand came out to save her and whether he'd ignore the commotion if he was too busy inside with the mostly naked blonde. As she debated, Madelyn glanced at her tablet in her hands.

"Also, you should know, Ms. Patel, that I believe Mr. Connor Henry, your former paramour, is here."

Asha glanced sharply at Madelyn. "What do you mean? Durand revoked his membership." Didn't he? That's what he told her, anyway. Had that been a lie as well?

Madelyn cocked her head to one side, a superior smile curving her mouth. "I believe he's in the ballroom now, or technically, the smoking room on the north side, if you'd like to ask him."

Asha hesitated. She knew she couldn't trust Madelyn. It was likely a trick. And yet... She glanced at the burly security guard in black, ready to do Madelyn's bidding. She had little choice but to leave. She might as well see what the hell Connor was doing here. If Durand felt so little about her, what really was the point in staying?

CHAPTER THIRTEEN

"PUT SOME CLOTHES ON, Your Highness," Durand instructed the naked Swedish princess, as she tried to press her body against him mere steps from the hotel ballroom. He didn't appreciate being ambushed in the small office off of the kitchen, and there wasn't much room to maneuver here.

"Is that the way you treat an old friend?" Princess Lilly asked, blond eyebrow raised, as she thrust out her impressive, gravity-defying chest. Durand realized then that Madelyn had set him up. She'd known about the naked princess. Had led him here on purpose. To distract him from searching for Asha. Were there no lengths that woman wouldn't go? He'd thought she'd let go of her petty jealousy, but now he realized he'd been wrong about that.

"This will not help reinstate your membership," Durand said.

"Come on now, I made one mistake." Princess Lilly grabbed the lapels of his jacket.

"You tried to turn one of my events into a sex party," he said.

"That's just a little fun." She shrugged one bare shoulder.

"No. That is not what the Sphinx Society is about. If you want a sex club, form one yourself."

Princess Lilly laughed and pulled him closer. "You didn't seem to mind the sex when we had it."

Durand untangled the woman's fingers from his jacket, suddenly regretting his choice of lifestyle up until now. It all seemed so shallow, so short-sighted. He was here dealing with a woman whom he didn't care about, when the one he wanted more than anything was most likely wandering the ball-room by herself, fending off advances from other men. He was wasting his time here, just like he'd wasted much of his grown life until now. Avoiding love… Why? Because he was afraid. A coward. All he wanted to do was end this meeting as soon as possible so he could go find Asha.

In fact, he wanted to find her so badly, he thought he might have heard her voice outside the door. Or did he imagine it?

"Your suspension will be over next week, and then you can attend the year's Masquerade Ball," Durand said. This, of course, was the most sought-after invitation in the Sphinx Society, where all the guests went overboard with full costumes, outfits that made the Met Gala look…tame. "Unless you want to try to bribe me, and then I'll have no choice but to extend your probation."

Princess Lilly searched his eyes and then snatched her wrap dress from a nearby chair and pulled it around her. "I'm not trying to bribe you. I'm just being friendly." She glanced at him once more. "So, I'll be able to attend the Masquerade Ball this year?"

That's what she was really worried about, after all.

"Yes," he said and nodded. "So if that's all the business we have, I need to be on my way."

"Of course." Princess Lilly nodded her head and stepped aside. He threw open the door and nearly collided with Madelyn.

"Have you seen Asha?" Durand asked as he looked down the corridor but found it empty.

Madelyn glanced at her tablet, deliberately not making eye contact. "I believe she's searching out Connor Henry."

"What is he doing here?" Durand growled. "His membership is revoked."

"I attempted to tell you before, but…"

Durand recalled the conversation on the balcony, when he'd cut her off. She'd deliberately not led with the important news, and he'd been distracted by thoughts of Asha, and then with the Princess of Sweden. "You should have told me."

"I tried, sir." Madelyn glanced up quickly, but

then lowered her lashes. Her growing inability to separate her personal feelings from her work was becoming untenable. At a calmer moment, he'd have a very serious discussion with her about just that.

"We'll talk about this later," he said. "Where did Asha go?"

"I believe she's in the smoking room."

"Then, that's where I'm headed. We will talk about your insubordination later."

Asha saw Connor first, sitting in an oversized leather chair by the fireplace, brandy glass in another, and an unlit cigar butt in his mouth. He wore a simple black mask, and a red velvet jacket with black lapels. The small red-carpeted smoking room with the marble fireplace and the four chairs arranged in front of oak shelves lined with books seemed too small all of a sudden. Connor looked smug, his floppy brown hair was perfect, as usual, and he seemed every inch like one of the spies he played in the dozen or so movies he'd starred in. Asha glanced around for any sign of Kayli, that model he'd been dating, but found none. Had he come solo? And if so, why?

"What are you doing here?" Asha asked him, stalking right up to his chair and standing in front of him, arms crossed.

"I'm in Berlin for the premiere of *Gunshot*. And

it's good to see you too, Asha," he said, his brown eyes giving her a slow once-over, his dimple just visible in his cheek as he grinned. "You look good enough to eat."

"As if you'll ever get that chance."

"You sound a little jealous. I heard you went to the last party looking for me."

"Hardly worth finding. You'd better get out of here before Durand finds you."

Connor took the butt of the cigar out of his mouth and tucked it into the empty ashtray on the golden side table near his chair. Then, he picked up his glass of brandy and cradled it in one hand. "I'm not scared of Durand."

"So he did revoke your membership."

"I don't care if he did or not. I'm planning on enjoying myself." Connor pulled a phone from his pocket. "Selfie?" he asked as he gently put down his brandy glass next to the ashtray on the side table.

"Those aren't allowed. The first rule of the Sphinx Society is no pictures." Just as she'd finished her sentence, he clicked a photo of her.

"Give me that!" she cried, and lunged for the phone, but missed. He held it aloft, and when she got close enough, he clicked a picture of them together. "Stop that." She lunged again, but he once again kept the phone out of her reach.

"Why do you care? I've got many more pictures. Of former presidents, actresses, pop stars.

You name it. Most of them are still recognizable even beneath their masks."

"That's against the rules." Asha knew Durand wouldn't like it. Rich and powerful people didn't go to secret balls if they wanted their identities known. Durand would most certainly not like it. Not one bit.

"You can't do that," she said.

"Why not?" Connor snapped off his mask, that cocky grin plastered on his face. She noticed for the first time his nose was crooked and wondered why she'd missed the flaw before. "Why do you care?"

"Just give me that phone." She stretched forward. He held the phone to his chest.

"Take a real picture with me, and I will." Asha considered this. If she took the picture, then maybe she'd get the phone. And she could delete that one... and all the rest while she was at it.

"Fine," she managed, and she leaned in and smiled, as he clicked a selfie of the two of them together. "Okay, give the phone to me." She held out her hand.

"Give me a kiss first," he demanded.

The nerve. He was the last person on earth she wanted to kiss.

"I absolutely will n—" But Connor had grabbed her wrist and yanked her into his lap, laying a wet kiss on her mouth against her will. She struggled against him, but he held her in a vise grip, his tongue lapping at her closed mouth. How had she ever thought he was even remotely sexy? He kissed like a dead fish. Plus, he was a jerk. What he was doing was technically assault. She squirmed, but he held her fast, and as she worked to free herself, she heard a familiar voice behind her.

"Am I interrupting?" The French accent was unmistakable, and she knew even as she freed her lips from Connor's who she would find when she turned and scrambled off Connor's lap.

Durand was standing just a few feet from the chair, his face looking like he was only barely restraining his temper, his blue eyes flashing fire and retribution.

"Durand," she managed, realizing from the anger in his eyes that from his perspective on the other side of the chair, it probably looked like she wanted to be on Connor's lap. Not that she went there against her will. "This…this isn't what you think."

Durand didn't look at her. He kept his focus on Connor. "You're trespassing," Durand said, voice low and lethal. She could tell his whole body was tense, every muscle ready to spring to life.

"I'm enjoying a brandy in the smoking room of one of my favorite hotels," Connor said, crossing one leg casually over the other. "And I'm a guest here, so, no, I'm not trespassing."

A muscle at the side of Durand's jaw twitched.

"You should go, Connor," Asha warned him. "Why make a scene for your publicist? Don't you have a premiere to worry about?"

"Yes, it would be a shame if your publicity photos were marred with a black eye," Durand added dryly. But his face said he was deadly serious. Asha glanced at Connor and then back at Durand, both men frozen in some kind of primitive staring contest. Connor blinked first. Of course he would. He wasn't half the man Durand was.

"This room is getting too crowded for me, anyway." He stared at Durand. "Enjoy your *party*." He grabbed his brandy glass and then nodded at Asha. "Good to see you again, Asha. If you get lonely later, feel free to come see me in my room. I'm in 305."

Durand's nostrils flared just a bit, his eyes on fire, but he managed to keep his hands still by his sides, Asha noticed.

Durand cursed in French, beneath his breath, but Connor ignored the remark as he left the room, closing the big oak door behind him. He was just out the door when Durand exploded.

"What were you doing *kissing* that man?"

"I wasn't. I was fighting him off." She crossed her arms and turned her back to him. Durand grabbed her shoulder and turned her to face him.

"What do you mean?"

"He *forced* me into his lap. That's what. I was

trying to fight him off." She clenched her teeth. "That's more than I can say for you and the nearly naked what's-her-face."

Durand stopped then, dropping his hand from her arm. "What do you mean?"

"I *saw* you. The Nordic beauty in the expensive lingerie? Waiting for you in the office near the kitchen? You seemed to go more than willingly. And *you* were the one who talked of *me* being faithful."

"I didn't touch Princess Lilly."

"No? Not what your assistant told me."

Durand blew out a frustrated breath and turned, running both hands through his hair. "You cannot trust what she says."

Asha knew this was true. But she'd seen Durand go into that room with her own eyes.

"Why do you still keep her around? She's gone behind your back twice now, and she should've been fired ages ago."

"She's worked for me for years. It's complicated."

"Right. Maybe you have feelings for her, too." Asha snapped off her own mask and threw it on the ground. "Maybe I'm wasting my time and I should just go up and be with Connor."

Durand laughed, a growl. "You mean to make me jealous?"

"No," Asha lied, searching Durand's blue eyes, her heart hammering in her chest.

"You do." He took a step closer to her and she could smell him: the clean fresh scent of his hair pomade. He reached out and touched her wrist, and she felt the heat in the touch.

"I don't care if you're jealous."

"You lie, ma chère." He pulled her close now, her heart thumping as he pressed her body against his. "I can feel you lie. Just like I can feel your want." He pressed his hand against her bare lower back. "It's like a perfume, calling to me," he whispered in her ear.

"No," she lied again, trying to resist him, but his hands, the smell of him, his strength, they all tempted her. His hands teased her with the promise of what they could do to her if she let them.

"Admit to me that you want to make me jealous," he said, tightening his grip. He laid a gentle kiss on her bare neck, and a shiver ran down her spine.

"Why?" she asked, hoping to sound strong, but it came out a croak, a weakened plea.

"Because you care for me. Admit it." He traced her lower spine with his finger, dipping to the edge of the fabric draped against her lower back.

"Yes," she managed in a low whisper.

"Tell me that you do not care for Connor Henry. That he bores you."

She glanced up at him. "He bores me," she said truthfully, as Durand studied her eyes. In that moment, she knew he *was* jealous, that Connor had gotten to him. Interesting. It was a fact she could use later, once her senses returned, *if* they returned. Right now all she could focus on was Durand's gentle touch on her bare back.

"Tell me you will never have him in your bed. Promise me." Durand pressed against her lower back.

"Why?" she breathed, their lips close enough to touch. She glanced up at his blue eyes, ablaze with jealousy.

"Because you belong to me."

Asha laughed, though the merriment died in her throat. "And do you belong to me, as well? Or will you be fucking the next princess who offers herself up to you?"

"I do not want anyone else. I did not touch that woman. Nor do I want to touch any other woman."

"And I don't want any other man."

Then, he covered her mouth with his, and all her thoughts shattered into a million pieces. All she could think about were his lips on hers, his tongue lashing her own. How clumsy Connor had been, how unskilled. Not like Durand, who took her breath away, who made her knees weak with want. She pressed her body against him, and he clutched her closer, his hand roaming down the snug lines of her dress. His hands found the backless drape of the dress, and then they were inside her dress, against her bare bottom, cupping her, owning her.

"You are bare," he whispered, voice thick with want.

"A panty line would ruin the effect," she murmured back. Her dress was so thin and tight that she wore nothing beneath. Even the thinnest thong would show through. Plus, she realized, she'd planned for just this moment, had wanted to surprise Durand, give him a naughty little gift.

She clutched his neck, kissing him with a ferocity she didn't know she had, as he walked her backward. She went, and suddenly her back was against the smooth wall, as he lifted her knee up, pressing fully against her. He devoured her mouth and she wasn't sure where he ended and she began, all her thoughts on his talented tongue, his wet mouth. A desire, stronger than any she'd ever felt before, rose in her belly. She wanted him. No, she needed him. She needed him now.

Yet, would he break his own rules? After all, sex was not allowed at one of his parties. Absolutely against Sphinx Society rules. What would his rich and powerful members think?

Then, she heard the zip of his fly and knew he needed her as much as she needed him. He yanked on her skirt and suddenly it was at her waist, the cool air on her bare thighs. She barely registered the fact they were still in public, that anyone could

open the door to the smoking room and waltz right
in, seeing them as they were. But she didn't care.
All she wanted was to be filled by him, now, owned
by him right here in the small smoking room of
this hotel. His very party guests right outside the
unlocked door.

"I want you to be mine," he told her, his eyes
hot with want.

"I'm yours," she managed, eyes flicking back
and forth between his, just as he entered her, fully,
completely, making her gasp with the shock of it.
Her body accommodated him gladly, and she had
no thought of anything else but him. His body, his
cock, his mouth. She wanted it all, and she wanted
it now. Her breath came hard as the wall beneath
her back absorbed each and every one of his urgent
thrusts, and she didn't care. He held her against the
wall, deliciously pinned. She'd never been so reck-
less before, never had sex in a public place, as her
heart raced with the naughtiness of it. Her climax
was building in her before she could think to stop
it, and as he took her, quick and hard, she found
herself tumbling over the edge, into the pool of pure
pleasure, biting her lip to hold back her cry. Durand
came too, then, fast and hard and hot, burying his
face in her neck.

The door creaked open then. "Excuse me, Monsieur Durand." Madelyn stood at the doorway, tablet in hand.

Durand withdrew quickly, zipping himself up. Asha pulled down her dress but not quickly enough. Madelyn had seen most everything, she assumed. She stared at Asha with a blank, unreadable face. A dark strand of hair fell into Asha's face and she pushed it back quickly, even as she pressed her sticky thighs together.

"What do you want, Madelyn?" Durand growled, protective, almost, as he put his body in front of Asha's.

"I'm sorry to interrupt, sir, but it's Mr. Henry. He took pictures of the guests."

"He what?" Durand adjusted his tie and scowled. "Did you call security?"

Madelyn nodded. "They've escorted him out now. But…"

"But what?" Durand's voice was annoyed, brittle.

"He sent Asha the photo. She's posted it on one of her social media accounts." Madelyn lifted her tablet and a photo of Asha and Connor came up. The one he'd taken when she'd been trying to take the camera from him. From that vantage point, it looked, of course, as if she was happy to pose with the man.

"I didn't post that," Asha said, taken aback. Somehow he had hacked her account.

"Is that you in the picture?" Durand demanded.

"Yes, but…" But she was trying to get the

camera. She was trying to help. And she'd never planned to post anything like that. Ever.

"Was this your plan all along? Did you just want to boost your own profile?" He glared at the account online. "You have already many thousands of likes."

His words felt like a cold spike through Asha's chest. How could he accuse her of that? This wasn't a ploy. This had never been a ploy.

"Were you and Connor even broken up?"

How could he ask that? Of course she didn't care about Connor Henry. How could she after being so fully possessed, fully pleasured by Mathis Durand? The two men weren't even in the same category. Plus, she wasn't in love with Connor Henry. Never had been. Why couldn't Durand see the difference?

"I am not working with Connor. How can you even think that?"

"I'm afraid I don't think that's true," Madelyn said softly, as her attention darted from Durand to Asha and back again. She swiped to another picture. "Connor just posted a new one." Madelyn showed the new picture then, one of Durand and Asha kissing, him pressing her against the wall. No nudity was present, but it was implied. The tag line beneath the photo read, "The host and his secret sex party?"

Durand cursed in French, and Asha could feel his anger, his rage.

"You planned this?" he managed, his blazing.

"No. Of course not!" How could she know that Connor would take such a picture? "I don't want that out any more than you do!" Her face grew hot. She imagined all the comments people would make, how it was probably spreading on every social media platform already.

"You were kissing him when I came in," Durand said, his suspicion clear on his face.

"He forced me. I didn't want to kiss him," Asha said, almost sputtering, feeling as if she were completely on her back foot, helpless against the onslaught of allegations, except that she knew she was innocent. She knew that as outlandish as it sounded, she'd been framed.

Durand paused, as if trying to work out whether to believe her or not. But he should automatically believe her. If they had anything like a real relationship, he shouldn't doubt her. Not like this.

"I didn't do this," she managed. "You have to believe me."

"Why? You haven't been honest with me. About your feelings. About your true aims."

"What do you mean?" Asha didn't understand.

"You played me all along. All you wanted was to increase your profile. Your followers. You never cared about me. About us."

"That's not true. It's not. You know it's not." Asha grabbed his elbow, but he shook her off, his eyes ablaze with anger, with betrayal. He truly believed she'd plotted against him. But how could he believe this? Did he not know her? "You can't believe this of me. I thought you loved me."

"I loved the woman I believed you were," Durand said. "I thought you were better than this. I thought I knew you, but it turns out, you are just like the reputation you fight so hard against. You're just out for yourself, and no one else."

A small, triumphant little smile broke on Madelyn's face. Asha saw then that she'd lost. Whatever she thought she'd had with Durand wasn't at all what she thought.

The insult felt like a shard of glass lodging itself into her chest. "You can't believe that."

"We're done, Asha. *C'est fini.*"

CHAPTER FOURTEEN

A WEEK LATER, Asha sat in her father's huge office in his massive Cloud headquarters in Seattle and wondered what had happened. She'd asked a few of her contacts in the building if they'd figure out how her social media account had been hacked. She'd changed her password since, and had had no other problems, but she wondered how those pictures had managed to get there in the first place. She'd never betray Durand like that. She hadn't even *cared* about her social media presence since the two had met. She'd been too busy obsessing over Durand himself to even worry about what her follower count had managed to tick up to this week.

She stared out of her father's windowed office, to the gorgeous view of Puget Sound. A single seagull flew by, white wings outspread, and the sun glistened off the calm blue water. Her father came into his office then, his salt-and-pepper hair combed back from his forehead, wearing his company's casual wear of a logoed polo and jeans.

"Asha! What are you doing here?" He opened his arms wide, and she went into them, suddenly feeling emotion choke her.

"I wanted to see you," she said, hugging her father, leaning into the secure feeling of his strong arms around her. Even if they didn't agree on her career path, she still needed him. Her father hugged her back and then slowly released her, stepping back and studying her face.

"Does this mean you'll finally take over the company?" He looked so hopeful, but she'd have to dash his desires.

"No, Dad. I'm afraid not."

He looked disappointed for a moment, but then recovered. "I'll never get you to take over the company, will I?"

She shook her head. "No, you won't. But you'll always be my dad. And I need you." His face softened a bit.

"Come on, have a seat. Talk to me. What's wrong?"

She sank into his plush sofa near the beautiful view of the water. The rare sunshine glinted on Puget Sound.

"I fell in love. But I think it's all ruined," she admitted. She told him about Durand, about the

Sphinx Society, about the stupid pictures that some-how had been posted to her account.

"I deleted them, but they're already out there. People have copied them, reposted them else-where." She bit her lip. "I know it's going to be bad for the Sphinx Society. Already there are ru-mors that members are leaving the club."

"Simply because of a little publicity?" Her fa-ther shook his head. Her father thought there wasn't any such thing as bad publicity. That was one of the cornerstones of his business.

"It appears so."

"Have you figured out how someone got into your account? I can look into that." He took a seat opposite her, face earnest.

"I've got some of your people working on it al-ready." She shrugged one shoulder.

"You do, do you?" He shook his head. "And you say you don't want to run my company? Though you don't mind using its assets?"

"Of course not. I'm just practical. Just like you, Dad."

Father and daughter shared a smile. She reached out and took his hand, and he glanced down at hers covering his.

"I understand." He nodded and patted her hand. "I was just like you, you know. Headstrong. Stub-born. Sometimes...impossible."

"Hey!" she whipped her hand away in protest.

"*But* that's what makes us Patels who we are. I can't blame you for wanting to make something of your own. And do not worry about this Durand fellow. He'll come around."

"I'm not so sure." Asha remembered the look of betrayal on his face. The anger. She wasn't sure he'd come around at all.

"Well, you have an enemy, someone who is trying to undermine you with him." Her father studied her face. "And knowing you, I bet you already know who it is."

"Madelyn," she said, instantly. "She's his assistant. She's in love with him." Asha tapped her finger against her bottom lip, thinking. "But how did she get into my account?"

"*She* may have been the one working with Connor," her father suggested. "It's what I would do, if I were trying to discredit a rival. As for the password to your account, would he know what it was? Or, perhaps he just stole it from your phone. One of our competitors is working on such a technology. It's bringing corporate espionage to a new level."

"Really?" Asha bit her lip, thinking. If this were true, then it would all make perfect sense. Connor just wanted revenge against Durand for kicking him out, and Asha for...well, causing him to be kicked out, and losing the social status he so craved. Madelyn simply wanted Durand for himself.

With her out of the way, maybe she thought her odds would improve.

"*If* this is what happened, how do I prove it, though? How do I make Durand believe me?"

Her father leaned back in his chair, thinking. "Let me talk to some of my programmers. See what we can do."

Durand sat in his Paris office, staring at the Eiffel Tower out his window, but not really seeing it. He couldn't believe he'd been so easily played, so easily led by his emotions. Asha had played him from the start and he should've seen it. Should've anticipated it. All she'd ever wanted was to boost her own image, to gain more followers and make more money, even if it made him look like a fool. Or perhaps *because* it made him look like a fool. Maybe all this time she was just fooling him. Stringing him along. Playing to his weaknesses. He should've known better. He should've seen it coming. But he'd let his emotions blind him, and now, he was about to lose everything.

More than anything, he understood how his father must've felt. He couldn't believe he was feeling sorry for the man. Couldn't believe he'd actually take pity on him. Perhaps it was because he was about to lose the only thing his father had ever given him: the Sphinx Society, his inheritance.

And he was beginning to realize for the first

time in his life the power of love, and for the second time in his life, love seemed to be destroying everything. Maybe it would always get him in the end. Maybe it was a force he simply couldn't overcome.

All he could think about was Asha. She betrayed him. There was no other logical explanation. Even as he struggled to once again gain control of his feelings.

"Sir?" Madelyn popped her well-coiffed blond head in his office door. She'd left her hair long and loose, forgoing her usual tight updo, not that Durand cared. She could've pranced around naked in front of him and he'd barely notice. His mind was filled with Asha. Her betrayal. "Do you have a minute? We really have to find some way to control the slide. Members are suspending their memberships at a record rate."

He barely heard her. The fallout from Connor Henry's posts continued. Many of his rich and well-connected members were skittish, worried that Connor's exposing them would tarnish their reputations. Others were quitting simply because they felt he was a hypocrite, demanding that they refrain from sex during his parties while he partook all he wanted. Durand had worked hard all these years to make sure the Sphinx Society's reputation wasn't tarnished with lewdness, and now he'd single-handedly ruined it all by not being able to control his impulses, not being able to resist Asha Patel.

And it was all because he'd seen her in the lap of another man. His primal, protective instincts had taken over, blinding him to all common sense. And now he was about to lose everything. Or maybe he'd lost all that really mattered already. Asha wasn't returning his phone calls. What did it even matter if the Sphinx Society went under? Asha was all he cared about, he realized. She was all that mattered.

Madelyn was still talking, still running through messages on her tablet, but he was barely listening. He kept his eyes on the Eiffel Tower, his thoughts elsewhere.

"Monsieur? Did you hear me?" Madelyn prodded.

"What?"

Madelyn frowned. "At this rate, we'll have to call off the Masquerade Ball. Already, people are declining their invitations."

She showed him a string of texts from members, politely declining. He took the tablet from her and scrolled through them, barely reading them. She was right to be upset. The Masquerade Ball was the most prestigious invitation in the world. Declining an invitation was unthinkable even last week. Now, the idea of people turning up their noses at the world's best party was growing. Madelyn, frustrated, paced in his office, in front of his ornate antique desk. Until, far back in her text history, he saw a single number, not attached to a name. He hit it, curious, and that's when he saw not messages, but photos. Photos sent from Madelyn's tablet.

"What's this?" He glared at the photo, the one of him and Asha in the study, so completely wrapped up in their passion that they hadn't seen the photographer, hadn't bothered to notice the door had opened. His mind worked out the puzzle before him. The damning photo was one she'd sent. "You took this photo."

"No! Absolutely not." Madelyn swiped the tablet from his hands, but he saw the guilt on her face.

"You did this. *You* betrayed me." Fire burned in Durand's belly. He saw it all so clearly then: Madelyn's jealousy, her love gone wrong, and her complete irrationality about it all. How she'd cut off her own nose to spite her face. She hadn't even cared about what she'd do to the Sphinx Society. She'd just been too threatened by Asha's mere presence.

Tears welled in Madelyn's eyes as she sank into a nearby chair.

"No. I was…only trying to help."

"By sending Connor this picture? Tell me, did you hack Asha's account? Or did he?"

"He posted the picture. He had some way of getting into her account," Madelyn admitted. She reached out to try to take his hands but he whisked them away from her. The last thing he wanted was her touching him.

"You betrayed me."

"No! I was thinking of you. I was trying to free you."

"Free me?" he thundered, anger still pulsing in his veins.

"From this obsession that had taken over your life. Your good sense. You were not yourself. You told me you'd never love anyone, and so I knew you would never love me, but then *she* came and…" Tears choked Madelyn's voice.

So this was all about Madelyn's unrequited love.

"I was never going to love you, Madelyn," he said. "I thought you knew that."

"I did, and I was all right with that. As long as you never loved anyone. But…but…you love her."

"Yes, I do." The admission came instantly. Durand loved her still. And now…he realized that he'd pushed her away, accused her of betrayal, when she'd been innocent all along.

"She was too much of a distraction, Monsieur Durand. I am so sorry. Please forgive me. I…"

"No. You are not forgiven, Madelyn." He shrugged off her touch. "You are fired."

"No! Please." She clasped his elbow in desperation. He glanced at her white knuckles and all he felt was disgust. "Where will I go? Please?"

"I cannot trust you." He whipped his elbow away, glaring at her.

"But I—I love you," she managed, tears streaking down her cheeks. "I have always loved you."

"I have never loved you, Madelyn. I never will love you," Durand said coldly. "Especially now that you have destroyed all that I have built. You have sent away the only woman I have loved. Or will love."

A sob wracked Madelyn's whole body as she buried her face in her hands.

"Your services will no longer be required now or ever, Madelyn," Durand said, voice low. "I never want to lay eyes on you again."

CHAPTER FIFTEEN

DURAND STOOD IN the beautiful manicured grounds of the Le Chalet Des Iles in Paris, the venue granted to the city by Napoleon III, surrounded by Lake Inferior, and accessible only by boat. The moonlight glistened on the water, and Durand waited, watching the opposite shore for signs of life. The grounds and the chalet were bathed in beautiful twinkling white lights, and the effect was magical. It looked like something out of a fairy tale, and that was the idea. He glanced at the empty waters, feeling disappointment rise in his chest. The water was supposed to be covered with rowboats, manned by Masquerade Ball staff, an army of boats like the ones who'd ferried the twelve dancing princesses to their enchanted ball to dance the night away.

Behind him, the beautifully delicate notes of a quartet broke the silence of the night air, and Durand glanced at his watch, wondering how long he'd let them play to a nearly empty island. In the last couple of weeks leading into the year's final and most important gathering for the Sphinx Society, hundreds of members had bowed out, rescinded their RSVPs, made excuses about how they could no longer attend. Durand knew the truth: they were scared off by Connor's posts, worried that Asha's social media feed had outed them. No matter how much damage control he'd done, no matter how many missives he'd sent explaining what had truly happened, the tide had yet to turn. People were still afraid to come to his party.

Durand glanced up at the waiter who stood at the side of the lit outdoor ballroom, looking bored. He'd put down his tray of champagne on an empty high-top table. Durand moved towards him, and the waiter snatched up the tray, eager to serve, and offered him a glass. Durand took it, feeling morose, almost as if he planned to toast the very last event of the Sphinx Society. He glanced at his own cell phone, but found he had no service. There was no way of knowing if Asha had gotten his texts that morning, if she'd gotten the message that Madelyn had been the one to betray him and not her. He hadn't figured out exactly how she'd managed it, but he knew that Asha wasn't to blame. But now that he'd accused her of betraying him, now that he'd doubted her loyalty, he wondered if she'd ever come back to him.

Love was a tricky thing, yes, but he had come to the realization that he'd rather live a life with it than without. He glanced back at the waitstaff, at various corners of the open, lit grounds of the chalet, and wondered if he ought to just cancel the party. He didn't need the staff of twenty to wait on him. This had been a mistake. He should've canceled the party from the start. He'd known the RSVPs were down to near nothing. But his own stubborn streak refused to allow him to do it. He still held out hope that the people would come.

Now, looking at the dark lake, absent of boats, he knew he was wrong. No one was coming. His dream, the society he'd spent his life building, was dead. And it was partly his fault. He'd built it up on a lie: that he could keep every member safe in secrecy. But no matter how many masks a person wore, eventually, the truth came out. Even if one didn't know what that truth was themselves. Asha had taught him that.

He finished the last of the expensive champagne and then thought of hurling the crystal glass into the lake, a vent for his frustration. But as he wheeled back one arm, a light bobbed in the distance. Durand stopped, midthrow, and squinted, focusing on the light. A lantern someone let go from the shore? he wondered. Then he saw what was happening: a single guest, coming to his party. He had planned for hundreds of boats to line the water, but here was just the solitary guest. He wasn't sure if he was hopeful or saddened. One guest? Who could it be?

Durand's heart thumped in his chest as he scanned the shoreline. He walked briskly to the dock, eager to meet the first guest, hoping against hope that somehow, Asha would be the one. Even as he told himself this wouldn't happen. Asha was done with him, and who could blame her? He paced on the dock, as the white rowboat slid through the water, the occupants too far away to see their faces. And even when they approached, all he could see was a golden mask, and a lady wearing gold. He strained in the darkness to see the outline of her as the boat approached. Could it be? Could he dare hope?

The lady wore a costume of a fairy in a ball gown, her clear wings stretching far behind her, the train of her golden gown flowing across the boat. Her long, nearly jet-black hair flowed down her shoulders. A fairy queen, he thought, regal and beautiful, and dangerously seductive with her low-cut gown. When the lady reached the end of the dock, the servant rowing hopped out, and helped her to shore, and as soon as she put a golden heel on the dock, Durand knew.

"Asha," he called, sweeping her into his arms.

"I thought we were *supposed* to be anonymous," she replied beneath the golden mask covering her eyes.

"I'll always know you," he said. "No mask can fool me."

"Is that so?" She pushed up her mask as Durand pulled her close. He kissed her and felt his heart thump in his chest. This woman was made for him. There simply wasn't another explanation. "I am so sorry, ma chère. You were not to blame for—" he began, but she shushed him with a soft finger on his lips.

"I know. My father's team discovered that Connor and Madelyn worked together to hack my account," she said.

"Can you forgive me for blaming you? I will earn your forgiveness. I promise you that."

"Earn it?" She arched an eyebrow. "How?"

"Spending the rest of my life bringing you pleasure, of course." He pulled her close and kissed her again, feeling his heart soar as she kissed him back, fully, pressing her body into his.

"We might never get any work done," she managed as she broke free.

"Work? What is this?" He grinned back.

"I don't blame you, Durand," Asha said, growing serious. "You were just protecting your society."

"Some good it did. You are the only guest this evening."

"Am I, now?" She glanced backward over her shoulder, and Durand followed her gaze to the opposite shore. One light came on, and then another, followed by another. Hope squeezed his chest. Those were…lanterns on boats. Many, many boats, all bringing party guests to the chalet. Soon, another lantern bobbed, and then another, as they pushed off from the opposite shore, an army of guests headed his way. He glanced down at Asha.

"You did this."

"I might have told a few of my friends that they'd be crazy to miss out on the party of the year. I hope you don't mind a few party crashers."

At this point, Durand didn't mind. Not at all. His party was saved. "None of them have invitations, eh?"

"They have one from me." She grinned. "And they're all the new up-and-comers, the new influencers, the *new* new money. They'd all love to become members if your *old* members don't care to join the society. And I bet, once they do, your old guests will come clamoring back for their spots."

"Interesting." Durand's mind turned as he thought of all the possibilities. "Maybe you're right. Maybe making it too secret was the wrong thing to do. Maybe it should be very, very public." Durand hadn't even considered the possibility before now, but it made sense, and it was the one way he could keep his society alive. "That would mean I'd change the rules."

"You make the rules. You can change them," she said.

"Change them with me," Durand said, grabbing her hand. "Be my partner."

"Partner?" Asha flipped her golden mask to the

top of her head and searched his eyes. "But I don't even have a *membership*."

"You don't need a membership when you're part owner. Will you? Please, Asha. I need you."

Asha bit her lip. "Does this mean I get a say in *everything*?"

"Fifty-fifty," Durand promised. "I want you to be my partner in business…and in life."

Asha blinked fast.

"I love you, Asha Patel." Durand clutched her soft hands, amazed how easily the words rolled off his tongue, because they were so true. He felt, for once in his life, that he was his true self with this woman. He wore no masks, and neither did she.

"I love you, too," Asha said, and his heart lit up with joy.

"I want you to be my partner in business, in life, in every possible way. Will you do me the honor of being my partner?"

"Mathis Durand, are you actually proposing to me?"

He hadn't even thought about that possibility before. Hadn't he sworn off marriage his whole life? But marriage, like love, seemed the right step. The only step.

"Will you be my wife?"

"Yes, of course, yes," Asha replied, and then threw her arms around his neck and pulled him down for a kiss.

EPILOGUE

A year later

THE GUESTS CROWDED the golden ballroom of one of Stockholm's most premiere destinations, the Grand Hotel. Each one wore a golden mask, and their reflections in the mirrored walls made it look like the two hundred or so guests were many more than that. The scene was as beautifully breathtaking as it had been a year before when Asha had first met Mathis Durand, in this very ballroom, her first introduction to the Sphinx Society.

"Are you nervous?" her father asked her as he met her at the doors of the ballroom in his black-and-white tuxedo, looking still much like himself despite the fact, he, too, had half his face covered in a golden mask.

"A little," she admitted as she fussed with her white dress. This time, she'd blend right in at the white-and-black ball. Though blending in wasn't what brides were supposed to do. "The last time I was here, I wore bright red."

"I think white suits you better. You're a beautiful bride, darling," her father said, and laid a gentle kiss on her cheek.

Asha glanced once more at her reflection in the mirrored wall. Her original designer gown offered a full train, miles of hand-stitched beadwork, and a veil that completely obscured her face through thick white tulle. She could see out, but no one could see in.

Music began from inside the ballroom. "That's our cue," her father said, and offered his arm. She took it, the butterflies anxious in her stomach. Despite a perfect year with Durand, despite her absolute confidence he was the right man for her, part of her worried that somehow, somewhere, it would all go awry. She'd never felt this lucky before, this in love, and she worried that one day she'd wake up and it would all be a dream.

She and her father stood at the doors of the ballroom, and the guests parted, standing each to the side, making an aisle straight downward. At the far end of the beautiful room stood the reverend who would marry them, and Durand himself in a black tuxedo and white mask, looking striking and dangerous, and absolutely the man for her. She sucked in a breath and walked to the beat of the string quartet. As she approached, she saw his face light up, his blue eyes glistening with joy beneath the mask. Her heart felt as if it would burst from love, and she was impatient to close the distance between them, to have her hands in his, to become his wife.

She passed all the guests, their friends and family, beneath the masks, and shook her head. The event—and the reception afterward—had been the most hyped social event of the year. Thousands of people clamored for invitations, and the Sphinx Society had never been more popular. In fact, membership had tripled in the last year, and the two of them, partners in the business, had grown. It turned out, they made as good a team in the office as they did in the bedroom.

Asha felt a little thrill of satisfaction when she thought of the year to come: the social engagements, their "wedding tour" that would bring them to cities across the world, where Sphinx Society members wished to line up and raise a glass of champagne in their honor. Their wedding had turned into the very best thing that could've happened for the elite club.

Asha took another step closer to Durand. Another two steps and they'd be there. Her father paused as they approached and kissed her hand.

"You take good care of her," he told Durand.

"But of course," Durand said. "Though it is she who has saved me."

Her father withdrew his arm from Asha's, and

Durand stood before his bride. He lifted her veil, revealing her bare face. She wore no mask. Tears welled in Durand's eyes. Tears of joy and love, and Asha felt her own eyes grow wet with emotion.

"You are the most beautiful woman in the world, ma chère," he said. "You wear no mask, and neither shall I."

He took off his own and tossed it the ground, and Asha and Durand stood facing each other, without conceit, without masks to hide behind.

"Ladies and gentleman," the reverend in the white mask began. "We are here to celebrate the marriage of Asha Patel and Mathis Durand. First, these two would like to exchange their own vows." He nodded at Durand.

"Asha, a year ago, I met you here, in this very ballroom. You were then an uninvited guest."

"As I recall, you kicked me out," Asha said, and the whole room laughed.

"You might have come without an invitation, but you made yourself at home in my heart. You made your own home there. You have done what no other woman could, and convinced me of the value of love," he said. "You are my love, my world, and my savior."

Asha felt tears choke her. Surprisingly strong emotions gripped her, and she feared she'd cry out her mascara in front of all their guests.

"I promise to love and honor you, Asha," Durand continued. "I promise to be my real self with you, and never to wear this or any other mask." He pointed to the mask on the ground. "I promise to cherish you all the days of our lives, and I will be faithful to you, and only you. I promise you this, now and always."

Asha believed him, because he had been faithful completely to her this last year, and she felt secure for the first time in a relationship with a man. She'd come to realize that relationships weren't about power at all, that true love was about surrendering power. And as soon as she'd done that, she'd realized that everything would be all right.

He took a ring from his pocket, covered in diamonds, and slipped it onto her finger. "With this ring, I claim you as my partner, my wife, my everything."

Asha swallowed back her emotions, even as the light of the ballroom glistened on her ring.

"You have shown me what it means to love, what it means to truly give myself to someone else," she said. "I have made a home in your heart, and you have made one in mine. I want to spend the rest of my years building a life together with you. Because you are the love of my life."

"And I'm yours," Durand said.

"I couldn't have said it better," the reverend said. "Now, I pronounce you husband and wife. You may kiss the bride."

"I hope so," Durand said. "Come here, ma chère. Show me how much you love me." He grinned.

"Now and always," Asha said, stood on tiptoe, and kissed him. She barely heard the cheers and applause in the room, as all she could feel were Durand's lips on hers, and their promise of the years of happiness to come.

* * * * *

DATING THE REBEL

LISA CHILDS

MILLS & BOON

To Dr. Megan McNitt.

I am so happy you've become a fan of my books.
I am a fan of yours!

Congratulations on becoming an MD!

CHAPTER ONE

"WHAT THE HELL is he doing here?" The question exploded out of Miranda Fox just as she felt like exploding. Usually she enjoyed the size of her small office, the elegance of the brocade wallpaper and white-painted coffered ceiling, but right now it wasn't giving her enough room to pace and nowhere to escape. If she walked out, she would have to pass him in the reception area. And the office was too many floors up for her to safely jump out the window.

And she wasn't about to risk her life, or anything else, over Grant Snyder.

"He wants to become a member of Liaisons International," the receptionist, who was also her younger sister, replied, as if it was obvious.

But it wasn't. Nothing was ever obvious about Grant.

Miranda shook her head. "No, he doesn't. He's up to something."

He had to be. Why else would he have flown

from his office in London to show up at her business in Monaco? Sure, he co-owned a private charter plane company, so flying to him wasn't much different than driving, but still...

There wasn't even an airport in Monaco. He would have taken a helicopter or a car to travel from Nice to her office. Why take the time for a visit? Why hadn't he just called her? Then she would have been able to hang up on him.

Oh...

That was why he'd made the trip instead of calling. But what was his real reason for the visit?

"Maybe it's about Blair," Tabitha suggested.

Blair was Grant's younger sister and Miranda's best friend since they were little girls.

Tabitha's face twisted into a slight grimace of concern as she almost reluctantly continued, "Maybe something's happened to her."

Miranda shook her head again—with such force that the ends of her blond tresses struck her face and tangled in her long lashes. She could not even consider such a horrible thought, for so many reasons. One—she'd spent so much time worrying about her friend when she'd been a fighter pilot. Retired and flying planes only for the private charter business that she'd started with her brother, Blair was safe now. And because of Miranda's business, Liaisons International, she was also happy. "No, if something happened to Blair, *he* would never come to tell me."

Unless it had been Miranda's fault…

Then he would seek her out to lecture her just like he'd done when they were all kids. Like he was any better than she was…

Like he'd never gotten into trouble.

Hell, he was trouble—just the way he looked, so muscular, so big, so damn good-looking…

So charming when he wanted to be. He'd never wanted to charm her, though. He only ever wanted to warn her to stop messing up his sister's life. Not that she'd ever really messed it up except for a detention or two or three in school. And now that they were adults, the most she'd ever done was talk Blair into taking a break from work and into joining her dating service.

Was that why he was here now?

But Blair and Matteo Rinaldi were happy and too perfect for each other to be having problems already. In fact, the billionaire had just granted an interview in which he'd revealed that he was happier than he'd ever been—thanks to Blair and Liaisons International.

So if Teo was happy, Blair was, too. And no matter how big a jerk Grant had been to Miranda, he'd only ever wanted his sister to be happy and safe, which was probably why he'd been such a jerk to

Miranda. He'd been protecting his sister from her bad influence.

She hadn't purposely gotten Blair into trouble, but she hadn't always exercised the best judgment.

She had to know why he was here, so she drew in a deep breath and said, "I'll see him…"

Tabitha grinned and eagerly nodded. "You'd be missing out big-time if you didn't. I think he's gotten even hotter than he used to be."

Was that possible? While they'd talked on the phone when she'd called their business looking for Blair, she hadn't seen him in person in years.

She'd been counting on the opposite—on her teenage mind having overexaggerated how damn good-looking he'd been. Like how, in her child's mind, she'd remembered her father's house as having been so large and elegant, but when she'd finally been invited back to visit him, it had been small and sad. Like he'd been.

Tabitha opened Miranda's office door and slipped out, closing it behind her. But even through the thickness of the solid mahogany wood, Miranda could hear her sister giggling in response to a deep rumble that made her own traitorous pulse quicken with excitement. Then the door opened again, and she had confirmation.

It wasn't just possible. It had actually happened—Grant Snyder had gotten even hotter. Unlike her father's house, Grant was even bigger than she remembered. Taller. Broader. More muscular. His hair was a deeper gold, his eyes a darker blue, and that reddish beard trimmed so close to his skin only enhanced the rigid line of his strong jaw. *Damn him...*

Damn her...

This was supposed to have been a simple mission. Track down Miranda Fox and warn her to stop messing with his sister's life. Blair was in a good place—a great place—now; she didn't need Miranda talking her into playing hooky from work or from her new relationship. It was a mission Grant Snyder had carried out many times in his youth, albeit never successfully. Miranda had always ignored him then.

So had his sister.

Then Grant had left to join the navy and hadn't been around enough to monitor their many misadventures. He'd had no excuse for not catching and putting a stop to their recent one, though, since he worked with Blair now. He should have noticed what was going on with her, but he hadn't—until it was too late.

Until she'd been reduced to tears, and his sister, a former naval fighter pilot, never cried, not even when their dad had died. But Miranda had set her up with that billionaire and nearly gotten Blair's heart broken. Teo had proved to be a good guy, though, but no relationship of Blair's had ever lasted, usually because of Miranda's meddling.

Damn Miranda Fox…

That was her fault. And if he didn't step in and get her under control this time, she would no doubt make Blair cry again. He couldn't have that; he hadn't been able to protect his sister like he'd wanted in the past, but he would now.

But who the hell was going to protect him… from Miranda Fox?

She'd been a cute teenager.

But now she was all woman—with full lips highlighted with just a shimmer of gloss. Unlike the heavy Goth makeup she'd worn as a teen, she looked to be wearing barely any at all but for that shimmer. Given how pale her coloring was, her lashes probably weren't real, but they looked naturally long and black surrounding her silvery-blue eyes. Her dress was nearly the same color, in thin silk that clung to her every curve. And she definitely had more of those than he remembered.

Unfortunately she had the same sassy attitude she'd always had. "You better make this fast, Snyder. Since you don't have an appointment, I'm fitting you in between other meetings."

How long had he been standing there in the doorway to her small office? Probably with his mouth hanging open. He touched his bottom lip, checking for drool. Not wanting her to throw him out before he'd had a chance to issue his warning, he stepped into her office and closed the door behind him. "Would you have given me an appointment if I'd asked for one?"

"No," she admitted freely—almost rebelliously. She'd always been such a rebel, but she didn't look like one now.

While still petite, she was as elegant as a princess. Maybe that was why she'd moved to Monaco—in the hopes of becoming one. Her many-times-married mother had been obsessed with husbands, the richer and more important the better. Maybe her oldest daughter had inherited that same obsession along with the business.

Her office reflected her elegance and her small size. With the door shut, he didn't have much room between him and the desk, even though it was small with spindly legs. She stood on the other side of that desk. Was she purposely keeping it between them? He leaned back against the door and crossed his arms over his chest.

"Why not?" he asked. "Why wouldn't you let me make an appointment with you?"

"Because all you've ever done is yell at me and threaten me," she said.

He suppressed the instinct to flinch at her direct hit. Threatening her, so she wouldn't interfere in his sister's happiness, had been what he'd planned on doing today. "I've never yelled at you," he said in his defense. And he wouldn't have yelled at her today, either.

"You don't need to yell," she said. "You have that voice…" She shuddered.

"Like it ever got to you," he said. "You never listened to me, anyway." She had never heeded any of his threats to stay away from his sister, which indicated that maybe it was time he changed his tactics with her.

"So why would you bother coming here?" she asked. "When I have no reason to listen to you now…" The way her voice trailed off suggested she wasn't entirely confident of that, though.

Was she up to something?

She lifted her chin and squared her slender shoulders. "Blair isn't in any trouble. In fact, she's happier than I've ever seen her."

"I agree," Grant said. And he damn well intended to make sure his sister stayed that happy. But the only relationship Blair had ever maintained was her friendship with Miranda, which Grant suspected had cost her all the other relationships she would have had if not for her best friend's interference.

"So you have no reason for coming here," Miranda said, and she glanced down at the delicate gold watch on her wrist, as if implying he'd already taken up too much of her time.

"Don't you think that gives me every reason to come here?" he asked.

Her lips, with that tantalizing shimmer, curved into a slight smile, and she walked around her desk to lean against the front of it, her shapely bare legs crossed at the ankle. "Oh, are you here to apologize for the hard time you've always given me? Are you finally going to admit that you were wrong about me?"

With her standing this close to him, he was the one having the hard time—controlling the sudden surge of attraction pulsating inside him and his damn traitorous cock. How could he be attracted to a troublemaker like her?

Easily.

Grant had always been drawn to the greatest danger, to the biggest risk…

But unlike with the other risks he'd taken, he doubted there would be any reward with her. Only heartache, like all the hearts she'd broken as a teenager.

But still, he couldn't resist…

He straightened away from the door, which brought him closer to her, so close that he could feel the heat of her slight body. And his began to tingle with awareness.

"Oh, I wasn't wrong," he said, and he leaned over more as if there was some cable between them

pulling him closer. "Not about you. You're definitely trouble."

She uttered a soft sigh, her breath touching his
mouth—making him want those shimmery lips
to touch his instead. All he had to do was lean a
little farther.

But she reached out and pressed her palm against
his chest as if to hold him back, as if she'd read
his mind and knew how damn badly he wanted
to kiss her.

His chest tingled where her hand touched him,
where his heart pounded harder with the attraction
and desire coursing through his body.

Did she feel it, too?

"And you're still more trouble than I ever was,"
she informed him. "If all you've come here to do
is call me names again, you can leave." She used
her free hand to point at the door.

She definitely wasn't going to listen to him any
more than she had when she was a teenager. But
Grant had always been good at improvising when
the original plan for a mission had failed. If he
hadn't been, he wouldn't have survived.

"Have you considered that I might have another
reason for being here?"

She narrowed her eyes with suspicion. "Really?
What? You had a crush on me all those years ago,
and you're seeking me out now because of your
unrequited love?"

He tried to suppress the chuckle that bubbled up the back of his throat, but it slipped out before he could control it. Kind of like his attraction to her...

But that was new. He'd never been attracted to her before. Even though he was only a few years older than her and his sister, he'd always felt much older—too old to have ever looked at her the way he was looking at her now.

She arched a brow. "What? No unrequited love?"

"What about you?" he asked. He was well aware that some of his sister's friends had had crushes on him. But Miranda hadn't giggled and flirted with him like those girls, like her very own sister just had. No. She'd only ever glared at him, like she was glaring now.

And she laughed. But it sounded more forced than his had been. Of course, she'd never found him funny before. Why would she now?

A weary-sounding sigh followed her laugh, and again her breath brushed across his skin with the faint scent of cinnamon. He loved cinnamon.

"I really don't have time for your games," she said with another pointed glance at her gold watch. "Why are you here, Grant?"

He couldn't tell the truth—not now—not when she was already so irritated with his visit. She would probably coerce Blair into doing something stupid just to spite him—like he suspected she'd done when they were younger.

"I want to join your dating service, of course," he said, as if it was obvious.

She laughed again, and this time it didn't sound forced at all.

"Why is that funny?" he asked. "Blair had such success that, of course, I would be interested in—"

"Are you looking for a billionaire?" she asked, interrupting him. Then shaking her head, she added with pity, "What? Have you gambled away all your money?"

A curse burned the back of his throat, but unlike the chuckle, he was able to suppress it. He grinned instead. "Quite the opposite, in fact. I would make a great catch."

She laughed again—even harder than she just had, so hard that her beautiful eyes crinkled and a dimple pierced one cheek.

His breath caught, probably on the curse he'd choked back, over her beauty. She was stunning and, unfortunately, almost as damn aggravating as she had always been. He leaned back against the door so that her hand finally fell away from his chest.

She glanced down at it as if she hadn't realized it was still there.

Obviously touching him hadn't had her tingling with awareness like it had him. He crossed his arms so that he didn't reach for her, so that he didn't try to make her feel the attraction, too.

Could he...

Was that the new tactic he should take? Making her want him?

Damn, the challenge was just too tempting. *She* was just too tempting...

"Why do you think I'm not a good catch?" he asked.

She drew in a breath, as if she needed it to stem the laughter. "I didn't actually say that."

"Clearly, you think it."

"Come on, Grant, what are you up to?" she asked. "You don't want to join a dating service. You've never wanted anyone to actually catch you."

She and Blair were apparently even closer than he'd feared. Counting on his ability to bluff, he replied, "I've never said that."

Not like she and his sister had...

Unlike Blair's other little friends, who'd put pillowcases on their heads and pretended to be brides, Miranda and his sister had done anything but—swearing that they would never marry. That was why he was certain she was going to mess up Blair's new relationship.

"You've always showed it," Miranda said, "like when you left your prom date alone on the dance floor while you played poker with the chaperones in the janitor's closet."

A grin tugged at his mouth with the memory. "I won, too," he said.

"She didn't," Miranda murmured. "And neither would any of the members you might date if I were to let you join Liaisons International."

"You're serious?" he asked. "You won't let me join your matchmaking service?" He'd had no intention of joining it…until she'd told him he couldn't. That was usually what made him want something—being told he couldn't have it.

Like her…

She hadn't told him he couldn't have her, but the way she reacted—or didn't react—to him said it for her. He would never try to coerce or force a woman into being with him if she didn't want to.

But Grant had never actually had the experience of wanting a woman who hadn't wanted him.

Miranda Fox was a novelty in every way—always had been. She posed a challenge he'd never faced before. Could he make her fall for him?

CHAPTER TWO

MIRANDA DIDN'T LIKE the way Grant Snyder was looking at her. But she sure liked the way he looked—too damn much. Her skin tingled yet from the contact with his, so much so that she curled her fingers into her palm. Maybe she should have swung that fist at him to get him out of her office and out of reach.

Because she wanted to reach for him again. But this time, instead of holding him back, she wanted to curl her fingers into his shirt and jerk him up against her. She wanted to slide her other hand around the back of his neck and pull his head down to hers, to kiss him...

Deeply.

Passionately.

To thwart that temptation, she moved quickly around her desk so that, strategically, it was between them again. Keeping them apart...

Keeping her from reaching for him...

What the hell was wrong with her?

This was Grant—*Grant Snyder*—who'd always treated her like nothing but trouble. That had been so damn hypocritical of him since he was actually the worst kind of trouble—the heartbreaking kind of trouble. His prom date hadn't been the only girl who'd cried over him. And the way he was looking at her, it was like hers was the heart he wanted to break next.

"No," she said. "I won't let you join the service." Although maybe she should, because then he would definitely be off-limits to her since the company rule was No Dating Members. Miranda had determined long before even buying the business that she was not going to be her mother, but to make sure that her sisters wouldn't become Mother, either, she'd implemented the new rule.

"I've already joined the service," he said.

A pang of panic struck her. "No, you haven't." She'd made certain neither of her sisters could sign up a member without her approval.

"The navy," Grant said with a wiggle of his reddish-blond brows. "They took me."

"The rumor is that they didn't keep you," she said. "Or so your sister told me." Blair suspected there was more to the rumors she'd heard about her brother, though. That those rumors could be covering up something else he'd done or was still doing for the US Navy.

What the hell was Grant Snyder? And why was she still so damn curious about him? Curiosity had done nothing but get her in trouble in the past, like when she'd gotten suspicious about where one of her creepy stepfathers sneaked out of the house to go to and followed him to a strip club. If she hadn't taken pictures, Mother probably wouldn't have believed her. Her mother was not a good judge of character; Miranda was. To stay out of trouble, she could not risk being curious about Grant.

"So you and my sister have talked about me?" he asked, and he moved closer and leaned over the desk she'd put between them. Amusement glinted in his dark blue eyes, letting her know that he was entirely aware that she'd purposely put that barrier between them.

Did he know why? Did he realize that she was really attracted to him?

He'd teased her about having a crush on him. But how could he know?

She'd always been so careful to keep it from him, and to keep it from Blair, too. She hadn't wanted her best friend thinking that she was using her, like so many other girls had, to get closer to Grant.

Only her sisters had discovered the truth when they'd discovered where she'd hidden her diary. Damn them.

Damn him...

And that knowing grin curving his mouth—that

mouth she still wanted to kiss. She wanted to know how his beard would feel against her skin, how his lips would taste.

Damn him...

"You know Blair and I are best friends," she said. "We talk about all our problems."

His grin widened. "I am not a problem."

He was for her. "Maybe not for your sister..."

"Come on, Miranda, you and I haven't seen each other in years. You should be happy I'm here and that I want to patronize your business."

"Oh, you patronized me enough over the years," she assured him. "I don't need you doing it now. In fact—" She glanced at her watch again. "A potential new member should be arriving soon." And she didn't want the young woman to think she could date *him*.

"A potential new member is standing right in front of you now," he persisted. "What's the deal, Miranda? Why won't you let me join? Are you really hanging on to some grudge from the past? You have to realize that whatever I said or did back then was just because I was trying to protect my sister."

Blair was a former fighter pilot. She was strong and tall and fierce. She didn't need protection from anyone.

"From me?"

He arched a reddish-blond eyebrow over his

left eye. "Uh, damn right. You always got her into trouble."

Heat rushed to her face. "I—I hadn't meant to..." There had just been so many things she'd wanted to do, and she hadn't wanted to do them alone.

"But like I'm saying, that's all in the past," Grant continued. "I've let it go. Why can't you?"

She narrowed her eyes and studied his handsome face. "I was warned that you weren't very happy with me over Blair joining the service."

He shrugged his broad shoulders. "That was back when she was upset about it, about dating, but she's happy now. That's what I want, Miranda. To be happy."

Suspicious of his claim, she narrowed her eyes even more until she could barely see him through the thin slits. "You're not happy now?"

He shrugged again. "Sure, the business is good. Life is good. But you know...sometimes you just want someone to share all that with."

She knew. Occasionally she felt a twinge of loneliness herself. "And you need help finding someone?" she asked skeptically.

He grinned. "Are you saying that I'm too good-looking to have to join your dating service?"

She snorted at his arrogance. "You've met Matteo Rinaldi, right?" He was the billionaire she'd set up with her friend, which had caused an issue with her sisters. Setting up their most eligible member with a nonpaying member...

But Miranda had just known that they were meant to be together. Soul mates...

She swallowed a sigh. She never let anyone see her romantic side—although it had probably slipped out from time to time with her friend. It wasn't something she was proud of, though. And having inherited that from her mother made her think she'd probably inherited other bad traits, like her taste in men and her penchant for getting married many times.

Grant snorted now. "I guess he's all right..."

"If you like tall, dark and handsome." A wistful sigh slipped out now.

Grant leaned farther over her narrow desk. "I don't," he said. "I actually prefer petite, blonde and beautiful."

Her mouth dried out so much that it was as if her tongue was stuck to the roof of it, trapping her words inside so that she couldn't come up with a snappy reply to his comment. Was he flirting with her?

Her heart pounded wildly at the thought of any of her teenage fantasies about him coming true. Was it possible?

But until he'd walked into her office, he hadn't known what she looked like now, so he probably hadn't come here to ask her out.

"Just what the hell are you up to, Grant?" she asked him point-blank, refusing to be drawn into his games.

He played for stakes much higher than she was willing to pay anymore. She wasn't the rebellious teenager she'd once been. She was a woman trying to turn around a business. She had her sisters relying on her.

Maybe not all that much had changed, because she'd always had her sisters relying on her. They hadn't been able to rely on their mother, who'd always been chasing her next great romance.

Miranda had learned young that there was no such thing as a great romance; any romance was too risky. And nobody was riskier than a flirty Grant Snyder.

Just what the hell was he up to? Grant wasn't sure himself. But he knew that he wanted to see more of her, and not just as a member of her damn dating service. He'd really had no intention of joining.

But just as he committed to a bluff, he committed to the lie, persisting, "I want to join Liaisons International."

She snorted again, which somehow turned him on that she looked all elegant and ladylike but could still snort like that. She was so damn sexy…and sassy.

Her silvery-blue eyes glittered with all that sass

as she patronizingly remarked, "I had no idea you had so much trouble getting a date."

"I don't," he said.

"Then you have no reason to join."

He had every reason to join. *She* was every reason.

"I saw what you did for Blair and Teo," he said. "Don't you think you're good enough to get those results twice?"

"I'm saying you're not good enough," she replied, as blunt as she'd ever been.

It used to annoy the crap out of him when she'd talked to him like that; now he found it intriguing for some damn reason, just as he found every single thing about her intriguing.

He pressed a hand to his chest, which still tingled from where her palm had touched him. "Oh, you've wounded me. I had no idea you thought so little of me."

"I know you, Grant."

"You know I ditched a prom date to gamble with the chaperones," he said. "That was a long time ago. I would never treat a woman that way again."

"One of the most important promises I make to the members is that everyone will be open and honest with each other," she said.

"I won't be giving a false name," he said. Like his sister had given Teo Rinaldi. He knew, though, that Blair had had no intention of falling for any-one. It was Miranda pushing her to go out with the billionaire that had gotten her into the awkward situation, which had been just the latest of all the awkward situations she'd gotten her into over the years. And, like in the past, Grant had had to help her out of it.

Miranda sighed.

"Give me a chance," he said. "Give me a trial run, see if I meet your dating standards." His heart began to pound as he considered what he was about to do. This might prove one of the greatest gambles he'd ever taken.

"What kind of trial run?"

"Let me take you out and show you that I am the perfect date," he said.

She laughed and shook her head.

"And here I thought nothing scared Miranda Fox…" He clicked his tongue against his teeth and sighed. "I'm so disappointed." He turned for the door.

"You don't scare me," she said. "My sisters and I have a policy. We don't date members."

"But I'm not a member," he reminded her. "You won't let me join."

He reached for the doorknob. But he had no in-tention of opening it yet. If she wouldn't give him a chance to have another talk with her, he would have to have it here; he would have to warn her to stay away from Blair and Teo and just let them be happy without her continued interference.

But if she would agree to date him, he could keep her busy and out of their lives. And he knew just how he'd like to keep her busy…

He would run his hand over her shapely legs and push up that dress, and then he would…

"Grant?"

Was she waiting for him to leave? Or had she changed her mind?

He was going to assume the latter—to his benefit. So he turned back and grinned at her. "You won't regret it," he said. "I'll show you a good time. The best time you've ever had…" He reached for the door now. "I'll pick you up at six thirty. Bring your passport."

"Grant—"

He didn't stop this time, just walked out and closed the door behind him to shut off her protest. Her sister, the receptionist, was on the phone, but she'd covered the mouthpiece to laugh. So she'd obviously overheard most of their conversation. "See you later," she whispered to him. "And good luck!"

Miranda might refuse to go with him when he returned to pick her up. But that was just one of the chances he was taking…

The biggest risk was her actually going out with him. What was he going to do then?

He knew what he would like to do—*to* her, *with*

her—but he was worried that she was going to get him into even more trouble than she always had his sister. More trouble than he'd even gotten himself into.

And that would be a hell of a lot...

CHAPTER THREE

"WHAT ARE YOU going to wear?" Tabitha asked the
minute Miranda wearily closed the door on the reception area after her last potential client.

She wouldn't be signing up the woman who had
wanted proof that Miranda had other billionaires
available for her to date. For one, Miranda didn't
want a client like that—like her mother—who
wasn't looking for a match but for a meal ticket.
And for another, she wasn't going to show the
woman anyone else's financial information. She
did require that information, though, just to make
sure that she didn't sign up women or men who
weren't gainfully employed. She didn't want any
freeloaders in Liaisons International.

It was bad enough having one working for her.

Confused, she stared at her sister and asked,
"What do you mean?"

"For your date with Grant Snyder," Tabitha replied. "What are you going to wear?"

"Nothing."

Tabitha laughed. "Guess you've waited for him too long to play hard to get, huh?"

Heat rushed to Miranda's face, but she ignored her embarrassment and glared at her sister. "I meant nothing because I am not going out with him."

"She can't," Regina said, startling Miranda with her presence in the open doorway to her office, which was on the opposite side of the reception area from Miranda's.

Miranda was startled that Regina had come into the office at all. Usually the IT expert worked from home. Miranda glanced from one sister to the other, amazed again at how different they all looked from one another. Tabitha was willowy with brilliant red hair and bright green eyes, and Regina was tall with dark hair and dark eyes. But then, they each had a different father, only three of Mother's many husbands.

Putting together why Regina had joined them, she accused Tabitha, "You called her."

Tabitha nodded. "Of course I did. This is huge! You're going out with Grant Snyder!"

"No, I'm not," she insisted.

With that last appointment running longer than she'd thought, she needed to get the hell out of the office before he actually showed up, if he really intended to at all. He'd probably just been messing with her.

Regina released a shaky sigh. "That's good. I thought you were returning to your old ways."

Miranda narrowed her eyes and studied her dark-haired sister. The sisters were all as unalike in personalities as they were physical appearance. While Tabitha was easygoing, Regina tended to be uptight and judgmental.

"What do you mean—my old ways?" Miranda asked, and her temper began to spark.

"Your rebelliousness," Regina continued disapprovingly. Regina had always followed the rules. Since she'd rarely left her room except to go to school, it had been easy for her, though. "I thought you were going to violate our partner agreement about not dating any members."

"He's not a member," Tabitha said. "She wouldn't let him join—probably so she could date him without breaking any rules."

Miranda hated it when they talked about her like she wasn't there; they often did that to her.

"You need to stop listening at my door," she chastised Tabitha.

Too bad the young actress had been fired from her latest play. Hopefully she would find another role soon, so she would stop playing at being a receptionist.

"And the reason I didn't let Grant join has nothing to do with dating him and everything to do with not trusting him to date any of our clients. The last thing we need is him breaking the heart of every female member we have."

Regina sighed again and nodded. "Of course. That makes sense, especially after you already broke their hearts by giving up Teo Rinaldi to your bestie. That interview he gave is all over the news."

Tabitha was too focused on Miranda to listen to their sister now. "So you have no reason to not go out with him," she said.

"What?" Miranda asked, her head beginning to pound from their onslaught—coming so soon after the applicant's unreasonable demands.

"Grant is not going to break your heart," Tabitha explained.

Regina actually smiled at the remark, as if the thought amused her. "He can't break what doesn't exist."

"You're calling me heartless?" Miranda asked.

"It's a compliment," Regina said. "It's much better to be like you than like Mother."

Miranda couldn't agree more. But she was afraid she had more heart than her sisters realized, more heart than she could risk going out with Grant Snyder.

"It doesn't matter," she said. "I'm not going out with him. I'm much too busy."

"That's why you need to go out with him," Tabitha said. "You have to have some fun. It's gotta be killing you to be all work and no play nowadays."

"It's killing us," Regina said. "You're working us to death, too."

Maybe she did keep Regina busy with the website updates and social media marketing. And Tabitha had been putting in some long hours at the reception desk.

"It's only because I want the business to be successful," she said.

"Then you shouldn't have set up our most impressive member with a freebie date with your best friend," Regina said.

"If you were going to set up the Italian billionaire with a freebie, it should have been one of us," Tabitha said. "Not Blair…"

Her sisters had always resented her close friendship with Blair Snyder. They'd wanted her to be their friend like they were to each other. But as the oldest, she'd always felt responsible for them— more responsible than their mother had ever felt for any of them. Her matchmaking business, and the marriages it had led to for her, had always been her baby more than her daughters.

"I'm not going to have this argument again," Miranda said. She'd already grabbed her laptop bag and purse as she'd shown out the latest potential member, so now she pulled open the door to the hall. But she couldn't walk through it—not because of her sisters but because of the man filling it. The man who wanted to be a member.

And her date...

"Aren't you eager?" Grant teased, knowing full well that Miranda had probably been trying to escape before he'd returned for her. That was why he'd returned even earlier than he'd told her.

"Yes," she agreed—much to his surprise. Then she added, "To go home and have a glass of wine—a big glass of wine."

He shrugged. "Okay, if you want to skip the date and go straight back to your place, I'm not going to complain."

She glared at him. "You are not invited to join me."

"Yet..." But he intended to charm that invitation out of her. Hell, he wanted to make her beg him to come home with her.

But this was Miranda Fox...

She was going to be a far greater challenge than any he'd ever faced.

"Ever," she said.

"We have an agreement," he said. "You agreed to give me a trial run to prove that I'd make a great addition to your dating service."

"I did not agree to anything," she insisted.

And he chuckled at her indignation.

"You did," her red-haired sister chimed in from

behind her. She was much taller than Miranda, but then, pretty much everyone was. He felt massive standing in front of her.

"Did not," Miranda said, her words clipped as if she was gritting her teeth.

"You should have," said the dark-haired woman who appeared beside the red-haired one.

Her other sister. He couldn't remember her name, but then, he hadn't seen her very much. She'd only come out of their house once in a while. They'd lived just a few houses down the block from Grant's family; that was how Blair and Miranda had become such close friends.

"A trial run is a great idea," she added.

"Not for me," Miranda said.

"You're the boss," the dark-haired one said— with a trace of resentment. "You're the one who makes all the decisions on who can join. You have to do this."

Miranda turned to glare at her sister now. And the red-haired one reached over her shoulder toward him.

"Here's her passport," she said.

Grant grinned. He liked that the other women had ganged up on Miranda. He wasn't sure if they were doing it to help him or piss her off, though. "I'll make sure she has a good time," he assured them. "A real good time."

The red-haired one smiled and winked at him. "I'm sure you will."

He chuckled.

Miranda turned her attention to him, reaching for her passport. "Give that back to me," she said—in that haughty princess tone she'd adopted as an adult.

He liked it. "After our little trip," he told her.

"Does she need a suitcase?" the red-haired sister asked.

He shook his head. He hoped she would soon need no clothes at all. "Just the passport."

"So this is going to be short?" Miranda asked. "Just showing off your airplane?"

"Something like that," he said.

She sighed and begrudgingly agreed. "Okay then…"

"Don't do anything I wouldn't do," the dark-haired one told them.

"Don't listen to her," the redhead said. "There's too much uptight Regina wouldn't do. Don't do anything either of you wouldn't do."

"That makes no sense," Regina said.

"It makes perfect sense," the redhead said and chuckled. "There isn't anything the two of them wouldn't do."

"Neither of you makes any sense," Miranda admonished them. "And you wonder why I'm the boss…" Seemingly disgusted, she shook her head as she stepped out into the hall outside her suite of offices.

Now he wondered if she was only leaving with him to escape her sisters. He didn't care what her reason was, though. Once he had her on that plane...

He was going to take her for a great escape and prove to her that she would be lucky to have him as a member of her dating service.

Not that he intended to actually join...

But his pride was still stinging a bit over her outright refusal to let him join, as if he wasn't good enough for her clients—or for her.

Just as he wanted her to beg him to go home with her, he wanted her begging him to join Liaisons International soon. But that he would refuse to do.

He intended only to set her straight about his sister once and for all—so she would stop interfering in Blair's life. He'd overheard some of the sisters' comments about the freebie she'd given Blair. Did she intend to take it back?

Didn't matter what she intended, though. He damn well wasn't going to let her. But instead of lecturing and threatening her, he was going to charm her into agreeing to whatever he wanted. Like her.

Even annoyed—either with him or her sisters—she looked beautiful. Her lips, pursed into a slight pout, shimmered, and her blue eyes sparkled. And her body...

She was small but shapely and so damn sexy.

Damn, he wanted her.

But could he, the professional gambler, take such a risk? Miranda Fox wasn't a woman a man would easily walk away from.

CHAPTER FOUR

HE'S UP TO SOMETHING... Something that was not going to end well for her.

Miranda had never been a nervous flier, until now. For the flights she'd taken, she usually had a different Snyder as the pilot. The one she trusted. As she settled into the passenger side of the two-seater plane, she remarked, "Before we take off, should I check to see if you're wearing a parachute underneath your jacket?"

Grant's brow furrowed with confusion. "Why would I need it? I'm a great pilot."

"I was thinking that maybe you intend to bail out and let me and the plane crash into the ocean," she said.

He chuckled. "I hadn't thought of that. Not a bad plan..."

"So you do want to get rid of me!" she accused. She'd known he was up to something.

He flashed that wicked grin of his. "Would I have asked you out if I wanted to get rid of you?"

"I don't know why you asked me out," she said.

"I told you—it's an audition so that you can see what a great date I will be and let me join your service."

She shook her head. "I'm not buying it."

"Then maybe it's unrequited love."

She laughed at his blatant lie. "I'd sooner believe you were trying to get rid of me."

He shook his head. "Not by bailing out and ditching this baby. After what we just paid for it, Blair would kill me."

The plane was quite luxurious, with a leather seat so comfortable that Miranda had sunk deeply into it. The control panel was trimmed with mahogany. And when he started it up...

The engine wasn't loud at all, not like in the other small planes Miranda had ridden in with Blair. Or like the helicopter they'd had to take from Monaco to the airport in Nice. Grant hadn't been at the controls of that, though. He'd been a passenger like her.

She hadn't been nervous with that pilot, either. She'd been more nervous about the big man sitting so close to her that she'd felt the heat of his body. He had seemed nervous, though, so maybe he didn't like it when someone else had the controls.

If that was the case, he wasn't going to want to go out with her again. Not that she wanted to go out with him again. Hell, she hadn't wanted to go out with him now. She didn't even know why she'd agreed.

Except that it had been a long, taxing day…and she'd wanted a distraction from thinking of her current business woes.

And Grant Snyder was distracting, with his big, muscular body and deep golden hair.

"It is nice," she agreed, but her gaze had slipped down to his heavy thighs. She cleared her throat. "The plane is nice. But I don't think Blair would be upset about just it."

He glanced at her with a twinkle in his dark blue eyes. "Really? What else would she be upset about?"

"Me," she said. "I am your sister's best friend, you know. If you do anything to hurt me, she's going to hate you."

The twinkle dimmed, and he turned back to the controls. He was definitely up to something…something that neither she nor Blair was going to like.

He didn't look at her again until after takeoff, which she had to begrudgingly admit was extremely smooth. But still, her suspicions were not alleviated, and he must have noticed, because when he glanced back at her, he chuckled. "Stop being so nervous! I'm not going to hurt you."

She narrowed her eyes even more.

He chuckled again. "Seriously, I am going to be the perfect gentleman for this perfect date."

She laughed now. "So you're going to perform a miracle and turn into someone else?"

He wiggled his eyebrows. "Maybe I already have, and you just haven't noticed."

Was that possible? Was he different than he'd been when they were kids? He was bigger, more handsome, but his personality?

It seemed much the same.

Miranda had changed, though. So it was possible...

She was no longer the wild child she'd once been. Now she didn't seek to escape from responsibilities she hadn't chosen. The responsibilities she had now were ones that she'd chosen. Like making the business a success while staying true to her friendships.

Making Matteo Rinaldi and Blair the perfect match was more important than having him available to date more clients even though they were starting to lose clients.

"So it's going to be like that?" Grant asked.

She shook her head to clear her mind of the doubts her sisters had planted and focused instead on the one Grant had planted. Could he have really changed?

"What are you talking about?" she asked.

"The fact that you're not talking," he said. "You're going to make this audition tough on me, huh? Or is this what the women with your dating service are like? Suspicious? Uncommunicative? Uninteresting?"

She sucked in a breath as his insult struck her like a slap. "Did you just call me *uninteresting*?"

He sighed. "Well, I have to admit… I'm kind of bored."

She glared at him.

"And you, you haven't even noticed the view? You're just sulking over there."

Heat rushed to her face. She had been sulking. About her sisters, about him.

She glanced out the window, and while her stomach flipped at the height, she sighed over the beauty of the water beneath them. It was such a crystal-clear turquoise.

"Beautiful…" she murmured.

"Yes," he agreed, his voice gruff. But he wasn't looking out the window; he was looking at her.

She narrowed her eyes again. "And I have every right to be suspicious of you," she reminded him. "You haven't ever been nice to me."

His gaze ran over her like a caress, from her silver-tipped toes peeping out of her silver sandals, up her bare legs, over her body, until finally he stared into her eyes. And his mouth curved into a slight, sexy smile. "I would enjoy being nice to you. Very, very nice to you…"

"And," she continued, as if he hadn't spoken, because she really, really wanted to ignore what he'd just said. While she didn't react verbally, though, her body reacted to his words and to his gaze, which had been so hot—so wicked—that she'd nearly felt the heat of it. Her nipples tightened against the lace of her bra. And he hadn't even touched her...

And she didn't want him to. She really, really could not want Grant Snyder.

"And?" he prodded her.

Making her realize she'd lost her train of thought because of him. As usual.

"And," she said, "I never agreed to this audition."

"You must have changed, too," Grant said.

"What—why?"

"Because the Miranda Fox I knew never did anything she didn't want to do," he said.

If only that had been true...

But her mother's flightiness had made it necessary for Miranda to grow up fast—too damn fast. She let a wistful sigh escape before murmuring, "You didn't know me at all..."

Her statement jarred Grant, so much so he inadvertently jerked the yoke, and the plane, in her direction.

A little squeak escaped her lips now like that wistful-sounding sigh had moments ago. "You are trying to kill me," she exclaimed as she pressed a hand over her heart. But with the words coming through the smile curving her lips, she didn't sound afraid; she sounded excited as she stared out at all the gorgeous water.

That was the Miranda he knew: the daredevil who'd always gotten Blair into trouble with her many misguided adventures. But had there been more to Miranda Fox than he knew?

There was certainly more to her now: a sex appeal that had tension gathering low in his belly, in his groin. When had she gotten so damn hot? It radiated off her—totally at odds with that pale blond hair and those pale blue eyes. While she looked like an ice princess, she was too sassy, too smart, too sexy to ever be mistaken for one.

While he easily righted the plane, he struggled for control of his body, of his desire for her. Because another thing she'd said earlier kept reverberating inside his head: *I am your sister's best friend, you know. If you do anything to hurt me, she's going to hate you.*

He hadn't considered that.

For some misguided reason, Blair really did love this woman and considered her the sister she'd never had. It had just been him and Blair...

Their mom had been too busy trying to make their dad happy, and their dad had been so unhappy despite all their mom's efforts that neither of them had had any time for their children. So he and his sister were close, so close that she would understand.

Wouldn't she?

Not that he intended to hurt Miranda. He wasn't even sure that was possible. He'd been eavesdropping outside the office door before she'd opened it and slammed into him. He could still feel the softness of her body against his.

But her body was the only soft thing about Miranda Fox. Even her sisters didn't think she had a heart. So there was no way he could hurt Miranda, even if he wanted to. And he didn't want to...

He only intended to make sure that she didn't hurt his sister. And if she messed up Blair's relationship with Teo, like she'd messed up every other relationship his sister had had, she was going to hurt Blair very badly.

"I'm not trying to kill you," he assured her. "That would be a horrible first date, and there would be no way for you to enroll me in your service then."

She chuckled. "That might be your plan, though. You would be able to talk my sisters into anything."

"But not you?" he asked.

"Have you ever been able to talk me into anything?" she asked.

"I haven't tried..." She'd been too young for him to even look at the way he was looking at her now.

She snorted. "Every time you saw me you tried to talk me into making other friends and leaving your sister alone."

While Blair had had other friends than Miranda—

giggling, happy friends—Miranda had seemed to have only her. He'd wondered then if that was because she'd been so dark and brooding back then. But Blair had always laughed more with Miranda than she had any of those giggly, happy girls.

"Let's say I haven't tried then the way I'm going to try now," he amended.

She studied his face. "I knew it…"

"What?"

"You're definitely up to something."

"Six four," he said.

Her brow furrowed for a moment before she laughed. "Smart-ass."

"Takes one to know one." She was smart—as smart as she was sexy. So of course she'd already guessed that he was up to something.

He could have just come clean and told her what it was—that he didn't want her messing up his sister's new relationship. But as she'd just pointed out, every time he'd tried talking her into something in the past, she'd ignored him. He was going to make sure that she couldn't ignore him this time.

He was going to make her as damn aware of him as he was of her. He was going to make her want him, too.

CHAPTER FIVE

MIRANDA HAD BEEN so busy wondering if Grant was going to try to kill her that she hadn't bothered asking him where he was taking her. She wouldn't have been surprised if he'd bailed out of the plane over the water. Instead he'd landed it—it had seemed nearly on the water, but it had actually been on the island of Ibiza.

She shouldn't have been surprised that he'd bring her to a place known for partying. But with her head already beginning to pound, she wasn't enjoying the volume of the dance music blaring out of the speakers in the crowded nightclub. She also felt overdressed in comparison to all the bikini-clad dancers. Not that she felt like stripping down to a bikini…

Not with the way Grant kept looking at her, as if he was already undressing her. Heat rushed through her—from his sexy stare and from the humidity in the club crowded with sweaty bodies.

The dampness in the air molded Grant's shirt to his muscular chest; he'd discarded his jacket somewhere earlier and rolled up the sleeves of his white dress shirt. Miranda wasn't able to take off anything but her shoes, and with the way people were gyrating around, she worried that she'd lose a toe if she did that.

She groaned at how much her thoughts reminded her of Regina. Judgy and old beyond her years. That wasn't her. Or was it?

She had changed. She wasn't the fun-loving Miranda she'd once been.

"What's the matter?" Grant asked. Despite the loudness of the music, she could hear his deep voice.

He wouldn't be able to hear her, so she forced a smile and shook her head. For so long she'd secretly wanted to go out with him. But while he hadn't ditched her to play poker in a janitor's closet, this wasn't the date she'd imagined.

Hell, she hadn't imagined a date at all. She'd imagined kissing and more...even when she'd been too young to truly understand just how enjoyable *more* could be.

"Don't you want to dance?" he asked.

The kind of dance that sprang to her mind wasn't done in a crowded club but between the tangled sheets of a soft bed. With nothing but sweaty skin sliding over sweaty skin...

She cleared her throat, trying to clear the desire from it. But Grant must have thought she'd said something because he leaned close. Too close…

His hair brushed across her cheek, and the softness of it sent a shiver rippling through her despite the heat. She was so damn aware of him already, but with him so close, the scent of him filling her senses…

He smelled like what she and Blair used to call *boy*—that curious mixture of rain-scented soap and musk. But she couldn't call that smell boy anymore. Not in relation to Grant, anyway. He was all man.

And all too tempting.

She'd been so busy with the business that she hadn't been out with anyone in a long time. Too long…

So maybe she needed to push the business from her mind and focus on something else. Or someone else…

But focusing on Grant was dangerous. So she pushed past him instead to head toward the dance floor. Ignoring the pounding in her head and the vibration of the speakers inside her body, she began to move to that frantic beat.

She hadn't lost Grant. He'd followed her onto the floor, and he stuck close to her on it, his body moving in rhythm with hers. Because the floor was so crowded, they had to dance close, their bodies bumping into and brushing against each other. Her pulse quickened and her breathing grew shallower with every touch.

Despite all the bikini-clad women around them, Grant's gaze never left her. A thrill rushed through her that he seemed as attracted to her as she was him.

But was it all an act?

Part of whatever he was up to?

It had to be, because he'd never looked at her like this before, like he wanted her. And if he kept looking at her that way, she wasn't sure what she would do.

But she knew what she wanted to do...pull his head down to hers and kiss him—deeply, passionately. She wanted to press her body against the long, hard length of his. She wanted to...

Desperate to escape him before she made a fool of herself, she stepped back into the crush of dancers behind her—using the other bodies to shield hers from his. And she disappeared into the crowd.

But she knew they were on an island, so she wouldn't be able to escape him for long. And even if she could, she wouldn't want to, because he was her ride back home.

No. All she needed was a few moments to collect herself, to breathe...without him filling her senses and making her lose her common sense.

She'd ditched him.

That was a new experience for Grant.

Was she giving him payback on behalf of his long-ago prom date? He hadn't really ditched his date, though. He'd only abandoned her for a little while until he'd taken all the money off the chaperones.

And since that night...

Well, he'd had to abandon a few other dates, but that hadn't been his fault. He'd been called out on time-sensitive missions those times. If he'd taken the time to explain, lives might have been lost, including his own.

He doubted Miranda had ditched him for a mission. But why had she?

And where the hell had she gone?

Her passport was on his plane, so she wouldn't be able to leave Ibiza without him. So she couldn't have gone far if she ever wanted to go home.

But she wasn't in the ladies' room; he'd already asked a waitress to check for him. Not that he was entirely sure she'd told him the truth, since she'd seemed more interested in becoming his date than in finding the one he already had.

The waitress was too young and too eager to please to interest him. He wanted more of a challenge—like Miranda.

Sick of the noise and the heat of the club, he stepped outside. A faint breeze blew in across the water, drawing him toward the beach that was just yards from the club. Night had fallen while they'd been inside, but the moon was high and bright, illuminating the sand and the woman who stood barefoot on it, her sandals dangling from her fingers. That breeze played in her pale hair, tossing the tresses around her shoulders while it plastered her dress against her body, leaving nothing to his imagination.

But what he would do with her...

That he kept imagining, over and over again, how he would touch her, taste her, please her...

"Couldn't find a janitor's closet?" he asked as he joined her.

She turned to him, her lips curving into a slight smile. "I wasn't looking for a game, Grant."

And she was so damn smart that she knew that was what he was doing: playing with her. That was what he'd wanted to do...tease her until she wanted him as badly as he wanted her.

And then he would get her to promise to leave Blair and Teo alone...

Blair.

His sister was his reason for being here, but he'd had to remind himself. For a while, watching Miranda move so sexily on the dance floor, he'd forgotten why the hell he'd sought her out to begin with. He'd forgotten his own damn name. Everything but her...

Then she'd disappeared on him, and he'd felt a twinge of panic. That wasn't something he often allowed himself to feel. Panic was too debilitating. A distraction he couldn't afford. Like her...

She was a distraction he couldn't afford. But for his sister's sake, he couldn't abandon this mission. He had to persevere despite the risk.

"What are you looking for?" he asked.

She held up her face to that slight breeze and emitted a soft sigh. "Some fresh air and peace and quiet."

He could relate. The music pounded inside his head still, the beat of it making his body throb. No. That wasn't the beat; it was his attraction to her that made his body throb, his pulse pound, his heart race.

"I thought you would like the music," he said.

She arched a blond brow. "Really? Why?"

"You always dragged Blair to concerts with you," he reminded her and himself, "even skipping school to stake out hotels where the band might have been staying." He hadn't been happy about his sister skipping school. His parents hadn't really cared, though. He was the only one who'd cared about the trouble Miranda had gotten her into.

She chuckled. "That was a long time ago. I don't stake out hotels anymore."

She wouldn't have to...not with the way she looked now. All she had to do was bat those long, thick lashes and she could have any man she wanted—no matter how rich and famous.

Why hadn't she kept Matteo Rinaldi for herself?

Was she as determined as she used to be to remain single?

"Do you want to join me in my hotel?" he asked and braced himself for her to slap him. But before she could, he hastened to explain, "I could get you that big glass of wine you wanted earlier and something to eat."

Her silvery-blue eyes had narrowed as she stared at him. "You booked a hotel room for the night?"

No. He didn't have to since he owned the damn hotel. He didn't bother explaining that, though. And she didn't give him time.

"You said that I didn't need a suitcase. That this was just going to be a short trip," she said, her voice sharp and accusatory. "You lied to me!"

"I didn't lie." About the short trip. It hadn't taken him long to fly them from Nice to Ibiza. "You don't need a suitcase."

She raised her hand then, and he flinched in expectation of her slap. But instead she just patted his beard and chuckled. "You haven't changed a bit, Grant Snyder," she murmured. "You're still as much trouble as you ever were…"

"Me?" he asked, as if he was totally shocked. "You're calling *me* trouble?"

"You know you are," she said. But she didn't sound accusatory anymore. Instead her voice had a lilt of amusement to it.

"Hey, you're the one with the dirty mind," he said. "I was just saying that you don't need a suitcase to share some wine and a meal with me—"

"At a hotel."

"There are restaurants in hotels, you know." His had a damn good one. Room service was even better... But he wasn't going to let her know what he really wanted: her.

So he shook his head, and her hand slid away from his face—regrettably. He had liked the feeling of her palm running lightly across his beard. "You have such a one-track mind, Miranda Fox."

She stepped back on the sand, and the moonlight illuminated her beautiful face and the sparkle in her eyes. "So that's all you're offering? Just a glass of wine and a meal in the hotel restaurant?"

"Of course I am," he said. "I'm a gentleman, Miranda."

She let out a weary-sounding sigh and murmured, "Well, that's too bad." Then she turned away as if to head back toward the nightclub.

His heart slammed against his ribs with shock. But it took him only a moment to process that and to react to her teasing challenge. Then he caught her shoulders in his hands and gently whirled her around before he lowered his head and covered her mouth with his.

He'd meant to surprise her, but the contact between their lips jolted him as if a spark had arced between them. Once again he braced himself for her to slap him, but her hands only skimmed briefly across his face, over his beard, before linking over the nape of his neck. She held his head down while she kissed him back.

Her lips were as silky as he'd imagined they would be and tasted slightly of strawberries and champagne—maybe from that shimmery gloss she wore. He nibbled lightly on them, teasing her to open her mouth and let him in…

But Miranda, being Miranda, bit back, her teeth just grazing his lips.

He chuckled as his pulse leaped with passion. And when he chuckled, she slid her little wet tongue into his mouth. Then he groaned with a desire so intense, his knees got a little shaky. Maybe that was just from standing on the sand, though, and having to lean so far over because she was so short.

It couldn't be that Miranda Fox was so damn passionate she was about to bring him to his knees. He'd intended to make her beg for him, to get her so worked up that she would be willing to do whatever he asked.

But he was the one with the plea burning the back of his throat. *Make love with me…*

CHAPTER SIX

WHAT THE HELL was she doing?

Grant Snyder. That was what she was doing—or rather, whom. That kiss on the beach had just been the start of this, of a quick trip to his hotel with his hand sliding over her thigh as they rode in the back of a limo. Then a fast ride up in the elevator, their bodies brushing against each other's with the upward motion. If they had been alone…

But there had been other guests.

So it had continued with nearly a trot down the hall to open the door of a seaside suite that looked out onto the starry sky and the water reflecting it. She stood at the windows, staring at that view— not just the view outside but at Grant's image reflected in the glass.

He was so damn good-looking, his skin such a golden tan against that white shirt he wore. She wanted it off him, wanted nothing between them.

But he'd no more closed the door than there had

been a knock at it. He'd opened it to a room service trolley. A bill passed from his hand to the waiter's. "Thank you, Mr. Snyder," the young man gratefully replied. "Let us know if there's anything else you need."

"I have everything I need," Grant assured him as the waiter stepped into the hall and he closed the door on him. Then he turned back toward her. "Unless you've changed your mind..."

She should have. She'd had sufficient time to come to her senses, but she didn't want to. Not yet. She was tired of being good, of being so responsible for so long...as she'd been these many months since she'd bought the business from her mother. She needed a break from those responsibilities.

From reality.

She would pretend that this was just a dream— one of the many, many fantasies she'd had about Grant Snyder all those years ago. She closed her eyes and drew in a deep breath, and when she opened her eyes again, he was standing behind her. His hands hovered over her shoulders, but he didn't touch her yet...as if he didn't dare.

She'd actively participated when he'd kissed her on the beach. But maybe he wanted her to make the first move now so that he knew she was sure.

She was more than consenting; she was eager.

She turned toward him and lifted her hands to his chest. He tensed as if he expected her to push

him away. But instead she reached for the buttons
on his shirt, tugging them through the holes until
his shirt parted, exposing sculpted muscles with a
light dusting of golden hair.

He had to work out all the time to look that
damn good. And he looked so damn good that she
couldn't wait to work him out. She leaned forward
and skimmed her lips across his chest.

His heart leaped beneath her touch, and he audi-
bly sucked in a breath. "Damn, Miranda…"

"Have you changed your mind?" she asked him,
but her lips curved into a smile as she slid her hand
down to where his erection strained the fly of his
dress pants.

He groaned. "You're such a tease."

"Oh, I'm not teasing," she assured him. She
wanted him too badly to back out now. But she
stepped back and then she turned around.

"You're not?" he asked, his voice gruff with passion.

"No. I'm getting impatient."

He chuckled. "So you're turning your back on
me?"

"I'm waiting for you to unzip me." She could
have reached it herself, but it was more fun this
way…to have his fingers gliding down her bare
spine as he lowered the zipper. He was so damn
good that he unclasped her bra at the same time.
The dress pooled around her waist—until she

shimmied her hips and it dropped to the floor. She stepped out of it and her shoes before turning back around to him. Then she lowered the unhooked bra until she stood before him wearing only her thong.

"Damn, Miranda," he said again, but his voice sounded as if he was strangling.

Maybe desire was choking him like it was her. Just his fingertips on her bare back had her nipples tight and pointed toward him. If he touched her anywhere else...

And then he did, with just one fingertip.

He slid it under her chin and tipped it up. Ignoring her naked body, he stared deeply into her eyes and asked, "Are you sure?"

Warmth moved through her, through her heart, and a smile curved her lips. Maybe Grant Snyder was not the rogue she'd always thought he was. When she was younger, that might have disappointed her. But now she was impressed.

"Very sure," she replied. She'd wanted him too long to not take him when she had the chance. And to prove how sure she was, she unclasped his belt and pulled it free of his pants. Then she reached for his zipper, and as she pulled it down, she stroked her fingers over his hard erection.

He groaned.

"What about you?" she asked. "Are you sure?" She pushed down his boxers along with his pants, freeing his cock. It was long and thick and nearly pulsating with the same need that throbbed inside her.

His jaw taut, he shook his head.

And she pulled her hands away, holding them palms up. "You're not?"

"Oh, I'm sure you're the one who's trouble," he murmured. "And I'm probably going to regret this later…"

She smiled. "But now?"

"Now I would regret it more if you weren't here and if I wasn't about to bury my cock deep inside you."

A moan slipped out of her lips now. He would fill her up, he was that big. But she wasn't intimidated. She was excited—so damn excited—that she could already feeling the wetness dampening her panties.

"I don't know, Grant," she said, "you might just be all talk and no action."

He chuckled and flashed that wicked, wicked grin of his. But he pushed down his unzipped pants, taking the boxers off with them. Then he shrugged the open shirt off his broad shoulders, his chest and arms rippling as he stripped it off.

She nearly moaned again. He was so damn fine…

Then he reached for her, tucking his finger into the top of her lace thong and tugging her toward him. But he didn't close his arms around her; he didn't press her body up against his naked one. Instead he moved his finger from her panties up her body, on a straight line between her breasts to her chin. He tipped it up again, but this time he didn't stare into her eyes. He lowered his head to hers and kissed her.

No. Consumed her…

His lips nibbled. His tongue stroked and tangled with hers. She clutched his head, tunneling her fingers into his soft hair, as she kissed him back just as hungrily.

He was such a damn good kisser, so passionate. She nipped his bottom lip lightly with her teeth, and he chuckled.

"You're naughty," he chided her. But his cock had jumped and pushed against her midriff, so she knew he found it exciting, as exciting as she found him.

She stepped closer to him so that her breasts rubbed against his body. Her nipples peaked even more, and a moan slipped through her lips.

He reached between their bodies and cupped her breasts in his hands. Then he pulled back from kissing her and stared down at what he held. His hands were enormous—unlike her breasts. But they were full and round and incredibly sensitive.

She pushed against his palms and moaned again. He leaned over and kissed the top of one mound before protesting, "You're too short."

"You're too tall," she countered.

Then he lifted her, with his hands cupping her butt and hips, until her head was at the same height as his. He smacked a kiss lightly across her lips before lifting her even higher—high enough that he closed his mouth over one of her breasts and stroked the nipple with his tongue.

She clung to him, gripping his shoulders with her hands while wishing she could touch more of him.

His hands, cupping her butt, moved between her legs, and he stroked her through the panties already damp with her excitement for him.

For what she anticipated was coming...

He pushed the panties aside and dipped a finger inside her while he pushed his thumb against her throbbing clit. Then his teeth gently closed around her nipple, tugging at it as he stroked her.

And she came, his name slipping out on a low moan of pleasure.

"You're easy," he said.

Maybe she should have been offended, but she laughed. She didn't usually come this easily, but it had been a long time for her. Maybe she needed to use her vibrator more...

But she would rather use him.

"I have to taste you," he said. And he lifted her even higher, sliding her legs over his shoulders. Then he pulled her panties aside and slid his tongue inside her. He lapped and licked and teased with his tongue and his lips until another orgasm shuddered through her.

Limp with pleasure, she nearly fell. But he caught her, swinging her up in his arms. Then he carried her from the living room part of the suite into the bedroom. Light from the living room spilled into the room, across the big bed. Then she spilled across the bed as he flopped her onto it.

"Don't get sleepy," he advised her. "We're not done yet."

"Promises, promises," she remarked. But she reached for him now, wanting to give him the pleasure he'd given her. He stood next to the bed, silently refusing to join her. And he was so tall that she had to kneel on the bed to reach him, to slide her hand up and down his cock before closing her lips around the tip of it.

A bead of his pleasure slipped out, and she licked it away.

He groaned. And his fingers tunneled into her hair. He held her against him as she took him deeper in her mouth, in her throat, before he pushed her back.

"I want to be inside you," he said. "I need to be inside you."

She understood that need. Even after the pleasure he'd given her, she needed more and instinctively knew she'd experience that with him.

He pulled open the nightstand and grabbed a condom from the drawer. This hotel was truly full service. His fingers shook a little as he fumbled with the packet, so she took it from him. And she used her teeth to tear it open before rolling the condom over the length of him. He pulsed in her hand, hard and thick and tight with desire for her.

He was powerful, but she felt powerful, too, for making him want her so...

And he did. Sweat beaded on his upper lip and his forehead, and his entire body vibrated with tension. Then he knelt on the bed and pulled her on top of him.

She straddled his hips, but he lifted her higher, his sheathed cock stroking her mound. She reached down and guided him inside her—where she was already so damn wet and ready for him.

She arched as he slid inside—deeper and deeper—until he filled her. And so damn thick that his cock pushed against her clit, too.

"You're so tight," he said, his voice gruff. "So damn hot."

Clutching at his shoulders, she rode him—bucking up and down, rocking against him. His hands gripped her hips, and he matched her rhythm just as he had on the dance floor. Fast, frantic—the beat of desire pounding inside her head, inside her body...

Tension wound tightly inside her, pulling her

nipples taut—making her clit throb. As if he knew it, as if he felt it, too, he reached between them and rubbed her clit with his thumb.

And she came, the orgasm shuddering through her with even more intensity than the other ones he'd given her. She dug her nails into his shoulders and screamed his name.

Then he tensed and growled as his body pulsed inside her with his release. He lifted her up and off him and laid her limp body on the mattress, and then he disappeared into an open door of the bedroom.

And Miranda panted for the breath he'd stolen from her. He had not disappointed. Grant Snyder had entirely lived up to her teenage fantasies and then some...

What the hell had happened?

Grant had spent the night—the entire night— having sex with Miranda Fox. While he'd hoped for that to happen, he had learned to never count on anything where she was concerned. She was more likely to do the opposite of what he wanted than she ever was to do what he actually wanted.

Until now...

Now she'd done everything he'd wanted and some things he hadn't even realized he'd wanted.

She was insatiable. And she'd made him insatia-

ble. He'd never rallied as much as he had for her—
the desire more intense each time.

The first light of dawn streaked through the
blinds of the bedroom, painting lines across her
silky skin. She lay limply on the bed, on her stomach, her face turned toward the side. A slight smile
curved her lips. She was pleased with herself.

So was he.

Wasn't he supposed to ask her something now?
Demand something from her?

Something about...

He couldn't think of anything but her, of wanting her yet again. Damn it.

"Damn you," he murmured as his cock began
to stir again.

"I'm not even touching you," she said, and the
smile was in her voice, too. She was staring at him
now, though, and that was all it took.

He hardened, and the minute he did, she moved.
She must have tucked the condoms under her pillow
because she already had one in hand. She sheathed
him in latex and then in her wet heat as she straddled him.

She felt so damn amazing. So hot. So tight.

Her inner muscles flexed and rippled, stroking
his cock into madness again. Stroking him into
madness.

The sex with her was so incredible that it could

become addictive. The pleasure so intense and un-like any he'd felt before.

Her every movement, every touch affected him so damn much. She leaned over and pressed her mouth to his chest, teasing one of his nipples with her tongue, just like he'd done with her moments ago.

He cupped her breasts in his hands and stroked his thumbs over her nipples. Then he rolled them between his fingers, tugging gently at them.

She uttered a soft cry of pleasure as she began to move faster, more frantically...

Despite all her orgasms, she was greedy for an-other, too. Maybe she would become as addicted to him as he was becoming to her.

Or maybe they'd wear each other out before the sun fully rose. He wasn't sure. And he didn't give a damn.

He just had to have another orgasm, or his body was going to explode. He gripped her hips and moved her faster, harder.

She cried out, her body shuddering as an orgasm gripped her. And she gripped him, those inner mus-cles squeezing him as she came.

Heat rushed over him. He pumped harder and faster, making it last for her until his tension broke as he joined her in the mind-blowing release. Her name escaped his lips on a groan of pleasure. "Miranda..."

He was supposed to ask her something...but he

was too damn tired to remember exactly what the question—or the demand—was. And so was she as she dropped limply onto his chest. All he could do was wrap his arms around her and hold her close as he finally drifted off to sleep.

CHAPTER SEVEN

NOT WANTING TO do the walk of shame into the office in front of her sisters, Miranda had had Grant drive her to her apartment instead. But she refused to let him come inside. She knew exactly what would happen.

Her body already ached in places that hadn't been touched in so damn long. With as big as he was, maybe they'd never been touched.

He was so incredible…

And she was so exhausted. But she had to go to work. So she had to get rid of him.

"Goodbye, Grant," she said—on the sidewalk outside the high-rise building where she paid entirely too much rent for just a studio apartment. But the building had a doorman who stood at the door, waiting for her to walk toward the lobby.

She was safe here on the street bustling with people heading off to work or to sightsee. She was safe from Grant and safe from her desire for him.

But still, she didn't trust herself to kiss him and not want him again.

So she held out her hand.

He chuckled. "You want to shake?"

She was already shaking inside, her body all soft and Jell-O-like from how he'd made her feel last night—this morning—and from the temptation to let him make her feel that way again.

"I want you to leave so I can go inside and get ready for work," she replied honestly.

He chuckled again. "So you're going to be like that, huh? Got what you wanted and now you can't wait to get rid of me?"

A smile tugged at her lips. "I have to go to work," she repeated.

"You're the boss," he said as he leaned closer to her. "You can play hooky. I sure remember you talking my sister into skipping school a lot."

She glared at him. "I'm the boss," she said. "So I have to set a good example." Coming in late after a night of debauchery was not the way to do that. But she would try to hide the dark circles under her eyes and claim that she'd had a morning meeting with a potential member.

That wasn't entirely a lie. Grant had claimed he wanted to join. But she had no idea what he really wanted. Last night it had been her.

Over and over again. The man sure had some kind of stamina.

"Speaking of your business," he said, and he flashed his wicked grin, "did I pass the audition?"

She sucked in a breath as pain stabbed her heart before it turned cold. So now she had her answer—that was all last night had meant to him. It had been an audition for him to sign up to date other women. The sex hadn't been that incredible because he'd wanted her but because he'd been trying to prove to her how good a lover he was. He wasn't really interested in her. Never had been. Would never be…

But that was fine with her.

That flinch of pain she felt, though, reminded her of something else—her duty to her clients so that they wouldn't get hurt. And Grant was too much of a heartbreaker to not hurt them.

"No, you didn't pass," she informed him.

His cocky grin didn't even slip. Instead he chuckled in arrogant amusement. "Really? That wasn't the best date you ever had?"

The best sex—definitely. But that wasn't what he'd asked. So she shook her head. "Not even close."

He sucked in a breath, and finally that wicked grin slipped away from his lips. "How can you say that? You came—"

She held her hand up to his mouth, stemming his words, before the doorman could overhear him. "You brought me to a loud club after I told you all I wanted was a big glass of wine. A glass of wine I never got, by the way."

"I had it delivered to the hotel room," he reminded her, his lips moving against her fingers until she jerked her tingling hand away. "You could have had the entire bottle if you'd wanted it, but wine wasn't what you wanted then."

She'd wanted him. Heaven help her, she still did.

"It had gone flat by then," she said. "And the food was soggy and cold." She shook her head. "So, no, it wasn't a good date at all."

"Miranda," he said.

"And now you're arguing with me on the street," she said. "So it's getting even worse."

He opened his mouth, then closed it and shook his head. After uttering a shaky sigh, he said, "You obviously just want to get rid of me now. So I'll let you go. But we need to talk about this."

She shook her head now. "Nothing more to say. You had your audition. You didn't pass."

He leaned down then, until his mouth was just a breath from hers. "Let me try again…" he murmured. Then he skimmed his lips across hers, nipping gently at her bottom one, pulling it apart from her top one so that he could dip his tongue inside her mouth.

She gasped and let him deepen the kiss, but she fought hard to keep her arms at her sides, so that she wouldn't reach for him and clutch his head to hers. Instead she stepped back until their mouths separated. "Give it up, Grant," she advised him. "This is one game you've lost."

Because she had no doubt that was all he'd been doing—playing some game with her. And she was far too busy for games, even ones that had given her as much pleasure as he had the night before.

Before he could stop her again, she rushed toward the door that opened for her. And as she passed the doorman, she murmured in French, "*Ne le laisse pas entrer...*" before passing the man a folded bill.

He nodded. "*Oui*, Mademoiselle Fox." And he closed the door behind her.

As she'd requested, he wouldn't let Grant into the building. But it was already too late.

She'd already let the man inside her; she'd let him get to her in a way nobody had in years, if ever...

She couldn't let that happen again.

Grant strolled into the office with a nonchalance he did not feel. This was his office—off the hangar at the airport in London. And it was already late afternoon, so hopefully his sister had left for the day.

Had Miranda called Blair?

She must have; they talked all the time. They told each other everything. She must have told Blair that she'd slept with her brother.

His hope that she was already gone was dashed when he heard her voice. But Blair paid him no attention, her focus on the cell phone clutched in her hand. But it wasn't Miranda to whom she was talking.

"I can't wait to see you, too," she nearly cooed into the phone. "I miss you so much, Teo."

He groaned. "How? You two are barely apart." But he knew now, after last night. The minute he'd left Miranda in Monaco, he'd started missing her. No. He'd started missing her before that, when she shut him down outside her apartment building.

Why had she shut him down?

Was the night before all she'd wanted from him? All that hot sex?

Because it wasn't enough for him. He wanted more.

"Oh, that's just Grant being grumpy," Blair said into the phone.

"Grumpy," he murmured; his voice so gruff that it sounded like a growl even to him. Yeah, he was grumpy. He was frustrated…with her damn friend.

Blair finally glanced up from her call to look at him and ask, "What? Did you lose a game?"

Suspicious, he narrowed his eyes and studied her face. What did she know? Had Miranda called her and bragged that she'd beaten him at his own game? He'd been playing a game with Miranda, trying to manipulate her into doing what he'd wanted. But he'd been so consumed with passion for her that he had completely forgotten about his mission. For Blair...

"If you did lose, Teo wants a rematch," Blair continued.

He glared at her.

And she giggled. Until Teo, it had been years since he'd heard his sister sound so happy and carefree.

Blair seemed to forget him again as she refocused on her call and her caller. "I saw the interview you did," she said. "You didn't have to mention me at all." Her face flushed, and her eyes sparkled at whatever her Italian billionaire said in the ear she had pressed against the cell phone. "I love you, too."

Grant groaned again—not over his sister's happiness but over his failure to make sure it was protected, that she was protected. He'd been such an idiot.

Blair giggled again and said, "Teo wants to know if you're jealous."

"Of what?" Grant asked. "Of your sickening display of emotion?"

"I can't say that to my brother!" Blair exclaimed into the cell. Then she held it away from her ear and clicked the speaker button.

Teo's voice emanated from the cell. "Sounds like somebody needs to get laid."

Grant had been laid—more than once. And it had been the best sex of his life, which said a hell of a lot to Grant. But even though he'd had the most mind-blowing orgasms he'd ever had, his body was all tense and needy again. Needy for Miranda Fox.

"Fuck you," he called out to Teo.

The other man's chuckle rumbled out of the speaker. "I'm taken."

He was. And from what he'd overheard outside Miranda's office, that and that interview was becoming a problem with her sisters and her business.

He needed to make sure that didn't become a problem for Blair. That Miranda didn't become a problem for Blair and her billionaire…like she had for every other boyfriend Blair had had.

"See you soon," Blair said before finally ending her call. Then—unfortunately—she focused all her attention on Grant. "What happened to you? You look like hell."

Her friend had happened to him. But she didn't seem to know. Maybe Miranda hadn't called her.

Maybe they didn't share everything…

"I see that you filed a flight plan to Monaco and then Ibiza," she said.

A twinge of unease passed through his heart. Had she checked it or had Miranda told her that?

"I didn't realize you were keeping track of me," he said.

"I was tracking down the plane you took," she said. "To see when you'd be bringing it back." She smiled. "I was hoping to use it."

At least she hadn't called him. If she had heard Miranda's voice...

"I didn't think I'd have it that long," he admitted. His plan had been to issue a quick warning to Miranda not to mess with Blair's happiness, but then...

"My plan changed," he continued.

"While you were gambling in Monaco, you heard about a game on Ibiza," she said, as if she knew him so well.

She didn't know him at all.

Neither did Miranda...

"From how bad you look, it must have been an all-night game," she said.

He hadn't changed out of his wrinkled dress pants and shirt. And since he'd just landed in London, he hadn't had time to go back to his house to change yet, either.

"And it doesn't look like you were all that lucky, either," Blair remarked with a teasing smile.

He had gotten lucky—with orgasm after orgasm—hers and his. But somehow Miranda thought she won.

Since he'd forgotten his mission about warning
her away from his sister, she had gotten the upper
hand for a while. But last night had only been the
first hand in a long game.

He wasn't done playing with Miranda Fox.

Not yet.

CHAPTER EIGHT

Whatever game he'd been playing with her must have bored him, because Grant hadn't called her. Hadn't texted or emailed.

He hadn't tried, since that morning a few days ago when he'd dropped her off at her apartment, to see her again. Not that he'd really wanted to see her. He wanted to join Liaisons International so he could see other women. Apparently she hadn't been enough for him that night.

Maybe no one woman would ever satisfy a man like Grant Snyder—a man who liked the gamble over the safe bet. Not that she was a safe bet...

Miranda was never going to fall in love and settle down. Or settle, which was what her mother had always done. That was why she'd chosen to buy her mother out of the business. She wanted to make sure that people found someone with whom they were truly compatible.

Like Blair and Teo...

That was what she'd tried explaining to some of the irate female members who'd called to complain that they hadn't been set up on dates with him. "You weren't compatible."

"Anybody is compatible with money."

That was why she'd set up Teo with Blair—because she knew her friend would see the billionaire for more than his money. That if she fell for him, it would be despite his wealth, not because of it.

Miranda wished she could blame the tension gripping her on the business, but she knew why she was so damn tense that she felt she might snap any moment.

Grant.

Because she'd been so edgy the past couple of days, she'd sent Tabitha home early this Friday. She hadn't wanted to snap at her sister—especially when Tabitha had worked so hard this week with all the calls they'd received.

But despite how busy she'd been, Tabitha had still had time to keep asking her about Grant.

"Is he a good kisser?"

"What does he look like naked?"

"How big is he?"

Miranda had learned young how to lie and get away with it. So she hadn't truthfully answered her sister. If she had, she would have only needed one word: *spectacular*.

He'd been spectacular at everything.

Instead she'd told her, "Do you really think that I would sleep with Grant Snyder when all he wants is to join our dating service? He doesn't want me. He wants other women. Probably rich women…"

Since that was what everybody calling wanted— a wealthy person to date.

Tabitha had believed her—too easily—which made her feel stupid. "Of course," her sister had said. "He wants a female Teo to support his gambling, no doubt. You were smart to not get involved with him."

She was smart.

Usually…

But her decades-long crush on Grant Snyder had made her a stupid little girl again. She hadn't been able to resist the temptation of finally living out her fantasy.

Maybe that was all it had been. Maybe that was why he hadn't called or texted or emailed. Maybe it had never really happened and she'd dreamed the whole night.

But her imagination wasn't that vivid; she couldn't have just imagined how incredible he had made her feel. How much pleasure he'd given her…

The release…

She needed that now, so badly.

Tabitha was gone now. She was safe. But anyone else who walked in the door or called might get subjected to her tension. She had no patience left.

If she didn't get a release again soon…

She knew that she might do something incredibly stupid…like call Grant. Or something almost as stupid as that and call Blair.

She'd been tempted to contact her friend and find out what Grant had really been up to, if he'd ever mentioned wanting to join the dating service. But her friend knew her too well.

If she mentioned Grant at all to his sister, she would give herself up. Blair would know that they'd crossed the line from old enemies to new lovers.

No. They weren't lovers.

They'd just had sex one night. And that was all that could ever happen between them.

She couldn't call him. So she needed to take care of herself. That was why she'd slipped her vibrator into her big purse.

She turned around her chair so that she faced the credenza underneath her office window. She opened the door behind which she stashed her purse. Instead of pulling it out, she reached inside and felt around for her special friend—the one that kept her from getting as damn desperate as her mother had always been for a man.

When Tabitha had left, she'd told her to lock the door, so she wouldn't be interrupted. But she'd just closed her fingers around the hard length of rubber and plastic and rechargeable batteries when hinges creaked. With the make-believe cock firmly in her grasp, she froze.

Damn it!

Tabitha could not even follow the simple directions to lock the door on her way out. Hopefully the actress's agent would call her soon with an audition—one back in the US or London. A twinge of guilt struck her that she automatically assumed that her sister hadn't locked the door. Maybe she had come back to the office or Regina had stopped in.

It was all the tension making her jump to conclusions. Tension she needed to relieve…

Tension that Grant, and his ability to give her orgasm after orgasm, had caused more so than even the business.

"Tabitha?" she called out. "Are you back?"

No one answered. And Tabitha was too chatty not to; it was her other sister who'd been giving her the silent treatment since Teo's interview.

"Regina?" she asked.

Not wanting her judgmental sister to catch her with the vibrator, she dropped it back in her purse, closed the credenza and spun her chair around to find her office door open. A jolt struck her heart, and she gasped.

Neither of her sisters stood in the doorway. As if he'd been there awhile, Grant leaned indolently against the jamb. He wore faded jeans and a black T-shirt that was just a little too tight. The cotton molded to the impressive muscles of his chest, the sight of which made her mouth begin to water.

She swallowed down the sudden rush of saliva and cleared her throat before asking, "What are you doing here?"

Me. She wanted him to do her. Now. On the desk. Or the credenza. Or even the floor.

She didn't care. She just wanted him. Anywhere...

"I want a second chance with you," he said.

Her heart flipped with hope. He did want her.

"I want another audition to show you that I can be the perfect date," he continued.

Her shoulders slumped with defeat as he dashed her hope. He was still more interested in dating other women than in dating her.

"Why would I do that?" she asked when seeing him now, looking so damn good, made it nearly impossible for her to keep her hands off him.

"I based that first date on the Miranda from all those years ago," he said. "I want to base this one on the Miranda I know now."

"You don't know me, Grant," she said. "And you didn't know me years ago, either." He had never made the effort to do anything besides threaten and warn her away from corrupting his sister.

She almost wished that was what he was up to now. But surely he would have done it already if that had been his purpose.

* * *

She was right. Not that he would admit that to her, though. He'd thought he'd known her, but until that night...

Until she'd blown his mind—and other parts of his body—like she had, he'd had no damn idea how passionate she was. What an incredible lover.

He wanted her again—so damn badly. But that had been his mistake. Taking things too fast...

He needed to slow down, to really seduce her into falling for him. That was what he needed her to do now, so that she would agree to whatever he wanted. Like leaving Blair and Teo alone so they could cement their relationship even more. But he also wanted her to do whatever he wanted, whenever he wanted. Like now...

He wanted to jerk her onto the top of her desk and take her there. Or on the credenza...

Or even the floor.

She looked so damn beautiful. Her suit jacket was draped over the back of her chair, so she wore only a thin blue chemise with the skirt from the navy blue suit. The desk with the spindly legs revealed her shapely legs—that she hadn't crossed since spinning her chair toward the door. He wanted to crawl under that desk and pleasure her like he had in the hotel room. He wanted to taste her desire for him.

But he also had to learn from the mistake he'd

already made with her. So he drew in a deep breath and summoned all his control—even as he acted as if he was totally relaxed and carefree.

He cared too much about getting a second chance with her. "So let me get to know you," he told her. And he was intrigued with her—more so than he'd ever been with any other woman. He wanted to get to know her better.

"Why?" she asked.

"You've been my sister's best friend forever—"

"So you should already know me," she said.

She was right. He should.

He'd thought he did, but now…he wasn't so sure. She was different than he'd thought she was—harder working, more serious and definitely a hell of a lot more sexual.

"Then our getting to know each other better is long overdue," he said. "Although I certainly know more about you than I did before." Like how she kissed and what she tasted like and how easy it was to make her come.

She leaned back in her chair and sighed. And he knew he was getting to her.

"Blair would be happy to know that we're getting to know each other," he persisted.

She snorted. "I doubt that. Did you tell her about Ibiza?"

He shook his head. "I thought you would."

Her pale blue eyes widened with shock. "What? Hell, no."

"You think she would be upset?" he asked and admitted, "I think she would be..." Because she would want to know the truth of what he was up to.

"She's wanted me for a sister for so long that I would be more worried about her planning our wedding," Miranda replied with a shudder of revulsion.

He should have been relieved that she wasn't as marriage-obsessed as her mother had been, but a little twinge struck his chest. She'd probably just pricked his pride again, because he sure as hell didn't want to get married.

He was probably even more averse to it than she was. If he hadn't had his parents' example of an unhappy marriage, he would have had plenty to pick from among the friends he'd made in the service and in the world of professional gambling.

Neither was a lifestyle that fostered healthy relationships, though. Which was probably partly why he'd chosen those careers. Or had they chosen him?

"Did the thought of marrying me scare you into leaving me alone?" Miranda asked him.

Realizing he'd fallen silent, he chuckled. "I don't scare that easily." Unfortunately neither did she, though, or she would have heeded one of his many, many threats to leave his sister alone before now.

"I don't, either!" she said, her voice sharp with defensiveness. Her body was tense, too, as if she was on edge.

Was she as sexually frustrated as he was? He doubted it. She could have called up any other guy to satisfy her. He only wanted her for some reason.

Maybe the novelty of it all? Once they had another night together, he would get over her. He would realize she wasn't any more special than any other lover he'd had.

But first he had to get her to give him another chance. So he goaded her, "You sure seem scared to me, or you'd let me take you out again."

She shook her head.

"Chicken," he teased. "But then, if I was you, I guess I'd be scared, too, that I would fall for me."

Now she laughed. "And you wonder why I won't let you join the service…"

"I do wonder," he said.

"You're an arrogant smart-ass."

"Yeah?"

She laughed again before spinning her chair around. She pulled her purse from the credenza then stood up and turned toward him. "Okay," she said with a sigh of resignation.

"Okay?" He tensed. "You're letting me join?" That really wasn't what he wanted. He wanted her.

She shook her head. "I'm giving you another audition. Prove to me that you can be the perfect date." Her eyes sparkled with the challenge that she obviously thought he would fail.

She might have won the first hand, but he was taking this one and the whole damn game.

CHAPTER NINE

HOW THE HELL had he done it? He'd found the perfect rooftop restaurant from which to watch the sunset over the water. He'd found the perfect bottle of wine, a sauvignon blanc chilled and crisp.

And the food…

Soft mozzarella sprinkled with fresh basil-covered sweet slices of tomatoes. Chicken and shrimp followed with creamy risotto and truffles.

And just when she'd thought she was too full to eat another bite, the waiter brought out white-and dark-chocolate-dipped strawberries and champagne.

Grant lifted his flute and clinked it against her glass. "To the perfect date…"

He was smug. He knew.

And she was too happy to lie. So, the bubbles bursting on her tongue, she sighed in ecstasy and nodded in agreement. But she didn't let him take all the credit. "Who helped you?" she asked. "Blair?"

"I already told you that I haven't said anything to her about us."

So that left her sisters. Regina wouldn't have helped him, but Tabitha was as hopeless a romantic as their lovesick mother. "My backstabbing receptionist…" she murmured. Tabitha had to have been the one who'd let him into the office, too.

She didn't know whether to be furious with her sister or grateful to her.

"She was being helpful," Grant defended his co-conspirator. "She said you've been really stressed out and needed a good, relaxing evening."

She knew what would help most with the stress, and it wasn't food or wine. It was him. Just him.

But dare she bring him home with her? All having sex with him had done was make her want him more. But remembering the pleasure he'd given her, the toe-curling release that she needed…

She knew it was worth the risk, even if tonight was only half as good as the other night with him had been.

She drained her flute of champagne and said, "The evening's not over."

He arched a brow. "What are you saying?"

"That you're coming home with me."

He'd planned on kissing her outside the door to the lobby of her apartment building. That was all Grant had allowed himself to count on this evening.

Good food. Good wine. Fun conversation.

And a wistful, longing kiss good-night.

Hell, he hadn't even counted on that; he knew all too well how stubborn she could be.

And now he knew how surprising.

Even after having the waiter pack up their dessert and the chauffeur drive them to her apartment building, Grant expected to be stopped on the street—especially when the doorman eyed him suspiciously as he approached with her.

"*Il est en sécurité,*" Miranda said in French.

Grant chuckled as he translated to English what she'd said. "I'm safe?" He didn't feel safe; he felt very uneasy, on edge, and it wasn't just because he wanted her so badly.

Or at least that was only part of it. He wanted her so badly and was worried that she was still going to toss him out. But at least he got past the doorman, who held open the door for him, however begrudgingly.

Despite the man's unwelcoming attitude, Grant slipped him a big bill. Maybe that would soften him up some.

Had the wine and the food softened up Miranda?

Was now the time for him to talk to her about Blair and Teo? He'd forgotten all about them last time he'd been alone with Miranda. This time he'd been reluctant to bring up anything that related to her business. Tabitha had told him that was why she was so stressed—because Teo's interview had pissed off so many of their female members.

Apparently everyone wanted a billionaire of her own—even Tabitha. Why didn't Miranda?

Why hadn't she gone out with Teo herself?

Oh, because of her rule...

The one that meant if she ever signed Grant up for the service, she wouldn't go out with him again. Maybe he shouldn't have made this date so perfect...

"I think you're scared," she said.

He glanced up and realized that she stood inside the elevator, holding open the doors for him. He hadn't even realized it had arrived; he'd been lost in thoughts...of her.

He'd rather be lost in her, though. He stepped inside with her, but a pang of regret struck him that they were not alone. An older woman stood in the corner of the elevator; she held a small dog in her scrawny arms. The dog bristled and growled at Grant, and he wasn't sure how long the woman would be able to hold on to it.

Used to dealing with unpredictable creatures, Grant emitted a high-pitched whistle for only the dog to hear. It dropped his head down to the woman's arms and stared at him balefully.

"What did you do?" Miranda asked, her pale blue eyes narrowing in suspicion.

She was young enough that she must have heard it. The dog's owner was blissfully unaware.

"And can you teach me how to do that?" Miranda continued.

"Dogs love me," Grant said. "You know they're excellent judges of character."

She chuckled—that sexy, naughty chuckle that had his blood pressure rising like the elevator moving from one floor to the next. He wanted the old lady and the dog off it. He wanted Miranda alone. But when the elevator stopped on ten, she was the one who stepped through the doors. When he hesitated, she asked, "Are you coming?"

"Soon…" he murmured—hopefully.

A slight smile curved her lips, and she sighed. "And here I just expected you to show me to my door like the perfect gentleman would do on the perfect date."

She was teasing—he hoped.

"You didn't think the wine was too dry?" he asked. "The risotto too sticky?"

Her smile widened as she walked down the hall. It was an older building with the wallpaper and carpet worn and in need of replacement. But it was clean and safe.

"Nope," she said. "It was all perfect." She stopped at the second door from the end of the hall. "This is my place." As she reached into her purse, her face flushed—almost as if she was embarrassed.

"Can't find your keys?" he asked.

She shook her head as she pulled them out. The metal jangled as she unlocked and pushed open her door.

Grant tensed, waiting for her to stop him there with the offer of another damn handshake like she'd done the morning after their incredible night. But before he could react, she reached out, grabbed his T-shirt in her hand and pulled him inside the apartment with her. She slammed the door and shoved him up against it.

Almost giddy with relief, he laughed. This was the Miranda he loved—no, not loved. He loved nobody but his family and some really close friends. This was the Miranda who intrigued and excited him.

She took the takeout container from his hands and put it on the table in the small foyer. Then she linked her arms around his neck and pulled his head down to hers. She kissed him like he'd wanted her to kiss him—with all the crazy passion she brought out in him.

She nipped and nibbled at his lips until he opened his mouth again. But he wasn't laughing anymore. He was panting for breath. His heart raced. He wanted her so damn badly.

He cupped her butt, her sweet, curvy little butt, in his hands and lifted her. She wrapped her legs around him, clinging to him, as he walked. He didn't go far. The apartment was a tiny studio. A small kitchen stood on one side and a living room on the other with a bathroom door open off that. "Where's the bed?" he asked, his voice gruff with the need gripping him.

Her lips curved against his. "You need a bed?"

"Don't you have one?" he asked. "What? Do you sleep hanging upside down?"

She laughed now and, unlocking her legs, she slid down his body, over his straining erection. "You really should be worried that you're going to offend me if you want to be the perfect date."

He didn't want to be the perfect date anymore. He just wanted her.

"I never offended you before," he said. "Even when I tried."

She wrinkled her nose at him. "I wouldn't be so sure about that..."

A twinge of regret struck his madly pounding heart. Had he ever hurt her feelings before? He'd been harsh with her sometimes, out of concern for his sister, but she'd never seemed to let it faze her.

"I'm sorry," he said sincerely.

She tilted her head and studied his face, as if uncertain if she should believe him. "I'll let you make it up to me," she said. "If you can find the bed."

"Are you going to give me a hint?" he asked—because he wanted her so badly he was thinking about taking her up against the door where she'd slammed him. But he wasn't sure his knees would hold him up; they were beginning to shake as desire overwhelmed him.

She twirled around in the middle of the living room space, like she'd twirled on the beach that first night they'd gone out—the moon casting a glow like a spotlight all around her. She was so stunningly beautiful that he had to look away for a moment, as if she was so bright she might burn his eyes. Or his heart.

That was when he noticed the wide armoire standing against the wall next to the bathroom door. Nothing sat on the hardwood floor in front of the antique piece of furniture, or maybe it had been purposely distressed to look as if the white paint was wearing off it. He opened the doors and pulled down the mattress of the hidden bed.

She giggled now, as if she was as excited as he was. He turned toward her and arched a brow. He hadn't ever heard her giggle like that. Only Blair's flighty friends had giggled like that.

She'd clasped a hand over her mouth, as if the sound had surprised her, too. Her eyes were wide above her hand, wide and bright.

He closed the distance between them, leaned over and brushed his lips across the back of her hand. But that wasn't where he really wanted to kiss her. Where he needed to kiss her.

When she'd wound her legs around his torso,

her skirt had ridden up—bunched nearly around her waist. He pushed it up the rest of the way and reached for her panties, sliding them down her bare legs. She stepped out of them, and when she parted her legs, he parted them wider and slid his fingers inside her. She was already wet, already hot, all ready for him.

But he had to taste her…had wanted to taste her again all night…

He lifted her onto the edge of her mattress, then he knelt in front of her, like he'd wanted to kneel in front of her desk. Parting her legs wide, he moved his mouth over her mound. He kissed the short curls before stroking his tongue between her soft lips.

She moaned and flopped back onto the mattress. And he pulled her legs over his shoulders and went down on her as if he was starving. He licked and lapped at her, teasing her with his tongue and his fingers until she came, screaming his name.

His face damp with her desire and his perspiration, he pulled his shirt over his head. Then he unbuttoned and unzipped his jeans and jerked them off with his boxers. He couldn't wait to be inside her. Deep, deep inside her…

His fingers shook as he ripped open the condom packet. But before he could roll it on, she took it from him. And before she rolled it, she took him deep in her mouth. Her tongue swirled around his cock, then she sucked him deeper. But it wasn't deep enough...

He wanted more.

He pulled her chemise up. It must have had a built-in bra in it, because her breasts bounced free and naked. He tugged on one of the nipples with his lips before grazing it with his teeth.

She clutched at his head and moaned. But then she pushed him back, just slightly, so she could roll that condom over him. Before he could reach for her, though, she crawled higher onto the bed and turned onto her hands and knees and pointed her sweet ass into the air. Then she reached between her legs and closed her hand around his cock, and she guided him into her vagina. A small scream escaped her lips as her inner muscles clutched at him, as if she was already coming again.

The woman was so damn sensual. She ground her butt against his hips, thrusting back, so he began to move, driving deeper and deeper inside her. He used one arm on the bed to help support his weight while his other hand found one of her breasts. He stroked and squeezed it as he continued to thrust into her.

Over and over again...

Her muscles gripped him tightly before rippling with an orgasm. And once again she screamed his name. Then his body tensed, and he nearly screamed her name, too, as an orgasm shook him.

It was so powerful. She was so powerful.

He'd probably filled the condom, so he pulled out and hurried into the bathroom to clean up. When he returned, she lay limply on the mattress. She'd shimmied out of her skirt, so she was completely naked now. And completely spent...

"Dessert?" he asked.

She chuckled. "I think I might need a little time to recover."

He didn't. His cock was already hardening again at just the sight of her. "How about the restaurant dessert?" he asked. He walked the short distance to the foyer, where she'd left the takeout container on the table. His bare foot struck her purse, knocking it over.

A vibrator rolled out onto the hardwood floor. She really was insatiable. Now he understood why she'd acted embarrassed when reaching into her purse. So he suppressed the chuckle rising in his throat. And he bent down to pick it up and slide it back into the bag. The vibrator wasn't the only thing that had fallen out, though. Her checkbook had, too, open to the ledger. He picked up that after the vibrator.

And something sounding almost like that whistle he'd released for the yippy dog rent the quiet. A hiss of outrage...

"What the hell are you doing?" she asked, her

voice shaking with anger. "Why are you going through my stuff?"

"I accidentally knocked over your purse," he explained.

"Yeah, right," she scoffed. "Put down my checkbook. Stop going through my stuff!" And she hurled his stuff at him, flinging his jeans and his shirt toward him. She threw his shoe like a football in a straight line right toward his face. He ducked just in time, and it went over his head and struck the door instead. He stayed low, waiting for the next one to fly. But she must have kicked it because it just rolled across the floor toward him.

"Get out!" she yelled at him. "Get out and don't even ask. Even you must know that you failed this audition, too. I will never trust you again and I will never put any of my members in the position of having to trust you, either."

Members?

He didn't know what the hell she was talking about—then it dawned on him. Liaisons International…

He'd forgotten all about telling her that he wanted to join her damn dating service. He opened his mouth to set her straight and to do what he'd really intended all along—to tell her not to mess with Blair and Teo. But before he could say anything, the bathroom door slammed behind her, and the lock turned.

Water started running and a fan began to rattle.

Even if he tried to shout through that closed door, she wasn't going to listen to him implore her to leave Blair and Teo alone. In fact, she might mess with them just to spite him with as angry as she was.

No. The smartest thing for him to do was get dressed and leave.

And he wasn't sure that he should ever come back...

CHAPTER TEN

SHE'D KNOWN HE was up to something. But what? Was he trying to figure out how much money she had? The balance in her check register must have disappointed the hell out of him if he was looking for a mark.

Was that why he was so determined to join the dating service? Just like everyone else, he was looking for a billionaire.

Maybe his gambling wasn't going so well. Or he'd spent too much money starting the charter business with Blair.

Or maybe all that money his sister thought he won gambling, he'd actually attained by other means, from women. What if he was a con artist?

She'd been smart to not trust him. But she never should have let him touch her, either.

And she damn well never should have touched him.

Because even as angry as she was with him, she

still wanted him, wanted him to fill the hollowness she'd never been aware of having before she'd had him as a lover.

And that hollowness only grew the longer it had been since she'd seen him...

It had also been too long since she'd seen his sister, so a week after throwing Grant out of her apartment, she met up with Blair for dinner. Unfortunately Blair had chosen the same rooftop restaurant where Miranda had watched the sun set with Grant.

Blair swallowed a spoonful of crème brûlée and emitted a soft moan of pleasure. "It's so good," she said with a lustful sigh.

Miranda pushed hers across the tablecloth toward her friend. "You can have mine, too."

"You're not hungry?" Blair asked with surprise. She always teased Miranda that she didn't know where she put everything she ate, since she was so petite.

Miranda had choked down some of her salad, but she hadn't had much of an appetite lately. At least not for food...

Her appetites had changed after she'd had sex with Grant. Now he was all she craved. But that was crazy.

She couldn't trust him, so she shouldn't want him anywhere in her life—not even in her bed. If only she could get him out of her mind as well.

"It's no wonder you don't like this restaurant," Blair said.

Miranda tensed. Did she know? Had Grant told her after all?

"Why's that?" she asked.

"Grant recommended it to me," Blair said. "And you two do not like the same things at all—most especially each other."

Miranda laughed—like her friend obviously wanted her to—but it sounded hollow, as hollow as she felt. She and Grant had more in common than she'd ever realized. Sex…

They were both very good at it.

"I thought Tabitha would have recommended the place," Miranda said. Since her sister had been the one who'd told Grant about it.

"No. Grant's been here a couple of times over the past couple of weeks."

"Do you know why?" Miranda asked.

Blair shrugged. Then after swallowing the spoonful of crème brûlée she'd taken from Miranda's bowl, she replied, "I have no idea, but that's nothing new with my brother. I don't think I'll ever know what he's really doing most of the time."

Miranda reached for her glass of sauvignon blanc and swirled the pale amber liquid around inside it. The sun streamed through the glass, casting rainbow patterns onto the tablecloth. She stared at the wine, trying to sound nonchalant, when she asked, "Do you still think he's a Navy SEAL or some other kind of special forces?"

Blair nodded. "Definitely. There's so much of his life that I know nothing about…"

"Too much," Miranda agreed—because if Blair didn't know it, there was no chance that she would ever learn about it, either.

"If that's what he's doing, he can't talk about it," Blair said, coming to her brother's defense. "Being part of something like that involves total discretion and secrecy." She sighed. "So no wonder he's single."

Still skeptical, Miranda snorted. "Yeah, that's why. It has nothing to do with his gambling and carousing?"

Blair chuckled. "Well, there's that, too. A couple of weeks ago he came into the office looking like hell, like he hadn't slept in days. Must've been a hell of a poker game."

Or the morning after the first night they'd had sex…

She'd looked like hell after that sleepless night, too.

"Do you think he's been losing a lot?" Miranda wondered aloud. That would explain why he wanted to join Liaisons International—to find a rich significant other like his sister had.

Blair laughed.

And Miranda furrowed her brow, confused. "That's funny?"

"It is with how much shit he's been buying lately. He just got a helicopter, for some reason."

"Won't that help out with the business?"

Blair nodded, but it was almost begrudging. "Yes, and when I come to visit you since there's no airport close by, but I don't know why he suddenly needed it."

To visit her?

Had he wanted to keep seeing her?

No. He'd made it clear he'd only been auditioning with her so he could join the dating service.

Blair shrugged again. "Probably makes it easier to get to his games. I think he's got one planned for tonight."

"And he needs a helicopter to get there?" Miranda asked. Why was she wondering where he was going to be? Or what he was? She had more than enough on her plate without dealing with him anymore.

She should have been happy that he hadn't tried to contact her since she'd tossed him out. But all she felt was that strange hollowness...

Blair chuckled. "No. But maybe he wants to make a splash." Her lips pulled into a slight frown. "I hope he doesn't crash that new bird into the sea."

"So you know where the game is?"

"Yeah, that hotel on Ibiza. I have a feeling he might own the place."

The way the staff had treated him suddenly made sense; they'd seemed to know him and kowtow to him. At the time Miranda had thought they'd just offered excellent service, like the condoms in the nightstand. Now she wondered…

Blair laughed again. "He probably won it in a poker game."

Won it or conned it out of someone?

"Do you think he cheats?" Miranda asked.

Blair laughed again. "He doesn't need to. He's so damn good at bluffing."

"So you mean he's a good liar?" she challenged her.

"Ouch," Blair remarked, her dark blue eyes twinkling with amusement. "You really don't like him any more now than you used to."

"Probably even less," Miranda admitted.

"You're really good at bluffing, too," Blair said. "So does that make you a good liar?"

Amusement tugged at Miranda's lips, making her smile.

"Finally," Blair said. "You haven't smiled since you walked up to the table."

Probably not since it was nearly the same one she'd shared with Grant a week ago.

Blair reached across the table and patted Miranda's hand. "I'm worried about you."

Miranda forced a wider smile. "Why?"

"You've been so busy lately, I've hardly seen you," Blair said. "I was hoping that was because the business is going well, that Teo's interview helped bring in new members, but that must not be the case at all."

Miranda swallowed down the stress she'd been struggling with over her business. She didn't want to dim her friend's happiness, but she didn't want to outright lie to her, either. They were too close friends for that. So she admitted, "Some women were upset that they didn't get dates with Teo, too."

Blair smiled. "I don't blame them."

Neither did Miranda—if they'd really been interested in the man and not his bank account. An image flashed through her mind of Grant looking at her check register. After seeing her dismal balance, it was no wonder he hadn't tried to contact her again.

"Is that why you're not happy?" Blair asked. "Taking some abuse for not spreading Teo around to more members?"

"Mostly just from Tabitha," Miranda answered honestly and smiled again. "It's nothing I can't handle, though." And she would.

She'd told her sisters to stop complaining about what was done and focus on what they could do to bring in new clients. They needed a new marketing hook—one that focused on what she wanted the business to be now—a place for people to date safely and with excitement.

Her sisters' only suggestion had been to let Grant Snyder join Liaisons. Sure, Grant covered the excitement part, but he wasn't safe—for her or for any of her members.

Grant had lost another hand of the game he'd been playing with Miranda. With her thinking that he'd been snooping in her purse, he wasn't sure he would ever be invited back to her table to play again.

So he'd found another game. Actually, he'd set up this one himself. It would be played by his rules—which usually meant there were no rules.

For once he'd limited the stakes, though. He'd lost too much lately to risk financial loss as well. He'd lost something he'd never even realized he'd wanted: Miranda's trust.

Which was stupid, since he'd been lying to her from the minute he'd showed up in her office, pretending he actually wanted to join her dating service. But he hadn't cared then that he might destroy her trust; he hadn't wanted it.

He'd only wanted her to leave Teo and Blair alone in their new love. But for some reason, every time he got near her, he'd forgotten his mission. Because she was so damn beautiful and sexy and passionate.

Maybe instead of a poker game, he should have

arranged a hookup. A lot of his old lovers had expressed interest in seeing him again—if only in the bedroom. But there was only one old lover he wanted to see again.

His imagination must have conjured her up, because when he looked away from his cards, he saw her standing in the doorway to the suite. Had she come here to see him?

This was the room in which they'd spent that first night together.

Maybe he should have booked a different one—because he kept seeing her everywhere he looked in it. Because she really couldn't be here...

Especially dressed like that, like the good girl going bad in that musical she and his sister had watched over and over again in the basement family room. The black leather pants and vestlike shirt were something his imagination would have conjured up to reveal her every tantalizing curve while making her look badass sexy.

Then she did something even sexier—something that had him smothering a groan and shifting in his chair. She slid her hand into the front of the black vest, into the cleavage the tight leather top had helped create, and she pulled out a wad of bills.

Where the hell had the money come from? Definitely not her bank account...

What was she up to? Or was she even real?

The hostess, to whom she'd handed the money,

walked over to the table he'd set up in front of the windows. "Sir, Ms. Fox would like to join the game. Is that possible?"

"Hell, yes," the player to his right answered before he could.

"Make sure she sits next to me," another said.

"Fox is sure as hell the right name for her," a third said with a low whistle of appreciation.

The hostess smiled and murmured, "That's what I thought…"

He'd booked Alberta to host the game because she was good at handling unruly players and didn't try flirting with any of them. But that was the first time he realized all the players were usually men… until now, until Miranda had showed up wanting to play.

Alberta was definitely flirting with her as she turned her smile toward the petite blonde. Alberta was tall with long, dark hair and a killer figure of her own, one showcased in the short skirt and low-cut top she wore.

Miranda must have taken the hostess's smile as her acceptance into the game because she crossed the room to join them at the table.

"I didn't say she could play," he told Alberta.

"What?" Miranda asked. "Afraid I'm going to beat you again?"

The man who'd whistled once did so again.

"Whoa, boy, she beat you, Snyder?" He dropped his cards onto the table. "I fold."

Grant wanted to fold as well; hell, he wanted to throw everyone but her out of the suite so they could do what they'd done last time they'd been here together—screw each other senseless.

He must have not regained his senses yet, because he found himself pointing toward an empty chair at the table. "You can take a seat, Miranda," he told her. "But you're going to regret playing me…"

Her lips, which she'd painted a bright crimson, curved into that slight, sexy smile. "Oh, you're not as good as you think you are, Snyder."

His pride took the hit directly, and he flinched… while everyone else chuckled with amusement. He would show her how damn good he was.

First at cards.

And then after everyone else had left them alone, he would show her just how good he was when he made her beg for sexual release…

CHAPTER ELEVEN

WHAT THE HELL had she let Teo and Blair talk her into doing?

Teo had crashed her dinner with Blair, and when Blair had shared that they'd been talking about Grant, he'd lamented about losing money to his lover's brother. "Where is he playing?" he asked. "I should try to get my money back from him."

"It's a good thing you have more to lose if you're going to have a rematch with Grant," Blair had teased. "I don't know anyone who's ever been able to beat him." Then she'd finally pulled her gaze from her Italian lover and focused on Miranda. "But maybe you…"

Panic had clenched Miranda's heart. She did know about them!

"You've played him?" Teo had asked.

"No," Blair had answered for her. "But she could. She's good. Grant taught me, and I taught her."

"So you should be able to beat him, too," Teo had said.

Blair shook her head. "I can't bluff like the two of them can. And that's the only way to win if the cards aren't going your way."

The cards hadn't been going Miranda's way lately—at least when it came to business. She shook her head. "I haven't played for a while…"

But for those sexual games with Grant.

"And I don't have the time or the desire to throw my money away," she added. All her desire was for Grant, and temptation tugged at her.

She wouldn't mind seeing him again. If he showed her no interest, then he was only after money, and she should be relieved that she'd figured it out before she'd done something stupid… like let him join Liaisons.

She wasn't about to fall for him—even if he wasn't mercenary, though.

"Throw my money away," Teo offered.

Miranda chuckled. "Why?"

"I owe you for setting me up with the love of my life," Teo said. "And I owe Grant some payback for getting me drunk and robbing me blind."

Blair laughed now. "That's right. And also another good reason for Miranda to take him on. She can probably outdrink him, too."

She'd held up her hands. "I'm sorry, guys. I really don't have time for this—"

"You deserve a break," Blair interjected. "You've been working so hard. And it took me forever to get a smile out of you tonight."

"You think Grant is going to make me smile?" she asked.

"Taking his money will," Blair pointed out.

And she wasn't wrong. If that was all he was interested in, Miranda would love to take away his money. And his clothes...

And his will to do anything other than sexually please her...

Blair clapped her hands together and startled a gasp out of both Miranda and Teo. "And I have the perfect thing for you to wear."

Miranda shook her head and reminded her long-time bestie, "You and I haven't been able to borrow each other's clothes since we were eight." Blair had sprouted up and out way before she had.

In fact, Miranda was still waiting to sprout up.

"No, I had a friend of Teo's design this outfit for you—"

"Tony said you designed it," Teo interjected. "And that you're brilliant and beautiful and that I'm one lucky son of a bitch." He grinned as broadly as his lady love did over his compliment.

Miranda hadn't had much of an example of real love, but she knew it when she saw it. And she was seeing it now. She grinned, too. "Man, when I'm right, I'm right..."

"Yes, you are," Blair agreed. "I was going to save this present until your birthday. But you've done so much for us, you deserve it now."

"And Grant deserves to get a little comeuppance," Teo added as he pulled out his wallet.

Miranda chuckled. "I'm not going to argue with that." They had no idea how much he deserved to lose.

"Is the draw that funny?" Grant asked, drawing her back to the present where she sat at the table with him and the other players.

She glanced at her cards, relieved she'd actually been dealt some good ones this time. The other hands she'd had to bluff. And she remembered why she didn't often play. She hated that there was no control over the draw. Whatever you were dealt, you were dealt...

Miranda didn't like relying on luck and hated feeling out of control. And, with members leaving Liaisons International left and right, she'd already felt like too much was out of her control.

But finally, with the pile of chips growing in front of her, she was proving that there was more to life than luck. There was strategy, and it also helped that Grant seemed quite distracted...

His gaze kept going to her cleavage.

Was it the outfit? She'd laughed when she'd opened her early birthday present from Blair. They'd spent entirely too much of their adolescence watching *Grease*. And Miranda's favorite part had been when Sandy had dressed up like the badass.

In this leather outfit, Miranda felt like a badass, too. And she wouldn't have had the cleavage without the tight top.

She suspected, though, that it wasn't just the outfit unsettling Grant. It was the way his friends, or whatever the other players were to him, reacted to her.

They flirted outrageously, even when she took their chips. The hostess kept flirting, too. If Grant was like most of the men Miranda knew, that was probably distracting him most...with fantasies of a threesome.

Every man's not-so-secret, cliched fantasy.

She'd been invited to join couples, but she knew from her mother's divorces—more so than her marriages—that inviting someone else into the bedroom rarely ended well.

Miranda, also, did not like to share. She'd had to do too much of that growing up with her younger sisters. She liked a man's attention all to herself.

And she liked to focus only on him, like she was focused now on Grant. He was so damn good-looking. His short beard clung to his strong jaw. His golden hair was a little spiky and incredibly sexy...like the silk shirt he wore that molded to the sculpted muscles of his chest.

Heat rushed over her as she found herself getting distracted. And she couldn't afford that now.

Not when Grant must have been dealt good cards, too. Because he kept raising the ante. Or maybe he was just that much better at bluffing than she was.

Either way, she didn't want to lose.

But one of the other players called it…and when she and Grant turned over their cards, he had the better hand this time. Was he cheating?

Was that how he always got such a good deal from the deck?

How he won enough to buy hotels and helicopters?

"You wiped me out," one of the older players commented. As tired as he looked, he might have been talking about more than his lost money. "Time for me to call it a night."

Another player groaned. "Me, too." He turned toward her. "Although I'll stick around if you are… or I'll leave if you'll come back to my room with me."

She laughed and disengaged the man's hand from her knee. "No, thanks."

"Leave," Grant told the man, his voice gruff and his words clipped as if he'd ground them out through gritted teeth. A muscle twitched in his cheek.

He really didn't like anyone else touching her.

What if she touched someone else.?

As if she'd read her mind, the hostess leaned over her shoulder and whispered, "You need to up your game if you want to beat Grant. Kiss me…"

So Miranda turned her head and did just that, brushing her lips across the soft ones of the dark-haired hostess. The woman deepened the kiss, swiping her tongue across Miranda's lower lip.

The only excitement Miranda felt was generated from knowing that Grant watched them, and—if she played her cards right—she might be doing more than kissing him soon.

Because she couldn't deny that even though she didn't trust him, she wanted him.

Badly.

He wanted her.

So damn badly.

Watching her kiss another woman probably should have excited him. It certainly excited the other men left in the suite as they whistled and cheered.

Grant didn't feel like cheering. He felt like firing his best gaming hostess. But he didn't blame her for this display. He blamed Miranda. He knew she was just trying to get to him. And she was damn well succeeding…

Just as she always had.

He clapped his hands together, and the two

women stopped kissing and laughed at him. "I think it's time for a break," he announced.

"Do you need to go be alone for a while?" Leo Decker asked. "I know I do..." He pushed his chips toward the dealer and said, "Cash me out."

Not that he had a whole hell of a lot left.

What Grant hadn't taken from him, Miranda had. She was good. How the hell had he never known that she played?

And of course, like everything else she did, she played damn well.

But this was his game, and she was not going to win.

He was so confident that he decided to up the ante but just with her. While the other players cashed out during the break, she walked over to the bar in the corner of the suite. Alberta stood behind it, mixing drinks for the losers who were leaving. But she dropped those on the bar to turn to Miranda. "What would you like?" and she wiggled her eyebrows at the blonde.

A powerful emotion gripped Grant, making his stomach churn and his muscles tighten.

This must be jealousy...

He wasn't sure if he'd ever felt it before, and he didn't like the sickening surge of emotion churning inside him.

"She wants me," he burst out, making everyone turn toward him.

Miranda arched one of her blond brows and asked, "Really? Why would you think that?"

"You're here, aren't you?"

Her lips curved into a slight smile. "Maybe I just felt like getting a little action…"

He hoped like hell that was why she was here— for some action with him. He needed to release all that tension building inside him before he exploded.

"A little card action," she clarified.

"I didn't even know you played," he admitted.

She sighed. "We've already established that you don't really know me, Grant."

After she'd kissed Alberta, he was beginning to wonder just how well he did.

"Sauvignon blanc," he told the hostess. "That's what she drinks." At least he knew that about her, but that was only because her sister had taken pity on him and helped him plan that last date so it would be perfect.

It would have been, had she not gotten so angry with him.

Was this payback? Her showing up here looking sexy as hell and flirting with everyone but him?

Probably.

Alberta poured a glass and handed it to her. "If you need *anything* else, just let me know."

"Oh, I will," Miranda promised with that sexy little half smile of hers.

Grant gripped her elbow and guided her away

from everyone else, toward the bedroom doorway. He stopped himself from dragging her inside with him and peeling all that leather from her sexy body. "What the hell are you doing here?"

Besides making him crazy.

Undoubtedly that was what she'd wanted, though, and she had somehow enlisted Alberta to help her. Who else had she enlisted?

"Playing poker," she replied. "Your sister taught me years ago."

He shook his head. "Blair's not that good."

"No," Miranda agreed. "She has too honest a face."

He leaned closer and studied hers. "You don't."

She smiled. "Neither do you."

Realization dawned. There was only one way that she could have learned about his poker game. "Blair put you up to this."

"Teo, actually," she said. "He staked me so I could try to get his money back from you."

A grin tugged at his lips. He'd had fun taking that money off the billionaire.

She touched the low neckline of leather vest. "Blair was responsible for this, and for flying me here."

"What did you tell her?" he asked.

"Obviously I agreed, or I wouldn't be here," she said, as if he was an idiot.

"About us," he clarified—even though he knew

she knew what he'd meant. She was just messing with him. "What did you tell her about us?"

"Same thing you have," she said.

"So nothing."

She nodded.

"Then she won't be suspicious if I tell her that I'll fly you home," he said as he pulled his cell phone from his pocket.

"You don't need to do that," she said.

"I will when you spend the night here."

She chuckled. "What makes you think I'm going to spend the night?"

"Because you're going to lose the next hand, and what I want more than Teo's money is for you to spend the night with me."

She glanced over to the bar where Alberta poured another shot for one of the losers. "Just me?"

The sick jealousy churned in his stomach again. He didn't want anyone else touching her but him. "Yes, just you."

She uttered a sigh, as if she was disappointed, but her eyes twinkled.

"You should be grateful that I want to focus only on you," he said. "It's a win-win for you either way this game goes."

She shook her head. "So you're saying I don't get anything but money if I win?"

"What do you want?" he asked. And he hoped like hell that she wanted him as badly as he wanted her.

"For you to give up on joining Liaisons International," she said.

That was an easy bet for him, since he'd had no intention of actually joining, anyway. He shrugged. "Fine with me. I'm not going to lose."

"Don't be so confident," she warned him.

But he was…

Like everyone who didn't think she had a tell, she had a tell. If she had bad cards, she swallowed before she started bluffing, as if she had to choke down the lie.

To him, bluffing wasn't lying, so he had no tells. And he'd always had phenomenal luck when it came to cards.

Very rarely was he ever dealt a bad hand.

"If you're so sure you're going to win, why haven't you agreed to my wager yet?"

She blinked. "Oh, I thought I had. I am very excited…" She leaned closer to him, and her breath brushed across the skin of his neck when she murmured, "To beat you…"

He damn well better get good cards this time…

CHAPTER TWELVE

DAMN IT.

She'd tried; she had really tried to win. To reclaim Teo's money and to get Grant to leave Liaisons alone.

But somehow he'd drawn a straight flush…

"How the hell did you do that?" she asked. "You had to cheat. There's no other way." She'd had a full house. That should have been enough to win.

She'd even thought he'd been sweating it for a moment. But then he'd turned over his cards…

She stared down at them on the table and shook her head. "It's not possible."

"So you're a sore loser," Grant remarked with a chuckle.

She shook her head. "No. It just doesn't make sense."

"It's called skill," Grant gloated. "Just admit that I have more of it."

That was undoubtedly true. She hadn't played cards in years, but she'd thought she'd done pretty well. And when she'd drawn two more cards to get the full house, she'd thought she'd beat him for sure.

A twinge of disappointment had struck her heart then—that she wouldn't have this last night with him and that he would have no reason to audition as a date again. So she was probably going to win more by losing.

She wanted him so damn badly.

She glanced up from the table and realized that everyone else had left. He must have silently shown them out because she hadn't noticed them leaving.

"You can still beat me if you like," he said.

"You want to play another hand?" she asked.

He shook his head. "No. I was just thinking you might have a whip to go with all that leather you're wearing."

"Thinking or hoping?" she asked.

He flashed that wicked grin at her.

"I didn't realize you were into kink," she said.

"Says the woman who suggested a threesome."

"I did not," she said. "I thought that's what you wanted."

He shook his head. "Just you…"

Her heart did a strange little flip. But she drew in a deep breath to settle her excitement. He just meant for tonight. He didn't want her for keeps. No. He wanted to sign up to date other women.

Not that she wanted him for keeps. She just

wanted him for tonight. Maybe if she had sex with him again, she would get sick of it, sick of him…

Or even more addicted to him.

"This is a bad idea," she murmured—more to herself than to him.

He pointed toward the door. "You can leave. I won't hold you to the bet."

Warmth spread through her heart. Maybe his acting a gentleman on their last date hadn't been just for the audition. Maybe he really was one.

She shook her head. "No, a bet's a bet." She flinched though.

And he sucked in a breath. "Not if you're going to be miserable delivering on it. The last thing I want to do is pressure you into something you don't want."

That was the problem. She wanted him—very much. "No, I was thinking that I failed Teo. I didn't make his money back for him."

Grant picked up a wad of bills from the hostess station near the door to the hall. "Here, give it back to him. I don't want it…"

"You don't need it?" she asked, and she wondered, just how did he make his money?

Cheating?

As if he'd read her mind, he said, "I didn't cheat you. I just got really, really lucky…" Then he took that wad of cash and held out his hand toward the front of her vest. "Isn't that where you had your money?"

He waited a moment—maybe to see if she'd push him away—before he dipped his hand, with that money, into her cleavage. She sucked in a breath, which strained the already tight top so much that the zipper on it began to slide down. His eyes darkened with passion, his dilating pupils swallowing that dark blue, as he saw what he was doing.

And he kept doing it until the top parted.

The straps had already been dangling down her shoulders, but now they slipped all the way off her arms as the top fell onto the floor.

"Maybe we should have played strip poker," he said.

"You want me to deal the cards?" she asked.

"No, I just want you to strip."

A smile tugged at her lips. She wasn't going to fight her desire for him. Not tonight...

She wanted him too much. So instead of arguing with him, she reached for the zipper at the top of her pants and tugged on it.

Grant's breath hissed out between his teeth like the rasp of the zipper as she lowered it. Then she shimmied out of the leather, which wasn't easy. The material had gotten warm and tight.

Grant chuckled. "A little trouble."

She giggled. "I might be stuck..." The leather

had molded to her thighs, so she wasn't able to roll down the pants any farther than her hips.

"I'll help," Grant offered, and he picked her up and carried her into the dark bedroom.

He lowered her back onto the mattress but left her legs dangling from the side, and he began to tug at the leather. She came with it, dropping onto her backside next to the bed.

"Ouch!"

"Sorry! Sorry!" he said, and he sounded sincere despite the twinkle of amusement in his eyes. "I'll kiss it and make it better."

"You better," she said as she rubbed her hip.

"Maybe we need scissors," he suggested.

She vehemently shook her head. "No. This outfit is a gift from Blair. I can't destroy it."

"I don't know whether to be grateful to her or mad at her," Grant remarked with a sigh. He knelt on the floor next to her and began to roll the leather down her legs.

His hands were so big, so strong, but yet his touch was so gentle—so seductive. His fingers skimmed along the inside of her thighs as he pushed down the leather—then over her calves. When he pushed the pants over her feet, he rubbed them—massaging her instep. She'd had the high heels to go along with the Sandy outfit, but they must had fallen off when he'd lifted her.

She moaned with pleasure over his touch. But it wasn't enough as tension wound inside her.

"Better?" he asked.

"That's not what hit the ground," she reminded him.

He leaned forward and moved his mouth over her hip to one buttock, pressing kisses along her skin—which tingled and sizzled with awareness. Everywhere he touched her became so sensitive.

He lifted her onto the bed again with just his hands around her hips then slid them up to her waist, which he nearly spanned. "You are so tiny," he mused. "I should think about how easily you can be hurt."

She shook her head. "I'm tough," she assured him. And she was—both physically and emotionally. She could handle whatever came her way with the business, with her family—even with him. "You won't hurt me."

But her words sounded a bit hollow, like she'd felt inside since she'd thrown him out of her apartment.

"No," he said. "I'll just piss you off."

"You're really good at that," she agreed.

"I really just knocked your purse over by accident," he said. "I wasn't snooping."

She was beginning to believe him, and that was dangerous. That was what her mother had always done with all her husbands. She'd believed their lies—about their fortunes, about their sexual preferences, about their fidelity…

Worried that she probably had the same blind spot with men that her mother had, Miranda had decided long ago to trust none of them and to never marry. That way she couldn't get her heart broken.

That was why she couldn't listen to Grant. So to shut him up, she pressed her mouth against his and kissed him. Deeply. Hotly—her tongue sliding in and out of his lips.

He pulled back, panting for breath. "I think I taste Alberta on you."

She smiled. "Jealous?"

"I was," he admitted, his voice gruff with seriousness.

"Good," she said. "I wanted to distract you, so I could beat you."

"And yet I won…"

She figured they'd both won—especially when he moved his mouth from hers, down her neck to her breasts. He tasted each nipple with his tongue, sliding it back and forth until she was nearly writhing on the mattress. Then he moved lower, kissing his way over her stomach to her mound. He knew just where to touch her with his fingers, with his tongue, to drive her wild. Just as she was about to come, he pulled back and she reached out to him in protest.

"Grant…"

Was this payback? Was he just going to tease her?

"What are you doing?" she asked, her voice throaty with the passion—and need—choking her.

"You know…" He had to stop and clear his throat, too. "I won you…"

"Yes, you did," she agreed, and she peered at him over her stomach. His face was as flushed as hers must have been, his eyes almost glassy with his passion. "Oh, so you're saying you first?"

"No…" And he went back down on her, his tongue swirling and teasing her before he drew it out and replaced it with his fingers. Then he licked her clit.

And she came.

The release shuddering through her, she screamed his name. But she knew this wasn't the only orgasm he would give her tonight. He really was the best she'd ever had—in every way.

He'd had his chance. He could have made her beg… maybe agree to anything…

Like leaving his sister and Teo alone.

But when she'd reached out to him and called his name the way she had, she could have asked him anything, and he would have given it to her. And he had…

Now she was giving it to him. She pushed him back so that he was standing—then she undressed him. And she kissed her way down his body like he'd kissed his way down hers.

She swirled her tongue around his nipples and then in his navel, making his stomach clench and his cock pulsate. And then she was there, closing her fingers around him. She pumped him in her hand, running it up and down the length of him. Then she knelt in front of him and, staring up at him with those beautiful pale blue eyes, she extended her tongue and licked him—up and down.

He groaned, and his legs began to shake a little as passion overwhelmed him. Then she closed her mouth over him and sucked him deep in her throat—as deep as she could take him. And her tongue swirled around him...

She could have asked him anything then and he would have happily given it, too. But she didn't pull back; she didn't tease.

On the edge of insanity since she'd walked into the suite in that black leather outfit, he came easily and powerfully—the release exploding out of him with her name.

Still staring up at him, she licked her lips. And despite what she'd just done, his cock stirred again. How could he want her so damn much?

"See?" she said.

And he furrowed his brow in confusion. "See what?"

"You shouldn't have been scared of having a threesome," she teased. "You could have kept up..."

He was up again. And he lifted her and lightly

tossed her onto the bed. "I wasn't scared," he said. "I just don't like to share."

"Oh," she said. "Now if she'd been more interested in you than me, you would have gone for it?"

"No," he said.

She was all he needed. All he would ever need.

The thought stunned him, and he pushed it from his mind. That was crazy.

He wasn't a forever kind of guy. Hell, he knew how short forever could be...especially with what he did when his country called on him.

They'd called again just that morning, with the offer of another dangerous mission.

And for the first time he'd hesitated over accepting it. Because he'd wanted to see her more...

Because those missions weren't the thrill they'd once been for him...

She was.

CHAPTER THIRTEEN

MIRANDA WAS LATE—which was crazy because she
was never late. She drew in a deep breath to quell
the anxiety gripping her before she pulled open the
door to the suite of offices for Liaisons International.

Usually she was the first one to get to the office. But Tabitha had beaten her in today and was
already on the phone. She released the breath she'd
been holding—at least she wouldn't have to answer
any questions about why she was late. Yet...

But before she could open the door to her private
office, Tabitha hung up the phone and remarked,
"Look what the cat dragged in."

Grimacing, Miranda turned back toward her sister. "I don't have a cat," she said.

"Maybe you should," Tabitha said. "Because
you're probably never going to let anyone else live
with you."

Miranda sighed. "You know my place is too
small for you to stay with me."

"I know. I know," Tabitha said.

And even if it wasn't, Tabitha probably would have stayed with Regina anyway. They'd always been closer to each other than to her. Probably because Miranda had had to act more like their mother than their big sister.

Tabitha was acting like her mother now, though. "You look like hell," she said. "Aren't you feeling well?"

She felt sick. Just not physically...

She felt sick that she'd let Grant Snyder get to her so much that she hadn't been able to sleep the past few nights because she hadn't heard from him. She didn't know why she even expected to hear from him. He never called or texted; he just showed up. But she would not be available the next time he showed.

If all it was between them was sex, she would have kept seeing him. But she was beginning to catch feelings for him—that was the illness she'd come down with...

Lying sleepless in the bed he'd once shared with her, wondering what he was doing, whom he was doing.

That was something her mother would have done—obsessing over a man. That was not Miranda. So finally resolved to push him out of her mind, she'd fallen asleep, and because she'd had so much missed sleep to catch up on, she'd slept in.

"I'm fine," she insisted.

Or she would be…

Clearly skeptical, Tabitha stared at her.

"Any messages?" she asked.

"I emailed them to you," Tabitha said. "There aren't any good ones."

Once she'd pulled them up on her laptop at her desk, Miranda had to concur. More women had called to cancel their memberships. And a Snyder had called…

Blair. Not Grant, though. There were no messages from him. But that was for the best.

She'd been getting too attached to him.

But what had happened? Had she offended him with teasing him that he wouldn't be able to please two women? Hell, with the extraordinary lover he was, he would be able to please all the women in Miranda's dating service—especially with the rate they were dropping their memberships.

She sighed. That was why she had to stop obsessing over him; she was going to lose the business if she didn't figure out how the hell to fix it. That was what should have been keeping her awake nights, not him.

Maybe she'd just been using him as a distraction, though, so she didn't have to think about what an epic failure the matchmaking business was turning out to be.

Except for one match…

"There's a good message in here," she called out
to her sister. "Blair's..."

She and Teo were so happy.

Through her closed door, she couldn't hear her
sister's response but imagined it was as snarky as
it ever was regarding her best friend. Her sisters
had always resented her relationship with Blair, but
since Miranda had set her up with the billionaire,
their resentment had grown.

Miranda wished Blair hadn't called the office
number, but she could understand why she had.
Miranda hadn't been returning her text messages.
After texting her that Grant was giving her a ride
back to Monaco, she hadn't texted anything else
to her friend—despite her questions about how the
night had gone.

It had been incredible—as it always was between them. Incredibly sexy. Incredibly fun...

And now incredibly done...

With a sigh of resignation, she picked up the
phone. She'd rather call back Blair than any of their
disgruntled members.

"Hey, stranger," Blair answered her phone. "I
haven't heard from you for a few days."

"I'm sorry," Miranda said. "I've been busy."

"So I hear..."

Not from Grant—since he hadn't been around.

"And I'm the one who's sorry," Blair continued.

"Teo thought his interview would help your business. Not hurt it."

"How do you know…" Tabitha. Of course. She'd taken Blair's message and had apparently given her one of her own. "I'm sorry. And truly, if those women were only members because they were looking to land a rich husband, then they didn't belong at Liaisons International."

In fact most—if not all—of the clients giving up their membership Miranda had inherited when she'd bought out her mother's business. When she'd done so, she'd explained that she wasn't operating her mother's matchmaking business, where the sole objective had been marriage. Her objective was for her members to have some fun and excitement with someone they enjoyed—not whom they wanted taking care of them financially or otherwise.

Blair chuckled. "Guess I didn't belong, then."

"What?" Miranda asked. "Are you…did you and Teo get engaged?"

"Not yet," Blair said. "But he's been hinting—probably so he doesn't scare me off when he drops down on one knee."

"And?" Miranda asked. "Are you scared off?"

"No," Blair said.

And Miranda could hear the smile in her friend's voice.

"Not at all."

Miranda released a shaky sigh.

"Sounds like you're scared for me," Blair said. "Aren't you confident of your matchmaking skills? You promised me Teo is a great guy."

"You know he is," Miranda said.

"So how come you can set me up with a great guy, but you don't want to find one for yourself?"

"I trust my judgment when it comes to other people," Miranda said. "But not myself."

If she'd had good judgment when it came to herself, she wouldn't have slept with Grant once—let alone all the times she'd had.

"You're too hard on yourself," Blair said. "And if things are getting hard with the business, let me know. Teo would love to help out somehow. We really owe you."

"You gave me a fun night out," Miranda reminded her. And it had been fun.

"Grant gave your winnings to Teo," Blair said. "Begrudgingly."

But she hadn't won...

"Then he took off somewhere and we haven't seen him since," Blair said. "Have you?"

Miranda choked on her own saliva. After she stopped coughing, she asked, "Why would I have seen him?"

"He's been making those trips to Monaco lately..."

"Must be for a game," Miranda told her.

He had to be playing games with her. Why would he want to join a dating service when he couldn't even consistently stay in touch with her?

What the hell was he up to?

"Speak of the devil…"

Despite how exhausted he was, he grinned at his sister's remark as he walked into the office off their airplane hangar. He'd just landed on his trip back from that dangerous mission. It had been dangerous—more so because he'd been so damn distracted with thoughts of Miranda than because of the mission itself.

"Tell Teo hi," he said as he dropped into the chair behind his desk.

"It's not Teo," Blair said. "It's Miranda."

His heart flipped, and excitement coursed through him—more excitement than he'd felt even once during his last mission. He'd thought the danger might get his mind off her, but it had only made him think of her more—at some damn inconvenient times. Like when he'd actually been able to sleep but his body had been too tense and achy over wanting hers.

"He must still be pissed over your beating him at poker," Blair said and chuckled.

He swallowed a smile over the lie he'd told. But he'd been too grateful to his sister for buying Miranda that leather outfit to keep any more of her boyfriend's money. Not that Teo would have even missed it.

"Yes, sure, I'll let you go," Blair said into the phone. "I know you're busy. And please, let me know if there's anything I can do to help you."

Fear clenched his gut over that. "What's up?" he asked. "What does she need help with?" Was she okay? Had something happened to her?

"Her business," Blair said, her forehead creasing with concern. "It's down—" she sighed "—a lot thanks to that interview Teo gave."

"Wouldn't that help her out?"

"That's what he thought," Blair said. "But women are angry they didn't get set up with him, and they're leaving."

A twinge struck his heart. He should have been happy that he'd been right about her friend, that he'd had reason to worry. But he just felt sick. "She told you that?"

"Of course not," Blair said with a chuckle. "Tabitha told me."

"But now you know…" Grant murmured.

And Miranda knew she knew. Would she ask Blair to give up Teo?

"Yes."

"You offered to help her," he said. "How?"

Blair narrowed her eyes and studied him. "Finding another good-looking rich guy for her might bring those female members back."

He shuddered at the thought of actually joining the service. "Was that what you meant when you said 'speak of the devil' when I walked in?"

Had they been conspiring about him?

No. Miranda didn't want him joining her dating service. She didn't trust him.

Blair chuckled. "Funny that you knew we were talking about you."

"Was Miranda asking about me?" he asked. Had she missed him like he'd missed her?

Blair shook her head. "No, I was asking her if she'd seen you. Where have you been?"

He shrugged. "Here and there…"

"Are you ever going to be straight with me about whether or not you're really out of the service?" Blair asked.

But having been in herself, she had to know her question was rhetorical.

He couldn't discuss what he did.

So he chuckled instead. "Service? You really thinking about having me sign up for Miranda's dating service?"

Blair shook her head. "I doubt she would take you. She has a thing about honesty."

"And I'm not honest?"

"We both know you're not," his sister said.

"Why does she have such a thing about it?" he wondered.

"Because she wants all the members of Liaisons International to be safe," she said.

"I'm not dangerous."

"But you are," Blair said. "Because you would break hearts with the way you go in and out of a person's life."

He heard the catch of emotion in her voice, and a twinge of regret struck him. "Have I ever hurt you?"

She smiled, but it didn't reach her eyes. "You've done so much for me. You're the best brother. But if you weren't related to me, I wouldn't want to date you."

He grabbed his chest as if she'd stabbed him. He expected her to laugh.

But she continued, "And Miranda would sure as hell never date you."

He nearly choked on the sudden rush of saliva welling up in the back of his throat. She had done more than date him; she'd screwed his brains out. After clearing his throat, he asked, "Why not?"

"Because of all her mother's marriages, she saw firsthand a lot of dishonesty—a lot of lying, cheating and sneaking around."

"Hey!" He wasn't a cheat.

"She won't put up with it in her own life," Blair said. "That's why she won't get involved with anyone."

But she was already involved with him. Wasn't she? Didn't she want him as much as he wanted her?

minding them that true love wasn't about money. It was about emotion, about a connection...

Despite her best efforts, Grant kept popping back into her head. Sure, they had a connection. But it was just sexual. That was all it was; it wasn't emotional.

And she had probably only been so drawn to him because he'd distracted her from her business woes. But she couldn't use him anymore.

She had to focus on her business. So every time he popped into her mind, grinning that wicked grin of his, she pushed him back out. She refused to be distracted.

And some of her effort paid off.

She managed to save a few clients, but she had to draw in some new ones. Ones who weren't tarnished with her mother's desperation to be married whether she'd met the right person or not.

What could she do to draw in new clients? Regina hadn't come up with anything to help their marketing. To help brand them as their new name for the dating service, Liaisons International.

Sure, they had clients from all over the world. But except for Blair and Teo, few of them traveled outside their sphere to meet with other members. Only members within that certain geographical area dated each other.

Was that the problem?

But then, most of the other members weren't

like Blair and Teo, in that they had access to private planes and could fly off at a moment's notice.

Her door burst open, startling Miranda into letting out a little scream. When she realized it was her sister, a twinge of disappointment struck her. She'd wanted it to be Grant. He'd had enough time to make the trip from London to Monaco. If he'd wanted to...

Grant could fly somewhere at a moment's notice. But that was the only part of her new branding that he fit; he wasn't safe.

Not at all...

"What is it?" she asked Tabitha.

Had her sister gotten an audition?

Instead of the relief she expected to feel, that twinge of disappointment struck again. As much as Tabitha and Regina annoyed her sometimes, she did love them very much. And because of that, she wanted what was best for them.

"Did your agent call?" she asked.

The disappointment was clearly all Tabitha's now when she shook her head, sending her red hair flying around her shoulders. "No," she said. "And I should probably fire him. But that's not why I came in here."

She paused for dramatic effect, saying nothing more for a long moment.

Then, as if sick of waiting for Miranda to give her the reaction she wanted, she burst out, "We have a potential new client! And he might be even better than Teo."

"Really?" Miranda asked skeptically.

Matteo Rinaldi was rich and good-looking and more importantly a really good man. That was a trifecta that was hard to find.

"He's a prince," Tabitha said, her green eyes wide with awe.

Miranda snorted. "And he wants to join Liaisons International."

Tabitha nodded. "He wants us to find his Cinderella for him."

"Do I look like a fairy godmother?" Miranda said. The last thing she wanted was to put someone in a situation that made them a target of the media. Even an article that was supposed to have been good, like Teo's, had wound up doing harm.

"You should at least meet with him," Tabitha said. "He already chartered a flight for you. Do you still have your passport on you?"

Miranda nodded. With the way Grant had been coming in and out of her life, she'd figured carrying it was smart. But meeting up with him like she had wasn't.

Not that she was falling for him or anything. She knew better. She was just using him. That was all she was doing. Using him for incredible sex that kept her mind off her business problems.

But maybe setting a few of her female clients up

with the prince would earn their forgiveness for her not setting them up with Teo—if he really was a prince. She had her doubts.

"Where am I going?" Miranda asked as she stood up from her chair. She could use a break from the phone. And there was something about the timing of this meeting that intrigued her, especially now that she knew Grant had resurfaced, at least at home.

Tabitha clapped her hands together with glee. "His private island."

"Okay…" She grabbed her purse from the credenza. "And whom am I meeting?"

"He wouldn't reveal his name until he meets you in person. I guess he doesn't want you alerting the press that he has to enlist a service to find him a mate."

"Okay." She could certainly understand his wanting to date discreetly, if he was truly royalty. But as she headed out the door, doubts flitted through her head.

Hours later, after a helicopter, plane and limo ride, she arrived at an elaborate villa in the middle of a very beautiful island full of leafy green trees and vibrant flowers.

And she wondered…maybe she truly was going to meet a prince. She was pretty certain that this island actually belonged to one from the crests she'd seen on street signs and in the foyer of the villa. The chauffeur had opened the double entrance doors for her and escorted her inside the space that was more courtyard than receiving area. The same trees and flowers from the grounds overflowed the foyer. She drew in a deep breath of fragrant air and something else…

That scent she and Blair had called boy. That she called man now. The chauffeur had gone back out the doors he'd opened for her, but Miranda was no longer alone. She turned around, but she didn't see him…just a dark shadow standing in another doorway, a doorway to a dark room.

Her pulse quickened with excitement and anticipation as, without ever seeing his face, she recognized the *prince*.

Even Grant couldn't believe he'd pulled this scam together so fast. Fortunately the man who owned the island owed him a favor and a whole lot of money from a poker game a few weeks ago. Grant had been the one who'd come up with the royal flush instead of the prince.

Seeing her here, looking all sexy in a wrinkled blouse tucked into a pencil skirt made him feel like he'd won again.

She might not feel as lucky to find out that he'd lured her here under false pretense though. Of course if she finally relented, he would join her dating service; the problem was that she was the only woman he wanted to date, though.

She was all he wanted—which scared him more than that last mission had. But she was worth the fear—to be with her again. If for only one more night...

Was she going to give him that night, though? Or was she going to turn around and walk out once she realized he'd tricked her into coming here?

Instead of walking toward the exterior doors, though, she turned and walked toward him. "Are you hiding from me?" she asked.

"Should I?" he asked, wondering how pissed she was. He couldn't tell from her carefully guarded expression.

Wasn't she happy to see him again? Sure, it had only been a few days since he'd seen her last, but he'd missed her so damn much.

Too much...

How was it that she affected him like no one else ever had? It must have been the sex, which was better than any he'd ever had. He hoped that was all it was. But what if it was more?

What if he was developing feelings for her other than sexual attraction?

Hell, maybe he shouldn't have come back so soon from that last mission. He'd been safer in a war zone than he was here—alone with her.

CHAPTER FIFTEEN

HE WASN'T A PRINCE, but she suspected Grant Snyder was more than the playboy gambler he pretended to be. He was hiding his real identity from her just as he was hiding in the shadows of the doorway behind him.

"Why did you go to all this trouble of getting me here if you're not going to talk to me?" she asked.

"Didn't your sister tell you?" he asked as he finally stepped out of the shadows.

Tabitha. Damn her. "She was in on it with you!"

"I'm not sure she even knew it was me," he said. "I told her that I'm a potential client."

"No, you're not," she said. "Just like you're not a prince either." But what was he really?

"I have a throne," he said. He tugged her inside the dark room with him. After flipping on a switch, a lone light illuminated a throne-like chair carved of highly polished wood with jeweled accents and a purple velvet cushion.

"Did you win it in a poker game?" she asked. Was that where he'd been the last few days that even his sister hadn't known where he'd gone?

He chuckled. "Not for keeps, just for a bit."

"So you've been playing poker the past few days?" she asked.

His lips curved into a slight grin as he stared down at her. "You missed me?"

She had missed him. Too damn much. But she didn't want him to know that, didn't want him to know he was getting to her. She shook her head. "No, it was a welcome reprieve."

"Really?" he asked. "You're the one who sought me out last, coming to that poker game."

She had, but she wasn't about to admit it. "Blair and Teo talked me into it. I just did it for them."

He snorted. "Like Blair has ever talked you into anything. It's always been the other way around." His grin slipped away then as his forehead creased with concern.

"Blair is not a child," she said. "She is a strong-willed woman with a mind of her own. I haven't ever talked her into anything she didn't really want to do."

He sighed. "She is strong or she wouldn't have made it through our childhood let alone her career as a fighter pilot."

"Exactly." She knew how hard it had been for Blair growing up with her disinterested parents. But she hadn't realized then that it might have been hard for Grant, too. He'd always seemed so unaffected by it all. So unaffected by everything…

But her.

She had affected him. He'd always lost his cool with her, warning her away from his sister. He was so protective of Blair.

"So why have you always given me such a hard time about her?" she wondered.

He drew in a shaky breath before grinning again. But it seemed forced, like it didn't quite reach his dark blue eyes. They didn't crinkle at the corners like they did when he was really happy. "I just like giving you a hard time…"

Her pulse quickened at the double entendre. She had missed him. So much…

And she'd worked so hard today, listening to so many complaints that she just wanted to forget about the business and lose herself in pleasure only. Lose herself in Grant…

Fear licked through her for a moment. She didn't want to lose herself—ever—in any man. She didn't want to become her mother.

"Are you okay?" Grant asked, his voice deep with concern.

She nodded. "Of course…" She was more self-aware than her mother. And she was more aware of Grant as well. She couldn't lose herself in a man who wasn't going to stick around anyway. "Let's not talk about Blair," she said. "Hell, let's not talk at all." She pulled his head down to hers and kissed him.

His breath shuddered out against her lips, but then he kissed her back—just as passionately as she was kissing him. Their lips nibbled. Tongues tangled.

She could have kissed him for hours. But he pulled back and trailed his lips down her throat, and the tension wound inside her as her body demanded more. Demanded the release that he could give her.

She reached for the buttons on his shirt, tugging them free, so that she could push the navy silk from his shoulders. But as she did, she noticed wounds on his muscular body—bruises and scrapes. "What the hell…" she murmured. "What happened to you?"

"I thought we weren't talking," he reminded her. Then he lifted her from her feet, swinging her up in his arms. But a grimace crossed his face as he carried her, and she knew he was hurt.

"Put me down," she said.

And he did, but not until he'd carried her through the throne room to another room where he dropped her onto the silk sheets of an enormous bed. He joined her on the bed and leaned over her. But she reached up for his shoulders, holding him back. "Grant, what happened to you?" she asked.

He shrugged. "I don't know what you're talking about…"

"These bruises and scrapes…you didn't have them the last time we were together…" She would have noticed anything marring the perfection of his muscular body.

"Well, you did get kind of aggressive with me," he teased.

And she knew he wasn't going to answer her. Why? Because he couldn't, like Blair suspected, admit what he really did? Or because he just didn't want to share anything of himself with her but his body?

"Grant…"

"That's your royal highness to you," he persisted in teasing her.

"Did you fight the real prince for this place?" she asked. "Is that how you got these bruises?"

He chuckled. "The real prince is nearly eighty years old so…"

"You beat up an old man?" she asked, teasing him back, because she knew that was all they were going to do. They weren't going to be honest with each other about themselves. She couldn't even be honest with herself about what she was beginning to feel for him.

Too much…

Too much concern and passion and interest…

He'd gotten to her more than she'd ever believed he would. And she didn't really even know him…

"He is a pretty tough guy," Grant said.

"Maybe we should introduce him to my mother," she said. "She's always wanted to marry royalty."

"I thought she didn't care who she married," Grant remarked.

She must have flinched because he quickly apologized.

"I'm sorry," he said. "I shouldn't say anything about your mother."

She sighed. "Why not? She probably hit on you in the past like she has every other man she's met."

He slid his finger under her chin and tipped it up, so their eyes met and held. "She didn't," he assured her. "And let's not talk about Blair or your mother..."

"Or your bruises?" she surmised.

He grinned. "Especially not those..." He leaned down and kissed her then, lightly brushing his lips across hers before trailing them down her throat.

Her pulse leaped beneath his mouth as he suckled at it. She wanted him, wanted this...too much to deny either of them. So she shimmied quickly out of her clothes while he shrugged off his shirt and shucked off his pants.

Then they were naked, nothing between them but those scrapes and bruises. She couldn't entirely ignore them—like he obviously wanted her to—so she kissed them gently, as if her touch would somehow heal them.

He sucked in a breath and murmured her name.

And she knew that he was as affected as she was by the attraction that burned between them. He wanted her just as badly as she wanted him.

He pushed her back against the mattress and closed his lips around a nipple then flicked his tongue over it.

She arched up from the mattress, needing his touch, needing him so badly.

As if he'd read his mind, he cupped her mound in his hand and slid his fingers inside her. He stroked her while he continued to tease her nipple with his tongue.

Desire throbbed inside her. And she shifted and arched against him, needing release. It came—she came—just a little, just enough that a soft cry slipped out of her lips.

He started moving lower, but she grabbed his shoulders. "I need you...inside me," she told him.

His throat moved as he swallowed hard. "I need to be inside you," he said.

He felt around under one of the many pillows on the bed until he found a condom packet. She took it from him, tore it open with her teeth and rolled it over his erection. Then she parted her legs wide for him.

He drove deep into her core—over and over again—building the pressure. She arched up, hooking her legs over his shoulders. Her thighs rubbed against her already taut nipples, adding to her pleasure.

And he drove even deeper before pulling slightly out again. Over and over he thrust. Faster and faster.

The pressure built inside her even more, making her feel as if she was going to explode. Then she came—over and over again. She couldn't stop coming...

The orgasm was never-ending as he continued to move. Then he tensed and yelled her name, his big body shuddering with the force of his release.

How was it like this between them every time? So damn incredible...

Grant felt exposed to Miranda in a way he'd never felt with anyone else. She'd seen more than his scrapes and bruises. And that knowledge had creased her forehead with concern.

He didn't want her to worry about him. Or them...

So he made sure to relieve all her concern and tension as he gave her orgasm after orgasm. He lay back against the pillows, panting for breath and said, "Now this has to be the perfect date."

"For you, maybe," she said as she leaned over him, her naked breasts rubbing against his chest. "But what do I get out of this?"

"At last count, I think about ten orga—"

She pressed her fingers over his mouth. "I'm not

a madam, you know. I don't let people join the service just because they're good at sex."

"Good?" he growled against her fingers. "Just good?"

She shrugged her naked shoulders. "Like I said, the perfect date isn't all about sex. You lured me here with the promise of royalty joining Liaisons International."

She was concerned about her business. Concerned enough to lure a particular billionaire back into dating? Grant wondered.

"The prince still owes me," he said. "I'll make him sign up for the service. His wife might not approve though."

"Is that where you got your bruises?" she asked. "Jealous husband?" There was something in her voice as she posed the question, something that almost sounded like jealousy.

"I don't mess with married women," he said.

"Just me?"

"Are you married?"

She shuddered in obvious revulsion. "God, no! My mother got married enough times for her, me and my sisters."

The tension was back in her body, the crease back in her forehead. He didn't want her worried right now—about anything.

"So what is your idea of the perfect date?" he

asked, to take her mind of her mother and her other troubles.

"Someone being completely honest and vulnerable with me," she said with a pointed stare.

And he knew his efforts had been futile all this time. He could never give her what she wanted; he could never be her perfect date. But for as long as she would stay with him in the villa, he could—at least—be her perfect lover.

CHAPTER SIXTEEN

THE IMAGE OF Grant with those bruises and scrapes marring his perfect body haunted Miranda. She couldn't stop thinking about them, about him, even during this business meeting with her sisters that was taking place in the reception area of the office suite after regular business hours. When she should be listening to them, she kept thinking about Grant. He'd not wanted her concern though, so he'd kept distracting her with sex and with silly jokes and fun games...

Thinking of his silliness, she had to swallow down the chuckle that tickled the back of her throat. But she couldn't keep the smile from tugging up her lips.

"You think this is funny?" Regina asked. "I quit my IT job to go into business with you, and there's no way we're going to earn enough to support the two of us, let alone all three of us. We need to do something."

Miranda sighed. "I am trying," she said.

"She really is," Tabitha said, surprisingly coming to her defense. "She stopped some of the members from leaving, and she met with a potential new one. A prince."

So Grant was right; Tabitha hadn't realized who he was. How good of an actor was he that he'd fooled the actress so easily? Not that Tabitha was that great an actress or she wouldn't have kept getting fired.

Regina arched a dark brow. "Really? Did you sign him up?"

Miranda shook her head.

"Why not?"

She sighed. "Because it wasn't really a prince. It was Grant Snyder pretending to be one."

Tabitha gasped and then giggled. "He's good. He really had me going."

And he'd had Miranda coming and coming and coming...

She was surprised she wasn't severely dehydrated after all the sex she'd had with him. She hadn't seen or heard from him since she'd come home, but it had only been a couple of days so far. She wasn't giving up on him yet—because she didn't think he was giving up.

On her?

Or on joining the dating service?

"And you didn't sign him up?" Regina asked.

"He lied and lured me out to a remote island," Miranda said.

Tabitha emitted a soft, wistful sigh. "Sounds romantic to me."

It had been, but Miranda wasn't going to admit it aloud. She'd tried to not even admit it to herself, but she couldn't stop thinking about it, about him...

She cleared the desire from her throat and asked, "How does that fit in with our promise of complete honesty from all our members?"

"At least he'd be a member. Blair wasn't even one when you set her up with our most eligible one," Regina said. "That wasn't honest, either, Miranda. You shouldn't have done that."

"Blair is my best friend," she reminded them— needlessly. They both rolled their eyes when she said it.

"And if Blair was really the great friend you think she is," Regina said, "she would give him up to save our business."

"Blair is my best friend," she repeated. So that was why she would never let her friend sacrifice her happiness for business, especially not when that friend was happier than she'd ever seen her.

"So she'll do it," Tabitha said.

Miranda shook her head.

"You two have always vowed how you'll never get married," Regina reminded her. "Ever. So what's the big deal if Matteo goes out on some dates with other women?"

Tabitha wiggled her red brows. "A woman like me?"

"That would break the rules—"

"Says the ultimate rule breaker," Tabitha interjected.

"I'm not breaking any rules—"

"Grant Snyder—"

"Is not a member."

"He should be," Tabitha argued. "He's sexy as hell and he must be rich, since Blair didn't have enough money to start that private charter business on her own."

"She's an equal partner," Miranda defended her friend.

Tabitha snorted as if she wasn't buying it. But they had never bothered to get to know Blair like she knew Blair.

Just as Miranda and Blair had vowed to never marry, they had also vowed to never let anyone have financial control over them. That was why they'd wanted their own businesses—to be in control and self-sufficient. Blair had taken out a loan to finance half of the business so that she would be an equal partner. But she'd admitted that Grant had offered to put up all the money. And he hadn't even needed a loan. Did he really make that much from gambling?

"And if Grant has money, I have no idea where it's coming from," Miranda admitted.

"Who cares?" Tabitha asked. "Even if he was broke, it wouldn't matter because he's so damn good-looking."

He was. Miranda could not argue that.

"Let him join," Regina concurred.

The thought of Grant dating other women made Miranda's stomach churn. Was she jealous? Had she somehow become possessive of him?

She shook her head.

"Why not?" Regina asked. "Do you want to keep him for yourself?"

"I can't keep what I've never had," she insisted. "I just don't trust him."

And that was the real problem between them. As much as she wanted him, she couldn't risk the lack of trust turning her into her mother—insecure and dependent.

"Then don't date him," Regina said. "And let some of our clients decide if they want to trust him."

She shook her head. "No. I have to protect them from getting hurt."

"That's your problem," Regina said. "You think you always have to take care of everyone else—like Blair. And you don't care about—"

A knock rattled the door, cutting off whatever else Regina had been about to say. Not that Miranda had wanted to hear it. She had proposed this business with her sisters to help take care of them. But it was clear they didn't appreciate what she'd been trying to do.

She jumped up from the reception area couch and opened the door to the hall. To Grant. And she was so happy to see him again that a smile immediately curved her lips. But he didn't return it.

Instead the corners of his mouth had turned down into a frown. His face was flushed, and his eyes were cold. What was he angry about?

Because she had no doubt that he was angry; she just didn't understand why.

Grant was furious. So furious that he had barely managed to resist the urge to break down the door and join in their shouting match. Even if he hadn't intended to eavesdrop—and he had—he wouldn't have been able to *not* overhear them.

These women really expected his sister to just give up the love of her life. Or worse yet, to share him with the desperate, money-grubbing members.

In order to support themselves...

He wanted to shout at them that it was cruel and immoral. And just as he'd been about to break down the door to call them that, they'd started talking about him.

Apparently the sisters didn't care if he was broke,

but Miranda did. She didn't trust him around those money-grubbing clients of hers.

And apparently she didn't trust him around her sisters, either, because she opened the door to her private office and gestured for him to proceed her inside. "You two can leave for the night," she told them.

They didn't argue with her now. Maybe they'd noticed how angry he was. She had—because the minute they left, she asked, "What's wrong?"

"I think you know what's wrong," he murmured. She was going to betray her best friend; he just knew that she would. To save herself and her sisters, she would betray Blair and Teo.

That was why he'd lied to her—to protect his sister. And she didn't trust him over that—because he hadn't been completely honest with her.

Hell, he couldn't be completely honest with anyone—not even his own sister. And he loved her more than anything. He loved her so much that he would seriously join this damn dating service if it would get Miranda and her sisters to let Blair and Matteo enjoy their happiness.

"You overheard that meeting," she murmured. Then she uttered a heavy, weary-sounding sigh.

"They're right, you know," he said. "Just let me join the damn service." Hell, he would pay her enough to take care of her and her sisters. He probably made enough in a week on the professional poker circuit to operate her business for a year.

She sucked in a breath. "You really want to join that badly?"

No. It was the last thing he wanted to do. But he would go out with a couple of gold diggers if it would ensure his sister's happiness.

He shrugged. "Why do you think I've been auditioning for you?"

"Because you love to play games," she said. "Because you wanted to mess with me for some reason..."

Because he didn't want her messing with Blair and Teo. And he'd obviously been right to worry about that—about *her*.

"We're not kids anymore, Miranda," he said. And he was suddenly weary, too.

He'd been having so damn much fun with her. So damn much amazing sex with her...

He'd been getting used to it—to her. Maybe even attached...

Damn...

Something must have gotten in his eyes—because he had to blink. Maybe it was just the red of anger blinding him.

"No, we're not," she agreed. "I have a business to run—to try to build. I can't take a chance on you—on the fact that you have grown up."

"Damn it, Miranda," he said. "What do I need

to do? Show you a tax return? I've got money, and that seems like the only thing your members are really interested in—"

"Not the members I want to keep," she interjected. "Not the ones I want to sign up. I don't want to run my mother's matchmaking business. I don't want dating to be all about desperation and the fear of being alone."

"What do you want it to be about?" he wondered.

"Fun," she said. "It should be fun."

"Haven't you had fun with me?" he asked. "Hasn't every date been fun?"

"Sure, until I caught you going through my purse."

"I told you that was an accident," he said. "I don't need or want your money."

She snorted. "That's good—because I don't have any. So what do you want from me, Grant?"

A strange stillness overcame her after she asked the question, as if she'd frozen into a statue of herself. She didn't move. She didn't breathe.

Did she care that much what his answer was?

Her stillness made him freeze. He didn't know how to answer her, so he asked a question of his own. "What do you want from me, Miranda?"

She stared at him so intently, for such a long time, before replying, "For you to be honest with me…"

He opened his mouth, intending to do just that—

to tell her about his initial reason for coming to see her—to warn her not to mess up Blair's happiness this time. But something kept him from giving her that kind of honesty. Maybe it was just his damn pride. "I have more money than Teo does," he said. "And I can show you the bank statements to prove it."

She flinched.

"What?" he asked. "Isn't that what you want?"

She shook her head. "No..."

"But you wanted honesty—"

"Honestly answer what you want from me," she said.

A strange sensation, like the ground shifting beneath his feet, unsettled him. This was important—this would change everything.

And he'd really been enjoying how things had been between them.

CHAPTER SEVENTEEN

SHE WAS FURIOUS— with him for eavesdropping on the business meeting with her sisters. Sure, they'd been shouting, but he could have knocked sooner. He could have let them know he was out there, listening to them talk about *him*. But as furious as she was with him, she was even more furious with herself.

How could she want him so damn much when it was clear he'd never really wanted her?

Tears stung her eyes, but she blinked them away. She was not going to cry over a man; she'd made that vow many years ago, after all the times her mother had brokenheartedly wept over another failed relationship.

This hadn't even been a relationship. It had just been sex.

That was all it had been—for both of them.

So she stopped waiting for the answer she already knew he was going to give her, and she turned to walk around her desk. But she hadn't made it a foot away when his hand closed around her arm and he spun her toward him—into his arms.

"I want you," he said.

Those traitorous tears stung again. "You don't even like me."

"You don't like me."

"No," she corrected him. "I don't trust you." But she had begun to like him very much. He was funny and sweet and protective of his sister. But none of that mattered when she couldn't trust him.

Because even though he said he wanted her, he also wanted to join the damn dating service. And even if he wouldn't break their hearts, she still didn't want him dating other women. She didn't want him dating anyone but her.

"You know I want you," Grant said. "That you make me crazy every time we're together…" He lowered his head then and covered her mouth with his.

She kissed him back—because she would rather kiss him than talk at the moment. Hell, she would rather kiss him than do anything else, except him.

She wanted to do him. One last time…

After today, she knew she couldn't see him again. She'd already let him get too close—close to making her care about him. Fall for him, even—and that could not happen.

Her anger and frustration heightened her passion, making her tear at the buttons on his shirt with such desperation that one pinged off and struck the wall.

He chuckled against her mouth, but he seemed just as desperate as she was. He pushed up her skirt and pushed aside her panties. Then he stroked her, over and over until her legs began to shake and threatened to buckle beneath her.

Before she could slide to the floor in a puddle of passion, he lifted and perched her on the edge of her desk. "I wanted to do this the first time I saw you in here," he admitted, his voice gruff. "Looking so damn sexy…"

He tugged at the buttons on her blouse until it parted and revealed her lace bra. Her breasts strained to escape the cups. Then he pushed it down and cupped them in his hands, his thumbs stroking over the taut nipples.

She moaned at the exquisite pleasure, at the sexual energy streaking through her—from her breasts to her core that throbbed with desire. She needed him inside her. Now.

"Grant…"

He kissed her again, quickly, passionately—lips nibbling, tongues tangling…

Then he lowered his head to her breasts, kissing them, tonguing her nipples…

And he dropped to his knees and tongued her clit. She grasped his shoulders as an orgasm rocked her and she cried out. It wasn't fair how easily he could make her come, how powerfully...

And how powerless she felt to resist him.

But she also felt power in that he wanted her just as badly. His blue eyes had turned dark with desire, the pupils swallowing the irises entirely. His face was flushed, a vein standing out along his neck.

Then she unbuttoned his jeans and lowered his zipper. And his cock sprang free, jutting toward her as if begging to come inside.

He groaned as she wrapped her fingers around him and pumped her hand up and down. Up and down the engorged length of him...

"I gotta be inside you," he said. "Now!" His hands shook as he fumbled with a condom, but he had it on in seconds. Then he entered her in one deep thrust.

She cried out again as pleasure overwhelmed her. How did he always feel so damn good? So perfect...

She locked her legs around him, riding him as he set the rhythm of this dance. Fast. Desperate. He built the pressure inside her again, making her writhe around as she sought to release it.

Then he touched her clit, rubbing his thumb over it, and she came apart, screaming his name. And those tears threatened again. She closed her eyes. So she didn't see him come. She only felt him tense and then shudder as an orgasm came over him. He buried his face against her throat and growled her name as his cock continued to pump. Then finally he stilled…

And he was gone…

He'd pulled out of her, and she'd been so limp with sexual satisfaction that she hadn't protested. Water ran in the bathroom off her office.

The sound of it jerked her from her inertia. She scrambled down from the desk and quickly adjusted her clothes. In her haste, she might had done up the buttons wrong, so she found her suit jacket on the back of her chair and pulled that on over the wrinkled blouse.

The water had stopped running, so she looked up and found him leaning against the bathroom doorjamb, staring at her. She didn't give him time to ask if he'd passed this audition; she was sick of that game, sick of playing all games with him. She just pointed toward the door to the reception area. "I want you to leave," she said.

"Mirand—"

"I want you to leave and never come back," she said. "No matter how hard you try to talk me into it, I will never let you join Liaisons International. I don't care how much money you have."

Because she knew she couldn't trust him not to break the hearts of all her female members…

Because she was pretty sure he'd broken hers.

* * *

Grant wanted to hit something.

Usually he didn't let anything get to him this much—make him this angry. But he couldn't stem the fury that coursed through him. She'd thrown him out.

Why was she so damn stubborn?

With how resolute she'd been, he'd known there had been no point in arguing with her. She'd made up her mind, and he doubted he could have changed it no matter what he'd done. Even if he'd showed her the bank statements like he'd offered...

He stomped down the hall from the hangar toward the office. It was late, so hopefully no one else was in the building. But when he walked into the office, two people turned toward him. They shared the chair behind Blair's desk as she sat on Teo's lap.

He shook his head. "I can't deal with this now," he murmured. With another damn reminder of his failure to get through to Miranda.

Blair jumped up and headed toward him. "What's wrong?"

He shook his head.

She pointed at his shirt, where it gaped around the missing button. "You look like you've been in a fight."

He had been...and as usual with Miranda Fox, he'd lost. "I don't want to talk about it," he said, his voice low with warning. Talking about it was only going to make him madder.

Teo was not intimidated. "I think your brother is just jealous," he said with a chuckle. "He wishes he could find what we have."

Blair laughed. "Grant has no interest in a real relationship."

Because of their parents' loveless marriage and all the other mismatches he'd witnessed during his lifetime. But then there was Miranda…

Thinking of her made him defensive—because he'd felt so defenseless with her. Nothing he'd said had made a difference to her. "You didn't want a relationship, either," he reminded his sister.

Her lips curved into a big smile. "But then I fell in love."

He shook his head. "It won't last."

She sucked in a breath. And Teo jumped up now.

"Just because you're in a bad mood, don't take it out on your sister," the businessman ordered Grant.

"I'm in a bad mood because of you guys," he admitted.

And Blair pressed a hand over her heart as if he'd stabbed her. "I didn't realize you had a problem with us."

He shook his head, further frustrated that it was all coming out wrong. But he needed to warn them. "I'm not the one with the problem," he said. "It's Miranda and those damn sisters of hers…"

Blair narrowed her eyes. "What are you talking about?"

"The sisters are pissed that she set you up with the billionaire there, and since he did that interview, they're losing clients right and left."

"How do you know all this?" Blair asked. Then she snapped her fingers. "That's why you've been going to Monaco lately. Not for poker games but for..." She tilted her head. "What the hell have you been doing, Grant?"

"Trying to protect you," he said.

She laughed. "I can protect myself," she assured him. "I've been doing it for quite a while now."

Teo was smiling, too.

They didn't realize how damn serious this was. "Your happiness is at stake here—don't you realize that?"

"How?" Blair asked.

"The sisters want Miranda to make you give Teo up."

Blair chuckled. "Of course they do."

"Doesn't that bother you?"

"They've never liked me," Blair said with a dismissive shrug. "They've always been jealous of how close Miranda and I are." She stared at him. "I don't think they're the only ones who've resented our closeness."

"I didn't resent it," Grant said. "I just worried

about it because she's always been able to talk you into doing stupid things."

She snorted.

"And giving up Teo would be stupid," he said. "I've never seen you this happy."

"I've never been this happy," she admitted. "And there's no way anyone could talk or pressure me into giving up the best thing that's ever happened to me."

Teo wrapped his arm around her waist and pulled her back against him. "*Ti amo...*"

Grant shook his head. "But you know how persuasive Miranda is."

"Yes," Blair agreed. "She talked me into going out with him."

"So you can understand—"

"No!" she interjected. "I can't understand why you think I'm such an idiot that I would allow anyone to talk me into doing something I didn't want to do in the first place. And I can't understand how you think my very best friend would betray me."

"Miranda—"

"Miranda loves me as much as you do. Maybe more—because she respects me," Blair said. "You don't."

Grant shook his head. "Of course I do. I know how hard you've worked. I know—"

About their shared past...

But Miranda had shared that past, too. She knew

Blair as well as he did—probably better. And as she'd pointed out, his sister was incredibly strong-willed. She wouldn't have let anyone talk her into doing something she hadn't really wanted to do.

"You don't know Miranda," she said. "Or you would know that she would never ask me to sacrifice my happiness for her business. Hell, she won't even let us help her with it, and we've both offered."

He groaned as that frustration coursed through him again. "I know. I offered to join her damn dating service, and she refused."

Blair laughed. "You were willing to make such a sacrifice? And she turned you down? I can't imagine why…"

He glared at his sister. "Neither can I." He dropped wearily into the chair behind his desk. He was so damn tired.

Teo chuckled. "Yes, you made such a magnanimous offer…"

"I did," he insisted. "I told her I would even show her my bank statements—since all her damn clients seem interested in his money."

"Ouch," Teo said. "Is that my only appeal?"

Blair glanced at him and nodded. "Yes. You're so damn ugly…"

Instead of being offended, her boyfriend laughed. He knew he was good-looking.

Grant was, too, though. "Her sisters tried to talk

Miranda into letting me join. They think I'm good-looking."

"You've always been mean to Miranda," Blair said. "Why did you think she would trust you to treat her clients any differently?"

"Because her clients aren't trying to mess up my sister's happiness."

Blair's brow furrowed. "But isn't that exactly what they're doing? They all wanted a shot with the man she set up with me. That's why they're angry and leaving or threatening to leave. Catering to them isn't going to save her business. Miranda already told me that. She wants new clients—not the ones she inherited when she bought out her mom."

His head was beginning to pound. "She said something about that…"

"But you weren't listening," Blair accused. "You never listened to Miranda. You just yelled at her—"

"I did not yell," he insisted. "I did everything but yell at her…"

Blair stepped closer to him and pointed toward his missing button. "What exactly was *everything*? Have you been harassing my best friend?"

"I've been auditioning for her," he said. "Trying to prove to her that I could be the perfect date."

Both Blair and Teo laughed—too hard and too long.

Heat flushed his face, but it wasn't anger this time but embarrassment. "I was doing it for the two of you," he said. "You should show some appreciation."

"That you thought so little of us and our relationship that we would break up for any reason?" Teo asked and shook his head. "No. I do not feel any sympathy for you, my friend."

"My sympathy is for Miranda," Blair said with a sigh. "I hope she forgives me."

"Forgives you?" Grant asked.

"She sure as hell isn't forgiving you," Blair said. "Not for thinking so little of her. And I don't even know what you mean by auditioning and I don't want to know."

His anger was gone now, leaving only this sick feeling in his stomach and this hollow ache in his heart. He'd screwed up his mission. And he wasn't sure if he'd ever be able to make it right—with his sister and Teo.

And especially with Miranda.

CHAPTER EIGHTEEN

"WILL YOU FORGIVE ME?"

Miranda hadn't expected to hear those words...
from Blair. She wasn't the Snyder who owed her
an apology. "For what?" she asked. "You haven't
done anything wrong."

Blair sat across the table from her—at that rooftop restaurant that reminded Miranda entirely too
much of one of her *perfect* dates with Grant.

"I know what my idiot brother has done," Blair
said, her blue eyes brimming with remorse. "And
I am so sorry."

"He told you?" Miranda asked, stunned that he
would have confessed to his sister the games he'd
played with her. That they'd played with each other.

Blair nodded. "I can't believe he thought you
would try to break up me and Teo so you could set
him up with other women."

"What?" Miranda asked, her head beginning to
pound with confusion.

"I know that's why he's been coming to Monaco," Blair continued. "To warn you away from me, just like he did when we were kids."

Miranda shook her head. "Oh, he didn't go about it the way he did when we were kids." He'd been so much subtler—so subtle that until now she hadn't even realized what he'd been doing.

Blair sighed. "I know he said he didn't yell, but he never thinks he's yelling—"

"It's his voice," Miranda interjected. It was so deep and rumbly and sexy…just like him.

"So he did yell?"

Miranda shook her head. "No, I didn't even know what he was up to. He claimed he wanted to join Liaisons International…" So he'd been lying to her—about everything…

Blair nodded. "Yes, he said he offered, so that he could somehow replace Teo. I actually think he was trying to help out your business."

"I don't want his help." All she'd wanted was him, but it had all been a lie.

Blair chuckled. "That's what I told him. That he'd disrespected both of us. That there's no way I would give up the best thing that's ever happened to me…" Her voice cracked, and tears sprang to her eyes.

Miranda reached across the table and patted her hand. She'd never seen her friend so emotional.

"And I hope you know that I would never ask you to…"

"Of course I know that," she said. "I know that you don't listen to your sisters. Unfortunately Grant was listening to them, though."

"He really thought that I would do that to you?" Miranda asked, and that hollow ache she'd had in her chest intensified even more so that she could barely draw a breath.

"He knows now that he was wrong," Blair said. "Hasn't he tried to apologize?"

He'd been calling, but she'd figured it was just to join the service. So she'd ignored the texts and emails and all the messages he'd left with Tabitha.

Miranda shrugged. "I don't want to hear it." It would be much safer for her heart if she never heard his voice again.

"I don't blame you…" Blair trailed off and reached for her glass, taking a long sip of her red.

And Miranda narrowed her eyes. "But?"

"He does feel really bad," Blair continued. "He's apologized to me and Teo so much that we've forgiven him. But he's still miserable."

Miranda could relate. She'd never felt like this before, and she never wanted to risk feeling like this again.

"He talked about going on auditions with you."

They were friends—close friends—but Miranda

couldn't talk about her lover with his sister. It was just wrong. She shook her head.

But Blair persisted. "He said he was trying to show you perfect dates."

"Yet he somehow kept screwing them up," Miranda said.

"But he lost to you in poker—"

She shook her head again. "He didn't lose. He just didn't want to take any more of Teo's money."

"Oh…" Blair's shoulders slumped.

"What?"

"I was thinking that he was falling for you," Blair said and smiled wistfully. "I was hoping he was…"

"Why?"

"I always wanted you to be my sister."

"That's why I didn't want to talk to you about this," Miranda said. "Because nothing's changed. I still don't ever want to get married. I don't want to be in love, even."

But she had the sick feeling that it might have been too late for that…that she'd fallen for the worst man for her. For one she couldn't trust…

"If you don't want to be with him, why won't you let him join Liaisons?" Blair asked.

And Miranda groaned. "Et tu, Brute?"

Blair chuckled. "This might be the one thing your sisters and I agree on—Grant would be a draw for your business."

Miranda shook her head. "I don't care about his money. I don't want clients who care, either."

"You want it to be about fun," Blair said. "And Grant is fun."

Miranda couldn't argue about that; she'd had a lot of fun with him. But she couldn't share that with her clients. She couldn't share Grant with anyone.

She wouldn't take his calls or return his messages. So Miranda had left him no choice—had given him no chance to apologize.

But when he showed up at her office, she was already gone.

"With your sister," Tabitha told him, and there was that trace of resentment in her voice. She and the dark-haired one who stood in the doorway to her office were really jealous of Blair.

His sister did have it all though—guts, brains, beauty...and now a billionaire. She also had the biggest, most loyal heart.

That was why he'd thought she might have been persuaded to give up Teo to save Liaisons International. But he'd been a fool to even consider it.

Blair loved Teo, and he loved her. Even if she had broken up with him, he wouldn't have started dating anyone else. Grant didn't want to date anyone else, and he and Miranda hadn't really even been dating.

"You're wasting your time," the dark-haired one

told him. If he remembered what Blair had said, her name was Regina. "She's not going to change her mind."

"Ditto," he said. "You guys are wasting your time, too, trying to get her to talk Blair into giving up the billionaire."

"We know," Regina said.

"She loves your sister more than she does us," the red-haired one resentfully remarked. Her name was Tabitha.

"Not more," he said. Blair had also explained to him how Miranda had always had to take care of her sisters because her mom was such a flake. "Just differently. She loves my sister like she's her sister—"

"But we're her sisters," Tabitha lamented.

As if she hadn't interrupted, he continued, "And she loves you two like you're her daughters."

Regina's mouth fell open, and her brow furrowed.

Tabitha laughed but then nodded. "She does act like a mother."

"Not our mother," Regina said. "Since our mother never acted like one…"

"At least I had a great stepmom," Tabitha said, and she turned toward her sister. "You and Miranda were the ones who didn't really have moms."

"I have a great dad," Regina said. "And Miranda had…"

"Blair," Grant said.

Tears sprang to Tabitha's eyes. "Oh my God…" She swallowed back a soft sob. "Because of our custody arrangements, we didn't have to spend that much time there. But she was always there, and she would have been alone…"

"If not for Blair," Grant said.

Regina uttered a ragged-sounding sigh. "We've been such bitches."

"Yes," Grant said.

"You've been an ass," Regina accused him.

And he nodded in agreement. "A total jackass," he acknowledged.

None of them had understood or appreciated how important Blair and Miranda's friendship was— to both of them. After her temper toward him had cooled off, his sister had explained it to Grant, and for the first time, he'd really listened and accepted how important Miranda was to her.

And to him…

"So what are we going to do to make it up to her?" he asked. Because he needed help.

Blair had already told him that she wanted nothing to do with it. Like her friend, she didn't trust him not to hurt Miranda.

Miranda was tougher than Blair thought, though. Or maybe she was more vulnerable than he thought.

"What do you mean?" Regina asked. "We already tried. You already tried. There's no way she's letting you join."

"I don't really want to join," he admitted. "I want to help."

"Joining would help," Tabitha said. "If you could market him, Regina…" She uttered a lustful-sounding sigh.

And heat rushed to his face. He hadn't minded laying himself bare for Miranda, but he didn't like her sisters undressing him with their eyes.

"Sounds like the business needs capital," he said. "I can buy in or give you a loan."

Regina shook her head. "I wish…"

"She won't allow that, either," Tabitha said.

"I thought you all owned this business together," he remarked.

"Set up with her having the most control and power," Regina said. "Miranda really has to be in control at all times."

He could correct them about that. He'd seen her out of control many times, screaming his name as she came over and over again.

But he'd already infuriated Miranda enough. He wasn't going to give her yet another reason not to trust him.

"It doesn't sound as if you two are very happy with the business," he observed.

"I'd rather be on the stage," Tabitha admitted.

"And I'd rather be at home," Regina added.

"So if you can't take a loan…how about selling your shares of the business?"

"To you?" Tabitha asked.

And he figured he was going to have to show his bank statements after all.

But Regina interjected, "We can't. Miranda set it up so that we can't sell without giving her first option."

"Well, she's not going to be able to buy you out." He knew what she had in her bank account, and even two-thirds of a flailing business was worth more than that.

"If you can't sell them," he mused, "can you lose them?" And he drew a deck of cards out of the pocket of his jacket.

Tabitha giggled.

And Regina asked, "You want us to lose our shares to you?"

"You might be able to beat me," he said.

"Miranda taught us how to play," Tabitha said. "We're actually pretty good."

"Not as good as she is," Regina said. "But we are pretty good."

"So what do we get if you lose?" Tabitha asked, and she was eyeing him that way that made him feel naked again.

"Money," he said. "And it won't be a loan…it'll be yours to put into the business."

The sisters exchanged a glance, Tabitha's red brows arching high on her forehead.

Regina rubbed her hands together. "Okay…"

He regularly played the best in the world, and he'd played their sister as well. So he easily beat them.

He could have thrown the game. But then he wouldn't have had any way of getting Miranda to see him again. And that was what he wanted most—a chance to plead his case, to get her to trust him.

Tabitha pushed back from her desk where they'd been playing and shook her head.

"I didn't take all your shares," he said. "I still want you both involved in the business, and when I infuse money into it, you'll get some of that."

Regina shook her head, too. "No, this was a mistake."

"I swear that you will still be involved," he promised. "I'm not taking everything away from you." He flinched. "But Miranda will probably be mad."

"This was a mistake for you," Regina said.

He didn't understand.

"Miranda will forgive us for gambling away our shares," Regina said.

"We're her sisters," Tabitha said. "Or, as you pointed out, she's our mother. She'll forgive us. She always does."

"But she won't forgive you," Regina warned him.

"For what?" he asked. "For winning?"

"You didn't win," Tabitha told him, as if she pitied him. "You lost more than we have…"

And he had an eerie feeling that she was probably right—that Miranda was not going to understand that he only wanted to help her.

CHAPTER NINETEEN

MIRANDA HAD COME up with a plan. Instead of apologizing for setting up the billionaire with the love of his life, she was going to expound on it. Matteo Rinaldi had the money to buy anything he wanted, but even he hadn't been able to buy love. Miranda had had to help him find it.

And she could help others—if they gave her the chance.

She could help others, but she couldn't help herself. Not that she wanted love.

Falling for Grant had just proved to her that she'd been right to worry that she shared her mother's poor judgment. Just like Mother, she'd fallen for the person she couldn't trust.

But she wasn't going to wallow in a pool of self-pity any longer. She was going to focus on the business—for her sake and for her sisters'. So after her dinner with Blair ended, she headed back to the office.

Her sisters would be gone now. But she would fill them in on her new marketing strategy in the morning. Eventually they would understand about her setting up Teo with Blair.

And someday they might forgive her...

She unlocked and pushed open the office door and stopped. The lights were off; everyone was gone. But there was a strange energy in the reception area, an almost familiar scent...

Boy...

That was what she and Blair had dubbed that rain-fresh and musk scent when they were young. But now Miranda called it *man*—which made her think of Grant. And her heart ached...

Damn him.

Even when he wasn't around, he could spoil her mood. No. She wasn't going to let him get to her. She was going to her office to work on her laptop before she forgot all the things she wanted to do.

Then she pushed open her office door to face the thing she most wanted to do: Grant. He sat in her chair, his feet on her desk, his head back as if he was sleeping.

Her traitorous heart swelled and warmed with desire and something else...something that scared her so much she lashed out. "What the hell are you doing here?"

But she was so distraught, she held up a hand before he could answer, "No. I know what you're doing. You're ignoring what I want. I told you never to come back here—that I never wanted to see you again, and here you are, doing what you want, not caring about what I want." Which was what her mother had always done. Going from man to man while ignoring her children.

"You want honesty—"

"And apparently you can't give that to me," she said. "You weren't really auditioning to join the dating service. You were spying on me to make sure I didn't mess with Blair and Teo's relationship."

He flinched. "Blair told you…"

"Yes," she said, her heart aching with his betrayal. "So all you've done is lie to me." She shook her head. "You need to leave. And this time, stay away!"

He shook his head and refused to budge from her chair.

"Grant, I don't want you in my life anymore."

He stood up then and planted his hands on her desk and leaned across it until he was nearly nose to nose with her. "That's not going to be possible," he said. "I am now your partner."

"What?"

"I just played your sisters for their shares of the company, and they're not as good as you are."

She shook her head. "No…"

But he nodded. "Afraid so. I guess I actually own more shares than you do right now."

She gasped as shock stabbed her heart. This was the ultimate betrayal...by all of them. And just like all those years ago, Blair was the only one she could truly trust. She had no one else.

And now she didn't even have her business. At least not control of it, and control meant everything to Miranda. Grant controlled the business now.

"Why would you do this to me?" she asked as those damn traitorous tears stung her eyes. "Do you hate me that much?"

Her beautiful face crumpled with a grimace of pain—pain he'd caused her. That pain gripped Grant's heart, squeezing it so tightly that he thought it might stop beating entirely. "God, no, Miranda."

"Then why would you take my company away from me? You must hate me..."

He shook his head, disgusted with himself for how he'd handled everything. Her sisters had warned him.

But he hadn't realized how angry she was until she'd lashed out at him. And then he'd gotten defensive and angry himself. But seeing her like this, so obviously hurt, his anger drained away to shame.

"I'm not taking it away," he assured her. "All I want to do is help, and you wouldn't let me join the service—"

"You still want to join?" she asked, her voice raw with the betrayal she must have been feeling.

And he finally realized fully what a fool he'd been. He'd been sleeping with her and telling her that he was only doing it so she would let him date other women. He dragged his hand through his hair and over his face. "No. I never really wanted to join."

"Then what was all the auditioning about?" she asked. "Just to have sex with me?"

He'd had some dangerous missions before, and this reminded him very much of the one where he'd had to navigate through a field of land mines. He didn't want to make one misstep, because it could cost him so much. It could cost him everything.

Then he remembered her one request of him: honesty. "I wanted to make you so crazy about me that you would do whatever I wanted you to do," he admitted. "And I wanted you to leave Blair and Teo alone. That was the reason I sought you out in the first place."

"And in the second?" she asked.

He groaned. "God, it's easier to lie than to be honest," he admitted. Because honesty was so dangerous. "I don't want to say you and the sex were in second place. But…"

"It's true," she said.

"It started out with me just protecting Blair," he said. "But then I wanted you, and once I had you, I wanted you more and more." Like now, he ached for her. But he didn't dare touch her. She was too angry and too hurt, and he didn't want to hurt her any more. "I wanted you so much that I forgot what my original mission was…"

It had all gotten so muddled for him, like now. He was struggling to explain himself to her, struggling to explain what she'd come to mean to him: everything. But the wrong words kept coming out.

"To destroy me?" she asked. "Is that why you're taking over my company?"

"No, Miranda. I want to help you. Your sisters said you won't let them take out a loan on their own, so I figured the only way I could put money into the business is if I owned part of it."

She shook her head. "I don't need you to rescue me, Grant. I need you to respect me. I figured out a way to make the business what I want it to be about."

"Fun," he said.

Her eyes widened; she must have been surprised that he remembered. "And love," she said. "Money can't buy love. It's just there or it isn't."

Did she have any for him? Or only distrust?

"I want dating to be about getting to know each other, having adventures—"

"Like us," Grant said. "We got to know each other. We had fun." More fun and excitement than he'd ever experienced. "We could figure out some way to incorporate my and Blair's business, Private

Flights, with Liaisons International—arrange dates in exotic locations."

"We could," she agreed—much to his surprise. But then she added, "If I could trust you. But all you've done is lie and play games with me. And I have no idea if what you're telling me now is the truth or if you're up to something else."

He sucked in a breath, but he couldn't come up with a valid argument to what she'd said. He hadn't been honest with her. Then.

"I'm being honest now," he vowed.

And she shrugged. "I have no way of knowing."

"Miranda…" He came around the desk and reached out to her now.

But she held him back, her hands out—her arms stiff—as if she didn't want him anywhere close to her. "I can't have a partner I can't trust, in business or in life…"

He understood what she'd meant about money not being able to buy love. No matter how much money he put into her business, she was never going to love him…because she was never going to trust him.

Over the years he'd had some missions go bad, but he'd always been able to adapt—to come up with a new plan—so that he had survived. For the first time in his life, he wasn't sure what to do. Except to give her what she wanted.

Honesty.

"I know I screwed up," he said. "Badly…and I know you're probably not going to believe me. But it's the truth…" Grant trailed off, struggling to find the words he'd never said to another woman. They were in his heart, so he pulled them from there and told her, "I love you."

She flinched as if he'd slapped her.

"You don't believe me," he said with a weary sigh. "Just think about this. If I really wanted to hurt you, I would have walked away. I wouldn't care about helping you with your business or about earning back your trust. I would have just left you alone like you wanted, because you wouldn't have mattered to me. But you matter, Miranda, more than anything…"

Tears trailed down her face now.

And his heart wrenched over making her cry. No matter what he'd said to her or how hard he'd been on her when they were younger, he had never made her cry. She was like his sister—tough.

And independent…

And his attempts to help her had just hurt and offended her. Just like Blair had felt over his meddling, Miranda felt disrespected.

"I'm sorry," he said, and his arms ached to reach for her. But he'd already done more than enough damage.

He'd made her cry.

"I'll do what you want from now on," he promised. "I'll stay away from you."

And before he could act on his selfish desire for her, he turned and walked out of her office.

And out of her life...

CHAPTER TWENTY

EVER SINCE SHE'D let him walk away a week ago,
Miranda had been kicking herself. She hadn't been
alone in that, either. Her sisters had been kicking
her, too. And even Blair...

This was the first time in a clash with Grant
that her best friend had sided with her brother over
Miranda.

"I know he's an idiot," Blair said from the cock-
pit of that two-seater plane Miranda had first flown
in with Grant. "But I believe him. He would not lie
about loving you. He has never played with anyone's heart like that."

"It feels like all he's done is play games with me
since he first showed up at my office..."

"Like I said, he's an idiot, but he's a well-meaning
one," Blair insisted. "He wanted to protect me."

She believed that; he'd always been protective of
his younger sister. "What about getting my sisters'
shares of the business away from them?"

"He wanted to help you," Blair said. "I know and you know that you didn't need his help, but that's what Grant does. Or at least, that's what I think he does when he disappears like he does. I think he's rushing off to someone's rescue. That's his first instinct."

"You're his sister," Miranda said. "You idolize him."

"So do a lot of other people," Blair said. "He's earned it. He's always taken care of me."

But nobody had ever taken care of Miranda. So she wasn't sure how to accept anyone's help...even though he'd had damn good ideas for the dating service.

She cared less about his ideas than him, though. He'd told her he loved her.

And she hadn't told him that she felt the same. She'd just let him walk away. She looked out the window on her side of the plane. "Are we almost there?" she asked.

"Yes," Blair said.

But Miranda didn't know how the pilot could tell for certain when all the aqua-blue water looked the same. She trusted her friend, though.

That was why she'd asked her to fly her to Rio. To the casino where Grant had signed up to play in a professional match.

He might be too busy to talk, but hopefully he would find time to listen. She had so many things she needed to say to him. But by the time Miranda arrived at the casino where he was playing, she was too late. The match had ended.

"Where is he?" she asked one of the players she recognized from the game on Ibiza, at Grant's hotel there.

"He should be down here celebrating his victory," the man replied.

If she'd missed him…

If he'd headed out to the airport she'd just left…

She would have been devastated.

"But he must have gone upstairs to his suite to count his money," the man continued.

"He has a room at the casino?"

"A suite," he said and gave her the number for it.

Her heart pounding, she rushed from the private room, through the lobby to the elevators. Her fingers shook as she pressed the button to his floor—the penthouse floor. The elevator was fast, so fast that she felt light-headed and dizzy when the doors opened onto a wide corridor. She stepped out and approached the double doors marked with the number the man had given her.

She drew in a breath, bracing herself, before she knocked.

"Go away," a gruff voice called out. "I don't feel like celebrating."

He must have thought she was his friend. She wanted to be—his friend, his lover, his everything…

"It's me," she called out.

The doors jerked open within seconds. "Miranda?" he asked as if he couldn't believe she was actually standing in front of him.

She wore his favorite outfit—the leather one Blair had given her.

Then he cleared his throat and asked, "What do you want?"

"You," she replied.

He stepped back as if she'd punched him. Hard. "What?"

"I'll play for you," she said. "Winner takes all…"

His forehead furrowed with lines of confusion. "What do you mean?"

"You just won this championship and you can't understand the rules of the game?" she asked as she stepped inside the suite and shut the doors behind her. Then she walked around him toward a table near the kitchenette part of the suite. A deck of cards sat on the table, and she picked them up. It was probably his winning deck, so maybe she should have asked for another. But she began to deal those.

"What are your rules, Miranda?" he asked as he joined her at the table.

Unlike the game in his hotel suite, this one must have been more formal, because he wore a tuxedo. But the tie was undone, and half the studs were loose on his shirt, leaving it partially open to expose his muscular chest. His scrapes and bruises had healed.

She had to blink to clear the desire and the confusion from her eyes and focus on his handsome face. Dark circles rimmed his dark blue eyes. He looked exhausted. She raised her hand and stroked his jaw. "Or are you too tired to play me?"

He shook his head. "I just need to understand what the stakes are," he said. "Are you trying to win your sisters' shares back? Because you don't have to. I'll just give them to you."

"I told you," she said. "You. I'm playing for you."

"But why?"

She drew in a deep breath; she owed him the truth. He'd given it to her. "Because I love you, too."

His eyes widened with shock. "But I thought you couldn't trust me?"

"Maybe I shouldn't," she said, but she smiled to soften her words. "But I will. I trust that you are a good man, Grant Snyder, and you have only the best of intentions for those you love."

"And I do love you," he insisted.

She nodded. "I know...so pick up your cards. If I win, you will be my partner—in business and life."

"And what do I get if I win?" he asked.

"Whatever you want..."

Grant reached out for the cards, but he never turned them over. He just tossed them aside. "I fold."

"You don't want to play?" she asked.

"I didn't say that," he said, and he lifted her onto the table. "But I already won."

"Congratulations on the championship," she said.

He shook his head. "I'm not talking about that. I won with you coming here, to me. With you trusting me…" Emotion rushed up to choke him, so he cleared his throat before adding, "With you loving me."

"I do love you," she said, and her smile widened. "I used to have the biggest crush on you."

"What? Now who's not being honest? You couldn't stand me."

"True," she said. "But even when I thought you were a dick, I thought you were super hot."

"And now?"

"You're still super hot," she said as she pulled the rest of the studs free on his shirt and pushed it and the tie from his shoulders. Then she reached for the button on his pants.

But he caught her hands in his and held them. "Do you still think I'm a dick?"

"You have your moments," she said.

And he laughed. She was always honest with him. He wanted to be the same with her. "I do," he agreed. "I also have some secrets I want to share with you, about something I still do occasionally for the government." He had a feeling he wouldn't be accepting as many of those missions, though. But he wanted her to know everything about him. So he told her what he wasn't supposed to tell anyone.

And when he finished, she was crying again.

"Damn it!" he said, as he pulled her against his chest. "I hate it when you cry."

She pushed her hands against his bare chest and turned her face up to his. "These are happy tears. You weren't supposed to tell me that, were you?"

"I'm not supposed to tell anyone," he admitted.

"But you shared with me," she said. "And you didn't need to… I am going to trust you."

"I want to make sure that I never give you any reason to doubt me," he said. "Or my feelings for you…"

She leaned forward and brushed her mouth across his. Then she lowered her head and brushed her lips across his chest, over his heart. "I don't."

His skin tingled from her touch, and passion surged through him. He reached for the zipper on her vest and tugged it down to free her beautiful breasts. Then he ran his mouth over them, and his tongue over her nipples. And then lower…

Her pants came off more easily this time. And she kicked them to the floor.

He pushed her back onto the table as he moved his mouth lower on her beautiful body. And he tasted her passion for him. She was so sweet, so wet…

She writhed before her body shuddered and

she screamed his name. Then she reached for his pants again. But he stepped back. He wanted her too badly for her to play with him. So he shucked off his pants and rolled on a condom himself. Then he slid deep inside her hot body and groaned.

"It's like coming home," he murmured. That was the feeling he'd had and hadn't recognized— because his home growing up had been too filled with tension and unhappiness to feel like a home. She did, though.

She smiled. "That's it," she said, and those tears glistened in her eyes again. "I didn't know…"

Because she hadn't had a happy home, either.

But now they had each other.

Love overwhelming him, he moved inside her, sliding deeper and deeper until he didn't know where he ended and she began. It was as if they flowed together. Then they came together, screaming each other's names.

He drew out and rushed to the bathroom to clean up, not wanting to be gone from her for long. But as he left the bathroom, he heard her cussing and hurried out to find her next to the table, staring down at the cards.

"You won," she said.

"I know."

"No, I drew two kings, and you drew four aces…" She threw down the cards. "How are you that damn lucky?"

He laughed. "I don't know. Just fate, I guess." Like them—they were fated to be together.

"Well, you won," she said. "And you never said what you wanted."

"You," he said, and he picked her up and carried her away from the table into the bedroom. "I want you to be my partner in business and life."

She smiled and murmured against his lips as he lowered his head to hers, "We both win…"

* * * * *

COMING SOON!

We really hope you enjoyed reading this book.
If you're looking for more romance, be sure to
head to the shops when new books are
available on

Thursday 21st
January

LET'S TALK
Romance

For exclusive extracts, competitions
and special offers, find us online:

f facebook.com/millsandboon

🐦 @MillsandBoon

📷 @MillsandBoonUK

Get in touch on 01413 063232